# FALLEN WOMAN

## A Pride and Prejudice Vagary

ARTHEL CAKE

ISBN: 978-0-578-44915-9 (paperback)

# TABLE OF CONTENTS

# FALLEN WOMAN

## A Pride and Prejudice Vagary

# PROLOGUE

June 1807
Pemberley Manor, Derbyshire

Fitzwilliam Darcy sat hunched forward in the chair beside his father's bed numb with grief. He had not left it since his arrival from Cambridge the night before. His usually fastidious clothing hung disheveled on his tall frame. He had not been shaved in nearly two days and the dark shadow of beard added to the image of a young man in emotional and physical disarray. Memories flickered and jerked through his mind like phantoms. His father leading him around the training ring on his first pony. His father taking him fishing in what became their favorite spot, showing him with endless patience how to cast a line. His father sitting with him in the music room while his mother played and sang, his face full of love for his wife. Memory after memory came and went until a soft groan startled Darcy from his reverie.

The wasted man in the bed stirred, his eyelids fluttered. Darcy took up his father's cold hand, holding it as if to lend the man his own warmth. Tears stung his eyes, and he blinked before they could fall. He felt like a boy again, standing at his mother's bedside to say goodbye as she failed. This was his father, the heart and soul of Pemberley; how could he be dying?

"Son. You arrived...in time."

The deep voice, so like his own, was a thin whisper. Darcy sat farther forward, his grip tightening. "Father. I came as quickly as I could."

Nothing, no response. Darcy's breath hitched, his chest constricted with pain. George Darcy gathered what strength he had, his fingers curled around his son's.

"Keys. Desk. Mr. Thatcher has...them. Locked drawer. Letter." His eyes opened wide, he struggled to focus on his son's face through a gray haze. "Burn...letter. Promise!"

"I will, father, I will. Whatever you want me to do."

The elder man's hand relaxed. For a moment his voice sounded almost as it always had. "Take care of Georgie. God bless you, Will." His eyes closed.

Darcy waited for more; there was no more. George Darcy was dead. A vast hollow chasm opened in Fitzwilliam Darcy's breast. At last he began to cry.

In the corridor outside George Wickham hurried away from the half-open door, making no more noise than a rat in a pantry. A look of triumph suffused his face. He knew which desk, which drawer. As he descended the stairs to the first floor he pulled a set of lock picks out of his waistcoat pocket. From the corridor two floors above he heard a muted stir. So his godfather and benefactor was dead. He would have a little time before anyone came near the study.

Inside the room with its walnut paneling and thick, silencing rug Wickham strode to the great mahogany desk. Soon his boyhood companion would take his place behind it as Master of Pemberley. Wickham's mouth twisted, his handsome features faded from a carefully practiced mask to an image of his real nature: cruel, greedy, heartless. William would inherit the huge Pemberley estate and all that went with it—wealth, prestige, privilege. All the things Wickham wanted and was denied. He was no more than the poor boy George Darcy had taken in as a favor to his Steward. Wickham had been given lessons, clothes, the companionship of the heir to Pemberley. But he was not the heir, and never would be and he never lost sight of that disparity for a moment.

It took him longer than he expected to find the right pick for the locked drawer, but at last the wards clicked into place. Wickham pulled the drawer open and began rifling through its contents. His mentor kept special papers there, those not important enough to be held in the safe inset into the wall, or too personal to reside there. He went through the documents quickly, forgetting in his eager search to listen for anyone in the hall outside.

There it was! Folded and sealed with Lady Anne Darcy's personal seal, "John Wickham" written on the outside. The name was its only direction. *My father! So...* Wickham snatched it up, tore the sheet of paper open. It took a moment to realize he had the letter upside down. With a curse he switched it around and read the first words:

"*Dear John,*
"*I want you to know how much comfort your friendship has given me in this time of trouble. We cannot meet at present...*"

"Give me that!"
Wickham's head snapped up at the stern voice. Mr. Thatcher the Pemberley butler advanced on him, his craggy face full of anger. He had been at Pemberley for nearly a half century and wielded almost as much power within the household as a member of the family.

"How dare you come in here to steal from Master George when he has just passed? You're nothing but a dirty thief. Give me that letter and anything else you've taken."

Mr. Thatcher had reached the side of the desk, outrage in every line of his gaunt body. A vein like a line of blue ink ticked beneath the white skin at his temple. Wickham, still holding the letter, wondered if he could knock the old butler out before he made enough ruckus to arouse others. He immediately abandoned the idea, He needed to stay at Pemberley for the present.

"Get out, old man. Its none of your affair."

The contempt in Wickham's voice fueled the butler's wrath. "Thieving from the man who gave you everything. You haven't an ounce of shame in you. What would your father say?"

The butler reached out suddenly with a speed that belied his age and snatched the letter out of Wickham's loose hold. Wickham snarled and raised his fist as the butler called loudly, "Tapman! In the study!"

Wickham dropped his arm, his fist still clenched. He knew the big footman was on duty somewhere in the downstairs area. There was no love lost between them. Mr. Thatcher retreated toward the door, giving Wickham a chance to reach the connecting door to the library. He went through it swiftly and was in the hallway before anyone appeared.

*To hell with it. I saw enough to know what the rest said. I should get a nice benefice from the old man's will, and now I have an ace in the hole I can use later, whenever I need cash. Darcy won't know I didn't read all of it. He'll pay me what I'm owed, many times over.*

Wickham quickly gained his rooms in the family wing. When he was called he wanted to be seem to grieve the news of George Darcy's death.

In the study, Mr. Thatcher refolded the letter without looking at it. He used a little candle wax to reseal the edges and stood immobile, holding the sheet of folded paper. He had seen Lady Anne's seal and his intimate knowledge of the family informed him the contents were private and possibly dangerous. It was young Mr. Darcy's property now, only he could decide what was to be done with it.

Slowly Mr. Thatcher put the letter into an inner pocket of his coat. Wickham might try to steal the letter again if it was left in the study. Using his duplicate key he relocked the drawer. He did not know if he should tell Master William about Wickham's actions. The poor boy had enough to deal with right then. Whatever the letter said and however much Wickham had read, it could be dealt with later. Mr. Thatcher left the study, determined to hide the letter in a place

Wickham would not find it, until he could apprise Master William of the situation and turn the letter over to him.

Three days later, shortly after the funeral of George Darcy, one of his oldest and most faithful servants suffered an apoplexy and died. It was as if Mr. Thatcher, like some ancient Viking retainer, had followed his master into the afterlife.

The loss of the Pemberley butler was a blow felt less keenly than it would have been had his death come at a time when the family was not in a state of grief over the loss of George Darcy. Georgiana was particularly bereft. When their mother died her five-year-old mind was unable to comprehend the full extent of the loss. Darcy had comforted his little sister as best he was able. Their father had been of little help. Although he had known his wife was dying the reality of her passing left him in a state of shocked anguish so complete he was unable to comfort his children.

It was their aunt Eleanor, Lady Fitzwilliam, who came and took them to Foxwood where they stayed for a month with their cousins. It was a time Darcy looked back on later as his first real awareness of his cousin Richard's staunch support. It was the time when their bond of kinship became one of brothers. Georgiana was now eleven, able to understand that her beloved father was gone, making the burden of taking care of her in the midst of his own terrible grief overwhelming.

Darcy was forced to put aside his own sorrow and watch over his sister as she adapted to the fact of their father's death. He saw that her governess also watched her for any signs of illness and distracted her as much as possible. When her spirits were particularly low, Darcy reminded her that her father was now in heaven with their mother and how happy he would be to see her, and that one day they would see both their parents again. After a time, Georgiana began to practice the pianoforte once more, quiet songs, the music giving her the peace nothing else could do.

At that point Darcy began to take up the reins of the estate; and remembered the letter his father had told him to burn.

There was no letter in the locked drawer. With a small chill of apprehension, Darcy opened the wall safe behind its decorative plaque to find only estate papers and the cash box from which the staff was paid and in which their mother's pin money had been kept when she was alive. In growing anxiety, he called Mrs. Reynolds, the Pemberley housekeeper, and asked her if anyone had been in the study since his father's passing. She assured him it had been locked since his father's last illness; it had not even been cleaned.

Mr. Niles, the under-butler, reiterated her statement. He proffered the keys carried by Mr. Thatcher. The study key was there as well as the key to the locked drawer. The only other key to the drawer was in Darcy's possession. The new master of Pemberley confirmed Mr. Niles to replace Mr. Thatcher, was thanked with dignified civility, and left with no answer to the question of the missing letter.

For days a quiet search went on in the great manor house. Although Darcy was as discreet as possible, the usual murmurs of concern and speculation followed its progress. Young Mr. Wickham followed the search as well, while seeming oblivious to it. In the end, Darcy concluded that either the letter had already been destroyed, or his father's memory, impaired by his illness, was at fault. He began to believe there was no letter and devoted his entire energy and focus to the estate.

And so life proceeded. Until the letter, and all it might mean to his beloved sister, was brought forcibly back into his life.

A letter arrived the day after Georgiana's thirteenth birthday. Darcy found it as he sorted through the post; for several heartbeats he simply stared at the handwriting, then started to rip the missive apart. He was not sure what stopped him. He had received a number of letters from Wickham—he refused to grant the miscreant the courtesy of "Mr."—each one increasingly abusive after the Kympton living became available. His refusal to grant Wickham the living, even though he had been well compensated for releasing any right to it, had inflamed the hatred Wickham already felt for Darcy. Eventually the letters stopped and no other communication from Darcy's former friend had been received: until now.

Slowly Darcy broke the seal of common candle wax and opened the single sheet. The paper was coarse, the sort provided by cheap hotels for their patrons; the ink proved similarly poor. Darcy read the first few words, his body stiffening. The writing blurred for a second. A man falling naked into a snowbank might have felt less frozen with shock.

Desperately, Darcy fought for control of his emotions. He focused on the words, rigid in his chair.

*Darcy,*

*Still looking for the letter my honored godfather asked you to burn? You can give up the hunt, I have it. I have kept it in reserve for the sort of financial deficiency I presently face. The money from the will and my foolish relinquishing of the Kympton living has disappeared and I am pressed by creditors, some of whom are threatening debtor's prison. The sum of £1,000 a month will do nicely to cover my debts and allow me to continue living decently. In the event you do not believe me, the following is a copy of the beginning of the letter, written by your esteemed mother to my father.*

*"Dear John,*

*"I want you to know how much comfort your friendship has given me in this time of trouble. We cannot meet at present but rest assured this proof of our stolen moments will be raised as a Darcy."*

*Should you choose to ignore my request, I am afraid I shall have to sell the letter to one of the broadsheets. I know for yourself you would tell me to do so and be damned, however there is pretty Georgie to consider. The scandal of infidelity and illegitimacy would destroy her socially, including any chance of her marrying when the time comes. I know you will not allow that to happen.*

*Send the money to my direction below.*

*Your old friend,*

*George*

Darcy sat for some time with the letter open on the desk before him, his body consumed with a rage such as he had never felt. Had Wickham been in the room, Darcy knew he would have killed the man, a realization that shook him more than the missive. Slowly he regained control. He folded the letter and put it in the locked drawer of the desk, rising to pace the room, his body stiff with tension.

His father had expended his last bit of energy demanding that his son burn the letter. He had not said who had written it or whom it was to, or what it contained. Could it be true? Darcy racked his memory of that summer. He had been eight years old and observant for his age. He knew their steward and his mother were friends. There were two bad harvests and a failed investment that took George Darcy to London for months on end, trying to salvage what he could for Pemberley's future. Alone and undoubtedly frightened, had Lady Anne succumbed to a need for comfort and turned to John Wickham?

He did not believe it, he would not believe it. John Wickham had been an honorable man, and his mother was always the soul of devotion to her husband. Darcy heard the words repeat in his mind. *This proof of our stolen moments.* He halted by the windows, staring sightlessly at the brilliant profusion of spring color in the gardens. His mother had loved Pemberley's gardens; like its more delicate blooms she had prospered here for a time, and then faded. An elegant woman, well-read for her time, she would never have resorted to the language of a romantic novel to express something so devastating as an illegitimate child.

Darcy returned to his desk. He did not doubt Wickham was capable of ruining Georgiana if his demands were not met. Even published anonymously the letter, however innocent, would be presented in such a way that its subject could be discerned. The subsequent scandal meant disaster not only for his sister and himself but for the Fitzwilliams. his uncle Lord Matlock's political enemies could not be handed a better weapon to use against him. No matter it had been altered or copied, the broadsheets used whatever came to them for their profit. It was blackmail and there was no recourse but to find Wickham and retrieve the letter.

That would take time. Darcy took out paper and pen. After some thought he wrote a short note without salutation or return direction.

*Send me a list of your current debts. I will pay them and advance you £100. I will consult with my cousin before any further action is taken. He will be most interested in your proposal.*
*D*

Darcy folded and sealed the letter and addressed it to the direction Wickham had given. Wickham had always been frightened of Richard Fitzwilliam, with good reason. Richard, a major in His Majesty's Army, was unlikely to stand by and wait for Wickham to act. The implied threat might be enough to make the cur think twice before doing anything to harm Georgiana. With the note in the post, Darcy ran both hands through his hair. He was unwilling to involve Georgiana's co-guardian unless it became necessary. Darcy was still not ready to condone Wickham's death by unlawful means. Not yet. It was a decision he came to bitterly regret.

## July 1812
## Longbourn, Hertfordshire

"Mr. Bennet, Mr. Bennet, what is it, what has happened?"

Elizabeth Bennet awoke to her mother's shrill cries echoing from the upstairs hallway. She sat up and swung her legs out of bed, wiping ineffectually at sleep-heavy eyes. An elusive breeze wandered through the room from her open window, smelling of lavender and summer roses. In spite of the breeze the air was thick with heat and she had only just fallen asleep. It took her several minutes to locate and pull on her dressing gown and shove her feet into her house slippers. The sense of foreboding that had weighed on her since her youngest sister had left for Brighton rose in a choking wave, causing her hands to shake and impeding her progress.

By the time she stepped into the hall, Jane was peering from her bedroom door, still in her night rail. Elizabeth heard voices from the entry and ran down the stairs to find her father still in his dressing gown, shirt and trousers, speaking to an express rider. Mrs. Bennet hovered nearby, holding her robe together with one hand and fanning herself with her inevitable lace handkerchief with the other.

An express at this time of night was never good news. Elizabeth heard the familiar creak of the worn treads at Jane's more dignified descent; her sister stopped on the last step just behind Elizabeth. Her long golden braid fell over her shoulder as she leaned forward to place a tentative hand on her sister's arm.

"Something must have happened to one of the Gardiners," she whispered. "Oh, I hope it is nothing too serious."

Elizabeth did not remind her that expresses were not sent for insignificant problems. A chill ran through Elizabeth's body. She watched her father open the express, waving the rider toward the rear of the house, where he would find a cold drink and something to eat. When the man departed with Mr. Hill, Mr. Bennet rapidly scanned the message. In the wavering light of the hall candle Elizabeth saw his face darken and then freeze in shock. He read a part of it over again before turning to Mrs. Hill, who waited in tense silence.

"Find Kitty and bring her here, immediately."

"Oh, Mr. Bennet," Mrs. Bennet stepped toward her husband, "please tell me what has occurred. Is someone ill, or—or injured?"

Mr. Bennet thrust the message into her reaching fingers. Elizabeth saw his hands clench into fists at his sides. She heard Jane's gasp as Mrs. Hill hurried upstairs past them. At that moment her mother screamed and clutched her chest, crushing the express against her bosom.

"Oh, my clever child! Only fifteen, and married! Goodness, oh, Lydia. I shall go distracted."

Mr. Bennet took the missive from her, saw Elizabeth and Jane and offered Elizabeth the paper. Both young women were staring at their mother, who continued to rhapsodize and fan herself.

"You might as well read this." His voice was more grim than either of his eldest daughters had ever heard it. "Please take your mother into the drawing room before she wakes the entire household."

Jane led Mrs. Bennet to the drawing room while Elizabeth followed with the letter. Mrs. Hill had lit a lamp, giving enough light to see the neat masculine hand. The message was from Colonel Forster of the —shire militia. Their youngest sister, Lydia, had been invited by the colonel's young wife to stay with the Forsters while the regiment was stationed in Brighton for the summer. Elizabeth held the missive close to the light as Jane joined her.

"No!"

Jane's moan of shock only increased Elizabeth's own sense of hovering disaster. She did not hear her father enter the room, or their younger sister Catherine's sobs. Neither sister was aware of anything but the news on the page they held.

"How could she?" Jane shook so badly Elizabeth was afraid she might swoon. She refolded the paper and put it in her pocket, her sister's voice wavering in her ears. "How could she be so lost to decency, to everything we have been taught from childhood? Surely they will marry. It is not right, but when she is married it will remove at least some of the stigma."

Elizabeth did not answer. She turned to see her father standing over a still weeping Kitty, angry and unyielding.

"Did you know about this infamous scheme of Lydia's? Tell me the truth, Kitty!"

She shook her head rapidly, dislodging her braid until it fell in long hanks around her shoulders. "N-no. I only…knew she liked Mr. Wickham, a-and he…he liked her. And she s-said what fun it would be to be married first of her sisters."

"So she did not share that they planned an elopement?"

"NO. It is the truth, Papa, it is!"

Mr. Bennet drew a visible breath. He glanced across at Elizabeth and Jane. Mrs. Bennet was still in raptures. "Oh, Mr. Bennet, you must give Lydia enough money to buy a trousseau. She will no doubt attend many balls and parties and she must have new gowns suitable for such entertainments. She..."

Mr. Bennet turned on his wife, glaring at her in a manner that silenced her immediately. "Madam, there will be no trousseau. Are you sensible of the fact that her presumed husband is a militia lieutenant with hardly enough income to live decently himself, much less support a wife and family? She has forsaken her family, disgraced her sisters, and possibly damaged Mary's betrothal to Mr. Clarke. I do not want to hear any more of your praise for a daughter so lost to all sense of duty or morality."

He motioned to Jane. She went to her mother and helped her to her feet. Elizabeth joined her, handing the letter to her father. The sooner they took Mrs. Bennet away from the opportunity to share her news with the servants the better. The Hills were safe, but the rest of the servants gossiped with those of other households. It would be hard enough to keep the matter quiet until Lydia was found without putting the story abroad for speculation and censure.

When Mrs. Bennet had been returned to bed with a mild dose of laudanum, Elizabeth left Jane sitting with their mother and returned to the drawing room. Kitty had disappeared. She found her father in his book room, sitting behind his desk, his head sunk in his hands. He looked up at her after several seconds. He seemed suddenly old, even his voice dull.

"I do not resent you, Lizzy, for being right about not allowing Lydia to go to Brighton. It was wise of you, wiser than I was. It never crossed my mind that she might do something to disgrace the entire family. Her silliness is one thing, but this," his words trailed away without a conclusion except to slam his fist on the express on the desk.

"Jane believes they will marry," Elizabeth said carefully.

Mr. Bennet's face twisted with anger. "Why would he marry her? She has nothing but a pretty face and an empty head. Her dowry is laughable. Wickham must know I cannot increase it. I might manage one hundred pounds a year with some economies. Can you really believe that would satisfy a man like him? No, Lizzy, he will not marry her, and I have only one choice now. I will be forced to disown her."

Elizabeth's hand flew to her mouth. "Oh, Papa, no."

"Child, what choice do I have? She has chosen her path she will have to live with it. My duty now is to the rest of my daughters. You know what happened when the Midlingtons' daughter came in the family way by one of their grooms. They were forced to withdraw from all society; they still live isolated among their neighbors. Sir William, my brother Phillips and myself are the only ones who recognize them. Is that what you want for our family?"

Elizabeth felt tears form in her eyes and shook them away. "Can you not wait at least until we know what has become of her? They could easily have traveled to Gretna Green, although it is a long way from Brighton."

"Too long. I wager they are no farther from the seashore than London. He is a cad, Elizabeth, and a rake. I knew from the start that he was shallow of character, and I rejoiced silently when you distanced yourself from his attentions. But I admit I never expected this level of immorality from either of them."

"You do not suppose—that my withdrawal from his company caused him to attach Lydia?"

Elizabeth sat down abruptly in one of the chairs before the desk. Her fear caused her father to say quickly, "No, dear girl, I do not. Lydia was simply the weakest link in the family chain. She is an irrepressible flirt. Some men take that to mean that she is not of a high moral character. In this case it seems Wickham saw it that way, and was justified." He waved her toward the door. "Go back to bed, Lizzy, there is nothing more to be done tonight. I shall write my brother

Gardiner in the morning, he can advise Mary what is best to do. I expect she will return home after this. I only pray her young vicar is of an understanding nature."

Elizabeth rose, accepting his dismissal. She desperately wanted to tell her father why she had withdrawn from Mr. Wickham's attentions, but it was impossible. At the Netherfield Ball the previous November she had used her dance with Mr. Darcy to accuse him of depriving his childhood friend of a valuable living. After the dance, Mr. Darcy had found her alone on the terrace and told her of Wickham's debts and seductions. Elizabeth was certain he had not told her everything he knew. What he said was enough to force her to take a closer look at her new friend. When Mary King inherited £10,000, Mr. Wickham dropped Elizabeth for the new heiress. It was enough to convince Elizabeth that Mr. Darcy spoke the truth. That she had allowed herself to speak to a man in private was a breach of propriety she could not share with her father, especially now.

The following morning dawned muggy and hot with a threat of rain in smoky clouds darkening the foothills. Elizabeth rose at her usual early hour, dressed and put up her hair, her mind occupied with the crisis weighing on her family. She decided to forgo her usual morning walk in the event news of Lydia arrived while she was out. Elizabeth knew all too well the penalty for breaking the rules of their society. A fallen woman disgraced her entire family, especially any sisters. It was assumed that if one were capable of infamy, all were. The unfairness angered her even as she accepted its potential for ruining the futures of herself and Jane and Kitty. No respectable gentleman would marry a woman from such a family.

Her father was not in the breakfast room, nor had Elizabeth expected he would be. She prepared two cups of tea and took them to his book room. Her tap on the door was not answered, alarming her enough to enter without invitation. Mr. Bennet sat in his favorite chair before the empty fireplace, still dressed as he had been the night before. Elizabeth's nose wrinkled at the faint odor of brandy.

He did not look up when she took the companion chair and put his cup on the table between them.

"Papa, you need to eat something. Let me bring you a muffin—"

He turned his head and Elizabeth's breath caught in her throat. Her beloved father had aged ten years in a night. She carefully extended the tea and after a moment he took the cup and drank it like a man parched. Elizabeth offered him her cup. He refused with a shake of his head.

"Papa, please, you must not do this to yourself! Lydia's behavior is not your fault."

His mouth twisted. "Whom else shall I blame? Your mother? Yes, she is partly responsible for this business, but it is my duty to control my family, including my wife. I have been worse than indulgent,, I have been irresponsible. And now my other daughters will suffer because of it."

"She may marry, Papa. We do not know for certain yet. Please, wait until more news is received."

Mr. Bennet closed his eyes wearily. "Very well, Lizzy. I will wait. Perhaps I will be able to formulate some plan to save the rest of you while I do so."

In spite of his words, Elizabeth felt the heaviness of fear press down on her. If Lydia did not marry, very soon, they were almost certainly lost. In a small community like Meryton such a scandal would provide gossip for months if not years. Some neighbors might be understanding, those they had known all their lives. Most, however, with daughters of their own to protect, would not. Mr. Bingley's defection had already left Jane the subject of talk and speculation; this would only justify the rumors. It was too late to cry, or regret. They could only wait.

The morning passed in wooden minutes and leaden hours. Mrs. Bennet kept her room, no longer ecstatic over her favorite's defection. Mr. Bennet had forbidden his wife to speak of the matter to anyone, especially the servants. In hope that another presence might enforce his edict, he asked Jane and Kitty to sit with her in turn. Elizabeth stayed close to her father in the event she was needed. She made no effort to read or do needlework, both were impossible under the circumstances.

She was sitting by the drawing room window when a rider turned into the drive from the main road. For one shining moment as she came to her feet, his red coat shouted *Mr. Wickham.* It took only that second for Elizabeth to realize it was Colonel Forster. She heard Mr. Hill stride to the front door and went to inform her father of the colonel's arrival. Both waited in the hall when Colonel Forster was shown in. He did not need to speak. His drawn face and dust-grayed clothing told them that his news was not good.

Silently, with only a brief bow as he passed Elizabeth, he followed Mr. Bennet into his book room. She was not invited to join them. Unable to leave the dim hall, Elizabeth stood silently staring at the green striped wallpaper without seeing it. After several minutes Jane joined her, taking her hand.

"Kitty heard someone arrive on horseback. Is it...?"

"Colonel Forster. He is with Papa." She closed her eyes for a moment. "I am afraid it is bad news."

"Surely not."

The desperation in Jane's face was reflected in her voice. Elizabeth shook her head sharply. "Mr. Wickham is not as he appears. He is a seducer, a man with no morals who preys on young, innocent girls."

Jane stared at her sister's angry face. "How can you know that, Lizzy? He seemed a pleasant young man."

"Because I was told so by someone who knows him far better than we do. This is not the first time; the only difference is that he chose a gentleman's rather than a tradesman's or cottager's daughter."

"Please, Lizzy," Jane squeezed her sister's hand, "let us wait until we know for certain. I cannot believe he is so evil."

Elizabeth put her arms around her dearest sister and held her. "We shall wait, Jane. I do not think it will be long."

It was not. The two men emerged after ten minutes and Mr. Bennet called for Mr. Hill. Without preamble, he addressed Elizabeth, "Take Colonel Forster into the drawing room and order tea. Jane, please fetch Kitty. I will speak to your mother myself, later. Mr. Hill, pack my traveling trunk and have the carriage brought around. I am going to London with Colonel Forster immediately."

"Papa," Jane's voice shook, "is there news of Lydia?"

His stony glare answered her. "I know of no one in this family named Lydia."

# CHAPTER ONE

December 1812
Middleboro, Hertfordshire

T he church of St. Eustace in the small town of Middleboro was filled to capacity to witness the marriage of their vicar, Mr. Clarke, to Miss Mary Bennet. The bride's small family occupied a pew in the front of the old stone building, except for Miss Elizabeth Bennet, who stood up with her sister. Curiosity murmured through the congregation as the bride's mother and sisters took their places, accompanied by a fashionably dressed couple who were said to be the bride's aunt and uncle from London. Mrs. Clarke, the groom's mother, sat in a front pew. She acknowledged her son's new family with a smile. It was widely known that the bride had resided with her mother-in-law-to-be for the past two months, and she was very fond of Miss Mary.

Light from narrow stained glass windows barely colored the rows of people. The day was chill and blustery with pelting rain, washing out all but the most intense hues of saints, darkening Goliath to a hulking outline and clothing David in pale shades of blue and green. Mary's arrival on her father's arm silenced the whispers. Mr. Clarke stood before the altar, his demeanor calm. The minister from the bride's church in Meryton officiated at Mr. Clarke's request.

The bride walked down the aisle on her father's arm, her step firm. Her dress of pale yellow silk brought out auburn lights in her chocolate hair and gave a soft glow to her brown eyes. When the last blessing was pronounced and Mary exited the church on the arm of her new husband, Elizabeth felt a great wash of relief mingled with happiness. She laid her hand on the proffered arm of Mr. Clarke's cousin who had acted as his groomsman, following the married couple. He glanced at her several times without speaking. When they reached the porch, he bowed, still silent, and left her.

*He knows. Or he suspects. He wonders if I am stained like my youngest sister. It is a look I shall see again, many times.*

The bitterness of the reflection made her want to flee from the gathered well-wishers. Her father handed her her cloak and nodded toward the covered carriage where Mary and her new husband were seated with his mother.

"She will be alright, Lizzy. Mr. Clarke is not another Mr. Collins. His Christianity is real, not self-serving. And his mother is a fine woman."

"Must we go to the wedding breakfast, Papa?"

Elizabeth looked up at him, half-pleading.

"I think we should make an appearance. Your mother is not well, we will not stay long in his weather."

Elizabeth glanced into the church where her mother made a slow progress toward the doors, Jane on one side and their uncle on the other.

*If she had not told our aunt Phillips, things might not have become so bad so quickly. She counted on her friends, people she has known since her girlhood, and they abandoned her. We are outcasts through no fault of our own, and Mama is failing.*

For the first time in Elizabeth's memory, her mother looked frail. Their friends and neighbors' desertion had aged her, taken all her joy in life. Perhaps she might be better if they could leave Longbourn, but it was all they had, their home. Where would they go, how would they live? Her father's words brought her back to the cold church porch and the cold reality of their lives.

"At least Mary has escaped the worst of the situation. It was kind of Mrs. Clarke to invite her to stay with her until the wedding. They get along well, it is a good prognosis for the future." He turned in time to see Mrs. Bennet shiver as a gust of icy air swept into the church through the open doors. It had begun to rain again. Mr. Bennet opened the umbrella he carried, went to his wife and took her arm from Jane. "Come, my dear. The carriage is waiting."

## April 1813
## Meryton, Hertfordshire

Elizabeth raised her eyes to the near-distant hills and Oakum Mount, her favorite destination on her long rambles through the countryside. The new green of fields separated her from it as from the past. She raised her face to the touch of the thin sun and the pale blue of the sky. It was barely spring, a fact the new buds pushing up through the ground refused to acknowledge. She left the crunch of the gravel path under her feet and made her way over grass and hardened mud to the newest grave in the Bennet family section. In two months the mound of dirt had subsided, grass was sprouting in a blanket of soft green stems. Soon there would be no difference from the other graves surrounding it.

*I stand in the midst of eight generations of Bennet lives, eight generations of honest, upright men and women. Eight generations of rectitude that cannot atone for one stupid child.* Elizabeth moved closer to bend and lay a small bunch of crocuses at the foot of the headstone: Frances Gardiner Bennet, beloved wife and mother. *I am sorry, Mama. I never told you I loved you often enough. I never realized how much you loved all of us, not just Lydia and Kitty.* A cloud drifted over the sun, temporarily shadowing the graves. It was an old churchyard, surrounded by tall firs. The smell of pine came to Elizabeth, sharply pleasant. *Papa is taking us to London. He has leased a small house somewhere near Sloane Square. Kitty will stay with our aunt and uncle Gardiner. She needs a woman to guide her and our aunt is wise and kind. Papa has turned Longbourn over to Mr. Collins and Charlotte. We will never live there again.*

Tears suddenly choked Elizabeth. She groped for her handkerchief and blotted her eyes. Kissing her fingers, she touched them to the top of the cold stone. *Goodbye, Mama.*

Elizabeth turned her back on the grave and the prospect of Oakum Mount and walked swiftly toward Longbourn. She found Jane in her room, the bed stripped, the rug rolled and pushed against a wall. Jane's closet stood empty; her trunk sat locked in the middle of the room. Mr. Hill appeared with their footman; they lifted the trunk and left without a word.

"I told Papa you had gone to the churchyard to say goodbye to Mama. He wants to be gone as soon as the wagon is loaded. Charlotte asked him to take the furniture in the attic that Mama changed out when I put my hair up. I did not think you would mind. It will save Papa having to buy new things for the London house."

"Mr. Collins did not object?" Elizabeth raised a brow.

"Charlotte said Mr. Collins does not want to be bothered selling the old things."

"Meaning she convinced him the neighbors would think he did not have enough money to live like a gentleman. Charlotte has been a good friend to us. I will miss her."

"So shall I." Jane's clear blue eyes filled with tears. "I wish we could turn back time, Lizzy. Is that not silly?"

"No, dear, just futile. Come," Elizabeth took her sister's hand, "we do not want to keep Papa, or our uncle Gardiner's drivers, waiting."

They left the house together to find Kitty already in their uncle's carriage and the luggage loaded. The Hills saw them off, Mrs. Hill blotting her eyes with her apron, Mr. Hill stoic except for his hands clenched at his sides. Mr. Bennet handed his two eldest daughters into the carriage, climbed in and the door closed. Kitty sniffed and blew her nose. Jane stared at her hands clasped in her lap. Elizabeth straightened in her seat, feeling only tired. She did not look back.

The life she had always known and loved was no more.

April 1813
Meadow Lane, London

The house was small, two stories of red brick with attics under the peaked roof. Elizabeth followed her father up the flagged walk to the door. While he turned the unfamiliar key in the lock she let her eyes wander to the overgrown flowerbeds and barren window boxes. The door was solid oak, varnished rather than painted, with an iron latch on the inside. It led to a miniscule entry, floored with dull red tiles. Jane stopped to close the door before joining her father and sister in the parlor—it could hardly be called a drawing room—with a soft sigh.

"It is not a bad house, Papa. Once we are settled we shall do nicely I am sure."

Mr. Bennet looked at his eldest daughter fondly. "My ray of sunshine. Yes, I expect we shall adapt as this is the best we can do for now."

Elizabeth heard the pain of failure beneath his words. Her father had changed so much in the past months she hardly recognized the man who had always been her rock of security. To hide her feelings she walked idly around the room. The window facing the road was not large, nor was the only other window, no doubt to avoid as much of the window tax as possible. The air had the stale smell common to rooms that have not been aired in some time. Elizabeth noted the dogleg grate in the fireplace and the black of old smoke staining the brick face beneath a painted wooden mantel. The wallpaper, originally a pattern of vibrant red flowers, had faded to an inconsistent grayish pink. The modest window in the north wall sent pale light creeping over the flowered carpet that covered most of the floor. It was the largest of the rugs Mr. Bennet had bought for the house. It did nothing, Elizabeth thought, to brighten what was essentially a dark and dreary room.

Elizabeth glanced at Jane and saw her own dismay reflected in her sister's face. As if aware of their feelings, Mr. Bennet indicated their surroundings with a gesture of his hands.

"I do not want you to worry," Mr. Bennet addressed Jane and Elizabeth, who turned immediately to give him their attention. "We are not destitute. When I offered Mr. Collins the opportunity to take over the entail early, I enforced certain conditions. I retain the rents from the two properties in Meryton for this year and next, and those rents already collected from our tenants. My brother Gardiner will invest the funds so we have an income. I am also in the process of selling what books from my library I no longer wish to retain."

Elizabeth took an involuntary step forward. "Oh, Papa, no! You cannot sell your books."

"I must, my dear. They are superfluous now. I am keeping the most valuable, including the 1623 Shakespeare first folio and the 1602 Islip Chaucer. If there is ever a need for ready cash they can be sold then. We have all made sacrifices, Lizzy. I find that my books are not such a great loss."

Elizabeth felt an emptiness inside. She knew his books were the great love of her father's life. If he gave them up to sustain his daughters, what did that portend for his own future?

"Do not be so upset, my dear. I have kept some of your favorites, and mine. Now, let us tour the rest of our new abode. There are two bedrooms upstairs, and a small sitting room as well as a bathing room. The beds have been moved in along with your dressing table and bench, Lizzy, and Jane's rocking chair. So have the soft goods you and your aunt purchased. I am certain we shall be quite cozy."

His attempt at lightening their mood was met with smiles from both Jane and Elizabeth that did not touch their eyes. For their father's sake they would make light of their present situation. Their gazes met briefly. This hollow pretense was to be their life. They must find a way to go forward whatever the cost.

Elizabeth followed her father into the hall and up the stairs. *I will not be beaten down because we have suffered for a sin we did not commit. There will be a way out of this and I will find it.* Adversity was a challenge to be met; she had never been cowed by a challenge, her natural courage rising in the face of intimidation. Head high, Elizabeth went to view their new home.

The following week was quiet. Through a local agency, Mr. Bennet engaged a Mrs. Hobson as housekeeper and cook. Mrs. Hobson lived with her married daughter and came in every day except Sunday, when she left food that could be easily heated for their Sabbath dinner. If heavy cleaning was needed she called in a young woman who also came one day a week to do the laundry. They had not looked for a maid and it soon became obvious one would be beneficial if not absolutely necessary.

"She's a hard worker is Nettie Glass." Mrs. Hobson held her reddened hands before her against a flour-dusted apron. "Her mum's a good friend of mine, I've known the Glasses all my life. Nettie's had a bit of training too, which I can show her anything else she needs to know. And if the young ladies could show her what's wanted, she'd make a ladies' maid soon enough."

Mr. Bennet consulted his daughters. An experienced lady's maid would cost more than they wanted to pay; if the girl was willing she could assume some of the duties of a maid of all work. An interview was arranged and precisely at the appointed hour Mrs. Hobson showed a thin, fair-haired girl of sixteen into the parlor. She curtsied and stood stiffly with her hands clasped in front of her. Her dress was plain stuff, a white collar emphasizing clear skin and large hazel eyes. Elizabeth and Jane were the only ones in the room. As she was primarily to serve them their father left the decision of hiring her to his daughters.

"Mrs. Hobson said you have had some training," Elizabeth began. "What sort of training?"

"Please, madam, I worked at an inn along the London Road. I was a maid of all work, but if a lady didn't have her maid with her, I helped with her clothes and hair. I'm not a lady's maid, but I'm a good worker and honest and ever so willing to learn."

"Do you sew?"

Jane's gentle voice and manner seemed to banish some of Nettie's nerves. "Yes, madam. I've helped my mum make clothes for my sisters. I—I don't do fancy work…"

Her voice halted. Jane smiled at her. "That is not necessary. Just plain mending and perhaps later assisting with making dresses when we are in half-mourning. You will be required to do our personal laundry. Will that be a problem?"

"Oh, no, madam. I've done ladies' washing before."

"Nettie," Elizabeth leaned forward a little, "what did you do at the inn?"

The girl had been holding herself very still and straight. For the first time she shuffled her feet slightly. "The usual, madam. Changed the beds and put out towels and tidied up and ran errands."

"Why did you leave the job? I am sure you made more than we can offer with gratuities as well as salary."

Nettie swallowed. She shifted her weight, her thin hands clamped together to stop their trembling. Jane spoke again, and as always Elizabeth marveled at her sister's ability to ease a situation with only a few words.

"You can tell us, Nettie. I am sure it is nothing to your discredit."

"It was—the gentlemen, madam. Some of them wanted more than just maid service."

"And you refused. Did the inn discharge you?"

"No, madam." The girl sounded miserable. "I left."

It was in Elizabeth's mind that this child was Lydia's age. She had quit what most young women of her background would consider an excellent post rather than compromise her morals. It was not only the Wickhams of the world who preyed on the innocent. Some *gentlemen* used their station in life and their wealth to corrupt those they considered beneath them, those with no ability to fight back.

"Would you like to start tomorrow, Nettie?"

The girl's face lit from within with gratitude. "Oh, yes, madam, please. I'd like that very much."

# CHAPTER TWO

May 1813
Darcy House, London

It was the same dream, the same nightmare he had suffered for nearly a year. Walking, wrapped in gray mist like a shroud, searching for her. The wavering figure appeared and faded before him just out of his reach. He called to her in growing desperation until at last she halted and then he could no longer move, only struggle against the enclosing fog.

"Elizabeth, please, stay. Do not leave me!"

"Why should I stay? You left me. You did not want me."

"I wanted you but it was impossible. I could not jeopardize my sister's future."

"What of my future? You knew what Wickham was, you told me he was evil. Why did you not warn anyone else?"

"I tried to protect you."

"How? I could not tell anyone what I knew without telling them how I knew; no one would have believed me. You could have stopped him but you were too proud, all you cared for was yourself. I would never have betrayed you as you betrayed me."

"I did not know about your sister…"

"You did not want to know. You took Mr. Bingley away from Jane, people talked. When Lydia ran away they already believed the worst of us. You could have saved her, saved us. You did not care."

*"I did, I cared too much. Elizabeth, forgive me, please!"*

*"Coward. It was your choice. You left us to be ruined."*

*"Let me help you now. I love you, Elizabeth."*

*"Liar. Go away. You mean nothing to me. I never want to see you again."*

*The mist thickened, her insubstantial shape faded. The mist grew colder, turned to freezing rain, to snow. He was cold, so cold, alone in a dark wilderness with no escape.*

*"Elizabeth...!"*

Darcy woke as always, struggling to free himself from tangled bedclothes, body slick with cold sweat. With a groan he rolled onto his side and wiped his face on the edge of the sheet, aware half the moisture was tears. He knew the accusations were his, not hers. She never expected him to behave any differently than he had. That was the worst of it.

Darcy rose feeling stiff, pulled a banyan over his damp body and went into his dressing room. It was nearly dawn. His cousin Richard Fitzwilliam was coming for luncheon at his invitation. Darcy stirred the banked fire, fed it enough coal to warm him. If he told Richard about Elizabeth—no. He could not tell anyone, especially now with his concern over Georgiana. It was his secret, his pain, never to be shared; his penance.

"I appreciate the invitation and the excellent port," Colonel Richard Fitzwilliam lifted his glass in salute over the spotless linen of the dining table, "now will you tell me what the hell this is all about?"

A professional soldier and experienced interrogator, the colonel was adept at hearing what was not said. Darcy sat back, tapping his fingers on the tablecloth. The dessert plates had been cleared, Darcy's untouched, and the footman dismissed. Richard noted that his cousin had spent the perfectly prepared meal pushing most of the food around his various plates without consuming it. Richard waited;

he was also adept at the skill of letting the other man break the silence. Darcy did not speak for several minutes, sipping his drink. At last he ran a hand over his face in a manner that told Richard he was more upset than he wanted to show.

"I am concerned about Georgie."

"Anything specific, or just in general terms?"

"Nothing I can put a finger on. Her first Season is nearly over and she suddenly seems to have little enthusiasm for any of the entertainments, or interest in any of the young men she has met. That is not like her."

"Well," Richard sipped his port, "perhaps there has been too much of a good thing. She has always been reserved—not unlike a near relative of hers—and the social dance can be exhausting."

"Do not waggle your eyebrows. You look like a pantomime clown."

"Sometimes clowns learn things that tragedians do not." Richard set his glass on the table and began to turn it slowly around and around, an old habit when he was considering a problem. "Mother has not said anything. Have you spoken to Georgie about it?"

"No." Darcy stared toward the window where drawn drapes allowed the clear light to slip in and fall like water over a stand holding a famile verte urn. "I have been immersed in estate business for the past five months, both at Pemberley and on the small estate in Scotland."

"Too immersed to speak to your little sister?"

"Damn it, Richard, I know I have neglected Georgie;, you do not have to remind me."

Darcy's hand slapped the table so hard the silver containers in the Georgian cruet set clinked like bells. He rose and began to pace behind the chairs, arms stiff at his sides. His cousin watched him with a certain speculation. He had known for some time that this man who was like a brother to him suffered from a heavy burden he refused to share. Richard suspected it involved a woman. What else could so disrupt the self-discipline of a man renowned for his cool detachment toward matters of the heart?

*Sooner or later he will tell me. He always does.*

"I am not blaming you, Will. I simply think you need to ask her what is troubling her. You have been more father than brother to her since uncle George died. She trusts you. You do not have to question her, just ask her about her Season, if she has made any new acquaintances, if she is enjoying herself as Mother's protégé. It ought to give you some insight as to whether there is a specific problem or not."

Darcy halted his pacing at the windows, gazing out at the side garden without seeing the perfectly manicured grass, the flowering shrubs, the small marble fountain sparkling with light.

"You are right, Cousin. I need to talk to her." Darcy swung around, his expression still tense but lacking the anger of moments before. "But first I will speak to aunt Eleanor. She will have some idea of Georgie's state of mind."

Richard rose. "An excellent idea. Mother has an instinct for anything that troubles her children, and she loves Georgie almost as a daughter. Is Georgie at Matlock House?"

"If she has bought out every ladies' shop in London she may be there. Your mother is kind to sponsor her."

"She is happy to do it, since you have no wife to do the honors."

"I shall never marry," Darcy said quietly. "Pemberley is not entailed to heirs male of the body. Let Georgiana's son inherit. So long as she marries wisely there will be no problem."

Richard looked at Darcy askance. "Is there any doubt she will marry wisely? You would never let her marry someone out for her dowry."

Darcy shrugged. "I would not. It is her innocence that troubles me. She has never been exposed to any of the *ton* outside our circle of friends. She is vulnerable. I do not want her to suffer the hurt of believing herself in love and finding out the man is not worthy of her."

Richard set his glass aside and rose. "If you are going to my esteemed parents' townhouse, I shall go with you. I want to speak to Father, always supposing he is not in a meeting somewhere."

Darcy walked with him to the entry sending a footman for their outerwear. His carriage had already been called for.

"Since Parliament is not in session at the moment I would think he had few meetings to attend."

"You do not understand how business is done in the government. There are more discussions and decisions taken off the floor than on it."

Darcy said no more as they entered his capacious carriage and began to thread the traffic on the streets of Mayfair. Without warning the driver pulled up the horses, nearly unseating the coach's two occupants. A jumble of shouts, curses and general noise filtered into the interior. Before Darcy could knock on the trap in the roof it opened and his chief driver Mr. Tombs said, "Accident up ahead, Mr. Darcy. Cart and a dray." Looks like it'll take some time to clear. I can't turn here. Do you want me to try and pull over, sir?"

Darcy looked at Richard. "Fancy a short walk?" When his cousin nodded he said, "We will go on foot from here, Mr. Tombs. Bring the carriage when you can get through."

The trap closed. A footman jumped down and put the step up. Darcy and Richard climbed out and stood for a moment to view the confusion ahead. Angry drivers swore and yelled at each other, each blaming the other for the collision. Such incidents were not uncommon even in the wealthy districts of London. Some of the watchers cheered one man or the other and some yelled in frustration at the chaos. The cart had lost a wheel and the dray was tipped partly on its side, its load of barrels threatening to spill into the already crowded street. As the event happened at an intersection traffic was snarled in every direction. Darcy cut rapidly through the bystanders with Richard at his shoulder to reach a lane that led to a mews. Once they were in the relative quiet of the mews he slowed to a fast walk. Richard recognized the space as being only a short way from Matlock House.

The butler admitted them with a significant glance toward the street. Richard said, "Two vehicles tried to occupy the same space at the same time. I believe that goes against the laws of nature."

Mr. Caldwell nodded. "Yes, sir. Good afternoon, Mr. Darcy."

"Good afternoon, Mr. Caldwell. Is my sister here?"

"I believe she has not yet returned from shopping with Lady Matlock. Would you like me to order tea in the drawing room, Mr. Richard?"

"I think we'll wait in my father's study, unless he is using it?"

"Lord Matlock is at his club. I expect him back for dinner."

With a knowing glance at Darcy, Richard led the way to his father's study.

"Georgiana, are you well, my dear?"

Lady Eleanor Fitzwilliam's beautifully modulated voice brought her niece out of a brown study of the passing cityscape. Georgiana Darcy forced a bright smile for her aunt, who was not fooled in the least.

"I am quite well, Aunt, I thank you."

"You have been rather—withdrawn of late. Is something troubling you?"

Georgiana did not answer immediately. She kept her pale head bowed so that the brim of her fashionable bonnet masked her face. Lady Eleanor smiled to herself. *She is the image of my mother-by-marriage. The same wheat-colored hair, the same turquoise eyes and delicate bones. The wedding portrait of her grandmother at Foxwood could almost be of her. It is the Danish blood.*

"Nothing is troubling me, Aunt."

"Very well. Perhaps you are just growing tired with all the activities. One's first Season can be exhausting."

Georgiana seized on the explanation too quickly. "Yes, Aunt, that is it. I am just a bit tired. I shall be fine for a little rest."

"Why do we not do this?" Lady Matlock took Georgiana's gloved hand in hers. "The Season will be over in about a month. From now until the end, why do we not only accept invitations to those entertainments given by friends? You have met all of the eligible young men, and some not so young, there is no need to be out every night. It might be well for you to take some time to think over all that has happened. If anyone wishes to call on you we can decide your course at that time."

"Thank you, Aunt."

Lady Eleanor squeezed her niece's hand and sat back. She knew perfectly well Georgiana was prevaricating. *I shall have to speak with Darcy. I do not believe it is serious, however as her main guardian he should be made aware of any possible problems before they arise.*

With her gaze once more on the perfectly kept houses passing by the carriage. Georgiana wondered how much longer she could sustain the masquerade. *I do not want to go to any more balls or soirees, or plays or operas or garden parties or picnics or listen to any further insincere compliments or self-serving descriptions of their estates or their prospects. There is only one man I want to call on me, and he will never do so.*

Fighting the tears that threatened to ruin her hard-won composure, Georgiana began to recount their shopping trip in great detail. By the time they reached Matlock House, she felt she was incapable of another word about fabrics or trims. She walked beside her aunt's elegant figure into the entry hall to find her brother waiting for them with a smile that washed away his habitually sober expression and showed his true age.

"Brother!"

Georgiana hurried to meet him, throwing her arms around him in a thoroughly undignified manner. He held her to him for a moment before she drew back so he was able to study her face.

"Have I any money left in the bank?"

"Only a little."

Georgiana kept hold of his hands. Over her head, Lady Matlock gave Darcy a significant look that meant she wanted to speak to him privately. Georgiana's cousin and co-guardian Richard Fitzwilliam joined them from his father's study.

"No greeting for me, little bird?"

Georgiana released Darcy's hands and curtsied deeply to her cousin. His response was to bow in reply and then hug her in turn. "Hello, Mother," he said as he let Georgiana go.

"I have not set eyes on you for a fortnight, and all you can say is 'Hello, Mother'?"

Her son knew the chiding tone was not serious. Richard took her hands, bent and kissed her cheek. "It is good to see you, too."

She smiled at her son, the favorite of her three children, took his arm and allowed him to escort her into the drawing room where she rang for tea before taking a seat on a sofa. At fifty-two she was still handsome, the bones of her face, which had made her one of the beauties of her Season covered by perfect skin with only a few wrinkles around the eyes. Her golden hair with its soft reddish lights had grayed at the temples without dulling its luster. The daughter of a baron, her marriage to the heir of the Sixth Earl of Matlock was the triumph of her year.

"I would have been home earlier," Richard was saying, "if I had not been kept in the north, playing errand boy for General Sternholt. We could end the war a year early if the man was capable of making up his mind."

"When will you have to go back?" Lady Matlock tried without success to keep her voice neutral.

"I am not certain. At present I am at the General's pleasure. Come, let us not talk of war or duty. The tea is arriving and I am famished."

"As usual."

"I am a soldier. I eat whenever food is available."

Lady Matlock smiled and waved the maid away to pour out the tea herself. Darcy had remained silent, watching his sister. She did look tired, he thought; he might have believed it was only the social rush of the Season had he not known her so well. Her face had a pinched look he had not seen since their father died. It told him Georgiana was keeping back some intense feeling. When tea was over, Georgiana excused herself to rest, the other three remaining in the drawing room. Darcy watched his aunt. She rearranged the tea tray taking time to gather her thoughts before meeting her nephew's gaze.

"Before you ask, William, I do not know what is bothering Georgiana. At first she enjoyed the Season, but recently she has withdrawn from several engagements she would otherwise have attended. She has met a number of eminently suitable young men, including the son of Viscount Tennerley, without any perceptible interest in any of them."

"She has not met any young men not of the *ton?*"

"No, Richard. I am perfectly capable of keeping her from the wrong sort of acquaintances. I do not know if the idea of marriage frightens her. She assures me it does not. She says she is just tired which I do not believe. She is seventeen, Darcy, the age I was when I married your uncle. If she does not marry this Season, she should go through the little season in the fall. Waiting too long will impair her chances of an appropriate match."

Darcy felt a stir of resentment. "Georgiana is hardly on the shelf. She is beautiful, wealthy, accomplished and has excellent connections. It is no matter to me if she marries this Season, next Season, or not until her majority."

"And that," Lady Matlock replied tartly, "is the problem. She has a duty to her name and family, as do you. You need to instill in her the obligation to marry and marry well. I realize you will not marry cousin Anne, even Catherine has eased her demands, but that leaves a number of debutantes you may choose from. For Heaven's sake, William, what is wrong with you? Do you not want an heir?"

Darcy wanted to rise to his feet and walk away. Instead he controlled an angry response by adjusting his perfectly tied cravat. When he was able to speak calmly he said, "My intentions regarding marriage are not the point. I will not have Georgiana pushed into a match against her will. She will marry when she is ready, as will I."

His aunt looked up at him as he rose. "Forgive me if I seem to meddle. I only have Georgiana's best interests at heart, and yours."

"I know. I will ask you to watch her, and if she will talk to you about her reservations I will be grateful for your opinion."

With a bow he left the drawing room and asked the butler to have his carriage brought around. Richard joined him after several minutes.

"Mother means well. She is just so used to running everything at Matlock House and ordering her children's lives she sometimes forgets not everyone appreciates having their future set out for them."

"I know. It is generous of her to sponsor Georgie. But it is not a law that a debutante must marry in her first Season, especially a young woman as sensitive as my sister. A bad marriage cannot be ended without time, money and above all scandal. I do not want Georgie to find herself forced into such a marriage, or one where husband and wife live separate lives, barely communicating with one another."

"My advice," Richard's hand rested briefly on his cousin's shoulder, a gesture allowed to very few men, "as useful as always, is to wait and see. I think Georgie will talk to you eventually."

"I hope so."

A footman brought Darcy's outerwear and assisted him into his overcoat. He left Matlock House still anxious for his sister. What could affect her in so obvious a manner was something he must discover, for both their sakes. Darcy knew that questioning her was not the way. He had to watch her carefully without seeming to and let her reveal the source of her pain herself. Lady Matlock's way was not the answer. Georgiana was not a prize mare on sale to the highest bidder. Darcy promised himself that whatever troubled her, he would never force her to violate her principles.

He rapped on the trap and ordered Mr. Tombs to take him to Angelo's fencing academy.

# CHAPTER THREE

May 1813
Meadow Lane, London

E lizabeth had grown tired of the barren window boxes and over-grown, weedy flowerbeds in front of the house on Meadow Lane. The low picket fence bordering the yard needed mending and a coat of paint. Straggling rose bushes should be pruned or taken out and replaced. Both she and Jane knew how to maintain a cutting garden and work in a still room, but the work required to improve the face the house presented to passersby required a gardener. Determined to explore the grounds in search of tools or any other useful objects, she made her way out the rear door into the yard behind the house. It had been graveled at one time, now only a scattered layer of small rocks covered packed dirt too hard for even weeds to survive.

The sweet odor of apple blossoms filled her nostrils from a burgeoning tree near what appeared to be an old stable. Cook at Longbourn always put up apple butter from their orchard as well as dried apples to be used over the winter. Elizabeth fought down a surge of nostalgia for those days when life was never valued as it ought to have been. The apple tree wore a face of pink and white blossoms that reminded her of Jane. There was no kitchen garden, only an empty space with a ramshackle fence where one might once have been. It was neither a pleasant nor a useful prospect.

Elizabeth refused to be discouraged. She squared her shoulders and sent herself striding toward a dilapidated structure at the rear of the property, not yet explored. It was indeed an old stable, its double doors leaning against one another for support, their hinges bright orange with rust. A single wooden handle on the right-hand door was the only means of entrance. Cautiously, Elizabeth pulled at it, felt the door move reluctantly. She pulled harder; with a loud screech of protest it swung out, its companion quivering at the disturbance before following to reveal the interior.

*Whoever this house was built for must have kept a carriage.* There was a small empty shelf next to the door, no doubt for a candle or lamp. She picked her way over warped boards that creaked and gave under her light weight. Two stalls stood open to the right, the near one with its half-door sagging on a broken hinge, the other stall's half-door long removed. The stale air retained a faint odor of horse. Elizabeth peered into dim space. *I should have brought a lamp. The sunshine barely reaches beyond the doors.* There was a narrow loft over the stalls with no ladder for access; a few bits of straw still lay here and there. She proceeded slowly past the stalls to a larger area where the carriage had resided.

A dim shape in the back of the space caught her attention. It looked like a rake or hoe. She could see it leaned against the corner next to an odd-shaped lump. A badly tarnished bridle sagged from a peg on the rear wall, its leather cracked, one rein cut off near the bit. As she approached the back of the open area Elizabeth was able to see that the lump was a wheelbarrow turned upside down, its wheel broken in half, the handles cracked. The implement leaning against the corner was the shaft of a garden tool, its unknown head no longer attached.

For a moment, Elizabeth stood and gazed around her. This was their life, this empty, useless, purposeless structure held together by the slowly failing remnants of its former solidity. She bit back the urge to cry. She had shed too many futile tears to indulge in more. Elizabeth straightened when she heard a tentative voice from the doorway.

"Madam? Are you there? Miss Bennet asked me to find you. You have a visitor."

Hoping it was their aunt, Elizabeth accompanied Nettie back to the house, straightening her dress as she went. For a moment she resented that their aunt Gardiner would not bring Kitty here, before she admitted it was best to sever as many ties to their younger sister as possible until she married. Neither she nor Jane had been close to Kitty or Lydia, a source of shame for both of them. They blamed themselves for not trying harder to curb their two youngest sisters' inclinations to flirt and act the hoyden. The guilt was only partly assuaged by the memory of their mother's indulgence and their father's indifference. Pushing the thought away, Elizabeth entered the house.

Elizabeth heard her aunt's voice as she approached the parlor door. She hurried forward to curtsy and then take her aunt's hands in hers. "I am so happy to see you, dear aunt. How is uncle, and how are my niece and nephews?"

Mrs. Gardiner hugged her niece, "They are all well, Lizzy. Catherine has been very good with them. I think she will make a fine mother one day."

They seated themselves and Jane rang for tea. She caught Elizabeth's eye then glanced toward the upstairs, indicating their father had declined to come down. Elizabeth was a little surprised. Mr. Bennet had not left the house since they moved in except to confer with their uncle Gardiner, however considering the debt they owed their relations his refusal bordered actual rudeness.

"How is my brother Bennet?"

Mrs. Gardiner sounded concerned. Lizzy bit her lip before she answered. "He comes down for meals, otherwise he remains in his room or the small sitting room, sometimes reading one of the few books he has retained, more often staring out the window at the distant prospect of Hampstead Heath."

"It will take time for him to readjust. I do not know if it was wise of him to bring you to London, however I understand his reasons. With so many of your neighbors turning against you, and Fanny gone, I am sure the house was like a prison. And there was little chance of anything changing."

"They killed Mama." Jane's low words were more bitter than Elizabeth had ever heard her. "I did not want to stay."

"We are here now." Elizabeth reached out to touch her sister's hand. "We will make the best of it."

Nettie brought in the tea and at Elizabeth's nod served it carefully. Mrs. Hobson had provided a plate of biscuits as well. When the maid had curtsied and gone, Mrs. Gardiner smiled.

"I see you have acquired a maid. She is quite young, is she not?"

"Sixteen." Jane sipped her tea. "She is quick and eager to learn. Lizzy and I are teaching her how to arrange hair and how to serve in a drawing room."

"Have you taken on a maid or a pupil?"

The three women laughed. As they drank their tea, Mrs. Gardiner became more serious. "I am not truly familiar with this area;, however I know there is a market at Bloomsbury. Not the big one at Covent Garden, but it has quite good produce and there are some shops. You must be careful, though. It is best to go by hansom if you can. St. Giles rookery is not far from here. Usually there is no trouble, however one never knows."

"Mrs. Hobson goes three times a week. She has been walking, but if you think it best we can send her by hansom."

"I do not wish to tell you how to run your household, my dears. I do not think a cook with a market basket walking in broad daylight is in any danger, but I would feel easier in my mind if either or both of you did not venture out alone. You are used to the country where a young woman alone tends to be quite safe. This is London. You must adjust to the very great difference."

"We shall take your advice, aunt." Jane glanced at Elizabeth. "As we are in mourning, we do not go out except to visit you and uncle and Kit—Catherine. Or to walk in Sloane Square."

Their aunt rose to go. "You will not always be in mourning, my loves. One day you will reenter the world again. Just remember I will be there to help you in any way you need."

It was not until Mrs. Gardiner's carriage pulled away that Elizabeth realized with a swift jolt of concern that she had not said "your uncle and I."

## July 1813
## Gracechurch Street, London

Catherine Bennet sat on the padded bench beneath the window in her room at the Gardiner's residence on Gracechurch Street and watched two sparrows busily engaged in searching the side garden for succulent insects. She wondered if Mr. Thurgood would call today. It was a subject much on her mind of late. She had grown used to being called Catherine rather than her family name of Kitty. After all, she was not a child anymore, she was a young lady of marriageable age, and Mr. Thurgood was the best prospect of the few men she had met. She understood why she could not have a regular Season where balls and parties meant introductions to many eligible young men. Lydia had made it an impossibility.

*Why, Lydie? You were always so pretty, you did not have to run away with someone like that and spoil everything. You could have married Mr. Fitzpatrick's son, he liked you so much. The officers were fun to flirt and dance with but none of them had enough money to afford a wife. You will be poor and miserable. I can at least expect a comfortable home and a family.*

Restless, she rose and made her way downstairs to the drawing room. The sound of voices in the entry came through the half-open door. Catherine recognized Robert Thurgood's educated tenor and her aunt's quiet tones. Her hands gripped the piece of needlework in her lap; she purposely relaxed them and took up her needle again. Mrs. Gardiner opened the door to admit their visitor. Catherine's eyes met Mr. Thurgood's for a second before she dropped them demurely, her cheeks coloring.

"Good morning, Miss Catherine."

Mr. Thurgood bowed and she curtsied as she replied, "Good morning, Mr. Thurgood." With a glance at her aunt, she added, "Will you not come into the drawing room? I will order tea."

"I—I hoped to speak to Mr. Gardiner if he is at home?"

"My husband is at his warehouse this morning. I expect him home for luncheon. You are most welcome to stay, Mr. Thurgood."

It was debatable which one of the young people blushed more profoundly. Mrs. Gardiner kept her amusement to herself as Catherine rang for tea to be served. Mr. Thurgood was a fine, solid young man. Not a gentleman by social standards, he had a responsible position with his father's soft goods business and an income substantial enough to afford a wife and family.

"I should like that, thank you, Mrs. Gardiner."

His eyes touched Catherine with admiration. Still keeping her gaze modestly lowered, she felt his inspection and wished she did not have to wear unrelieved black, even though the dress was new and fashionable. She tugged surreptitiously at the skirt to straighten a crease. Catherine was not aware that the matte black bombazine made her pale complexion appear translucent and emphasized the color in her cheeks.

Tea was served and they made small talk until Mr. Gardiner arrived. He noted Mr. Thurgood's presence with a smile, but grew serious when the young man asked to speak to him in private. Mr. Gardiner led the way to his study. It was a room familiar to Mr.

Thurgood from his own father's study, wood paneled, a Bokhara rug with a small seating area before the marble fireplace. Mr. Gardiner indicated the chair before his desk and went to a sidebar.

"Port or brandy?"

"Oh, a small port, sir, thank you."

Mr. Thurgood wanted to say, "I never indulge in brandy this early." He did not, afraid he might insult his host. When Mr. Gardiner handed him the glass, he sipped it and set it down. He could feel his palms sweating. Something seemed to have happened to his voice.

The older man took his chair behind the desk. "You wanted to speak to me, Mr. Thurgood?"

Mr. Thurgood swallowed twice before his voice returned. "My father is in the process of purchasing a weaving company from a supplier of his who is retiring. We will be able to produce our own cloth, including jacquards. It will save us the cost of purchasing from the factory owner. Father is sending me north to finalize the sale and take oversight of the factory. If I succeed he will make me a full partner." This was not what he had practiced. The words were jumbled in his ears and coming too fast. He stopped, breathed in deeply and clutched the arms of his chair. "Over the past two months I have come to admire Miss Catherine very much. She is a wonderful young lady. I—I want to marry her. I can take care of her and a family that is, we can have a family and she will never want for anything."

Mr. Thurgood stumbled to a halt, picked up his glass and drained it. Mr. Gardiner struggled with a sudden cough. When it was under control, he watched the young man before him with a brief memory of asking for Mrs. Gardiner's hand.

"You know her father lives in London?"

"You mentioned it once, yes. Do you think he will not approve of me?"

"No. But you should have his consent as Catherine is only eighteen."

Mr. Thurgood leaned forward a little. "How shall I obtain it, sir?"

Mr. Gardiner considered. "Let me contact him. He is of course in mourning for his wife, my sister. He has given Catherine into my care for the time being and I think he will be satisfied with my recommendation." Both men rose. "Do you wish to speak to Catherine now?"

"Yes, sir, if you will allow me to."

He followed Mr. Gardiner to the door. In the drawing room, Mrs. Gardiner sat with her niece as her husband and her potential nephew-by-marriage left the room. Catherine looked at her aunt in a mixture of apprehension and excitement.

Without being asked, Mrs. Gardiner replied, "I can think of no other reason he would wish to speak to Mr. Gardiner privately. Will you be happy if he offers for you, my dear?"

Catherine considered the question with a deliberation new to her. "Yes, aunt, I will. He seems kind and considerate. We will not have to live in strained circumstances. His family has been welcoming to me. I believe it is my best chance for felicity in marriage."

"You have not said that you feel affection for him."

Catherine shifted her weight a little on the sofa. "I like him very much. For now, that is enough. I believe I will come to feel affection for him in time."

Mrs. Gardiner was not certain if her niece's attitude surprised her as much as it might have. In the year since Lydia's infamous act, her next eldest sister had grown less romantic and more realistic. In a way it was sad, but her aunt believed it would serve Catherine in better stead than her old frivolous ways.

The two men returned after a quarter hour. Mr. Thurgood appeared nervous. Mr. Gardiner gave his wife a swift look of satisfaction before turning to his niece.

"I have allowed Mr. Thurgood five minutes to speak to you privately. Then we will go in to luncheon."

Mr. and Mrs. Gardiner left the young couple alone. Catherine resumed her seat and Mr. Thurgood came to stand before her, stiff with purpose. "Miss Catherine, as I have come to know you over the past several months, I have developed a great admiration and respect for you. You are a fine woman who will make a perfect wife. I know you are in half-mourning still, and I shall wait as long as necessary. But I must speak." Dropping to his knee, he tentatively took her hands in his. "Miss Catherine, would you consider…that is, will you agree…to accept my hand in marriage?"

Catherine looked into his face, so close to hers. She began to tremble as the enormity of what she was about to do overcame her. This was the rest of her life. She was committing her care and safety and happiness to this man until the day she died. Swift images of her mother and father flitted through her mind. It would not be like that, she was certain of it. She would be happy.

"Yes, Mr. Thurgood, I will."

Surprised at the steadiness of her voice, Catherine pressed his hands. He smiled tentatively, then a wide grin lightened his face. He rose, pulling her to her feet.

"May I?"

His eyes were on her lips. She nodded and he kissed her very gently, only for a moment. There was a tap at the open door, and her aunt looked in. The two young people jumped apart, but Mrs. Gardiner only smiled.

"Luncheon is served."

# CHAPTER FOUR

August 1813
Matlock House, London

Darcy heard Lady Catherine de Bourgh's imperious voice with an involuntary wince as he approached the drawing room at Matlock House. He respected his aunt without feeling any fondness for the woman. Lady Catherine treated any house she visited as if it were her own, ordering the servants about, criticizing anything not meeting her exacting—and totally arbitrary—standards. Her years-long campaign to force a marriage between Darcy and her daughter Anne was a burden he carried with no little resentment. Of late she had not importuned him as much as usual. He wondered as he entered the room if she intended to start up again.

"Well, nephew, it is about time. Where is my niece?"

Lady Matlock shot a glance at him from eyes already simmering with vexation. The animosity between the countess and her sister-by-marriage began when Lady Catherine opposed the marriage of her brother, heir to the earldom, to the daughter of a baron with a brother in banking. The financial connection smelled too strongly of trade for her aristocratic sensibilities. When he ignored her objections and their father the earl upheld his son's choice, Lady Catherine took a permanent dislike to her sister-by-marriage. It was a state that still existed more than thirty years later, and one Lady Catherine was only too happy to encourage at every opportunity. Darcy suspected some of Lady Catherine's pique was jealousy. Comparing the two women was like comparing a cow and a mare. Both might be prize animals, but the mare would always be more admired.

"Good morning, Aunt."

Darcy kissed her regally extended hand. In spite of the heat of late August she wore her usual dark clothing in the style of a previous generation; purple silk edged at the high neck and long sleeves with the finest lace. The drawing room drapes were drawn against the harsh daylight; the relative dimness of the room did nothing to soften Lady Catherine's hawk-like features. Darcy kissed Lady Matlock's hand as well and took a seat with a practiced flip of his coat tails.

"Georgiana is at Pemberley. She has not been well. Doctor Morrow recommended she remain in Derbyshire rather than undertake the journey to London."

"Nonsense!" It was one of Lady Catherine's favorite words and she exercised it with the diligence of its position in her vocabulary. "She needs to be here for the remainder of the little season. If you had let me sponsor her, she would be betrothed by now."

"And how would you have accomplished that, Sister?" Lady Matlock's voice was a shade too sweet. "Throw her into the arms of the first gentleman who came close enough?"

"I do not appreciate your attempt at sarcasm, Eleanor, although I understand it in view of your failure with the girl. She needs to be brought under control, not cosseted and allowed to reject perfectly good opportunities to marry into the highest levels of society, as is her duty."

His aunt's voice grated on Darcy's nerves. He said more sharply than he intended, "Georgiana is my responsibility. It was my decision to leave her at Pemberley. The little season is half over and the present heat will not benefit her. As to her marrying, that is her decision. It is her life that will be spent with her husband, she has every right to be as sure of her choice as possible."

Darcy dared say no more. For years he had dreaded this time, when Georgiana would enter society with the goal, at least for her relatives. of marriage. There was no way she could know her danger from Wickham, but Darcy was not sorry Georgiana seemed reluctant to choose a suitor. If only there was a way to ensure her future from disaster he would take it; at present there was not. The best Darcy could do was to fend off their aunt's meddling interference and wait.

"No wonder the girl has wasted her first Season. Your attitude tells me everything I need to know."

Darcy suppressed the urge to say *When it comes to my personal business there is nothing you need to know.* "I did not come here to discuss Georgiana's marriage prospects. How is Anne?"

Instead of the sarcastic response he expected his aunt's expression grew sober. She said reluctantly, "Anne is not progressing as well as I would wish. I have brought her to London to consult a specialist."

Darcy's stomach tightened. If his aunt wished her daughter to see a London specialist instead of the quack she employed for Rosings, Anne's poor health must be worse than previously. He caught a glance from Lady Matlock that confirmed his fears. His always fragile cousin was very ill.

"Has she seen anyone?"

"Sir Edgar Crane. He has not returned a diagnosis yet. I will meet with him tomorrow."

Lady Matlock rose and rang for tea. She resumed her seat, concern in her voice. "I hope Sir Edgar is able to help her. He has an excellent reputation."

"It is well earned," Darcy assured her. "A friend of mine saw him last year, he provided more help than several others my friend had seen previously."

Tea came and with it a pitcher of lemonade. "The conservatory is proving quite satisfactory." Lady Matlock poured a glass for Darcy and one for herself. "I am glad we added it in spite of the disruption the construction caused. Our gardener is going to attempt pineapples as soon as suitable plants can be obtained. Lemonade, Catherine?"

"No, thank you. Tea as I always take it."

Lady Matlock prepared a cup, offered her sister-by-marriage the server of tarts and biscuits. Catherine declined with a shake of her head. Darcy took a lemon tart. They were one of the pastry chef's specialties Darcy could never resist. He must behave as normally as possible. His aunt Eleanor was a perceptive woman.

"I cannot understand the necessity of building expensive glass houses to nurture plants that do not adapt to conditions in England, when we have a sufficiency of perfectly good fruits and flowers already." Lady Catherine sipped her tea, made a face and set the cup down.

"The tea is not to your liking?" Lady Eleanor did not sound surprised.

"It is no worse than usual."

"I am so sorry. It is a new blend from Porter's Tea Shop. Shall I send for a pot of bohea?"

"Do not bother. I am sure your maid has better things to do."

Conversation waned. They were finishing tea when Richard joined them. He wore his regimentals, from red coat to polished boots, with an élan his stocky build did nothing to impair.

"I took time to clean up a bit before joining you. The ride from Westminster is worse than usual right now. Hello, Mother."

He kissed his mother's cheek, made an elaborate bow to Lady Catherine and helped himself to lemonade and a plate of edibles.

"Acting the mountebank as usual," Lady Catherine snapped without humor. "I see you are still in London."

Richard swallowed the remainder of a tart and dabbed his lips with his serviette. "I expect to receive my orders at any time. There is bound to be a push now that the French are likely to retreat over the Pyrenees."

"Bonaparte still has followers," Darcy offered.

"True. But his *Grande Armée* is in tatters, and his Prussian allies are having second thoughts. Austria has already joined the Allies and after Vitoria, Boney may well replace Soult. The emperor can put up a good fight and I have no doubt he will, but I do not think he can win unless the Allies cannot field sufficient troops. That is why I am still in England, training recruits."

"I wish you could stay."

Lady Matlock sounded resigned. She knew her son was anxious to return to his regiment. He had been a soldier for ten years; nothing but serious injury or death would prevent him finishing the war with Bonaparte. She put a good face on her fears however much they darkened her life. He was the man he was.

Darcy rose as his cousin set down his glass and stood. "I have a business appointment this afternoon. Please let me know how Anne does."

Lady Catherine nodded without answering. In the entry the two cousins waited together for Darcy's carriage. Richard glanced back along the hall toward the drawing room, lowered his voice.

"I have news of a sort I wanted to tell you in private." At Darcy's raised eyebrow Richard said, "One of my men though he saw Wickham last night. I have them out looking for deserters and he was in the edge of Whitechapel when he saw a man in a militia uniform generally fitting Wickham's description. He followed as close as he dared for several blocks. A fight spilled out into the street and he lost the man in the crowd. He has never seen Wickham, so he is not certain it was him. I have increased our presence in the area. If he is there we have a chance of spotting him."

Darcy's eyes had grown hard and very dark. "Have you found Mrs. Young? They were together for some time."

"Finally." Richard's mouth twisted. "She runs a boarding house at the edge of Whitechapel populated by women who work mostly at night. It is not formally a brothel but it might as well be. She claims she does not know where he is. There was something strange about her response that leads me to believe she has information, but even the reward did not tempt her."

"Strange. If money does not move her she is deathly afraid of something."

"We will keep looking. He cannot stay hidden forever."

Darcy did not look as if he agreed. "Let me know at once if there is a positive sighting."

"I shall. I should tell you, too, that Anne is quite ill. I am not sure it is not because of that fake doctor our aunt employs and his potions. I just hope Sir Edgar can help her." His voice was more grim than might have been expected, a fact Darcy noted in passing.

"As do I. It is enough to worry about Georgie without having Anne worse."

"Georgie? What is wrong with my little bird?"

"The same thing that was wrong this spring. She claims she is not ill, however she is sinking deeper into melancholy. She will not talk to me about it, she will not even confide in Mrs. Annesley. She does not want to participate in the little season, or talk of the gentlemen she has met. She is not eating enough either. I am at my wits end."

Richard appeared thoughtful. "I wonder if something has occurred that frightens her?"

"Surely she would tell me, or at least aunt Eleanor, if that were the case." *I hope she would. If he has contacted her...* Darcy felt the hair rise on the back of his neck.

"She might wish to avoid any confrontation so long as nothing of a serious nature has happened." Richard sounded thoughtful but unalarmed.

Mr. Caldwell appeared with a footman bearing Darcy's hat, gloves and stick. "Your carriage is ready, Mr. Darcy."

Darcy took them, thanked him and pulled on his gloves. The fanlight over the door etched his patrician features in a soft chiaroscuro. "I shall have to think of how to approach her if that is in fact the problem. Your mother seems to feel she needs to choose a husband

and marry, but I will not pressure her to do so. If it is someone who has disturbed her peace of mind I will find out who he is and take whatever action is necessary."

Richard's voice was unusually sober. "Take care, my friend. Scandal is like fire, it consumes everything without discrimination."

Darcy made no reply. He knew the results of scandal on the innocent all too well; he had lived in its shadow for five long years. He put on his hat and took up his stick. Mr. Caldwell held the door open.

"Let me know when you must return to the Continent, Richard."

"I will."

The door closed behind Darcy's tall figure. Richard rubbed a hand over his face, shook his head. Where Georgiana was concerned, Darcy was unlikely to listen to reason. He would have to see what he might find out and without arousing his mother's suspicions. A task nearly as daunting as finding Wickham in the London rookeries.

August 1813
Janus House, London

In the drawing room at Janus House, the de Bourgh London town home, Anne de Bourgh stared out the nearest window and let her mother's voice slip over her like a chill draft. She often used this method of insulating herself from Lady Catherine's irritable and imperious sentiments. Anne watched the rainbow array of summer roses surrounding a splashing fountain and planned the garden she would have designed if she had ever possessed the vitality to take on such a project. But she was rarely even afforded the chance to walk in the gardens, let alone design them.

She hated the room; the elaborately carved and gilded furniture, the fussy, inlaid and gilded tables, the thick dark drapes and confused patterns of the upholstery, the oriental rugs, all in somber colors and two generations out of date. The chairs were so uncomfortable that Anne had to have cushions banked in them to sit for more than a few minutes. It reminded her of the main drawing room at Rosings that she was forced to occupy on the occasions she came downstairs.

Her mother would never allow the windows there to be opened, so the room frequently had a musty atmosphere although it was cleaned regularly. Altogether, she would rather remain in her own chambers most of the time. Over the past several years she had managed to slowly replace a number of the furnishings chosen by Lady Catherine with pieces that were more to her taste, discovered in unused guest rooms. Her mother did not visit her chambers often, and seemed not to notice the alterations.

Nearby, her companion, Mrs. Jenkinson attended to some mending, keeping her head bowed over her work. Her companion was terrified of Lady Catherine, as were most people who dealt with her. Even her new parson trod softly around his patroness in spite of a lack of subservience. Anne had not cared for Mr. Collins; the new vicar was a little better.

"I have just returned from meeting with Sir Edgar Crane."

Lady Catherine's sharp voice cut through Anne's thoughts with knifelike pain. Her mother seated herself in what amounted to a throne, a large oak chair upholstered in scuffed red velvet. The back rose a foot above her head; the arms ended in griffin heads. Its twin sat in the formal drawing room at Rosings. Anne hated it.

"Ring for tea," she ordered Mrs. Jenkinson, who immediately jumped up and went to the bell pull. "I am in need of restoration."

Anne waited. She did not have to ask for Sir Edgar's diagnosis, her mother would relay it when she deemed she had her daughter's full attention. Lady Catherine smoothed her skirt and raised pale blue eyes like gimlets to Anne's face.

"Do you not want to know what he said?"

"Yes, Mother." *Those are the words that define my life.*

"You are indeed ill. Sir Edgar says the medicines Dr. Lessing gives you are of no value and may even contribute to your fatigue. He recommends a special diet, mild exercise, and an herbal compound of his own devising to strengthen your constitution. I have sent the diet to Cook. It is quite practical and will do no harm." She turned to Mrs. Jenkinson. "You may take Anne for a brief walk in the garden before dinner. See that she is properly dressed so she does not catch a chill."

"Yes, my lady." Mrs. Jenkinson glanced briefly at her charge. Anne almost smiled. She would not be too properly dressed.

The tea came. The maid poured out before Lady Catherine waved her from the room. She added cream and three lumps of sugar to her own cup and allowed Mrs. Jenkinson to prepare Anne's and her own. When she had taken a long swallow, Lady Catherine set the cup on the tray with satisfaction.

"So much better to use the pure bohea rather than the fancy blends Eleanor is so fond of. It is always better to keep matters simple."

To change the subject before her mother started on Sir Edgar again, Anne said, "How is aunt Eleanor?"

"As supercilious as usual. She has added a conservatory to the rear of Matlock House. Foolish expense so she can serve lemonade and oranges and lord it over those who do not possess one. Stupid woman. It comes of my brother marrying beneath him."

"Her father was a baron. That is hardly beneath uncle Henry."

Lady Catherine glared at her daughter. "Not beneath an earl? Where do you get such an opinion? He could have had the daughter of a viscount, even another earl. He wanted Eleanor because she used her arts and allurements to capture him. Richard was also present, acting the fool. If I did not know better I would think Henry bought his rise in the military."

"Richard earned his promotions. He is a fine soldier."

Anne's voice sounded tight. Her mother searched her face; she found nothing more than her daughter's usual pale countenance. "No doubt. I do not know what he intends to pursue when this war ends. Perhaps he can use his military reputation to attract a wealthy wife. He will certainly get nothing of importance from the estate. And that reminds me. Darcy was there as well."

Anne drew in a breath and braced herself. Now the old harangue was inevitable. Of late her mother had not brought up the subject of her supposed engagement to Fitzwilliam. Anne knew the truce could not last forever; it was a subject Lady Catherine could no more leave alone than she could accept that her will was not to prevail.

"Your cousin Georgiana is still at Pemberley, he did not make her return for the little season. I do not know what ails the boy. She is not made of crystal, she needs to find a husband and marry. When she is settled, perhaps he will return to his duty and your marriage can be finalized."

"I am not strong enough to marry, Mother, you know that."

An unpleasant smile turned up Lady Catherine's thin lips. "Sir Edgar says if you progress as he hopes, in a few months you will be strong enough to marry. I asked him specifically."

"I am sure you did. And how long is this new cure to last?"

"Sir Edgar estimates it will be several months before you show any notable progress. Until then you will follow his regime precisely."

Anne wanted to rise and shout at the woman before her, *I will not! I will not have my life planned for me any longer, especially by you.*

"Yes, Mother."

"Good. Perhaps you will be able to participate in several events next Season. It will be the perfect time to announce your betrothal."

Anne motioned to Mrs. Jenkinson who rose and came to assist her from her chair. "I think I will rest for a little while before my walk."

"Yes," Lady Catherine returned to her tea, "a good idea. You do not want to overtax yourself. Time enough to gain strength before we make any specific wedding plans."

Anne walked from the room on her companion's arm as if each foot were made of lead. *Not again, not again, not again...*

# CHAPTER FIVE

August 1813
Meadow Lane, London

Elizabeth moved her chair back from the small escritoire in the dining room, put away her pen and closed the lid of the inkwell. The ledger before her had come to epitomize their life now, its gray fabric surface dull, frugal, empty, unlike the big leather-bound ledgers of Longbourn. The room was no larger than the other rooms, just enough space to hold a table, four chairs, Mama's china dresser and the writing desk. Its white-painted wainscoting rose half way up the walls to meet a dull green wallpaper striped in yellow and showing darker patches from previously hung paintings. The escritoire occupied the only window. Wall sconces holding candle lamps gave enough illumination for meals, but barely enough to read or sew even had there been room for a settee.

Their family had never been of high status; this was barely gentility. They were not starving, Mrs. Hobson came in six days a week and there was Nettie, although why she stayed when she was paid so little was a mystery. Elizabeth ran her fingers absently over the rough fabric. She did all of the household accounts now, her father did not even check them. They saw little of him unless they sat in the small sitting room upstairs where he spent his days and at times, his nights.

Elizabeth put the ledger away in a drawer of the dresser. She had paid the monthly rent and such other accounts they did not handle in cash. There was a modest amount of money coming in from the investment their uncle Gardiner had made for them. They might survive for years. Was that what she wanted, to survive, moving bleakly through day after day until true poverty overtook them? She and Papa might live that way but not Jane. Jane was drifting slowly into melancholy. Fear washed through Elizabeth's mind. Something had to be done and she was the only one to do it.

Elizabeth strode to the parlor. Jane sat by the side windows, the sun illuminating her golden head. She looked up from her needlework at her sister's entrance with the shadow of her old smile.

"I thought I would do a sampler for the sitting room. Something cheerful for Papa. He so rarely comes down, it is the only room he spends time in."

"That was thoughtful of you, dear."

Jane laid the sampler in her work basket and turned to watch her sister look out of the front window. Geraniums bloomed red and bright orange in the window box, among a profusion of spicy leaves. Half a dozen rose bushes were pruned into conformation and presented a picture of red, yellow and white blossoms. All weeds had been disposed of. Mulch now surrounded the roses and the flowering shrubs brought back from horticultural chaos. Elizabeth sighed. If only life could be tended like a garden and respond as well.

"Mrs. Bailey's son has done a very good job." Jane's voice echoed her sister's thoughts.

"Yes. I am glad he approached us. He is less expensive than a jobbing gardener and seems as competent."

"I thought Mrs. Bailey might call," Jane sounded wistful, "but I suppose she felt it was not appropriate."

Elizabeth turned from the window. "She certainly cannot know anything about us other than our names. If an older woman lived here she might feel more comfortable."

"Yes. Mama would know every lady in the neighborhood by now."

They moved to the sofa. Elizabeth sat close to her sister, her voice purposely calm. "I have been thinking. We are not doing badly, but we could save even more money if we took rooms when the lease is up next year. Nettie could stay with us as she lives in, and we could find another housekeeper, perhaps full time. If it was closer to the shops we would not have to take a hansom when we needed something, except to visit our aunt and uncle. Perhaps we could find a flat where Papa could have a book room. Our uncle Gardiner can help us find something appropriate. What do you think, dearest?"

Jane did not answer for a time. Elizabeth wondered if Jane was afraid her response might disappoint or upset her.

"You know I will go wherever you do, Lizzy. I just do not know how Papa would react to the suggestion that we reduce our household to a set of rooms."

"I do not think he cares. So long as he is allowed to spend his days in solitude he seems to care little where he is. If you are right, we will abandon the idea. It is only something to think on."

Elizabeth patted her sister's hand. Nettie came in from the entry hall with a small tray. "The post, madam."

"Thank you, Nettie." Elizabeth took the single letter and looked at the pretty, practical hand. "It is from our aunt."

Jane watched her sister break the seal and open the page. Elizabeth read aloud:

*My dearest nieces,*
*I will send the carriage four you at eleven this morning so you may visit with me and Catherine and stay for dinner. We have news I believe you will find joyful. I also have a surprise for you both. If my brother Bennet will come with you we will be most happy to see him. Your loving aunt*

"Oh," Jane sat up straight, "oh, I hope it is Catherine and Mr.

Thurgood. I would so love to see her happily settled. I know Papa still blames her in some part for not telling him of Lydia's attachment to Mr. Wickham, but they had both been flirting with the officers all summer, and she had spoken of preferring him to the others many times. Kitty could hardly know what was to occur."

"Papa blames himself more than anyone. I will ask him, but I doubt he will accompany us. He has allowed our uncle to assume the responsibilities of a father for Kitty. He will trust our uncle's judgment as to a husband for her."

Jane sighed. "I do not blame her at all. I do not blame anyone for Lydia anymore."

"Did you blame Mama and Papa?"

"Did not you? Mama always encouraged her to act the hoyden, cosseted and spoiled her. And Papa did nothing to stop it, although he might have. You spoke to him I know after—after Mr. Bingley came to Netherfield. He laughed at you. How could I not blame them when she threw away everything we had been taught since childhood to run away with the first man who asked her?"

Elizabeth was surprised at the resentment in Jane's usually gentle voice. "She intended them to marry. Her note to Kitty said as much. It is not an excuse for her behavior;, it only explains that her intentions were not so bad as they turned out."

"It is of no consequence now, what she intended. It was what she did that ruined everything. She is responsible, Lizzy, for Mama and for this." Her outflung arm encompassed more than the shabby room, the house itself, their well-worn mourning clothes.

Elizabeth sat without responding, the letter from Mrs. Gardiner in her lap, one hand over her eyes as she fought to find words for what she felt. Something stirred inside her, a darkness, a heat, the core of a banked furnace. She had felt it before when Mama died. She pushed it down and raised her head to find Jane watching her expectantly.

"When Papa decided to move us to London I was not sorry to

leave Meryton. I had seen how one person's disgrace destroyed lifetimes of respectability. I believed that here where we are not known, where our history is of little importance, we might make a tolerable life. I believed he would recover from Mama's death in time, enough to reach some sort of equanimity with the past. I was wrong. Not that we move, that Papa could heal. All our lives Papa treated her as if her sole function in life was to act silly so he might laugh at her. I never saw the truth—she was the balance wheel of his existence. Like a clock with the hour hand and the minute hand working at different speeds to tell the time. Without her, Papa is lost."

"What are we to do, Lizzy? I do not know how to mend this great rent in the fabric of our family."

"I do not think," Elizabeth rose, folded the letter and slipped it into her pocket, "that it can be mended. We will go to our aunt's and find out what she has to tell us. Perhaps if it is what we believe, it will make Papa feel a little better."

The creaking treads of the stairs accompanied Elizabeth to the first floor. *It may help. I do not think so. There is only time to dull the pain if it will. If only it will.*

To Elizabeth's surprise, Mr. Bennet scowled when she told him she and Jane had been invited to the Gardiners' for dinner and to hear some news.

"We think it is about Kitty and Mr. Thurgood, Will you come with us, Papa? Our aunt and uncle want to see you, and I am sure Kitty would be very pleased."

He put a finger in his book to hold the place and stared at her with an expression she had never seen before: severe disapproval. "No, I will not go. The food here is preferable to the foot of the table at your aunt and uncle's. Go if you like. If Kitty has caught a husband it is all to the good, even if she does not have the decency to wait until she is out of mourning."

Stunned, Elizabeth caught her breath. "Papa, what is wrong? I thought you would be happy for Kitty?"

"Happy? Courting at a time she ought to be mourning the mother who always favored her, and encouraged by those I trusted to watch over her properly? I think not."

He returned abruptly to his reading. Elizabeth went slowly downstairs. She debated telling Jane of his attitude, however she knew it would spoil her sister's enjoyment of the visit. *Perhaps Papa is simply upset and does not mean it. I will wait and see how he is later.*

Their aunt was happy to see them, embracing both her nieces and walking them into the drawing room where Catherine waited nervously. Elizabeth went to her and hugged her. While Jane was greeting their younger sister she watched Catherine's face, colored by a blush.

"So, what is the news you have for us?"

Mrs. Gardiner smiled and drew her nieces to sit on the settee. "It is Catherine's news."

"I am betrothed to Mr. Thurgood. We shall be married in October. He is very kind and I am sure we will be happy together. He is soon to be a full partner in his father's business. We will be living in Manchester where he will be in charge of a factory the business is purchasing."

"I am so happy for you, Kit—Catherine!" Jane rose to embrace her sister once more. "What is Mr. Thurgood's business?"

"Mr. Thurgood's father sells carpets and upholstery to the craftsmen who use them in their own businesses. The new factory has a Jacquard loom; it will broaden the fabrics they carry and save the money to the factory owner."

"You have become quite voluble in the matter of business." Elizabeth's smile erased any hint of censure. "When shall we meet him?"

Mrs. Gardiner said, "Soon, I hope. We are having a family dinner with him next week, I want you both to come. You are going into half-mourning, it is quite proper."

Jane bit her lip. "I am afraid we do not have anything appropriate to wear."

"I understand some modistes keep a few dresses that are nearly finished and can be fitted to any woman and trimmed to her taste. I am certain we can find something." Elizabeth sounded less sure than her words.

Mrs. Gardiner was beaming. "That is my surprise. Mr. Gardiner wants each of you to have a new gown for the dinner, and another for the wedding. He will be home for dinner and you can discuss it with him."

Jane's breath hitched. She looked at Elizabeth. "Oh, Aunt, you cannot. There will be Catherine's trousseau and the wedding…"

"My dears, Mr. Gardiner is doing very well. It is no burden, I assure you. I have made an appointment with my modiste for tomorrow. She can have the dresses ready before the dinner."

Jane was quietly pleased with the arrangements. She spoke of it as the carriage returned them to Meadow Lane. They went upstairs immediately to tell their father, meeting Nettie on her way down. She held a tray with a plate of food hardly touched, shook her head and passed by them. Mr. Bennet sat in his armchair in the sitting room, a book open on his knees, staring at the windows. He turned his head slowly to watch his daughters enter.

"How was your visit?"

Elizabeth heard something unusual in his voice, a harshness she did not expect. "It is as we thought, Papa. Kitty is to be married to Mr. Thurgood."

"Is that all?"

"Aunt is arranging for us to have new half-mourning gowns for the wedding and a family dinner next week. They want you to come, Papa. Can you not go for Catherine's sake?"

"No. I will do nothing for Kitty's sake. And neither will you. You are in mourning and you will stay in mourning for a full year. Your mother deserves that much from her daughters."

For a heartbeat Elizabeth thought he was not serious. The scowl he turned on her told her otherwise. "You will not allow us to attend our sister's wedding?"

"Go if you like, but you'll wear black. I'll have no disrespect for your mother."

Elizabeth bit back the response that rose like bile in her throat. *Like the respect you always showed her as your wife?*

"The dinner is to introduce us to Mr. Thurgood's family. It will be very small and quiet." Jane was pale with shock that trembled in her voice. "Do you not want to meet Kitty's new family?"

Mr. Bennet's tone cut her with sarcasm. "Is your hearing defective? You are in mourning! If *Catherine* is willing to forget that it does not surprise me, but you ought to know better. She already has a new family—my brother Gardiner's. He has done enough to make me look incompetent already, I refuse to allow him to suborn the two of you. Now get out and let me have a little peace."

He picked up his book. Jane said softly, "Yes, Papa," fighting tears as she left the room.

Elizabeth did not move. "What is wrong with you, Papa? Our uncle has done nothing to harm any of us. Have you forgotten who came to our aid when you gave up Longbourn and moved us here?"

She was startled by the venom in her father's voice when he stared at her. "Have *you* forgotten who is the head of this family? If you do not like my orders you can get out and go live with the Gardiners or whomever you like."

He turned his shoulder to her and began to read. Elizabeth left him without another word. Mr. Bennet tried to turn the pages of his book without success, his hands shaking. He laid it on the table beside him, put his head back and closed his eyes. Elizabeth found Jane in the dining room writing a note to their aunt. She wiped ineffectually at the tears streaking her face. Elizabeth went to her and put both arms around her. Jane laid the pen down and put her head on her sister's shoulder.

"What has happened to him, Lizzy? He has never been vindictive or cruel. Why has he turned on Kitty and our uncle and now on us? I do not understand."

"Nor do I. Perhaps it has all been more than he can stand. He has done nothing but brood since we came here. We should have stayed at Longbourn. At least there he had a few friends and the work of the estate to occupy him. We would have managed. I do not believe he came here for us, I believe it was for himself, an escape from too many memories."

"He has escaped nothing, Lizzy. And now he does not even want us to remind him of what was."

"Well, there is no help for that." Elizabeth's mouth set in a grim line. "I will not abandon Kitty and I will not abandon Papa. Somewhere there is a way to get through this and I will find it. Perhaps our aunt will have some ideas."

It was not Mrs. Gardiner who responded to Jane's note however, but her husband. He arrived at the house as they were finishing breakfast and was shown into the dining room by Nettie, who curtsied and left quickly. Mr. Bennet acknowledged his brother-by-marriage with a sneer.

"Come to plead *Catherine's* case, brother?"

"May I speak to your father in private Jane, Elizabeth?"

The two sisters rose and left immediately. Elizabeth closed the door behind them. She saw Nettie hovering in the hall that led to below stairs and shook her head to indicate that nothing was needed for their visitor. When Nettie left, Elizabeth pressed her ear to the door. She was able to distinguish between the voices, still too low for her to understand words. Jane came to stand near her. She looked more frightened than Elizabeth remembered since Lydia's elopement.

"I have come," Edward Gardiner said quietly, "to ask why you are ignoring the marriage of your daughter. Mr. Thurgood is a fine young man; kind, honest, hard-working, and very much in love with Catherine. He will soon be a partner in his father's business. What is your objection?"

Mr. Bennet threw his serviette on the table. "My objection is that you could not wait a decent year of mourning to marry *Catherine* off. Did you have Mr. Thurgood waiting for her?"

"Catherine met Mr. Thurgood when he visited with his father. And, yes, Bennet, *Catherine* not Kitty. She is a grown woman not a little girl. There is nothing wrong with her given name. My sister named her after all. There is nothing wrong with a couple marrying when one is in half-mourning. Mr. Thurgood will be moving to Manchester as a full partner in his father's business, a business he will one day inherit. He needs a wife. He will make her a good solid husband."

"Unlike I made Fanny. Maybe she should have married into trade as well."

Mr. Gardiner shook his head. "I do not know what has come over you, Bennet. You have never been a cruel man or a coward, yet to punish your daughters for your own failures is both cruel and cowardly. You gave Catherine into my care because she was not able to read her sister's mind. Spoken partiality for a man does not indicate a desire to run away with him. If you want Jane and Elizabeth to observe a full year of mourning for their mother, that is your business. I am sure they are happy to do so. But why act as if it is some sort of penance?"

"You take a particular interest in my daughters, Gardiner. They are not your concern."

"They are my blood too, my sister's children. I want nothing but the best for them. For heaven's sake man, what is wrong with you?"

Mr. Bennet came to his feet. "You and your wife constantly showing my daughters the life they could have had if I had not been an incompetent fool! Stay away from Jane and Lizzy, Gardiner. And stay away from my home, both of you."

Elizabeth barely reached the parlor doorway when the dining room door flew open and her father slammed up the stairs. Mr. Gardiner followed more slowly. He stepped into the parlor to face his nieces, his expression more concerned than angry,

"It seems your father thinks I am trying to take his place with you. Has he been like this long?"

"No." Elizabeth looked more shaken than her uncle. "It began

48

last night when we returned home. We told him of the engagement and that our aunt wanted to have half-mourning dresses made for us for the wedding. He became outraged and spoke harshly to Jane and to me, forbidding us to go into half-mourning or accept the dresses."

"He was like someone we had never met," Jane added. "We have no idea why."

"Has he had a fall lately? Struck his head?"

"No. He spends nearly all his time in the sitting room, reading or looking out of the window. Do you think his mind…?"

"I do not know." Mr. Gardiner looked grim. "Do not go against him. If he will allow you to attend the dinner do so, in mourning. I have known Ralph Thurgood for a number of years, he will understand. However, if your father refuses to let you attend your sister's wedding, I will see to it that you are present. Catherine deserves to have her sisters with her on that most important day."

"Thank you, uncle. Please give aunt Margaret our thanks as well."

Nettie crept into the entry with his hat and gloves. The sisters saw him to the door before returning to the parlor.

"You can clear the breakfast things," Elizabeth directed. "We are finished."

# CHAPTER SIX

September 1813
Hephaestus House, London

"Mr. Hurst, sir."

Mr. Chapman, the butler at Charles Bingley's townhouse, stood aside for a strongly built man in a finely made tweed coat and buckskin breeches. The clothing told Bingley his brother-by-marriage had ridden over from his own home rather than take his carriage. Hurst entered the study, strode across the room as Bingley rose and came around his desk, his hand held out and a welcoming smile on his face.

"Miles, how are you? How is Louisa?"

Mr. Hurst had obviously built up a head of steam on the short ride. He shook Bingley's hand briefly but did not sit down. His usual languid nature was not in evidence. With a foreboding that he already knew the answer, Bingley braced himself for whatever problem Hurst felt needed his personal attention.

"She would be considerably better if you kept Caroline away from her. Good Lord, man, my wife is six months gone with child and she has been sick from the beginning. I will not have her upset by her sister, who insists she is perfectly well and ought to come out to entertainments during the little season. The only reason Caroline wants

Louisa to join her is that my wife is welcome at places her sister is not. It has got to stop, Charles."

In the face of his brother-by-marriage's agitation, Bingley felt a sinking in his stomach. Caroline had been involved enough in the social clamor to leave him in some peace. *I should have known it would not last. But our own sister...*

"I am sorry, Miles, that she is imposing on Louisa." Bingley moved to the side bar. "Port or brandy?"

"Whisky, a small one." Hurst finally sat down.

Bingley poured the whisky and a small brandy for himself and brought the drinks to chairs by the scrubbed, empty fireplace. It was more than warm enough in the room without a fire. The drapes were drawn over tall, narrow side windows letting only a little light seep in at the top. The air had the dense feel of trapped heat from a too-warm night.

"Thank you." Hurst extended his booted feet and relaxed a little. "I was out this morning at Tattersall's looking at a hunter. Damned fine horse, but too round a sum for me. When I got home, Louisa was almost in tears. The accoucheur prescribed rest and quiet. Louisa cannot be upset. If she is and its bad enough she could—well, it could be very bad."

Bingley sipped his brandy. Caroline was getting completely out of hand. Money poured through her fingers like water, she alienated the servants, treated him as a cross between a banker and a bird-wit, and now this. It was past time he put a stop to it.

"I am sorry, Miles, I did not know. Caroline has always been hard to handle. Our father spoiled her I am afraid. She was always a precocious child and able to talk him into almost anything. Louisa tried to control her, but Caroline just ignored her and Mama would never go against Father."

"That is no excuse for her behavior." Hurst set his glass down with a thump. "She's a grown woman, dammit. She ought to care more for her sister's health than her own social life."

"You are perfectly right. Let me find out where she is." Bingley rang for the butler.

Mr. Chapman came at once, but was not helpful. "I am sorry, sir, I was not informed of Miss Bingleys' itinerary. Shall I ask her maid?"

"Yes, find out, please, Mr. Chapman. The moment she sets foot in the door, find me."

The butler closed the door softly behind him. No one saw a satisfied smile momentarily touch his face. In the study. Bingley rejoined his guest. Hurst watched him without expression.

"What are you going to do, Charles? You know she is out of control."

"Caroline is not to visit her sister without sending word first. If you are not at home, she is not to go. If she ignores the sanction, you have my express permission to toss her out on her dignity."

"It will not stop her." Hurst sounded unconvinced. He knew his sister-by-marriage all too well. "I shall inform my butler if Miss Bingley arrives and I am not at home he is to refuse her entrance. Be sure she knows that ahead of time. She abuses your servants, I will not have her abusing mine." He set his glass down and rose. "Sorry I barged in on you, Charles. Thanks for the drink."

Bingley watched him go with a weary sigh. *Why is it always Caroline? She has everything a woman could reasonably want, yet she is never satisfied. And now Louisa. Has she no feeling for anyone?*

He knew the answer and it troubled him more than he was willing to admit.

September 1813
Pemberley Manor, Derbyshire

"Georgie, what is wrong? Something is troubling you. Can you not tell me what it is ?"

Georgiana did not meet her brother's eyes. She shook her head. Darcy sat beside her on the sofa and took her hand in his. He had returned to Pemberley from London at a note from Mrs. Annesley, his sister's companion, expressing her concern over Georgiana's growing depression. They sat in the music room with the windows open to a cool breeze from a fall day of leaves like patchwork quilts thrown over trees and ground. Darcy felt a growing anxiety as he watched his sister. Like their mother, Georgiana was adept at hiding what she felt from those who did not know her well.

"You know you can tell me anything, sweetling. Surely it cannot be so bad that you are unable to share it?"

Her soft voice was barely audible. "You will think me an ungrateful wretch."

Darcy took one of her slim hands in his. "I would never think that of you. Is it something about the Season? Our aunt has said nothing to me of any difficulties."

Georgiana bit her lip. For a moment the gesture reminded him so much of Elizabeth his breath hitched. "aunt Eleanor has done so much for me I cannot bear to disappoint her, but she expects me to choose a husband on the strength of a few dances at balls and conversation over dinner. I do not want to decide the rest of my life so." Her tone was growing more agitated. Her cerulean eyes glistened with tears. She wanted so badly to unburden herself to William, knowing she did not dare to do so. She had no proof of what she felt. She could only avoid any direct indication of her disquiet.

"Aunt Eleanor would have liked me to be engaged by the end of my first Season. She kept taking me to events where certain gentlemen were sure to attend. And she would point out the advantages of being married to a nobleman. But I did not *want...*"

She stopped abruptly. Her shoulders were stiff, the Bruges lace at the neckline of her day gown quivered with her breathing.

"You do not want to marry?"

The gentleness of his words calmed her. Georgiana gathered

herself, still not looking at her brother. "I want a man of intelligence and discernment. Some of the gentlemen are—are obviously more interested in my dowry than in any interests we might have in common."

Her words intrigued her brother at the same time they sent a vague alarm through his mind. "What do you mean, Georgie, more interested in your dowry? Have any of the men spoken to you about it?"

The tension left her abruptly, Darcy could feel her withdrawal as if she suddenly realized she stood on uncertain ground. "Not directly. I only mean I do not want a husband who thinks only of his own needs and sees a wife only as an accoutrement to himself. I want a husband who talks to me, who values my opinions. A—a man of courage and foresight, like Richard. aunt Eleanor is only concerned that I marry well. I know she wanted me to go through the little season. I could not face it, Will, not so soon."

Darcy almost said *I know a young woman who would completely agree with you.* Now he was the one on dangerous ground. He was silent for a time, still holding his sister's hand. He knew Georgiana's explanation was not the whole story, as well as he knew he would get no more from her now. If their aunt indeed wanted her niece to choose a husband, she was capable of subtly pressuring her to do so. "Did aunt Eleanor express her opinion in so many words?"

Georgiana looked down at their joined hands. "N-no. But she talks of my opportunities to meet gentlemen when I have not been in the marriage market before. Next Season there will be other, newer debutantes to draw their attention. I am afraid she feels I will be a failure if I do not accept someone of status and wealth."

She dared say no more. Darcy raised her hand to his lips and kissed it, smiling past a stirring disapproval. He was grateful to Lady Eleanor for sponsoring Georgiana, but he had not expected her to push his sister to marry before she was ready, in spite of her comments during their earlier conversation.

"I will have a word with her, not" Darcy stopped Georgiana's protest with a raised finger, "a confrontation. I will ask her opinion of the young men you have met. Depending on what she says and her attitude toward you marrying, I will let her know I do not want you to feel any obligation to choose a husband. As for the little season, it is nearly over, too late for you to join it. We will wait until next spring."

"I hope she will not blame me." Georgiana returned her gaze to her lap. "She has been very kind and enormously helpful."

"I will see that she does not. Now, is it not time for you to practice?"

"Yes, brother." She rose in a rustle of silk. "Thank you, dear Will."

October 1813
Meadow Lane, London

The wedding of Catherine Bennet and Robert Thurgood was indeed a small family affair. Held in the church where the Gardiners worshipped, the congregation consisted of a few close friends, the groom's family, and the bride's aunt, uncle and sisters, including Mary and Mr. Clarke. Mr. Gardiner walked his niece down the aisle before joining his wife and the others in their pew. Mr. Thurgood's sister stood up with Catherine, and his cousin acted as groomsman. Catherine's gown of sheer pale pink silk crape over a white satin underdress gave her an ethereal aura; the groom could hardly take his eyes from her.

After the ceremony Elizabeth and Jane accompanied their aunt and uncle to Gracechurch Street for the wedding breakfast. In the carriage, Mr. Gardiner studied the sisters with an expression of uncertainty drawing his brows together.

"Thomas refused to attend?"

"Yes." Elizabeth bit her lip. "I asked him again this morning. He said there would be enough of an audience without his presence. But he made no objection to our coming."

"Gracious of him."

Jane spoke quietly but with intensity. "Uncle, something is wrong with Papa. He hardly leaves the sitting room, he eats almost nothing. He is growing so thin. We are worried for him."

Mrs. Gardiner touched her husband's hand in support. "Have you consulted a doctor?"

"He will not see one," Elizabeth's fingers tightened on her reticule. "I have tried several times to suggest he see a physician, but he only gets angry and forbids me to call anyone."

She did not have to tell her aunt she was at her wits' end. Mr. Gardiner contemplated the two young women with sympathy. "Why do you not find a doctor somewhere nearby and call on him? Explain the situation. He may have a helpful suggestion or some idea of what is wrong with Thomas."

"Nettie will know someone." Jane brightened at having something concrete to do. "We can ask her. I do not like to involve Mrs. Hobson, but Nettie is discreet, and she knows everyone in the neighborhood."

"Thank you, Uncle."

Elizabeth felt a small rise of hope as the carriage pulled into the driveway at their uncle's home. At least it was better than waiting and watching as their father declined. They stayed only half an hour at the wedding breakfast. As they were preparing to leave, Mr. Clarke and Mary approached them.

"You look very well, Mary." Jane smiled at her younger sister. "I know you are happy."

Mary leaned forward so only her sisters would hear her. "I am with child. The baby will come in February of next year."

Elizabeth hugged her. "I am so happy for you, my dear sister. I wish…"

She did not finish the sentence. As Jane hugged Mary in turn, Mr. Clarke said quietly, "Mary would like to see her father. Do you think he would object?"

Elizabeth glanced at Jane. "I do not think so. He has

grown—capricious at times, but he has not spoken of Mary since your wedding."

"Then if you will allow us to take you home, we will try a short visit."

The Clarke's carriage was not new and not particularly comfortable, but it filled Elizabeth with hope that seeing Mary and her husband might bring Mr. Bennet some pleasure. She went upstairs first to where he sat in his chair by the window. He turned a stern gaze on her before she was able to speak.

"I heard a carriage stop and voices below. I hope it is not Gardiner."

"No, Papa. Mary and Mr. Clarke attended the wedding, they want to visit with you."

"Mary? Drove a long way for little enough. Yes, let them come up. I would like to see Mary and her vicar."

Relieved, Elizabeth conducted them to the parlor, Jane following. Her gaze met Elizabeth's and she relaxed visibly. The Clarkes sat on the sofa with Jane. Elizabeth sent for tea and seated herself in a chair near the empty fireplace. Mr. Bennet asked Mary about her life; it was safe conversation and lasted until the tea came. When Nettie curtsied and left them, Mary sat forward a little.

"Papa, I am with child."

For the first time in weeks, a true smile played across his face. "A little olive branch, eh? When is he or she due to make an appearance?"

"Early February. Near Lizzy's birthday. If it is a girl, we would like to call her Frances."

"Your mother will like that."

Mary's alarmed gaze went to Elizabeth. Her husband caught her hand in support; she managed to smooth her features but the tension in her body remained. Mr. Clarke kept hold of Mary's hand, his voice calm.

"It must be a comfort to you to know Mrs. Bennet is in a good place."

Mr. Bennet contemplated the sampler Jane had made. *With God All Things Are Possible.* "Yes. She deserved better than she had."

They spoke of general subjects then for another quarter hour until Mr. Clarke rose to go. Mary kissed her father's cheek. He patted her hand. "Take care of yourself, Mary."

Mr. Clarke approached as his wife and sisters-by-marriage left the parlor. "Father Bennet, would you like me to pray with you?"

Mr. Bennet looked up at the comforting voice. Slowly he nodded. "Yes, son."

In the downstairs parlor, Mary blotted her eyes with a handkerchief. "I am sorry, I know you warned us, but it was such a shock to see him look so thin and ill."

Jane said slowly, "I think our uncle Gardiner's advice is well taken. We should speak to a doctor, at least it may give us some course to follow."

"We will pray for him. Poor Papa."

The Clarkes left and Elizabeth and Jane sat alone in the parlor, more weary than if they had attended a ball. Elizabeth heard Nettie in the hall and called to her. She put the tea tray from upstairs on a small table and curtsied. Elizabeth motioned her closer to where they sat on the sofa.

"Is there a physician anywhere in the immediate area?"

Nettie's face showed alarm. "You are not ill, are you, madam?"

"No, Nettie, I am quite well. Please just answer me and do not say anything to anyone."

"Yes, madam. Dr. Griswald lives two streets over. He is not very active, but he still takes local cases."

"Can you give us his direction?"

Nettie obliged. Convinced her mistress was not in need of medical care, she went back to her duties with a light heart. When she returned to the kitchen, Mrs. Hobson turned from the stove with a glance at the stairs to the ground floor.

"I happened to be passing and heard you mention Dr. Griswald. I hope nothing's amiss with our young ladies?"

Nonplussed, Nettie tried to decide how to respond and settled on the simplest answer. "No."

"Always good to be prepared, ain't it? Never know when somebody'll need a doctor. Old Mister don't look well to me. Shouldn't wonder if it was for him."

"I'm sure I do not know."

Nettie put the china and silver in the wash tub and left Mrs. Hobson stirring her soup pot. "It's him, never fear," she muttered darkly. "We'll likely be out of a job soon."

They had dinner without Mr. Bennet joining them. Elizabeth left the dining room as Nettie cleared the table, her stomach tight with apprehension. She would visit the doctor tomorrow and hope for some helpful advice. At the moment it was her only hope for their father. She found him where he had been when they left him earlier, in his chair with a book open on his lap. His stillness alarmed her, she crossed the room and stopped where he could see her.

"Papa?"

Mr. Bennet did not look up. He rubbed his forehead slowly, his brow furrowed with pain. "What do you want, Lizzy?"

"I wondered if you would like a tray? You did not come down for dinner and you only had a little tea earlier. Mrs. Hobson made a pot of soup, it is very good."

"I am not hungry right now, thank you."

Elizabeth came closer to his chair. His face was drawn; it had a grayish cast she found alarming. "She can make you something else if you like. You have hardly eaten anything today."

Her father raised eyes that scarcely seemed to see her. "Fanny talks to me."

Elizabeth felt cold chills race down her arms and across her chest. "Mama?"

"She chattered at me for twenty-six years, why should she stop now? She misses me." He spoke as if in a dream.

"We all miss Mama," Elizabeth said carefully. "I am sure she watches over us from Heaven."

"Yes. Heaven. I hope they will let me in. I want to be with her."

"Oh, Papa," Elizabeth's voice trembled, "you will join her someday. Now you need to rest."

Mr. Bennet did not reply. He closed his eyes, his breathing slow but steady. Elizabeth pressed both hands tightly to her chest. She left the room and fetched her pelisse from the bedroom, calling for Nettie. When Jane met them in the hall, she was tying on her bonnet.

"What is it, Lizzy, what has happened?"

"I have to see the doctor right away. Oh, Jane—he says Mama talks to him!"

Dr. Griswald's home was a small cottage set closer to the street than most, fronted by a neat, well-tended garden. The doctor was in his consulting room when Elizabeth and Nettie arrived. His housekeeper showed Elizabeth to a waiting room and took Nettie to the kitchen to wait for her mistress over a cup of tea. Ten minutes later Elizabeth was shown into the consulting room to be met by a short, wiry man of her father's age. *Pince-nez* glasses sat on his aquiline nose above a small gray mustache. He gestured to a chair and resumed his seat behind a wide oak desk. Elizabeth expected the room to smell of the usual medicinal odors, carbolic and herbs. Instead an open window allowed the scent of verbena to infuse the air.

"Now, then, young lady, what seems to be the trouble?"

Elizabeth drew a breath and straightened her shoulders. "It is my father."

Dr. Griswald listened to her explain the situation with as little of their family background as possible. When she finished he took off his spectacles, polished them on his handkerchief, and replaced them on his nose. His gray eyes, enlarged by the lenses, held her gaze.

"You understand that without examining the patient I cannot give a diagnosis, only a guess. Of course, doctors do that a good deal of the time even when they see the patient. The problem may have arisen simply from the radical changes in your father's life in the past year. Losing his wife after so long can may have affected his mind, especially as he chose to move from the country, where he had always lived, to the city. However," the doctor looked at his hands, square and competent, resting on the desk, "the onset in such cases is rarely so sudden or so radical. I have to suspect that your father may have suffered a small apoplexy."

Elizabeth felt herself go cold all over. She tried to speak, swallowed, unable to form the words. Dr. Griswald rose, poured a glass of water from a carafe on a sidebar and handed it to her.

"I know the idea is frightening, Miss Bennet, but if he has indeed had even a little damage to the brain he might very well act as he has. I can only counsel you to keep him as calm as possible and watch for any further changes in his behavior. If you require my services, send Nettie and I will come as soon as I can."

Elizabeth set the glass on the table beside her chair and rose. "Thank you, doctor. How much…?"

"Nothing for a bit of speculation. Let us all hope for the best."

She thanked him and left with Nettie. Dr. Griswald resumed his seat at the desk with a grim face. He had chosen not to mention the other possible diagnosis for Mr. Bennet's altered behavior, a growth in the brain. No need to put the lady through more grief than necessary. He reached for a medical text in the low bookcase behind his desk. He had a feeling he had not seen Miss Bennet for the last time.

The walk back to the Meadow Lane house seemed to take an hour. Jane waited in the entry. She took Elizabeth's arm as soon as Nettie carried away her sister's pelisse and bonnet. They went into the parlor and Jane sat with Elizabeth on the sofa, an arm around her sister's shoulders. The room was warm and pleasant with afternoon light but Elizabeth felt only a cold dread.

"He thinks Papa may have had a—a small apoplexy. Oh, Jane, how much more are we to suffer? Lydia and then Mama, and now Papa!"

"I do not know, dearest. We can only follow the doctor's advice and hope for the best. And pray."

Elizabeth raised her head. She refused to give in to despair, it had never been in her nature. Whatever her own fears, she must be strong for Jane.

"Yes, we will pray. Papa may get better."

Jane hugged her sister. She kept her head averted so Elizabeth could not see the anguish she felt reflected in her face.

## November 1813
## Janus House, London

"Dr. Crane's regimen is doing well for you. You look much better than you have for some time. You have gained enough weight that your gowns do not hang on you like wash on a line."

Lady Catherine observed her daughter with speculation. Anne's color had improved; she looked closer to her real age than the sick child she previously resembled. Anne did not respond. Her opinion was neither expected nor wanted, she was simply a sounding board for her mother's comments.

"If you continue to improve you will need some new gowns. I have decided to remain in London for the holiday season. I am sure there will be entertainments you can attend without jeopardizing your improvement."

"What sort of entertainments?"

"Oh, family dinners, perhaps the theater if it is something light."

"We do not keep a box."

"Your uncle does. So does Darcy. We will be invited if I let Henry know I wish it for your sake."

"Darcy."

Anne let the name drop into the cool air of the drawing room.

The windows were not open; the drapes had been pulled so the clear sharp light of afternoon made shafts of pale yellow on the oriental rug. Her mother's brows drew down in irritation.

"It is time you were seen in public with him. When your engagement is announced it will not come as a complete surprise to the *ton*."

"It would not come as a surprise to anyone in the home counties who has ever spent ten minutes in a room with you."

"Are you trying to be clever or are you growing defiant?"

Anne passed a thin hand across her eyes. "I have never wanted to marry Darcy. You refuse to believe me or him, Mother, but it is never going to happen no matter how many times we are seen together! Why do you continue with this fantasy of yours that Fitzwilliam and I will marry?" Anne's voice shook a little in spite of the firmness of her resolve.

"Fantasy? How dare you say that? He is promised to you! It has always been so, since you were infants. How can he turn his back on duty, responsibility, honor?"

"Honor? He has never proposed to me. We are not betrothed. He can marry where he wishes."

Lady Catherine's face darkened, her hands clenched on the carved arms of her chair. "Not betrothed? When it has been my wish for all your life? When it was his mother's wish? He has no right to contravene his almost nearest relative's wishes or his own dear mother's. How can he turn from all that is right and proper?"

"I do not know, Mother," Anne said shortly. "Perhaps you should ask him?"

"I shall do more, never fear. I shall go to my brother, Lord Henry. He is the head of the Fitzwilliam family, he will soon set my nephew straight."

Anne stiffened her spine. In spite of the hard knot in her stomach she had backed down from her mother's tyranny one time too many. "I suggest you think carefully, Mother, before you do so. Uncle Henry may be the head of our family, but Fitzwilliam is head of the Darcy family. He makes his own decisions."

Lady Catherine stared at her daughter. Anne was not as pale and fragile as her mother was used to see her; there was something in her tone, the stiffness of her slim neck and shoulders, that caught Lady Catherine's attention. "Do you not feel betrayed?" she asked harshly.

Anne closed her eyes for a moment and drew in a shallow breath. She was not as perpetually tired as before, she felt less ill of late, although still not strong. Her life had been one long struggle to rise, live though the hours, sleep to rise and do it all again. If she could only reach a point where that was over, perhaps she might yet achieve a life of her own.

She rose. Mrs. Jenkinson immediately hurried to assist her, but she shrugged off the woman's hand. "You ask if I feel betrayed. No, Mother, I do not. I have told Fitzwilliam several times that I have no wish to marry him or anyone else. I do not know if he has found someone else, I only hope if he has she can give him the healthy heirs, and the companionship I can never afford any man. The plan to marry us was *yours*, Mother, not mine. I am sure Fitzwilliam will not appreciate your interference in his private affairs, and I have no intention of joining you in such an ill-advised venture."

Lady Catherine bristled with indignation. She had been a handsome woman in her youth, but years of self-aggrandizing arrogance and an inflated opinion of her own worth and consequence had marked her face as it had marred her soul. She stared at her daughter with hauteur mixed with disdain.

"Selfish, disloyal, ungrateful child! I have tried all your life to secure Pemberley for you, to join our two great families into one. This is how you repay me."

"I have never wanted Pemberley, Mother, you have. I already have Rosings."

"Yes," Lady Catherine sneered, "and you cannot even manage it. Your condition will never allow you to expend the energy and strength it requires."

"True," Anne agreed. "That is why you are managing it. If I cannot even manage my own estate, how do you expect me to manage the duties of mistress of an estate like Pemberley, which is three times the size of Rosings? No, Mother, I have long understood your interest in marrying me to Fitzwilliam. You want to control Pemberley through me as his wife. As if he would ever permit such a thing. If I died in a year, from disease or childbearing or some other affliction, you think you would still have a say in matters. At the very least, you would continue to control Rosings." Suddenly weak, Anne said, "I need to lie down, if you will excuse me, Mother. I have no more to add to your schemes."

Leaving Lady Catherine sputtering with resentment Anne took Mrs. Jenkinson's arm and walked slowly from the room. Lady Catherine glared after her in furious disbelief. Her concern for her daughter's health had vanished in outrage. She followed as far as the hall. With a last angry grimace at Anne's retreating form on the landing, she strode back into the drawing room.

*She will come around. Anne will always do as I tell her. I will ask Henry to include us in family gatherings, Darcy will be there whether Anne likes it or not. I will have my way, never fear. A spring wedding will be the social event of the Season.*

Satisfied, Lady Catherine rang for fresh tea, berating the maid for not making sure it was brought without being told.

# CHAPTER SEVEN

December 1813
Meadow Lane, London

Elizabeth Bennet stopped on the threshold of her father's room with an involuntary shiver. The atmosphere seemed saturated with the stale smell of sickness. In spite of a small coal fire in the fireplace the air was chill. Outside the single window, fogged with condensation, snow fluttered like summer moths.

She carried a small tray with a teacup and a bowl of porridge. Mr. Bennet opened his eyes as she approached the bed. Elizabeth felt she was looking at a frail stranger; bones pressed the translucent skin of his face, his eyes sunk in lavender hollows. She put the tray on his bedside table and pulled a chair closer to the bed, fighting the fear that threatened to choke her.

"How are you feeling, Papa? I brought you some porridge with sugar and a little warm milk, the way you like it."

He turned his head to look at her as she sat down. "Thank you, Lizzy. You were always—a good girl."

The words were barely a whisper. Elizabeth struggled to maintain her countenance. "Will you not eat a little, Papa, please? Just a few bites. You have had nothing since yesterday morning."

"Later perhaps." The effort of even so little speech drained him. "I want to... talk to you, my Lizzy. While there is time."

"Papa, you will be well again, Dr. Griswald is very good—"

"Please, my dear, do not...waste my strength with...false hopes. He gives me...pain medicine. It is enough."

Mr. Bennet reached a trembling hand toward her. Elizabeth took it in both of hers; a cold tingling ran down her spine at the feel of the chill flesh. "Yes, Papa."

The words came slowly, punctuated with short breaths and pauses. "I never want you or Jane...to blame yourselves...for any of this. It is...my fault alone."

Elizabeth held her father's hand as tightly as she dared. She had to force words out through a throat constricted by fear. "Please, Papa, do not do this. It is over."

The pause was longer this time. Mr. Bennet closed his eyes and Elizabeth sat rigid, watching for the next inhalation. When it came it was with a shudder that shook his wasted body.

"No, Lizzy. It is...just beginning." Then on a gasp, "Letter—desk."

His hand tightened on hers. Elizabeth did not move, did not breathe. Her father's body stiffened, his hand in hers went limp. Shaking with pain and fear, Elizabeth stumbled to her feet and ran out into the hall. Jane was in the entry way speaking to the young medical assistant they had hired to care for their father's personal needs when he became bedridden.

"Mr. White!" Elizabeth gripped the stair rail to keep from falling. "Papa..."

With one look at her bloodless face Mr. White loped up the stairs and ran into their father's room. Jane stared at her sister then buried her face in shaking hands, sobbing. Slowly Elizabeth made her way downstairs and took Jane in her arms. They held each other and cried together until Mr. White returned, his face solemn.

"I am sorry, ladies. Mr. Bennet has passed."

The next two days were a blur of grief so intense Elizabeth felt she was moving through a thickened atmosphere where even breathing became an effort. Their uncle Gardiner arrived with their aunt, who gave the necessary instructions to Nettie and Mrs. Hobson in her nieces' stead. Arrangements were made, the undertaker and his assistant did their work. Mr. Bennet was laid out in the parlor for one night in a plain, varnished wood coffin. Elizabeth and Jane sat with him, close together, sometimes in silent prayer or speaking softly of memories. For the most part they simply held hands, like children. In the morning the undertaker came again, and the coffin was loaded into a closed van and taken away. They stood on the small porch, shivering with cold, until the van disappeared in the snow-wrapped distance.

When they returned inside, the parlor was empty of any sign of death. A fire burned brightly in the hearth, the front drapes were drawn, the side windows only half masked. Light as gray as their spirits seeped into the room. Before they had time to sit down, Nettie appeared with a tea tray, her eyes red from crying. Elizabeth thanked her absently. It was Jane who spoke quiet words of comfort to the maid. She returned to her sister, sat beside her on the sofa, and poured out tea for both of them. Elizabeth rarely took sugar in her tea; the heavy dose Jane put in surprised her by its calming effect.

"He is with Mama," Jane repeated as she had the night before. "It is where he wanted to be. Uncle has made all the arrangements, we can do nothing more."

"We cannot even be there to visit their graves."

Elizabeth's anguished words came from a parched throat. She drank another swallow of the tea. Watching her, Jane's eyes filled with tears. Lizzy had always been so strong, it pained her to see her sister so vulnerable. Jane loved their father, but Lizzy had been his child, the one he felt most comfortable with, the one who understood him best. The loss was somehow worse for Lizzy than for any of them.

"Perhaps we can go later," she offered tentatively. "Uncle will see that everything is done properly."

Elizabeth made a conscious effort to control her emotions rather than upset Jane any further. "Uncle has been extraordinarily kind. We will have to repay his expense, at least for the funeral and—and burial."

"Do not think of that now. Lizzy, you need to rest. You have not slept in nearly two days."

"Neither have you. I do not think I can sleep yet. If I could go for a walk—"

"You know what aunt Margaret told us. It is not safe, not like ho—Meryton."

Fury shook Elizabeth to her core. "Meryton! I never want to see that town again!"

Softly, Jane said, "It would have been the same anywhere. Please, Lizzy, try to rest. Let us lie down for a while at least. We can talk later."

Elizabeth sat without responding one hand over her eyes as she fought to find words for what she felt. Something stirred inside her, a darkness, a heat, the core of a banked furnace. She had felt it before, when Mama died, when Papa became ill and it was apparent he would not recover. It frightened her as nothing else she had ever experienced. She pushed it away and raised her head to find Jane watching her with alarm in her clear eyes. Suddenly Elizabeth felt unutterably weary.

"Yes, let us rest for a time. I am—so tired."

Jane took her sister's arm and they climbed the stairs together, neither one looking toward the bedroom that had been their father's.

In the morning their aunt Gardiner called. She sat in the parlor with them, her face full of the concern she felt. "I am sorry I could not come yesterday, my dears. Randall has a cold, his chest is not strong and I did not want to leave him with Nanny as he calls for me when he is ill. Your uncle had to go to his office this morning, but if you feel well enough we want you to come to dinner tomorrow. Everything went well with the burial, you need have no worry about that."

"We understand," Jane assured her. She glanced at her sister, "We are sorry our uncle has had additional expense on our account."

Mrs. Gardiner shook her head. "There was no particular expense. We need not discuss it now, but several of Thomas' friends and our brother Phillips made the arrangements and took on whatever expense there was. I will let Edward discuss it with you."

"Sir William Lucas?" Elizabeth asked.

"I believe so, yes, and a Mr. Goulding. And the vicar, a Reverend Placet?"

"Plakett." Elizabeth raised her head, her voice thick with disgust. "They are the only ones who stood by him. A pity more of his 'friends' did not do so."

Mrs. Gardiner took Elizabeth's hand and squeezed it. "Try not to be bitter, Lizzy. There is no changing the past. God will make all right in the end."

December 1813
Matlock House, London

The Darcy carriage stopped before the portico of Lord Matlock's London home in a brilliant fan of light from two gas lamps, one on either side of the walk. Darcy handed Georgiana out and tucked her hand in the crook of his arm. As they made their way toward the steps leading to the front door where a bewigged and liveried footman stood, Darcy watched the light paint a stark picture of the garden and lawns, frosted shrubs and white swaths of snowy ground delineated by areas of inky shadows.

"Uncle Henry wants to use gas to illuminate the house," Georgiana told her brother as they climbed the steps, "but aunt Eleanor is afraid it might blow up or cause a fire. He told her that Westminster Bridge is to be gas lit on the 31st of the month. If the bridge is still standing on the first of January he will go ahead."

Darcy smiled. *Sometimes she sounds so grown up, then suddenly she is a girl again. She needs a woman to guide her, and I am not sure our aunt is the right person.* He knew who was, and pushed the thought roughly out of his mind.

Lady Eleanor met them in the entry foyer. Polished marble tiles reflected a hazy image of the chandelier overhead. Its many candles glinted on the countess' jewelry and simple silver embroidery accenting the bodice of her gown. There was no receiving line as it was strictly a family celebration. Georgiana handed her cloak and gloves to a waiting maid. Darcy divested himself of his hat, gloves and greatcoat, then took his aunt's hands, leaning to kiss her cheek.

"I am so happy you came tonight. Georgiana, you look stunning. Come into the drawing room, both of you, and get warm."

The smells of Christmas surrounded them from all sides, bringing memories of childhood. The air was redolent with the scent of pine boughs cut fresh and transported from the Matlock estate of Foxwood in Derbyshire. Their sharp green wound through the balustrades of the main staircase decorated with red satin ribbons and bows. Pomanders stuck with bits of nutmeg and cloves and tied around in gold ribbons hung among the greenery. There were mistletoe balls above the doorways. In the main drawing room the mantle of the Adam fireplace held holly branches, two candle lamps and more red and gold ribbon. The German tradition of a live tree was not widely in use, but a yule log burned in the hearth, sending out a steady wave of warmth.

Georgiana halted on the threshold, her face aglow. It was the happiest Darcy had seen her in months and he rejoiced in her pleasure. Perhaps the worst was over.

"Sofia is here," Georgiana noted her cousin, the youngest of the Matlocks' three children. "I hope she is well, the baby is due in four months."

"She looks well. Adele is here also with Brentmore."

"I noticed."

With a glance at her cousin-by-marriage, Georgiana detached her hand from Darcy's arm and crossed to where Sofia sat with Anne de Bourgh. The wife of the heir to the earldom was not popular with most of the other ladies in the family. The granddaughter of a French count driven to England during the Terror, she behaved with a superiority that did nothing to endear her to her female relatives. The fact she had already presented her husband with an heir, a second son, and a daughter in six years only added to her self-importance. Tonight she wore a gown of dark red velvet heavily embroidered in colored silks and edged with gold lace. An elaborate gold and ruby *parure* glittered in the candlelight from neck, ears and wrist.

Darcy suppressed a grimace. *Beside Sofia and Georgiana she looks like one of those exotic. birds Brentmore keeps. Perhaps that was the attraction, someone a little out of the ordinary.* His mind instantly presented an image of a young woman in a simple white ball gown, green silk ribbons wound through her ebony curls. *Why does Elizabeth torture me when I shall never see her again?*

"Dear Georgiana," Viscountess Chadwick's rather too sultry voice with its faint accent carried to Darcy as he accepted a glass of wine from a footman, "how very grownup you look tonight. What a shame you cannot wear more colorful gowns, but that *sweet* pale green suits you admirably."

"Thank you, Cousin Adele," Georgiana smoothed the silk with an innocent smile. "I enjoy some decoration I admit although I cannot help but think too much embellishment is just a bit—*outré*, especially as a lady grows older."

Sofia suffered a sudden fit of coughing. Adele, Viscountess Brentmore, clamped her mouth shut and found she suddenly wanted to talk to a cousin she had not seen recently. Darcy took a quick sip of his wine. He noticed his aunt, Lady Catherine's, smirk; she and Adele were too much alike to do more than tolerate one another in company. Her light eyes flashed to her nephew before he could look away. The triumph he read in that brief look unsettled him more than it should have.

It was the usual sort of family gathering. The men talked politics, estate matters and horses. The ladies talked of children, fashion and gossip. After a time Darcy made his way to the windows looking out on a side garden and stood gazing at the prospect. It was snowing once more. The glare of the gas lamps only made a glow near the front of the house, all else was wrapped in silent white. Eventually the sounds of the gathering faded; the rise and fall of voices, clink of glasses and cups, even the snap and hiss of the fire.

*Where are you, Elizabeth? Are you in some cottage in the country, are you well, do you have enough to live in comfort? Will you celebrate the birth of our Lord with family or only your father and sisters? Surely Mr. Bennet made provision for his daughters, he had some resources outside the estate. Have you even found a man who will look beyond the sin of one woman and love you as you should be loved?*

That last thought sent pain ripping through his chest. He caught his breath just as Richard Fitzwilliam's voice broke into his consciousness.

"Will, are you well?"

"Yes." Darcy got hold of his emotions straightened and turned to his cousin. "Quite well."

Richard did not look convinced. "You do not look it. I need to talk to you, privately, before dinner. Library, ten minutes."

Darcy gave a small nod. Richard laughed as if his cousin had said something witty and walked away. Darcy moved back into the room, set his glass on a tray carried by another footman. Georgiana was engaged in conversation with Sofia; Anne watched him intently, then dropped her gaze. The others in the room paid no attention as he moved to the door and stepped into the hall. He found Richard in the library, standing stiffly before the low fire in the grate.

"What is going on?"

"Aunt Catherine, as usual." Richard looked more angry than Darcy was used to seeing him. "You know she came to father a fort-night ago and demanded he force you to marry Anne, as if he were

73

the final arbiter of your personal life. He sent her packing. She has said nothing since, but you know she never forgets or forgives what she perceives as an insult. She is more determined than ever to impose her will on you and Anne."

"None of which is surprising."

Richard's expression tightened. "Anne sent me a note this morning. They are here tonight because her mother has some scheme to trap you into marrying her. Will, I need you to tell me once and for all if you have any intention of offering for our cousin."

"I have told the entire family that I do not." Darcy sounded irritated. "Why must I keep repeating it?"

"Because I am going to marry her."

Seconds ticked away on the gilt bronze mantel clock. The fire reflected orange tongues of light across the worn hearth rug. At last Darcy found his voice.

"You are—?"

"Going to marry Anne. I spoke to Father about it when our aunt first brought her to London to see Sir Edgar. At that time her health was so precarious the whole question of marriage was moot. She has improved greatly, although she is still fragile and always will be. What Lady Catherine has told no one is that it is Anne's heart."

"How can you know that?"

"Let us say I am adept at finding out secrets. Father has given his blessing so long as Anne agrees. He would, of course, because it means I will control Rosings. The note alone would compromise her if I were to reveal it, however I would rather not use such a method."

"And Anne wants the marriage?"

Richard ran a hand through his hair, ruffling the short thick locks. "She wants to get away from her mother. I will not tell you that either of us feels for the other what one could call deep affection. I am fond of Anne and she says she is content to be my wife. A good many marriages have started with less."

"She cannot give you an heir." Darcy spoke in a hesitant voice.

Richard considered a moment before he said, "I know. It is not a marriage you would be comfortable with, Will, but it suits Anne and me. There is a strong probability Anne will not survive me. In time I may marry again. That is not the issue. Our aunt is half mad. I want Anne out of her clutches before Lady Catherine does something to irrevocably harm her."

"What of the war?"

There was a pause while Richard pondered his response. "We will marry very shortly, before I have to rejoin my regiment. I believe this campaign will end the war. When it is over, I will resign my commission. If—things do not work out well for me, Anne will still be safe with father and mother."

Darcy held his hand out. "I can only say I wish you happy, Richard. I will be glad to see Anne settled and safe at last."

There was a tap at the door. Both men turned at the sound to see Anne de Bourgh slip in. Her face had lost what color she had shown earlier. Darcy saw the flutter of her breathing and the rapid pulse at the base of her throat. She hurried to them and took hold of Richard's arm.

"Mother told me to prepare myself." She barely got the words out, a hand to her chest. "She is going to announce my engagement to Darcy at dinner. She says he cannot deny it or I will be ruined and he will never do that!"

Richard took her hand. "I will have a quick word with father. Do not upset yourself. Everything will be taken care of."

Anne immediately quieted, although she remained visibly shaken. "After I sent you the note, I had Mrs. Jenkinson pack my traveling trunk and hide it in a box room. She has a portmanteau for herself. I will not leave her to face Mama alone."

"You have done well. We will send a carriage for her and your things. She is welcome here."

Anne's breathing had returned to nearly normal. She watched Richard with complete trust. Her reaction was all Darcy needed to assure him the marriage was best for both cousins. He offered Anne his arm. "Let me walk you back to the drawing room before you are missed."

In the hall smelling of spice and forests, Anne walked with her head down. "I know you wonder why I consented to marry Richard."

"It is between the two of you. I have no say in the matter."

Her mouth turned up at the corners. She looked up at him through her lashes, her large hazel eyes serious. "I will tell you, however. It may ease any doubts you have. I have loved Richard since we were children. I want to spend whatever time I have with him. I know he marries me to save me from Mama's machinations. I marry him for love."

Darcy squeezed her hand on his arm. "You have not told him?"

"No. It is best kept to myself, for now."

Lady Catherine appeared in the doorway of the drawing room, her eyes raking over them. "I wondered where you had gone off to."

Darcy released Anne's hand. She hurried past her mother. Lady Catherine spent a searching look on her nephew. When what she saw did not alarm her, she turned abruptly and followed her daughter. With a grimace, Darcy went after them. He had barely entered the room when dinner was announced. As it was a family gathering there was not strict precedence except that Lord Henry took Anne in and Darcy offered his arm to his aunt Eleanor. Richard took in Lady Catherine, who was seated mid-way down the table. Lord Henry put Anne on his right and Sofia on his left with Richard next to her. Viscount Brentmore sat next to Anne. Somehow his wife was seated across from Lady Catherine. Darcy remained at the far end of the table next to Lady Matlock. Across from him a cousin was pleased to be seated by Georgiana.

As soon as the general noise of settling and speaking to dinner partners quieted, Lady Catherine puffed out her chest and made to rise. Before she was able to do more than lift herself off the chair, Lord Henry rose with a large smile on his face and gestured to a footman. Champagne appeared on trays passed to the guests. While he stood no one dared to interrupt him. Lady Catherine sank back without losing her gloating expression.

"Ladies and gentlemen, family all, I have a joyous announcement to make." He reached his free hand to rest lightly on Anne's shoulder. "My dear niece, Miss Anne de Bourgh, has consented to accept the hand of my son Richard in marriage. Please join me in wishing them all the happiness in the world."

He raised his wine flute and drank. Around the table a babble of congratulations and surprised exclamations momentarily overwhelmed Lady Catherine's outraged cry.

"WHAT? No, Anne will NOT marry Richard. She is promised to Darcy, they are engaged!"

Her outburst instantly stilled the guests. Lord Matlock's face turned stony. Lady Catherine came to her feet, her face red and twisted with wrath; she pointed a shaking finger at her brother. "This is your doing, Henry! You have always wanted Rosings, but I tell you Anne will marry Darcy or no one!"

Lord Henry placed his glass carefully on the table. "Anne is past her majority. There is no formal arrangement with Darcy or anyone else. She may marry where she pleases. You have no say in the matter. If you had not precipitated this announcement, it would have been made in a more conventional manner. Now sit down and stop disrupting dinner."

The whip crack of the last words quieted even Lady Catherine for several seconds. She remained on her feet, staring in near hatred at her daughter. "Anne, get up. We are going home."

Slowly Anne raised her head to face her mother. "I do not want to marry Will, I have never wanted it, nor does he. I shall marry Richard."

Lady Catherine leaned forward, her voice grated out the words. "It does not matter what *you* want or what *he* wants, it is what *I* want and his mother wanted that will prevail. If you defy me I will see that you regret it. Get up and come home."

Something in Anne de Bourgh gave way; some small reserve of courage inherited from her father rose against her mother's tyranny. She had spent the years since her twelfth birthday listening to Lady Catherine make plans to wed her to her cousin Fitzwilliam, a marriage neither of them wanted or intended to fulfill. Anne felt she was suffocating under the weight of expectations imposed on her like chains. It was time she threw them off before they crushed whatever spirit she still retained.

She said clearly, "I am home."

Slowly Lady Catherine's murderous gaze turned on Darcy. He met it with cool disdain. She raised her head, once more turning on her brother. "I see. You are all in this together. Very well, Henry, enjoy your triumph. It will not last long."

Lady Catherine picked up her wine flute and hurled it against the wall in a tinkle of shattered glass and spraying champagne. Her exit was less dramatic. Lord Henry motioned a footman to accompany her to the front door and seated himself as another footman cleaned up the broken flute and its contents.

"My friends, I apologize for this unseemly display. Now let us have a quiet celebration."

Four days later Darcy stood again in the formal drawing room at Matlock House after a small, private wedding at a chapel. where he had served as Richard's groomsman. Georgiana had been curiously reluctant to stand up with her cousin; she had performed her duties as if it were a play and she was uncertain of her lines. After the ceremony there was a small opulent wedding breakfast for the few guests. Lady Catherine was reported to have returned to Rosings Park the day after the dinner at Matlock House. Her silence was more troubling to her daughter than a raging tantrum.

"I have had Janus House closed." Richard stood in a corner with Darcy, his voice low so it did not carry to his bride. "We will stay here for two days, and then I must take up my duties. Wellington is chasing Soult over the Pyrenees. After Leipzig the French were reduced by sixty thousand killed or captured and over three hundred guns lost. By the time they crossed the Rhine they were down to about seventy thousand, with thirty-five hundred or so stragglers, and typhus reported. If Boney cannot pull it all together, it will be a short campaign."

"For all our sakes, I hope so." Darcy fell silent. He sipped his wine to gather his thoughts before he continued. "Lady Catherine has been too quiet. Your father can handle her under normal circumstances but this is the end of a twenty-five-year obsession. She will bear watching. I will do whatever I can to protect Anne while you are away."

"I am well aware of our aunt's tactics. Watch your back."

It was excellent advice.

January 1814
Hurst Townhouse, London

"Caro! What are you doing here?"

Louisa Hurst sat up on the pink silk chaise in her boudoir as her sister strode into the room like a sudden frost in a spring garden. A crystal vase of early roses on a gilded table dispersed their sweet perfume into the air. It was a room of light colors, entirely feminine. Louisa wore a loose morning gown of pale pink silk embroidered with a pattern of white flowers that emphasized the delicacy of her skin.

"I came because I had to speak with you. You are my sister after all."

Louisa replied obliquely, "Does Miles know you are here?"

"Why, will her throw me out if he finds I have not obeyed his and Charles' silly restrictions?"

Caroline's smirk caused her sister to shift her position minimally. "You know what he and Charles agreed. You are not to call without sending word first."

"Nonsense." Caroline plopped into a brocaded chair. She surveyed her older sister with a raised brow. "You have had a child, not a dangerous disease."

"I was ill nearly the entire time, and the birth was—very difficult." Louisa looked away. She did not choose to tell her sister it was unlikely she could ever have another child. "I am still weak. The accoucheur tells me not to worry, but nothing helps except rest. I do not need further upset," she added pointedly.

"You have missed the entire little season. When is your jailer of a husband going to take the locks off the doors and let you out?"

Louisa began to feel annoyed. "I have told you, Caro, it is not Miles. I do not feel like socializing, I can still barely go down to dinner. Most days I take a tray here. Why do you refuse to understand?"

"Because you are not trying to help yourself. Lady Darrington gave a ball for Twelfth Night. She asked after you. You could have gone for an hour or two—"

"What do you really want, Caroline? You have no concern for my health, so why do you not tell me your real reason for being here?"

Caroline folded her arms at Louisa's tone. Her mouth tightened, forming small white lines around the corners. "Dear Georgiana was there. She came with her aunt the countess and her cousin Mrs. Fitzwilliam.. You know she married the earl's son Colonel Fitzwilliam just after Christmas?"

"I read of it in the *Morning Post*."

"Mr. Darcy was not at the ball. He is living like a recluse;, Charles rarely sees him anymore. I have had no opportunity to even speak to him in months. If you were to rejoin society and give a ball or entertainments you could invite him."

Louisa lay her head back on the watered silk of the chaise. The interview had begun to wear on her delicate condition. She had lost a great deal of blood at the birth, so much her body needed time to renew its supply. The accoucheur's diet was slowly restoring her, it just did nothing to speed the healing process.

"What is this, Caro, your fourth Season? If you cannot manage to acquire a husband in that length of time, I cannot help you."

"I have no intention of 'acquiring' any husband but Mr. Darcy. It is not him, it is *dear* Georgiana. She is playing him for a fool. She should have married last Season, she had half the young men in the *ton* after her, and she turned them all down. If I had her dowry and her connections, I would be mistress of Pemberley by now."

Louisa tried without success to keep her vexation concealed. She knew perfectly well that her sister's only real concern was her own desires. It had long annoyed her, now it was threatening her precarious health. She sat up so she faced Caroline directly.

"You will never be mistress of Pemberley. When will you admit that Mr. Darcy has no interest in marrying you? Find a man you can accept and marry him."

"Like you did Miles, just because he is a gentleman? A nobody with a property one can hardly call an estate, and a face like a white bull?"

Louisa felt anger swell in her stomach, hot as boiling tea. "Who are you to judge, sister? Miles has been good to me. After Mr. Rudolph kept calling and Papa sent him away, he told me he would never marry his daughters to men in trade. You need not believe it, but a handsome face and great wealth do not make a good man. Miles is a good man, he cares for me and I care for him. Now go away. I need to rest."

Before Caroline could respond a male voice spoke sternly from the doorway. "Yes, it is time you left, Caroline. And do not call on my wife again without prior notice. She needs rest and quiet, not the upset you always bring."

Caroline snapped her gaze from Louisa to her husband. Miles Hurst regarded her implacably from the doorway to his wife's bed chamber. Without a word Caroline flounced from the boudoir and down the hall. Miles came to occupy the chair his sister-by-marriage had vacated, taking his wife's hand.

"Mr. Land told me she was here. I am sorry I did not arrive sooner. What is her complaint this time?"

The lightness of his tone soothed Louisa. She squeezed his hand. "The same as always. She wants what she cannot have and thinks I can help her get it."

"And she has upset you, as usual. I am sorry to say it, Louisa, but the woman is insufferable."

"She is also determined, Miles. I hope she does not do something that will actually reflect badly on all of us."

Hurst brought her hand to his lips and kissed the soft knuckles. "She is the proverbial tempest in a teapot. Do not worry. Nothing will harm you or our child. I swear."

Louisa smiled. She touched her husband's cheek. "Thank you, Miles. I shall let Caroline go her way and think of it no more."

It was a promise Louisa Hurst wondered in her heart if she could keep.

# CHAPTER EIGHT

February 1814
Meadow Lane, London

*Dear Sisters,*

*Mary and I wish to share our joy with you at the birth on 7<sup>th</sup> February of our daughter Frances Ruth Clarke. Praise God, mother and child are doing well. We could not be happier with our beautiful girl. Mother has been an enormous help and comfort to us both, and will assist with the house and the baby until Mary recovers.*

*Please convey our blessed news to your aunt and uncle. Mary sends her love and will write when she is stronger.*

*Your brother,*

*John Clarke*

"Oh, Lizzy, we are aunts!"

Jane's happy exclamation made Elizabeth smile. Yes, they were aunts and Mary had survived the dangers of childbirth to give them a healthy niece. *How happy Mama would have been, a granddaughter named for her and Mr. Clarke's mother. I can hear her exclamations and see her fanning herself with her handkerchief. And Papa would smile and say "Well, well, I am a grandfather."*

"Lizzy? Are you not happy for Mary?"

"Of course, dear. I was just thinking of how thrilled Mama would have been."

Jane touched her sister's arm gently. "I am sure she is happy. And Papa too." Jane folded the letter and laid it on the table. "We must tell aunt and uncle Gardiner at once. Shall I write them or will you?"

Elizabeth rose to put more coal on the fire. The February day was cold with an icy north wind seeking out every crevice in the old house to produce little unexpected, chilling drafts. From the hearth she said, "Why do you not write them? We are invited for dinner tomorrow for my birthday, but I do not think we should wait that long to share the news."

"I shall, then." Jane went to the escritoire beneath the front window. "Do you think it will snow tonight?"

Elizabeth shrugged. "Uncle will send his carriage for us. So long as the streets are clear it will make no difference."

On the morrow she would reach her majority. Twenty-one years old. Elizabeth felt that she had lived twice that in the past two years. Before, they had been a family; not perfect, not always in harmony, contentious, noisy, a group of individuals bound by blood. And by love. She replaced the fireplace poker feeling a wave of memory so intense it left her hollow with pain. How had everything gone so terribly wrong? Lydia, yes, but that was not the heart of the matter. When crisis came they had simply fallen apart. The bonds had shattered like glass with hardly an impetus except the censure of their neighbors.

Had it all really been so fragile—their faith in one another, their belief in themselves? Had Mama depended so heavily on friendships nurtured more on petty rivalry than mutual trust and caring? Had Papa really been so blind to his family's need for a strong parent rather than an indolent caretaker? Had she and Jane and Mary failed their younger sisters because they were so content with their own lives they made no real effort to improve the understanding and behavior of Kitty and Lydia?

"Lizzy?" Jane's alarmed voice beside her shook Elizabeth out of her thoughts. "Are you ill? What is it?"

"N-nothing. Just remembering."

"Oh, Lizzy, dearest, do not do this to yourself. Nothing can change what has been. Come, sit down, I will have Nettie bring us tea. I can finish the letter to our aunt later."

"No, I am fine, really." Elizabeth drew away. "Finish your letter. I am going to see what Mrs. Hobson needs when she does the marketing."

Elizabeth left the parlor quickly. She could have rung for the housekeeper but she needed the effort of seeking her out to dispel her feelings. Jane was right, there was nothing she might do about the past. She pushed the baize door to below-stairs open and went down the steps to the kitchen. Her head rose, her shoulders squared.

*I will never again take life for granted. I will never again be a victim.*

The following day dawned with a heavy gray sky but no snow. The carriage arrived promptly for the trip to Gracechurch Street. They spoke little on the way, each wrapped in their own thoughts. Elizabeth felt no desire to celebrate; if it were not for Jane's happiness, she would rather have let the day go by without commemoration. Their aunt Gardiner met them at the door. As soon as their outerwear was handed to the maid they followed her into the drawing room where tea already reposed on a piecrust table. It was, Jane thought, and had always been their second home. She sensed her sister's sadness, wishing she could do something to alleviate it. Perhaps the day would lift Lizzy's mood a little.

After wishing Elizabeth a happy birthday and discussing Mary's baby and partaking of the little cakes served with tea, Mrs. Gardiner set her cup aside and contemplated her nieces.

"If you do not mind my asking, are you going into half-mourning?"

Elizabeth glanced at Jane, then turned to their aunt. "We are. We have mourned Mama for over a year, and then Papa. I believe we are both agreed that there is no reason to continue past May. I truly do not think Papa would want us to do so."

"Before," Jane colored slightly at the memory of their father's treatment of their uncle, "it was not about our grief. It was because Papa missed Mama so. And he was ill."

"Poor Thomas," Mrs. Gardiner's honest sympathy was apparent in her voice, "he lost so much so quickly. But that is in the past. You remember the offer we made you at the time, of dresses for half-mourning? It still stands. Your uncle and I want to have several dresses apiece made for you appropriate for the next six months. The seamstress Edward employs at his warehouses is perfectly competent to produce them by the end of May. And please do not think of repaying him in any way," as Elizabeth began to protest. "It is something he wishes to do."

Wondering a little at their aunt's insistence, Jane said, "It is very generous of him. Of both of you."

Elizabeth echoed her sister's sentiments with no less reserve. It was not only generous, it was unprecedented. Ashamed of her misgivings, she smiled at her aunt and took up the subject of her Gardiner niece and nephews.

## March 1814
## Matlock House, London

"Mr. Caldwell, what is the meaning of this?"

Lady Matlock stared coolly at the butler who was somewhat less composed than usual, a sign of great distress. A commotion in the entry dominated by the strident voice of Lady Catherine de Bourgh with another male voice in counterpoint invaded the drawing room. Anne Fitzwilliam tensed at the sounds. Her breathing grew rapid, she pressed a shaking hand to her chest.

"Lady de Bourgh, my lady. She has brought an—ah—official person and is demanding he search a part of the house."

Eleanor Countess Matlock rose and went to her new daughter

placing a reassuring hand on Anne's shoulder. "I shall deal with it, Mr. Caldwell, thank you."

"I knew she would not let it go." Anne sounded choked. Lady Matlock said, "Mr. Caldwell, find Mrs. Jenkinson and have her sit with Anne, please."

"Yes, my lady."

He hurried out, followed by his mistress. Lady Matlock swept into the entry with the presence of a queen. She raked her eyes over her sister-by-marriage, noted the overwhelming arrogance of Lady Catherine's posture and expression, and let her gaze rest on the constable who stood next to her, hat in hand. His attempt to look official was rapidly failing.

Lady Matlock ignored Lady Catherine completely. "What is the meaning of this invasion, constable?"

"He has a warrant to search for stolen items," Lady Catherine interposed. "A pair of pearl earbobs are missing from my jewelry case."

Still passing over Lady Catherine, Lady Matlock held the obviously uncomfortable official's eye. "Why should they be sought here? And why now? Surely a valuable pair of earbobs would have been missed earlier? We have not seen Lady Catherine since before the holidays, and she did not stay at Matlock House. Why not search Janus House where they most probably will be found."

This time the man answered before Lady Catherine was able to override him. "I am sorry, my lady, the complainant," he jerked his head at Lady Catherine, "swears they were in her possession when she came to Town before Christmas. She only looked at the jewels two days ago and found them missing. A search has been made at the residence with no results."

Lady Catherine, kept from a new tirade, saw Mrs. Jenkinson start into the drawing room and pointed a finger like a dagger at the companion. "There she is, constable, the thief. Arrest her!"

Constable Shotts, well aware of where he was and somewhat uncertain about the accusation, looked at Mrs. Jenkinson's shocked face with a hint of sympathy. "There'll be no arresting until something is proved, my lady." He returned his attention to Lady Matlock. "If you will allow me, my lady, the search is only for the rooms and belong-ings of a Mrs. Jenkinson. I'll be as quick as I can," he added. "If you like, you can have one of your servants go with me to make sure noth-ing else is touched."

Lady Matlock gestured the frozen Mrs. Jenkinson to enter the drawing room. "I will send my butler, Mr. Caldwell, with you, con-stable. I will appreciate as little disruption as possible."

"Yes, my lady."

Mr. Caldwell, who had been hovering in the background with an expression of disbelief, adjusted his face and came forward. He de-parted with the constable. Lady Catherine made to follow her sister-by-marriage into the drawing room, only have Lady Matlock turn on her with the face of an avenging fury.

"If you say so much as one word to Anne, I will have you bodily evicted from this house. You have caused her enough suffering in her life, you will not cause her more."

"Sooner or later she will have to know that her companion is a thief. If I prosecute, she will be convicted and hanged for it. Unless Anne agrees to have her so-called marriage annulled."

Lady Matlock surveyed Lady Catherine as if she were something so foul its mere odor was sickening. "So that is your plan. I had thought you mad, now I see you are evil. Not—a—word!"

They sat together in the now silent drawing room, Lady Matlock still and vigilant, Lady Catherine glaring at Mrs. Jenkinson, who stayed by her charge in spite of her obvious distress. Anne had rallied and did not look at her mother. She remained pale, but her heart had returned to its regular beat.

Ten minutes passed, fifteen. There was a small tap at the door and the housekeeper entered at Lady Matlock's summons. She knew the housekeeper would not have interrupted her for anything less than something urgent.

"Yes, Mrs. Banks, what is it?"

Mrs. Banks, a solid middle-aged woman in a simple dress and starched apron, held her hands together in front of her. "I beg your pardon, my lady, but something has come up of a disturbing nature."

"Can it not wait for now?"

"No, my lady, I do not think so. There is a constable searching the yellow room with Mr. Caldwell. I understand it is for a pair of valuable earbobs. Are these the ones?"

The housekeeper took something from her apron pocket and held out her hand. A pair of pearl earbobs gleamed like small moons in platinum settings. Lady Catherine gave a strangled cry and came to her feet.

"Those are the ones. Give them to me."

Mrs. Banks recoiled a step. Lady Matlock said crisply, "Not so fast, Catherine. Mrs. Banks, where were they found?"

"Not found exactly, my lady." She handed the earbobs to Lady Matlock and retreated closer to the door. "I caught the new maid coming out of the white suite in the family wing where she had no reason to be. She was going toward the far end of the corridor where Mrs. Fitzwilliam has her rooms. When I stopped her she looked guilty so I made her turn out her pockets. Those were in one of them."

"Its not true.," Lady Catherine had turned an alarming shade of red. "She is in this with Jenkinson!"

"Enough!" Lady Matlock did not have to raise her voice to command obedience. "Mrs. Banks, did you check the maid's character reference before she was hired?"

"Yes, my lady. She worked for Lady Hatchert who gave her a very good character."

Lady Matlock's eyes narrowed. "Is not Lady Hatchert one of your oldest friends, Catherine?"

"I—I know Lady Hatchert, of course."

Lady Matlock sat straighter if that were possible. "Mrs. Banks, if Mr. Caldwell and the constable find what I expect them to, which is nothing incriminating, you will dismiss the maid without a character."

"Yes, my lady." Mrs. Banks curtsied and removed herself, grateful to have an employer who did not blame staff unfairly.

"Lady de Bourgh," Lady Matlock's tone was icy, "as soon as the constable returns, you will tell him your earbobs were found in a suite here you sometimes occupy. False accusations are looked on severely by the law, especially in capital cases. Then you will remove yourself from my home. You are not welcome here. What Lord Matlock may choose to do about this unconscionable act will have no effect on my decision."

Five minutes later constable Shotts reappeared in the doorway, his face flushed. Realizing he had not knocked although the door was open, he tapped it lightly and faced somewhere between the two noblewomen.

"I'm afraid there was nothing recovered. Mr. Caldwell stayed while I looked for the earbobs. They are not there, my lady."

"We know that, constable." Lady Matlock looked significantly at Lady Catherine.

"I—I am afraid there has been a mistake. The pearls were found in a—a chamber I sometimes use when I stay here. No crime has been committed."

The constable looked nonplussed. "If I might suggest, my lady, you maybe ought to have looked here before you called me in."

Lady Catherine did not deign to answer. She rose, not looking at anyone in the room, took the earbobs Lady Matlock handed her and flung out of the house with a thoroughly annoyed constable in her wake. Immediately Lady Matlock went to Anne and took her hand.

"Are you well, my dear?

"I think...yes, Eleanor, I am. I am quite well."

Mrs. Jenkinson asked tentatively,. "Did she intend to have me arrested?"

"I doubt it." Lady Matlock straightened. "It was another maneuver, her last, to end Anne's marriage to my son. She will not try again,

Lord Matlock will see to that. I am going to have a word with Darcy as well. The sooner he marries, the better."

## March 1814
## Darcy House, London

The Darcy townhouse in Mayfair stood on a lot of its own, large by neighborhood standards. It had been built by Darcy's paternal grandfather during the early development of the area and stood as elegant and reserved as its master. That master was currently occupying his favorite room in the house, the oak paneled study where he enacted the business of running both the London establishment and Pemberley, his Derbyshire estate.

It was later than his usual time of taking up the post to decide what his schedule for the day was to be. He had escorted Georgiana to Almack's the previous night, where she wished him to meet Viscount Tennerley's son. Sir Frederick. Darcy wondered if it was because Georgiana had some interest in the nobleman. He hoped not. Sir Frederick did not impress him as someone he would want his sister to marry. The young man was too full of himself for Darcy's liking. He had not gotten to bed much before dawn which explained his late start to the day.

Darcy had just finished separating the various documents from the morning post into stacks and was perusing the more important ones when Mr. Burgess tapped at the door. Raising his head, Darcy called him in, only to have the butler step rapidly aside as Charles Bingley virtually pushed past him. He nodded and the butler withdrew, dignity intact, closing the door behind him. If his demeanor was a bit ruffled it would never show to the casual observer.

Bingley stared at Darcy with a face paled by shock. His usual amiable expression had been replaced with one of confusion and pain.

Darcy went to his friend, led him to a chair before the flickering fire and retrieved two brandies from the sidebar.

"Drink."

Bingley obeyed, gulping down a large swallow that brought a gasp as it burned down his throat. Darcy took the other chair and put his glass down untouched.

"Is it your family, Charles?"

The calm inquiry steadied the younger man, he shook his head and ran a distracted hand through his sandy hair. "No, as far as I am aware my family is well." Bingley gripped the glass in both hands, his fingers trembling. His voice came low and intense. "My God, Darcy, you should have seen her. Her cloak was not heavy enough for this weather and her half-boots were caked with mud. If she had not been walking she would have been blue with cold. And her face…"

Darcy felt a grinding pain in his chest. He breathed in deeply before he spoke, willing Bingley's answer to be other than he feared. "Whom, Charles?"

Bingley met his friend's dark gaze. "Miss Elizabeth Bennet. If she is in such straits, Miss Bennet must be—oh, God, I cannot think of it."

Darcy closed his eyes for a moment. He forced his voice to remain neutral in spite of the cold seeping through his body. "Tell me how you came to see her."

"I was riding near Bloomsbury. I thought it a shortcut but it took me down a lane perhaps a mile from the small market." He drank the rest of the brandy, shivered and set the glass on the marquetry table between the chairs. "She was walking toward me with a little maid behind her who looked about twelve years old. At first I thought I must be mistaken, until she was closer and I could be certain. I called her name and she looked up as if she thought I meant to accost her, then just halted and stared at me." Bingley put his head in his hands for several moments before he sat up wearily. "She was in mourning. The dress was too thin for this time of year and obviously not new. I—I asked after her family. Darcy, her father is dead."

It took an effort of will to keep Darcy from groaning. Miss Elizabeth had always been close to her father; losing him so soon after her mother's death and the whole ruinous scandal that had destroyed her family's social position must have seemed the final blow. Bingley stared unseeing at the finely appointed room. He seemed adrift in his pain. Darcy took command of himself as so many years of training and self-discipline allowed, but his heart beat as if to escape his chest.

"Did she say how he died?"

"I did not ask. She said it was last winter, I think two or three months ago. I offered my sympathy for both her parents' deaths. There was not more to say. She obviously wanted to be off, and I cannot blame her. I acted abominably, Darcy, you know I did. Then Caroline kept the news of Mrs. Bennet's passing from me until I decided to return to Netherfield Park. By the time I arrived the family had gone and no one knew where. I think Mrs. Collins knows but I could hardly question her with her husband always nearby." Bingley turned to his friend, desperation in his eyes. "Darcy, what am I to do? I do not know how to find her." He meant Miss Bennet, Darcy thought. "She could be starving, sick, I have to know, I have to reach her, but how?"

Taking firm hold of his own wrenching thoughts, Darcy said quietly, "Charles, stop and think for a moment. She had a maid with her, so they must be able to keep at least one servant. They are likely in reduced circumstances, however they have family in Town who would not let them live in penury. The dress was most likely made for her mother's mourning period and she is unable or unwilling to have new dresses made for her father's. Miss Elizabeth is a strong woman, she will take care of her sister, they are as close as twins. Do not let your imagination run away with you."

"You know how Miss Elizabeth was in Hertfordshire, always smiling, teasing, full of life? Darcy, she looked like a ghost of that young lady. Her eyes are old. If not for civility I believe she would have told me to go away and leave her alone. I feel as if I have, in some part at least, caused her misery. I could have married Miss Bennet, it would have erased the scandal for her and possibly helped the other sisters as well."

"What it would have erased is any standing you have with the *ton*."

Bingley rose abruptly to pace several strides across the oriental carpet's intricate pattern before he turned on his friend. "Damn the *ton*! I have never been a part of it except for your patronage, and I never will. My children, perhaps, if I have any, but not myself, and not Caroline whatever she may think. I gave up the only woman I have ever truly loved because her sister—a spoiled, willful, stupid child of fifteen—ran off with a scoundrel. Why should that ruin her other sisters when they were all ladies of superior morals?"

"Because that is how society works. I do not like it any more than you do, Charles, but if you wish to keep your status you must live within Society's rules."

Bingley walked back as Darcy rose, until they stood face to face, his hands clenched at his sides. "Status is a thing one may lose at any time. Jane Bennet is a living woman. She is more important than an abstract concept that changes at the whim of people I care nothing for. I *will* find her, Darcy, and if she will have me I will marry her. Nothing you or anyone else can say will change my mind."

"Very well." Resigned, Darcy laid a hand briefly on his friend's shoulder. "How will you go about it? You can hardly go door to door asking after them. Miss Elizabeth was always a great walker, they could live anywhere within five miles of where you met her."

"I do not know." Bingley ran his hand through his already ruffled hair again. "I looked at property sales when I first thought they might be in London, there was nothing."

"I do not doubt they are on a lease or renting. Mr. Bennet gave Longbourn over to the heir of the entail, he must not have realized much from whatever was left. Not enough to both buy a house and produce a sufficient income." Darcy hesitated. He knew of one way to reach at least their relatives. Reluctantly, he said, "Have you tried locating their uncle? He has a business here."

Bingley started visibly. "Good Lord, I had forgotten all about that! What was his name? I never met the man but they spoke of him often. Something with a 'G', Grant, no, longer, Garrison, Grantham—damn!"

"Gardiner."

Bingley gripped Darcy's arm briefly with a grin. "Gardiner. Bless your excellent memory, my friend. I can find him easily I think. I may not be welcome but I will prevail if I have to camp out on his doorstep."

"Caution, Bingley," Darcy advised as he accompanied his friend into the entry hall. "She may not want to have the past thrust upon her."

Bingley was helped into his overcoat, donned the hat and gloves Mr. Burgess handed him. "I can try, Darcy. She is an angel, she may be able to forgive me. I pray it will be so."

The door closed and Darcy walked slowly back to the study. He dropped heavily into the leather chair behind the broad mahogany surface of his desk, leaned his elbows on the leather writing pad and dropped his head in his hands. Images from the past rose in his mind; a soft oval face, creamy skin, a mass of ebony curls, a neat, light figure, and the most beautiful eyes he had ever seen. When he fled to London the day after the Netherfield Ball, Darcy had made a herculean effort to put Elizabeth Bennet out of his mind. Marriage was impossible. She had no connections, no fortune, a silly, vulgar mother, an indifferent father, and four sisters, two of whom were un-disciplined hoydens. He owed a duty to his family name and his sister to marry a lady of his own class. One who would bring stature to the title Mistress of Pemberley.

Darcy had known certainly that if he remained in Hertfordshire he would offer for her. After the debacle of the youngest sister's elopement with that cur George Wickham, Darcy could only believe his flight had been the right action to take. He tried to make himself believe that wherever she was, Elizabeth had found peace. That she had made a new life beyond Lydia Bennet's devastating act of defiance. The thought of her marrying pained him as it always did; if only she was happy, he could bear it.

Instead, he thought bitterly, she haunted him by night and day. Thanks to Bingley's accidental meeting, she had been brought back into his life. The image of those wonderful eyes dulled by grief and the undeserved condemnation of those she had called friends was unbearable.

Darcy rose abruptly to pace to the windows, railing at himself. It was impossible. Bingley might be willing to throw away years of making a place for himself and his younger sister on the lower levels of the *ton*; Darcy had no such option. Georgiana's unresolved withdrawal still haunted him. This was her second Season., If she did not find a suitable husband it was unlikely she would marry now, perhaps not even later. He could not, he *would not* jeopardize her future. Even when Georgiana was appropriately wed Darcy dared not even think of marriage to a lady with the social deficits of Elizabeth Bennet. There must be no shadow of scandal in his sister's life. He owed her, and his parents, the protection of a spotless reputation.

And there was Wickham, always Wickham. The dark shadow that blighted their lives like a lurking disease.

Darcy battered his emotions back under his control. If marriage had been impossible before, it was now completely out of the question. He could not let his desires guide his actions. He retrieved his glass, drank the remainder of the brandy in a gulp. He would suffer the nightmare, he would suffer the thought of her so close and never attainable, he would suffer whatever he must for his sister, and his honor. Twenty generations of Darcys demanded it.

"Elizabeth," he whispered, his eyes shut in pain so intense he wondered if his heart had literally broken apart. *"Elizabeth..."*

March 1814
Meadow Lane, London

Elizabeth paused in the doorway of their parlor the air assailing her nostrils with a faintly acrid whiff of coal smoke. They had not been able to open the windows for two days while rain slithered and slid down the panes. One reason she had walked to the market this morning, other than to spare Mrs. Hobson's rheumatics, was to escape the staleness of the house. She wished now she had let the housekeeper go by hansom instead.

Jane sat in a well-worn armchair where light from the side window fell onto the mending in her lap. Her slender hands rested on the material unmoving, her golden head turned to gaze at the prospect of the willow tree in the side yard. Elizabeth straightened her shoulders and stepped into the room, attempting to speak normally.

"Jane, dearest, I am back. I bought some turbot for dinner, and vegetables so Mrs. Hobson can make another pot of soup. It will be good in this chill weather, do you not think?"

Jane turned her head slowly, trying to smile. "Yes, very good." She watched Elizabeth take the companion chair before she returned her mending to the work basket by her feet and pulled her shawl closer around her shoulders. "Did you have any trouble? I am always concerned when you walk alone."

"No trouble. The fresh air does me good, and I had Nettie with me."

Elizabeth looked up as Nettie came in with a tea tray. There was a pot of tea and a small plate of biscuits. "Mrs. Hobson thought you'd want some tea to warm you, madam."

Elizabeth smiled. "Thank you, Nettie, that was thoughtful of her."

"Yes, madam."

Elizabeth poured out. No doubt there was a cup of tea waiting for the little maid in the kitchen. When they were alone, she passed Jane a cup and drank a swallow of her tea. It was not the best grade, however it was what they could afford and it did warm her after her cold walk and the shock of seeing Mr. Bingley. Elizabeth still debated whether she ought to tell Jane about the incident. Jane had struggled for so long with the pain of his abrupt abandonment; was it foolish to bring even so little of his presence back into their lives?

"What is it, Lizzy?"

Jane watched her closely. Elizabeth set her cup down carefully on the tray, composing herself. "Something—unexpected happened this morning as I was on my way to the market."

"Unexpected? Tell me, Lizzy. You know you can never keep secrets from me."

*Can I not? I have done so in the past.* "A horseman approached us coming from the Strand. I did not look up until he called me by name. It was Mr. Bingley."

Jane's hand began to tremble so the porcelain cup rattled against the saucer. Elizabeth took them from her and put them back on the tea tray. She took her sister's hands in hers and squeezed them. "I only spoke to him for a minute. He said he was unaware of Mama's passing until several months afterward when he was returning to Netherfield. He tried to find out where we had gone but no one knew. He—asked after you. I said we were both well, and went on. That was all."

"You d-did not tell him where...?"

"No, dearest, I told him nothing else, and he would not have asked in any event."

Jane's eyes closed in pain. "Returning to Netherfield. If Papa had only waited a little longer..."

Tears began to slide down her face. She cried silently, holding Elizabeth's hands, her body rigid. Elizabeth put her handkerchief into Jane's hand and moved to the arm of the chair. She wrapped her arms around her sister, holding her tightly, rocking her a little, like a child. They had both cried for their mother, at their father's passing and before as he wasted away, only not like this overwhelming storm. As if the weight of Jane's despair had broken through a shell of acceptance to find release.

"Darling, please, you must stop." Elizabeth stroked Jane's hair. Her throat ached from helpless distress. She wanted only to comfort her dearest sister, but for once her presence accomplished nothing. Elizabeth felt ashamed that she had not realized how much Jane endured quietly rather than distress her with her own suffering.

"I am sorry I told you, I did not think it would upset you so badly." Jane shook her head sharply. Slowly the tears subsided. Jane wiped her eyes and blew her nose, brushing ineffectually at the wet patch on Elizabeth's shoulder where her face had rested. She struggled for words before straightening and dropping the soaked handkerchief on the floor. Her voice sounded unnaturally strained.

"It is not him. I am glad to know at least that he had some feelings for me. It is everything we have lost." Jane lowered her head. She hesitated to go on even though she had begun and she knew Lizzy would not let it rest. Slowly she said, "Sometimes I sit here with my needlework and close my eyes and pretend I am in the morning room at Longbourn and Mama is preparing to visit our aunt Phillips and Papa is in his book room and if I try hard I can smell the roses from the garden and hear the crows in the distance bickering in the fields." Jane lifted her head to look at Elizabeth. "It is so real sometimes that when I open my eyes I am uncertain for a moment where I am."

Elizabeth swallowed hard. She stroked the damp hair from her sister's cheek. "Darling, we cannot go back. You have said yourself the past cannot be changed, however much we might wish it. Memories can only console us if we do not let them rule our lives."

Jane found her own handkerchief, holding it tightly in one hand. Her voice strengthened. "You are right, Lizzy. The past is beyond mending. We no longer have the life we did, we must live in the one we have now. Our aunt Gardiner is ready to help us re-enter society. We need to accept the opportunity."

Elizabeth poured the remnants of their tea into the slops bowl and refilled their cups. Jane seemed almost too determined. It left Elizabeth apprehensive so that she went on cautiously.

"As we are talking about the future, I have something else I have been considering." Jane watched her without responding. Elizabeth took a moment to gather her thoughts before she continued.

"Papa leased this house for two years. The lease will need to be renewed in April. I have been thinking the two of us do not really need a house, a flat or rooms would suit us better. We spoke of this before, however it has become a decision we will have to make soon. Uncle might help us find something we can afford in a respectable area. I am sure the rent or lease would be less than we are paying now."

"Especially if the owner of this house raises the rent on a new lease." Jane finished her tea and set the cup down, grateful for the distraction.

"We could sell any of the furniture we do not need and perhaps buy something better. Or have several of these pieces re-covered. We could keep Nettie with us if she is willing, and arrange for another housekeeper-cook full time."

"Lizzy, it could be a new beginning. We might even make friends. I should like to have someone to visit."

"Of course we might make friends." Elizabeth forced a smile. The idea of strangers calling with their inevitable questions about a new acquaintance's history sent a chill through her. "First, though, I think we should consult uncle Gardiner. He will better understand what is needed."

"You are right, Lizzy." Jane attempted to sound confident. "We are to see our aunt next week to select fabrics and for the seamstress to take our measurements. We can ask him then."

Elizabeth rang for Nettie to take away the tea things, her mind unsettled. Jane's unquestioning acceptance of her plan bothered some deep instinct. Elizabeth wondered if it was only a reaction to this morning's news of Mr. Bingley, or if the unrealized spell of grief and loss was broken. She could only wait and pray that her sister was not more damaged than she seemed.

# CHAPTER NINE

March 1814
Hephaestus House, London

"You heard WHAT?"

Caroline Bingley sat down abruptly on her dressing bench, her face echoing her shock. Colette, her French maid, quailed, twisting her hands in her dress.

"I—I thought you would wish to know, madam."

Caroline Bingley grasped at her composure. It would never do to let a maid see her in a state of uncontrolled emotion. She took several gulps of air and forced her expression to calm. Rising, she said, "Where did you hear this nonsense?"

"I overheard M. Eaton talking to M. Phipps. He said master was discomposed when he returned from M. Darcy's house because he had chanced to meet a Miss Bennet while he was out."

Worse and worse. "At Mr. Darcy's house?"

"No, madam. He did not say where. If it had been at M. Darcy's I am certain he would have said so."

Caroline felt as if her stomach had tied itself into an extravagant cravat knot. "He did not say which Miss Bennet?"

"No, madam."

"Very well, Colette, you may go. If you hear anything more come to me at once."

"Oui, madam."

Colette escaped, happy to be without bruises. Caroline paced her dressing room for several minutes in a state of furious distress. The Bennets were a bad memory, one she had put out of mind for nearly two years as of no further threat to her status. How could they surface now, when she was so close to securing Mr. Darcy? Charles would certainly have shared the information with his best friend. Charles' valet said he had "chanced" to meet a Miss Bennet. Her informant in Meryton had relayed that the middle sister was married to a local minister, so it was not her. He would not have been discomposed by meeting the younger sister. Caroline pressed both hands to her head. She was developing a migraine. It had to have been either Eliza Bennet or Jane.

*Oh, not that, not again! I worked so hard to separate him from that sweet-faced ninny and suddenly she has reappeared and I shall probably have to do it all over again. Unless I can stop it before he has the notion to chase after her. With the scandal her youngest sister caused I do not understand how he could expose himself to the censure that such a connection would cause for both of us.*

Caroline's hands closed into claws at her sides. She stomped from her room, slamming the door behind her. The door to Mr. Bingley's chambers was closed. She struck it with her fist rather than knocking and barged in, startling his valet into dropping the shirt and cravat he carried.

"Where is Charles?"

Mr. Eaton straightened. "I am afraid I do not know, madam."

"Do not prevaricate, Eaton. You always know where my brother is."

Mr. Eaton, noting the lack of the courteous "Mister," wondered hopefully if his master had already left the house. Miss Bingley tapped her foot, not a good sign. Mr. Eaton was secure in his position, however the edge of Miss Bingley's tongue was preternaturally sharp.

"He is most probably downstairs, madam."

Without a "thank you," which he did not expect, Miss Bingley marched out of the room leaving the door open. Mr. Eaton sighed, picked up the fallen clothing and closed the door, quietly, behind her.

After washing off the dust of the morning and changing from his riding clothes into a fashionable suit, Charles Bingley retreated to his study to plan his campaign. His father had been widely known and respected among London's merchant community. It ought not be too hard to locate Mr. Gardiner and arrange to call on him. He remembered the name vaguely from years ago. The man dealt in imported textiles, silks, cashmeres, luxury fabrics so beloved of the *ton*, none of whom would acknowledge him on the street. Newly disgusted, Charles was about to see if his carriage was ready when the door of his study swung in with a perfunctory tap and his sister entered.

Her color was a little high, not alarmingly so. On her way downstairs Caroline thought better of confrontation for the moment. Charles did not respond to open resistance as he used to do. Somehow he had become more sure of his choices, less willing to be urged to follow her lead. She assayed a smile of sisterly interest and modified her tone.

"Are you going out again, Charles?"

"Yes. I have a luncheon engagement at my club."

*Well, he is not likely to find any Bennets there.* "Oh. I wanted to ask you if you have any objections to a small dinner party?"

Bingley turned to regard her fully. "I do not usually have any objection to your social events."

"I understand Mr. Darcy and dear Georgiana are in London, although I have not seen her at any entertainments. I thought I might invite them. We have not seen Mr. Darcy in some time. I met Lady Addington's niece at her soirée, a lovely girl. Her father is a baronet. And there is Mr. Burkhalter, and Sir Eldridge,,,"

"It is your dinner party, Caroline, invite whomever you please. Just do not pair me with some vapid heiress whose dinner topics consist solely of gossip and the weather."

Bingley's tone was curt, something Caroline found annoying. He might at least reply civilly. She said as much only to find him unrepentant.

"The point of your dinner is to bring Darcy here since you cannot call on him alone, and if you call on Miss Darcy he will not appear. It will not work, Caroline, but by all means try if you do not mind the disappointment."

Caroline drew herself up. She was taller than the average woman of her time; it brought her eyes nearly level with his. "Really, Charles, now you are being purposely objectionable."

"I have no desire to be, nor do I wish to engage in the old argument that you need only a little more time to attach Darcy. We both know you have done everything in your considerable power to catch him, if you will pardon the phrase, to no effect. By all means invite him, his sister, and all his relations. It will change nothing. Now, if you will excuse me, I have to leave. I do not wish to keep my guest waiting."

Caroline swallowed a sharp retort and stepped aside. This was going to be more difficult than she had anticipated. She walked slowly back to her chambers biting her lip. She had tried to match her brother with a number of pretty, socially prominent ladies to no avail. Lady Addington's niece was no more likely to succeed than any of the others. Her pigheaded brother's affection was still fixed on Jane Bennet. If only she could find some way to get to the Bennets first—

She hurried to her writing desk, took out paper, pen and ink and began to compose a short letter. All thoughts of invitations and dinner parties were temporarily forgotten. Someone in Meryton knew where they were, someone vulnerable to a clever woman. With an unpleasant smile she began to write.

## White's Gentlemen's Club
## London

Bingley's luncheon guest was a shipbuilder Darcy had introduced him to several months before when Bingley was looking to diversify his investments. Mr. McFadden exited his carriage at Bingley's arrival. Bingley conducted him to the dining room since the man was not a member of the club, and ordered drinks.

"I appreciate you coming, sir." Bingley poured a glass of claret for each of them. "I hope you can assist me. You must know all the merchants who import goods from the East."

"I do." McFadden's large, square hand, clean but callused from years of personal involvement with his business, raised his glass in salute. "Your health, Mr. Bingley."

"Yours, sir."

They drank, neither man wishing to initiate the conversation. After several minutes, aware he was failing to act as a host ought, Bingley waved the waiter over and asked for the day's offerings. When they had decided on selections from the *hors-dœuvres variées*, they proceeded to the main course. Once they had ordered, both men settled to wait for the food and take one another's measure.

"I can't say I wasn't surprised to hear from you, Mr. Bingley, since you didn't seem interested in a partnership in the *Juno's Swan*. I take it this has nothing to do with that?"

Bingley heard a slight accent in the shipbuilder's otherwise London speech putting his origins somewhere north of the Clyde.

"No, sir, it does not." Bingley twisted the stem of his wine glass, took a sip, and sat back. "Will you tell me anything you know about a Mr. Gardiner who owns an import business?"

"May I ask first why you want to know?"

Bingley hesitated. "I may be doing business with him. I like to know something of a man before I meet him." It was lame, he thought, but his inquiry was not personal enough to raise McFadden's suspicion of some ulterior motive.

Mr. McFadden paused while the waiter brought their first course and departed. He placed his serviette on his lap before meeting Bingley's eyes.

"Edward Gardiner does most of his shipping with Traquil and

Marchand, now and then on an East Indiaman. He inherited the business—Gardiner Imports—when it was a small concern mostly bringing in cloth from India, and built it into a business that has made him a wealthy man."

Bingley moved his salmon sauced prawns around his plate. "How is he with business contacts?"

"Honest, shrewd, a hard bargainer but fair. I've been trying to talk him into a partnership I'm putting together to build his own ship. I think I've nearly got him convinced."

Fond of prawns, Bingley ate a little of the seafood without tasting it. His mouth was dry but he did not want to consume too much wine and give the impression he was a drinker. "Family man?"

"To the core. Has a lovely wife and three children. They live in Cheapside, not far from his warehouses. Something Street, can't remember the name right now. If you want to talk to him on business see him at his office, its in the main warehouse on Brixton Street."

Bingley thanked Mr. McFadden for the information and they continued their meal, the shipbuilder entertaining his host with stories of incidents along the docks. They parted without further talk of Mr. Gardiner, the shipbuilder repeating his offer to go over the new partnership with Bingley if he was interested. At that moment an investment opportunity was the last thing on the younger man's mind.

*I have to see Mr. Gardiner before anything else. If he sends me away...* The thought was so painful Bingley closed his eyes with a groan. *I will not give up. I lost my angel because I gave up too easily. That will not happen again.*

He would have Caroline to fight and possibly Louisa, a fact he no longer considered a deterrent. For the first time in his adult life, Charles Bingley had no concern for his sisters' opinions. He entered his carriage and directed his driver to take him home. As soon as possible he would call on Mr. Gardiner and begin the quest for Jane Bennet's hand. He did not allow himself to think of failure.

## March 1814
## Gracechurch Street, London

"Mr. Porter, may I present my nieces Miss Bennet and Miss Elizabeth Bennet? Ladies, Mr. Porter,. a friend of the family."

Jane and Elizabeth curtsied as Mr. Porter bowed. Elizabeth noted her sister's reticence as she took a seat beside Jane on the sofa. The drapes were drawn back, cool light spread over the polished floor. It made the pale flowers of a broadloom carpet into a dreaming garden. Mr. Porter was a man in his early forties, dressed conservatively in a suit of fine wool and excellent tailoring. A businessman, Elizabeth judged, successful, well off. Perhaps it was only coincidence the man was calling on the same morning they visited; Elizabeth did not think so. Mildly vexed, she touched Jane's hand in reassurance and turned her attention to Mrs. Gardiner's cheerful voice.

Their aunt confirmed her niece's speculation. "Mr. Porter owns a tea business. He has brought several samples for me to try. I am sure he would be interested in your opinions as well."

"I would appreciate your comments very much, ladies." Mr. Porter's long, serious face showed only affirmation of their aunt's words. "I try out new blends several times a year. Mrs. Gardiner has an exceptional palate. She has never missed the mark on what will sell well and what will not."

Mrs. Gardiner blushed at the compliment. "You are very kind, Mr. Porter. I must say you rarely bring a blend that I do not find enjoyable."

She rang for tea to be brought. The maid appeared with a large try on which sat three small teapots and nine china saucers. Mrs. Gardiner poured tea into the first three saucers—she had not needed to send for additional saucers, Elizabeth noted—and handed one each to Elizabeth and Jane. The tea was fragrant, it seemed to be a mix of several flowers with a slight fruity undertone. It was quite delicious. Mrs. Gardiner watched her nieces with hardly less interest than Mr. Porter. Both praised the brew. Smiling, Mr. Porter turned to his hostess.

"Something for an afternoon tea." She sipped again and set her saucer down. "I like it, Mr. Porter, although I would not particularly want it at breakfast."

"It was designed with afternoon tea or perhaps a garden party in mind. I think you will find the next blend a little more hearty."

The second blend was stronger, a black tea with enough added spices to enliven it. Jane tried only one sip and put her saucer down.

"I think gentlemen would prefer this rather than ladies," she said softly.

Elizabeth liked her tea strong; she said, "I agree, except for ladies who enjoy a robust drink. I like it."

Mrs. Gardiner glowed. "I believe both my nieces are correct, Mr. Porter. This is more a man's tea than a lady's."

"I shall advertise it as such, then." Mr. Porter seemed perfectly comfortable with the comments. "The third is something different. Have any of you ladies ever drunk green tea?"

There was a general denial of the experience. Mr. Porter smiled. He had good teeth and a pleasant aspect. Elizabeth found herself warming to him. He had not once stared at Jane with the thinly -disguised intensity so many men showed on first meeting her. It struck Elizabeth suddenly that he was most probably married, and she relaxed her protective watchfulness a little.

"This," he said as Mrs. Gardiner poured from the third pot, "is yellow tea. It is a derivative of green tea where the leaves are allowed to oxidize more slowly. Please tell me honestly what you think."

The tea was indeed a pale lemon color. Elizabeth took a sip. "It is quite mellow," she said. "I can see it used for someone with a delicate stomach."

"Originally, green tea—in fact, all tea—was probably used for medicinal purposes. It may be a little mild for most people."

Jane finished the sample. "It is very pleasant, Mr. Porter. Even a child could drink it quite easily."

"Nursery tea." Mrs. Gardiner rose and rang for the maid to remove the tea samples and bring regular tea and refreshments.

Amused, Mr. Porter said, "I think I shall advertise it that way. Thank you, ladies, for your honest assessment of the samples. It is of great assistance to me."

Tea was served with cake and biscuits, the conversation passed to general subjects. In another quarter hour Mr. Porter was ready to take his leave. He bowed to Jane and Elizabeth who curtsied in return. They exchanged pleasantries before Mr. Porter hesitated and then spoke respectfully.

"I realize you ladies are in mourning. My sympathies on your sad loss. In time, perhaps you will visit my shop on Bond Street. I would be more than happy to give you a tour of our tea blending operation. It is quite small, of course, as most of my blends are prepared in the East. I think you would find it interesting."

Elizabeth thought such a visit would be interesting indeed. She was surprised when Jane answered, "I think that would be delightful, Mr. Porter. Thank you for your kind offer."

When the tea merchant departed, the sisters took their seats again. Mrs. Gardiner returned from seeing her guest out to find her nieces talking quietly. The conversation stopped when she reappeared, not guiltily although she wondered what they were discussing in her absence.

"Edward has known Mr. Porter for several years," she informed them from her favorite chair. "He lost his wife at a young age and has spent the past few years devoting his energies to his business. The *ton* buys from him over most other tea merchants. Perhaps when you are in half-mourning we might agree to his offer of a tour?"

Resigned to their aunt's gentle matchmaking, Elizabeth agreed. The stated purpose of their visit was to walk to their uncle's warehouses so that the seamstress could take their measurements for the half-mourning gowns. They left directly after luncheon. The day was brisk, clouds scudding across a sky like pale blue muslin. A wind off the Thames blew their skirts around their legs and tugged at their bonnets. It smelled of salt, spices, tar, sawn wood, fish, and mud stinking with the inevitable detritus of the great river. It smelled, Elizabeth thought, of the greater world beyond the boundaries of ordinary lives.

Mr. Gardiner greeted them warmly and conducted them to an upstairs room where they were introduced to a Mrs. White. She was younger than Elizabeth expected, in her late thirties, her fair hair pulled up severely in a bun. She wore a stuff dress like a maid, with a full apron covering it from chest to near the hem. The apron was clean but patterned by loose threads and fluff from various materials.

"I was fortunate to find Mrs. White free," Mr. Gardiner informed them. "She has quite a busy enterprise in her home, sewing for several of the modistes. When you are done here," he turned to his wife, "bring the ladies to the sales rooms and they can choose the fabrics and trims they want."

He left them to Mrs. White and their aunt. In half an hour they were measured and ready to depart for the show rooms. After several minutes of general conversation on patterns and fabrics, Mrs. White addressed them directly.

"I not only sew for modistes, I also take private customers. If you have need of my services Mr. Gardiner has my direction. I keep a number of fashion plates as well that can be adapted to a lady's taste."

"We will keep that in mind," Elizabeth agreed when Jane thanked the seamstress.

They did not intend to impose on their uncle's generosity and the gowns to be made for them would need supplementing sooner or later. Purchasing mourning clothes for three daughters when their mother passed had been a major expense, even though Mrs. Hill had dyed two of their older dresses black. After more than a year it had become obvious they required replacements. Elizabeth suddenly wondered if some of Mr. Bingley's shock on seeing her had been the condition of her attire.

The showroom was not as crowded as Elizabeth had seen it.

Several well-dressed ladies were perusing the more expensive offerings, one of whom smiled when she saw Mrs. Gardiner. She was an older lady of a very upright bearing. Her gray hair had been arranged in a becoming twist under a fashionable felt hat decorated with yellow silk roses. Mrs. Gardiner stopped to greet her and introduce her nieces. The lady's companion, a young lady more modishly attired who was obviously a friend or relative, cast a casual glance at the three women before returning to the fabrics.

"It is good to see you, Mrs. Gardiner. This is my niece, Miss Lambert."

At her aunt's words the young lady turned and curtsied briefly. Mrs. Gardiner returned the civility before she replied. "May I introduce my two nieces, Miss Bennet and Miss Elizabeth Bennet? Lady Addington and Miss Lambert."

Elizabeth and Jane curtsied. Miss Lambert shifted her weight although she made no move to leave her aunt's side. Lady Addington noted the black dresses and said, "I see you are in mourning. My condolences on your loss."

"Thank you, my lady." Jane replied softly.

Miss Lambert's eyes, a clear blue, focused on Jane for several seconds before dropping to her hands. Elizabeth had seen the expression many times before when a young lady took in her sister's beauty compared to her own. *Do not worry, Miss Lambert. Jane is no one's rival.* Although she knew if they were ever admitted to society again, Jane would outshine any other lady.

After several minutes of general civilities, Elizabeth and Jane excused themselves and moved on to the fabrics set aside for them. Mrs. Gardiner remained in conversation with Lady Addington and her niece. Jane immediately chose a dark blue silk, while Elizabeth preferred a gray. Although all of the materials were matte, it had threads of lavender that gave it a soft variation in color she found attractive. There was muslin as well. Jane chose a dark violet and a medium blue with dark blue figures; Elizabeth a chocolate brown and a darker green. Their aunt joined them as they were indicating their choices to a sales assistant.

"I have known Lady Addington for over a year," she explained. "We are both involved in several charities, one that assists young mothers with children, who have no resources. Some have no families and others have families that are unable, or unwilling, to assist them. With this terrible war going on and on there are also many young women who have lost their husbands. We try to see that they find adequate housing and receive a stipend for food and necessities. We also find work for those able to accept it."

"I cannot understand why a family would turn from a woman who is in need, especially if she has children."

"I find it difficult as well," Mrs. Gardiner agreed. She did not say that the alternative for many was the streets. Seeing that Jane especially seemed distressed by the idea, she added, "We have been quite successful. Now, let us return to the house and rest a bit before dinner."

The walk back to Gracechurch Street found a chill in the wind that penetrated their clothing. The sky had darkened, pearl-white clouds frosted the horizon. Against them, Elizabeth saw ships' masts in the near distance raise a denuded forest of bare shafts that rocked with the tide. They hurried to the house and entered the front hall to be met by the Gardiners' butler. He indicated a package on a table while they removed their pelisses, bonnets and gloves.

"It was hand delivered a short time ago, madam."

Mrs. Gardiner took up the package. "Thank you, Mr. Tucker. I will see to it."

They settled in the drawing room. Mrs. Gardiner opened the wrapping and took out a short note. "It is from Mr. Porter thanking us again for our assistance and sending me the enclosed. As there are three packets and I cannot use them all, I hope you will each accept one."

It was yellow tea.

## April 1814
## Darcy House, London

Colonel Richard Fitzwilliam settled into the leather armchair before the hearth in his cousin's study, a small brandy in hand, and stretched his legs out to the warmth of the low fire. He was leaner than Darcy remembered seeing him in years. His face looked worn; a new scar marred his left temple. Richard adjusted his left arm, still in a sling, and grimaced.

"We defeated Soult again in Italy," he continued while Darcy took the matching chair and settled with his own drink. "After Marat went over to the Austrian side he advanced to occupy Rome, Ancona and Bologna." He sipped the drink and shifted position to better cushion his arm. "Marat started negotiations with Eugène that went on until news of the advance on Paris reached us. At that point the war was effectively over."

"You were already on your way home by then?"

"Yes. Napoleon's troop strength was severely reduced, but he put up a hard fight before the inevitable caught up with him. He has abdicated in both his own name and his son's. He is now emperor of Elba with a stipend and not much more."

Darcy looked into his brandy glass as if it were a gazing ball. "Do you think he will be satisfied with that?"

Richard started to shrug, but thought better of it with a wince. "Perhaps. He has never been predictable. I am out of it and I am not going back. Anne is doing well;, she is stronger than I remember her since childhood. I am resigning my commission and we will be removing to Rosings Park as soon as I straighten out some things with my new mother-by-marriage."

"You have been told what she attempted with Mrs. Jenkinson?"

"Oh, yes. Anne told me, and mother filled in the blanks. Lady Catherine will be staying in the dower house unless she wants to set up her own establishment. She will have no say at all in the running of the house or the estate. If she makes any further trouble, Father and I will look into having her sent to a private nursing home—preferably somewhere in the Outer Hebrides."

Darcy drank a little of the brandy. He was not truly interested in Lady Catherine's fate. Lord Matlock had gone to Rosings Park shortly after her attempt to have Anne's marriage to Richard annulled. The result of his visit was their aunt's removal from the manor house to the dower house with a skeleton staff, under threat of her brother assuming complete control of the income from the trust set up by her late husband, of which he was trustee.

They sat in companionable silence for a time, so used to one another after a lifetime of friendship and mutual accord they did not need to fill the stillness with words. Richard studied his cousin's face surreptitiously. Darcy looked like a man carrying an unbearable burden he cannot put down. Richard had seen that look in the field; it disturbed him to recognize it in a man who rarely was at a loss in the face of a serious problem.

"I saw Georgie at home, she was visiting Mother and Anne. Have you learned anything of the reason for her discomposure?"

"No." Darcy set his glass aside. "She has gone to a few entertainments this Season and says she is nearly ready to choose a suitor."

"But she does not." Richard straightened in the chair, finished his brandy and declined another. "There is one area of life, Will, where I have far more experience than do you: women."

"Experience of a certain kind, I grant you," Darcy replied wryly.

Richard ignored the jibe. "What of you, Will? You still have not chosen a wife."

Darcy stiffened. He did not meet his cousin's steady gaze. His hands closed on the chair arms so hard his knuckles became whitened knobs. He swallowed past a dry throat but did not reach for his glass.

Richard settled the sling on his arm. "Whoever she is, whatever the impediment, sooner or later you will have to take action. You are not a man who can ignore a problem indefinitely. If you try, it will eat you alive."

Darcy rose abruptly, pacing across a carpet like a dark sea to the windows. The side garden burgeoned in spite of the intermittent rain that had marked this April. Bright flowers mixed with darker shrubs. White blooms covered the boxwood hedge between his property and the next. He stared sightlessly at the panoply of nature. *Richard is right, I have lived with this ceaseless torment for two years. It has become almost too much to bear.*

Slowly Darcy turned from the window. Richard saw his shoulders tense. He started to apologize when his cousin spoke in a low voice.

"Do you know who Miss Elizabeth Bennet is?"

"She was at the ball Bingley gave a couple of years ago at the estate he was leasing in Herts. Sister of that stunning blonde Bingley seemed entranced with. He did not marry her, though."

"No."

"I remember riding back with you in the carriage the next morning. You were sour as a green apple. In fact, you have not been yourself since. Is she the reason?"

"In a manner of speaking."

"At first I did not consider it might be a woman. You have always been immune to the beauties of the *ton*."

"She is not of the *ton*," Darcy said harshly. "She is herself and no one else." He drained his glass, retrieved the decanter and poured another for both of them. He took his seat and drank half of his at a swallow.

Richard raised an eyebrow. "Keep that up and you will not be able to tell me the problem."

"The problem is I realized that night I could never marry the one woman I have met that I—that I wanted to marry."

"Did you chase Bingley off her sister for the same reason?"

The question came a little too close to the truth. Darcy stiffened, then sat back. "I did not 'chase' Charles off of Jane Bennet. Caroline did, with Louisa Hurst's help. I did nothing to stop them. It was his decision."

"I will not debate that statement at the moment. So you believed you could not marry her. What were your reasons? She is gently born after all."

"If her social status had been the only concern I would not have hesitated. There were other things."

"Such as?"

Richard's practicality sometimes annoyed his cousin. He saw everything in terms of pros and cons which could either be reconciled or not. Darcy gritted his teeth, but he continued. He wanted Richard's opinion, or at least his understanding.

"Her mother was a crude, vulgar woman from a trade family. She was worse than a debutante's mama trying to marry off her daughters to any man who looked at them twice. Her father was a bookish man who took more care with his library than his estate or his family. The middle sister had a tendency to sermonize, otherwise she was proper enough. As for the two youngest…"

Darcy grimaced. Richard contemplated his drink thoughtfully. "Dowry?"

"A thousand pounds when the mother died. Which happened just over two years ago. And there are still relations in trade."

"Is that the entire indictment?"

"I wish it were. The summer after the ball, her youngest sister ran off with that cur Wickham. They were not able to find her and she was irredeemably lost. The Bennets were ruined, shunned by their neighbors. I heard nothing of it for months as I was at Fenwick, my Scottish estate, all winter and into the early spring. Bingley did not know until after the fact that Mrs. Bennet had passed. By the time he decided to run his own life instead of letting Caroline run it for him, it was too late. Mr. Bennet had turned Longbourn over to the inheritor of the entail and removed without leaving a forwarding direction. If anyone knew where they were they would not say. I have not seen Miss Elizabeth since the fall when Bingley leased Netherfield."

"I understand he has given it up?"

"Yes. He is buying a modest estate in Derbyshire not too far from Pemberley."

Colonel Fitzwilliam raised an eyebrow. "You shall no doubt have Miss Bingley visiting constantly then."

"No. He says she will stay in London until she reaches the age of five-and-twenty or marries. That is less than a year according to Bingley. He learned a great deal from Netherfield, not all of it about running an estate."

"Had she been a more agreeable lady, I might have offered for her myself." Colonel Fitzwilliam grimaced, but Darcy passed over his humor. "It was Wickham who caused it all. Miss Lydia was silly and a bit wild but she would never have done what she did without Wickham seducing her. If I could get my hands on the bastard I would choke his rotten life out."

"I would help you. Unfortunately he has disappeared, I have had men looking for him for desertion with no success. He slipped into the cesspit of St. Giles and no one has seen him since."

"Even if we found him it hardly helps the Bennet sisters."

"True." Colonel Fitzwilliam turned a speculative eye on his cousin. "Still, most of your objections either have been eliminated or are rather specious."

Darcy glowered at him. "I do not follow you."

"Miss Elizabeth's mother is dead. You need not associate with the relatives in trade, although I have met a few tradesmen who are more honest and at least as well educated as half the members of White's. You do not need the dowry, in your case it is only society's expectation that you marry wealth. The only major barrier is her sister's conduct. Is it certain they did not marry?"

"She had nothing but youth and a pretty face. You know Wickham. What do you think?"

"True. I am afraid the other sisters will never marry now, or not matches one would wish for them. Of course, if one of them did marry well—"

"It cannot happen!"

Darcy rose abruptly, nearly shouting. Richard saw the frustration in the gesture, even though he had been referring to Bingley. His cousin was well and truly hooked, sympathy now was worse than useless; it was an insult.

"Passion in matters of the heart should be soundly discouraged among our social class. It can only lead to unsound decisions and reckless actions."

Darcy turned on him, his voice dripping sarcasm. "I hope that particular piece of rot is a quote from your father?"

Richard grinned. Darcy threw himself into his chair once more. Now that he had taken Richard into his confidence words poured from him with a visceral intensity.

"Bingley saw Miss Elizabeth recently, walking toward the smaller Bloomsbury market. She is in mourning again, for her father. She had a young maid with her which means she has at least one servant and probably a housekeeper and cook, as I doubt either of the sisters is knowledgeable in a kitchen. I do not know why she did not use a hansom except she always liked to walk. He said the dress and pelisse she wore were too light for this weather, and looked well-used. I do not believe they are living in poverty, however they are certainly in reduced circumstances. And I can do nothing to assist her. I almost wish Bingley had not seen her."

Richard heard the "almost" and stared into the fire without responding while Darcy calmed himself. "Did Bingley tell you anything else?"

"He did not have to. He was so upset he could barely get the story out. He intends to find their relative in trade, I suppose to ask after Miss Bennet. I was wrong about it being another one of his transitory affections. He has never gotten over her."

"Well, if he is willing to take the plunge it will certainly be to her advantage. It may destroy him with the *ton* though. What about his sisters?"

Darcy shrugged. "He will have to deal with it. It does not change my position. I have Georgie to think of, I cannot risk the faintest scandal touching her life, especially now." *Not with Wickham holding the letter over my head. He will appear if Georgiana becomes betrothed, damn his black soul!*

"You will probably throw me out on my head if I say what I am thinking."

Darcy had calmed somewhat, enough to take Richard's words lightly. "If you landed on your head it would likely do you no damage."

Richard remained serious. "She has nothing. You are capable of improving her situation tremendously. Make her your mistress."

He waited for the explosion that did not come. Darcy stared straight ahead his eyes dark with pain. "I know it is what you would attempt and it has its merits, only not for her. She would never accept me, not after what happened with Miss Lydia. She would likely refuse to ever speak to me again. I do not believe I could even ask it of her."

"You have considered it, though."

Darcy did not reply. Yes, he had considered offering Elizabeth Bennet *carte blanche*, settling her in the house at Twickenham with a trustworthy staff. He could easily spend time with her there and she loved the area, away from the City's clamor. Darcy had considered it—and the potential reasons she would reject such an offer. Her sister's disapprobation, the gossip that sooner or later would link their names, and worse, the prospect of a child. If they should have a son, he could never inherit Pemberley, even if he proved to be Darcy's only child. There were too many barriers. Darcy had rejected the idea with finality.

"Yes. It is impossible."

Richard nodded. "Well then, if there is nothing you can do there is nothing you can do. Do you want to find out where she lives?"

Darcy's head turned sharply toward his cousin. "Do you read minds now?"

"Only simple ones." Richard sipped his drink. "You know she lives in London, somewhere within two or three miles of the Bloomsbury market. Probably a row house or cottage. If her father bought it the sale will be recorded. If its rented or leased, a street vendor with a penchant for chatting to servants will find her. At least you will have some idea of her situation."

Darcy considered the idea. He had no intention of hunting her down as if she were some criminal. She would be justifiably furious at him for invading her privacy. But a discreet canvass of the area could be kept quiet.

"I appreciate your help, Richard. Bingley looked into sales but none were recorded, so they are most likely renting or under a lease. Finding her may be unnecessary if Bingley can convince her family to let him see Miss Bennet. Still, I should like to know her exact situation."

Richard raised his glass to study the amber liquid within. "I have just the man. I shall let you know what he finds out." *For better or worse.*

Both men drank in silence.

# CHAPTER TEN

April 1814
Matlock House, London

"Georgiana, you really cannot afford to offend the viscountess. Lady Jersey is a friend of hers and she is socially prominent. I do not understand your reluctance to accept her invitation. After all, it will be a party of people you either know or have at least met, and Sir Frederick will be there."

*That is the source of my reluctance.* Georgiana did not voice the thought, however Lady Matlock was adept at reading expressions and sat back with a little huff.

"Sir Frederick is obviously attracted to you, Georgiana. He will be Viscount Tennerley one day. His family is well off and well placed. You could do worse."

"I do not wish to offend anyone, Aunt. I just do not understand why the viscountess is holding this outing at their country house at this time of year."

Lady Matlock chose to soften her approach. It disturbed her that Georgiana seemed to wish to withdraw from society rather than become a part of it. "Lady Tennerley is fond of the country. It is a beautiful home at the edge of the Heath. You can ride out rather than take a carriage. I am sure you will enjoy the day if you allow yourself to."

Georgiana sighed inwardly. Her aunt was not going to let her escape the outing. "Very well, aunt Eleanor, I shall go. Shall I write my acceptance or will you?"

"I think you should write." Lady Matlock hid her smile of success. Perhaps it only took a little encouragement to engage her niece's cooperation. "The weather has been quite fine, Lady Tennerley will probably serve luncheon *al fresco*."

## Viscount Tennerley's Manor
## Near Hampstead Heath, London

Georgiana remembered the words as the group of laughing, chattering young people approached the Tennerley mansion. To her discomfort Sir Frederick had insisted on riding next to her, regaling her with anecdotes of the races at Newmarket his stable had won and his trips to Bath and Brighton where he mingled with the highest ranks of the nobility. He had even attended a ball at the Brighton Pavilion, where the Prince Regent was in attendance. Georgiana did her best to be polite. Once she caught the eye of Sir Frederick's cousin Giles Worthington as he let his mount come abreast of hers; he had distinctly made a face of such boredom Georgiana had to develop a sudden cough to disguise her laughter.

Sir Frederick shot a glare at his cousin and said smoothly, "You ride extremely well, Miss Darcy. Most ladies would choose a carriage."

Giles Worthington dropped back and Georgiana recovered herself. "Thank you, sir. My family breeds horses. I have ridden since I was six years old." *For a man with a racing stable he should certainly know of the Pemberley thoroughbreds!*

Sir Frederick led the small group toward the manor house that appeared in the near distance. It was a modern structure built barely a decade ago. The lawns spread a sea of manicured green around three stories of golden stone, windows glinting in the late morning sun. Giles Worthington rode just behind Georgiana. His face did not show the anxiety he felt; Frederick was not a trustworthy man, he was deeply in debt from his gambling, and Miss Darcy provided a temptation his cousin was unlikely to pass up. This unexpected jaunt to the viscount's manor was too providential to be a coincidence.

"This was part of the original grant from Ethelred the Unready to a servant. Can you imagine giving six hides of land to a servant? The king must have been out of his mind."

"Perhaps the servant rendered some special service to King Ethelred."

"Indeed." Frederick laughed rather coarsely.

Giles' mouth drew down in disapproval. *This is not your mistress, Freddy. She is a lady. Treat her with respect or I will see that you do.*

The rest of their party gathered around them as they halted their horses and the two carriages in the driveway. Sir Frederick came to assist Georgiana down from her mare. He managed to run his hand along her back without seeming to notice the contact. Georgiana stepped quickly away from him, but he had already turned to his other guests. Giles came up to her as several grooms led the horses away. She smiled at him, causing a most peculiar sensation to flutter through his chest. Before Giles addressed her, Sir Frederick rejoined them and offered Georgiana his arm.

"Let us go inside. Mother has had a cold luncheon prepared, we can enjoy it in the gardens."

Georgiana laid her hand lightly on Sir Frederick's arm, whereupon he tucked it into the crook of his elbow. For a moment Georgiana fought the desire to pull her hand free; Sir Frederick smiled at her with a self-confidence that made her shiver. He walked toward the house and she allowed herself to be conducted to the entry where Viscountess Tennerley waited to welcome them. Georgiana had met the noblewoman at a ball and found her pleasant if somewhat vague. Lady Tennerley was in her late forties and tended to wear makeup, as well as fashions and coiffures meant for a younger lady. The result was to give her the look of an overdressed doll, which the fact her hair was obviously dyed did nothing to dispel.

She greeted Georgiana with speculation behind her professional warmth and smiled adoringly at her son. Georgiana knew her measure was in some way being taken; it left her more uncomfortable than before. She felt oddly relieved when Giles Worthington joined them in spite of his cousin's angry glances. Her brother had always told her she must listen to her instincts when they warned her about a situation or person. They had grown louder and louder at every encounter with Sir Frederick.

Georgiana went to the ladies' retiring room with some of the other female guests to wash off the dust of the ride and make herself comfortable. A maid was in attendance to brush the ladies' clothes. A quarter of an hour passed before the group made their way to the side of the house where a terrace adjoined part of the formal gardens. Tables were laid with china and silver and a buffet held an abundance of food. Servants helped the diners to their choices. Georgiana's stomach was not prepared to eat at the moment, however she chose several items at random: crème chicken, salmon mayonnaise, some bread and a poached pear with grapes. Wine accompanied the food; Sir Frederick insisted she sit with him, killing whatever appetite she retained.

Giles Worthington had taken a place a little farther down the table where he could observe his cousin and Georgiana discreetly. He seemed to possess no more interest in the food than she did. His scowl deepened when his cousin kept urging Georgiana to drink more and more wine. She declined gracefully, growing obviously agitated at his insistence. Sir Frederick's voice came to Giles at an inevitable lull in the chatter, causing him to press both hands on the table so hard his silverware clinked together.

"Come, Georgiana, have another glass of this," he indicated a servant who held a bottle of amontillado. "Surely you can manage a little more. It is imported from Spain in spite of the war, at quite a large expense. It is one of my mother's favorites."

She placed her hand over the top of the wine glass and shook her head at the footman. "I have tried it, it is very pleasant, but I do not wish any more, thank you. And my name is Miss Darcy, Sir Frederick."

"Oh, but I prefer Georgiana."

Georgiana raised her chin. "I do not when we are barely acquainted."

Sir Frederick laughed and waved the servant away. It was not a pleasant sound. Giles saw her start to rise, only to have Sir Frederick say something that made her stay at his side. At last the luncheon began to drift into languid conversation. The tables were cleared, dessert and champagne offered both of which Georgiana waved away. She rose as soon as politeness allowed and excused herself. Sir Frederick's narrowed gaze followed her. Giles watched him rise after several minutes to organize a game of lawn bowls for any gentlemen who wished to participate.

"Come, Giles, you are quite good at the sport. Show these friends of ours how bowls should be played."

The subtle command beneath the words sent Giles' hackles up. He kept his voice mild, almost lazy. "Why not? Come, gentlemen, let us have a little exercise after all of that food."

Half a dozen of the male guests joined him. Servants had already set up the equipment. As they sorted themselves out, Giles saw his cousin slip into the house unnoticed by the remaining ladies and the few men who declined to play. He excused himself and circled around the side of the manor, entering by a door into a small parlor. There was no sound in the hallway. Giles thought hard for several seconds; where would Miss Darcy go if she wanted privacy? At once the answer came, sending him in a silent sprint toward the front of the house.

He ducked into a doorway, crossed the carpeted drawing room in swift strides. The door to the music room stood ajar. Giles suppressed the tight sound of his breathing. Someone was playing the piano-forte with a mastery he had never heard outside of a concert hall. He edged the door a little farther open; Georgiana Darcy sat behind the elaborately carved instrument, her face calm, her hands moving as she created beauty without apparent effort.

Giles saw her start, her head came up and the enchanting sounds stopped with a jangle of mis-struck keys. She rose but did not leave the illusionary safety of the pianoforte.

"I wondered where you fled to."

Sir Frederick's tone held a deceptive lightness. Georgiana's face paled, she straightened to her full height. The gesture would have been a revelation to anyone who knew both Darcys.

"I wanted a few minutes alone. I am not always comfortable in crowds."

"Crowds? I only invited a dozen couples."

"I thought Lady Tennerley was the hostess."

Georgiana fought to conceal her growing unease. Giles saw Sir Frederick advance on the young woman. There was a stalking quality to his movements that made his cousin's blood pound in his ears.

"My mother does whatever I ask her to. I could hardly invite you to visit alone."

"Why should you wish to?"

Sir Frederick had reached the pianoforte. He placed both hands on the polished surface of the case and leaned over, the heat of his skin leaving white impressions in the gleaming ebony. His face was barely two feet from Georgiana's.

"Because it is the only way I can secure your hand in marriage. I realize I do not please you as a prospective husband. That matters nothing to me. You are beautiful, well connected, and have a very useful dowry. Once you are compromised you will have no choice. Do not fear, I shall teach you to like me, or at least pretend to."

The menace in his tone was unmistakable. Giles could not see Georgiana's hands but he knew they were clenched into fists, or perhaps gripping the skirt of her riding ensemble. Light from the windows spread a graying illumination into the room. With the sudden violence of spring storms, clouds had gathered over the estate, no less full of unseen menace than the scene in the music room. Giles heard the fear beneath her determined control and it increased his anger at his cousin. It was all he could do not to break into the room before Sir Frederick had declared his intentions.

"I will never marry you. My brother will see to that."

"Your brother will protect your reputation at all costs as it means his reputation as well. And I promise you both reputations will be in tatters if you refuse me. A whisper here and there is all it takes."

Georgiana's outrage momentarily overcame her fear. Her eyes burned into her tormentor. "How dare you threaten me, your mother's guest? I thought you a gentleman. I find you are a pig!"

Sir Frederick straightened. Before he was able to start around the pianoforte, Giles' voice exploded into the room as he jerked the door open and entered. "He is a swine, Miss Darcy, but not one you need worry about. Miss Darcy is in no way compromised, Freddy. I have been a third party to the entire disgusting encounter. I can even repeat your sickening words verbatim, and I shall—to your father. You know what his reaction will be."

"Get out! This is none of your business, you damned prig!"

Giles took a step toward his cousin, who retreated at the look on the other's face. Voices suddenly echoed from the hallway outside, unnoticed amid the drama unfolding in the music room. Giles turned to Georgiana, ignoring Sir Frederick's furious demeanor.

"Play, Miss Darcy, quickly. Whatever you can."

Georgiana sank onto the padded bench. Her hands trembled on the keys, she made a false start, then began to play the melody Giles had heard her play so short a time ago. First one then another of the guests entered the room. Sir Frederick stalked to the windows, his back to the others. One or two glanced curiously at him until the glorious music captured them. When Georgiana finished, there was applause and calls for another piece. She declined graciously in favor of any other young lady who wanted to exhibit. Giles could tell she was badly shaken. She made her way to his side, her voice lowered so no one else heard her words.

"Thank you. I hope you will not be harmed by coming to my rescue."

"I shall be fine, Miss Darcy. Sir Frederick is deep in debt from gambling, his father has threatened to disinherit him, although I believe it unlikely. This may be enough to make the viscount take drastic action."

She hesitated. "You will not use my name?"

"No, do not worry. I suspect Lady Tennerley had a hand in this, she indulges her son in whatever he wants. The viscount will not be happy about it if she did."

Rain suddenly hurled itself against the windows, rattling the panes of glass like hail. Georgiana startled at the noise, Giles saw her struggle to control her agitation. There were exclamations of distress from some of the ladies, answered by gentlemen in a superior fashion. All at once Sir Frederick turned on the crowd, the gleaming glass making a stark contrast to his shadowed form.

"I think it is time you all departed. I will see that carriages are arranged as soon as this downpour lets up. Good day."

He left them without another word. Georgiana heard murmurs of resentment at such cavalier treatment, none of them loud enough to be insulting. Sir Frederick was not popular with many of his set, however the idea of offending the viscount mitigated their response to his son.

"I will see you home, Miss Darcy, if you have no objection? We can take a carriage with one of the couples."

Georgiana smiled a little. "No objection at all, Mr. Worthington."

April 1814
Gardiner Warehouse, London

"Sir, a gentleman to see you."

Mr. Gardiner's chief clerk extended an engraved card to his

employer without exhibiting any of the curiosity he felt. Mr. Gardiner looked up from the bill of lading he perused, took the card and read it. A scowl briefly troubled his usually calm demeanor; then he dropped the card on his desk amid neat piles of paperwork.

"Bring the gentleman up."

"Yes, sir."

Whatever he might have expected from his unexpected visitor, it was not the tentative young man who entered his office and bowed. "Mr. Gardiner, thank you for seeing me."

Mr. Gardiner indicated a chair before his desk without rising. "Mr. Bingley, your name is not unknown to me."

"Nor is it particularly welcome, I expect." Bingley sat, his hands resting stiffly on his knees. "I cannot blame you, sir, for any reluctance to meet with me. I have acted badly and hurt someone I would never wish to hurt. I hope you will believe me when I say that I have suffered also, not least knowing my motives were unworthy."

Mr. Gardiner indeed saw lines of pain in the young man's pleasant countenance. It was not a face made for sorrow, or any strong emotion. The fact that he felt those emotions so clearly inclined Mr. Gardiner to listen to him rather than send him away as he had intended. He rose and went to a sidebar, poured two small brandies and brought one to Bingley, who accepted it gratefully.

Returning to his chair, Mr. Gardiner sipped his drink before setting it down and folding his hands on the well-worn mahogany of the desktop.

"Suppose you tell me exactly why you have come to see me?"

Bingley took a swallow of his brandy and set the glass down. He seemed to struggle for words for several moments before sitting straighter and gathering himself.

"My father was in trade in Newcastle as was his father before him. He made a large fortune in ironmongery, and decided I should be educated as a gentleman. I went to university and soon learned that a cit is always a cit. It was my father's intention to sell his assets, which he did except for the company my family founded, and buy an estate so I and my two sisters would eventually attain the status of gentry. Sadly he died before his plans were complete."

"I met your father on several occasions, I believe—Mr. Josiah Bingley?" At Bingley's nod he added, "He was a good man."

"He was. Much better than his son." Bingley paused. "Nearly three years ago I leased an estate in Hertfordshire. One of the neighboring estates was Longbourn. I met the family and became much impressed with the eldest daughter, your niece, Miss Bennet." With the tendency of those whose family runs to redheads, his fair complexion flushed. "I intended to make an offer of marriage, but my younger sister insisted to marry into the lesser gentry would spoil any chance of her making an advantageous marriage, and that Miss Bennet did not feel any strong attachment to me. I am afraid I let her convince me. If you knew my sister—but it was my decision."

Mr. Gardiner felt an unexpected sympathy for the young man before him. His own sister, rest her soul, had been demanding and frequently difficult to handle. And the sincerity of Bingley was impossible to disbelieve. He had made a bad decision and he had suffered for it.

"What do you want from me, Mr. Bingley?"

The words were not angry, and Bingley raised his head and leaned forward slightly. "I saw Miss Elizabeth two days ago near Bloomsbury. I thought the Bennets might be in London, but had no idea where. When I went back to Hertfordshire after I learned of Mrs. Bennet's passing, no one seemed to know their direction. I was—I was shocked at how she looked,, she seemed weighed down with grief. She said her father had passed. It must have been a terrible blow along with everything else that happened. She said she and Miss Bennet were well, but I cannot help but wish to know the truth. My friend Mr. Darcy remembered your name and I thought if I spoke to you, you might consent to allow me to meet with Miss Bennet, if she agrees, wherever you deem proper."

Having said everything he had built up his resolve to say, Bingley sat stiff with tension awaiting Mr. Gardiner's response. That gentleman contemplated the request with some misgiving. If Elizabeth had told her sister of the encounter, Jane would already know Mr. Bingley knew she resided in the area of Bloomsbury. Mr. Gardiner did not believe Mr. Bingley meant to find Jane on his own. Whether she wished to see the young man after what had passed between them was not a matter he could decide.

"I shall consult my wife on the matter. She is close to Elizabeth and Jane. If you will call here tomorrow I will have an answer for you."

He stood, and Bingley rose, bowing. They did not shake hands, Bingley too uncertain of his position in Mr. Gardiner's regard and the older man unwilling to exhibit a friendly overture that might be misunderstood as encouragement. When Bingley left his office, Mr. Gardiner glanced at the Pettigrew clock on a bookcase and decided he should go home for lunch.

Mrs. Gardiner was pleased to see her husband arrive home as lunch was ready to be served., She worried at times that he devoted so much time and energy to his business he did not take enough care of his health. The fact he was a vigorous man not yet five and forty did not assuage her wifely concerns, nor did his serious expression.

He bent to kiss her forehead. "Margaret, there is a matter I wish to speak with you about."

Curious at his serious tone Mrs. Gardiner said, "'Of course, Edward. May we discuss it over luncheon?"

The dining room was cool in spite of the warmth of the day. Wallpaper striped in blue, green and gold rose to the ceiling above a white chair rail. A place for the master of the house was always set in the event it was required. Mr. Gardiner took his place at the head of the table as his wife signaled for the soup to be served. When the footman departed, Mr. Gardiner regarded his wife soberly.

"I had a visitor at the office this morning: Mr. Bingley."

Mrs. Gardiner sat very still. She knew the name and the story of Jane's heartbreak. She did not ask the purpose of his visit. "What is he like?"

"He is not as I expected. He must be five and twenty, but his manner is that of a boy just becoming a man. He explained that he allowed his sister to influence him to leave Hertfordshire as she deemed a marriage to Jane the ruination of her chances to secure a wealthy husband. She also convinced him Jane had no strong feelings for him. Apparently he decided on his own to return to his leased estate this past summer, only to find my sister deceased and the family gone without a new direction."

"I am surprised he summoned the nerve to face you." Mrs. Gardiner ate a spoonful of her lobster bisque. "A man of that age who allows his sister to determine whom he will marry is not a promising prospect."

"Normally I would agree with you. However, I admit I felt some sympathy for him—Fanny could be impossible to ignore on occasion. Still, he is the head of his family and a grown man. He wants to know if I will allow Jane to see him in a chaperoned situation. I did not say that Jane may see whomever she likes as she is past her majority and not in my care."

"She would not go against your advice, Edward." Mrs. Gardiner leaned toward her husband. "What do you think of the idea?"

Mr. Gardiner rubbed a hand across his forehead. "He is a pleasant fellow. I can see why Jane was attracted to him, and he to her. I believe him to be sincere in his regret. I just wonder if seeing him again will bring back all the pain of that time, or if it may be Jane's salvation."

"You mean she is unlikely ever to marry if it is not Mr. Bingley?"

"I mean that marriage for any of our nieces is more a matter of luck than certainty."

Mrs. Gardiner pondered the situation while the main course was served. She had told her husband about Mr. Porter's visit, including his cautious response to both Bennet sisters and his offer of a tour of his tea business. Few men could look at Jane and not marvel at her classic beauty. Perhaps it was only because they were in mourning, but she was not willing to put too much faith in a favorable outcome.

The servant left the dining room. Mr. Gardiner began on his

mutton and new peas. They ate in silence for several minutes before he continued, his voice thoughtful.

"Mr. Thurgood knew there was some problem with the youngest sister. I indicated she eloped with a militia officer leaving a note that they were going to Gretna Green, and was lost to the family. It is the truth as far as it goes. The Bennets are not a prominent family and virtually unknown in London. There is little chance of the whole truth becoming known."

"Half-truths are dangerous, Edward. Still, Mr. Bingley knows everything, and he will never speak of it. As for his sister, she would be a fool to use the information. She would suffer for it more than her brother or Jane."

"I cannot speak for her, Margaret. I can only hope that Mr. Bingley has taken charge of his family and can control her."

They finished the meal without further discussion before Mr. Gardiner rose, gazing steadily at his wife. "Will you send Jane a note and tell her there is a matter we must discuss with her? You may want to write Lizzy separately about the situation we find ourselves in."

"She will tell Jane."

Mr. Gardiner assisted his wife to her feet. "I think not. She will want to hear everything before she comes to a conclusion. Thomas trained her well. And now I must return to my bills of lading."

He bent and kissed his wife's forehead. She accompanied him to the door and stood watching him stride away. There was a heaviness of foreboding in her breast. Edward Gardiner was a truthful man. He did not lie; the only reason he had glossed over the truth with Mr. Thurgood was in the belief that to do otherwise might rob their niece of the hope of happiness in marriage. Still, she thought, any distortion of the truth was dangerous. It could not be all so easy; things never were where scandal was involved. With an inward sigh she returned to the drawing room to write her nieces.

## April 1814
## Darcy House, London

Darcy was preparing to leave for an appointment with his accountant when he heard Lady Matlock's voice in the entry. She sounded agitated, something he was not used to. His aunt was an accomplished politician's wife, her self-control in the face of trouble was legendary in the family. Darcy put his papers aside and went to the door of his study. Just inside the front door Lady Matlock faced Mr. Burgess, who watched her with his head slightly inclined, the picture of solicitous efficiency.

"Is my niece awake, Mr. Burgess? I need to speak to her at the earliest possible moment."

"Aunt Eleanor, what is the matter?"

Darcy nodded to Mr. Burgess and took his aunt's hands. Her mouth thinned, she glanced past him to see the butler depart on her request. Darcy offered his arm and conducted her to the drawing room. She took a chair, straightening the skirt of her coral silk day dress. Darcy saw the tension in her neck and shoulders with a small instinctive jolt of apprehension. He remained on his feet while Lady Matlock composed herself, folding her hands in her lap as some long-gone governess had taught her.

Georgiana appeared in the doorway, her eyes went from her aunt to Darcy and he saw her go pale. She came in and curtsied to Lady Matlock. "Good morning, aunt Eleanor."

"I wish it were." Lady Matlock surveyed Georgiana with a mixture of uncertainty and discomposure. Georgiana seated herself on a sofa across from her aunt. She kept her arms folded across her stomach as if to hold in some strong reaction. Lady Matlock's expression softened. She looked from sister to brother and back before she spoke.

"Lady Tennerley called on me this morning. Do you know what it was about, Georgiana?"

"I am not certain. Sir Frederick I imagine."

"Yes, Sir Frederick. To make the matter short, she accuses you of playing with her son's affections and setting his cousin Giles against him."

Georgiana's mouth opened. No sound emerged, she gave a little gasping breath and looked as if she might faint. Darcy went to a sideboard, poured a very small amount of brandy into a glass and brought it to her.

"Sip. Slowly."

Georgiana clutched the glass in both hands. She took a tiny sip, coughed and took another, some color returning to her face. Darcy removed the glass from her trembling hands and sat beside her on the sofa. Lady Matlock's expression had gone from questioning to disturbed. Darcy took his sister's hand and squeezed it. He wondered briefly if he was about to find out what had been disturbing his sister so profoundly.

"No one is accusing you of anything, Georgie. We both know," with a glance at his aunt, "that you are not a flirt, much less a lady who likes to set men against each other. Tell us what happened and we will straighten out this whole matter."

"Indeed, Georgiana, I only want to know exactly what occurred yesterday. When you did not return to Matlock House, I was afraid you might have ridden home in the rain and taken a chill. I was completely astounded at Lady Tennerley's accusation."

"I was afraid he would keep his word." Georgiana felt tears of anger prickle her eyes and brushed them away. "He threatened to ruin my reputation. Now his mother will try to do just that. He wants to marry me and I cannot stands the sight of him!"

Darcy said slowly, "Is this what has been bothering you?"

Georgiana hesitated briefly. "Yes. At first I liked Sir Frederick, but then he kept pushing me to accept a courtship, and something about his attitude made me uncomfortable. He was too familiar, as if the matter was already settled. I tried to discourage him as politely as I could, but it made no difference. The more I tried to avoid him the more he kept after me. I did not want to go on the outing, but—Lady Tennerley was supposed to be the hostess. She welcomed us when we arrived, and we did not see her again."

Lady Matlock frowned. "Who acted as host?"

"Sir Frederick. He insisted I stay with him. Every time I tried to get away he made some excuse to keep me nearby. I finally went into the house after luncheon while he was organizing a game. I found the music room and sat down to play. I just wanted to compose myself, but he found me."

Georgiana halted, her hands twisted in the skirt of her morning gown. Darcy's face darkened. "Did he harm you?"

She shook her head. "He told me I had to marry him whether I liked the idea or not because I was compromised. He said I would be ruined if I refused. He said I would ruin William as well. I c-called him a pig and he started toward me when Mr. Giles Worthington came into the room. He had been listening to everything and threatened to tell Viscount Tennerley. The others were coming in because it had started to rain. Mr. Worthington told me to play something so they would think I had been entertaining them. Sir Frederick was very angry, but no one else thought anything of it."

"Bless Mr. Worthington," Lady Matlock said with feeling. She met Darcy's gaze, "This is still very serious, William. Lady Tennerley told me I was the only person she was calling on today. If we act quickly there should be no repercussions."

Darcy saw Georgiana's eyes fill with tears. She blinked rapidly, not willing to show how deeply disturbed she was.

"Act quickly how?"

Darcy felt a sudden disquiet at his aunt's reaction. He knew she disliked unpleasantness, and gossip of the kind Lady Tennerley was capable of initiating could reflect badly on her as well, as Georgiana's sponsor. But her reaction seemed out of proportion to her status in society.

Lady Matlock leaned forward intently. Darcy's shoulders tightened, he let his hand rest on Georgiana's arm. "I am reluctant to suggest it. I know you want Georgiana to take time to choose a suitor, but if this is to be stopped you must authorize a courtship with one of the most suitable young men Georgiana has met this Season. There are several choices who have impeccable reputations and are not fortune hunters. If there is gossip then, it will be put down to jealousy on Sir Frederick's part."

Darcy felt Georgiana shiver beside him. She looked ill. He kept his voice neutral in spite of a growing anger. "You want me to use a young man Georgiana hardly knows to stop gossip that has not yet begun and never may. I cannot believe you have so little influence that the word of a viscountess would be taken over yours."

Lady Matlock drew in her breath sharply, then sat back. She ran slim fingers over her eyes before she answered. "Lady Tennerley is not the problem. Her good friend Lady Jersey is."

Georgiana raised her head to meet Darcy's eyes. "William, what am I to do? If Lady Jersey believes her the truth will not matter. I do not want to involve someone else out of fear, it would not be fair to the gentleman. I have done nothing wrong, why must I be punished for Sir Frederick's actions?"

The panic beneath the words sent a cold surge of protective anger through Darcy. "You will not be punished Georgie, and we will not involve anyone but Viscount Tennerley. I will call on him in the morning. If he is unreasonable I can do more damage to Sir Frederik than he can do to either of you."

"William, you would not...not call him out?"

Both women looked at Darcy, Lady Matlock alarmed and Georgiana horrified. Darcy shook his head. "There are other ways."

"Very well, William." Lady Matlock thinned her lips. "If that is your decision. I have enough influence to counteract some of Lady Tennerley's assertions if need be." She rose. "Please let me know the result of your interview."

He walked her to the door. Georgiana had not moved when he returned. Looking at her bent head, the whole indrawn posture as if she wanted to minimize her physical presence, he saw another young woman who had been destroyed by scandal not of her making. *Not this time. Not Georgiana. Not if I have to ruin the viscount and his entire family.*

April 1814
Hephaestus House, London

"Charles, I need the coach. I am to call on Lady Greenwood this morning."

His sister's sharp demanding tone raised his old defensive instincts, he started to answer her with a placating explanation when a face rose in his mind's eye, a lovely, serene face smiling at him in gentle reprimand. His jaw hardened. He swung around to find Caroline standing in the doorway of the drawing room, her hands on her hips. She wore a dress in the latest fashion, of plum silk embroidered with trailing green leaves, and a lime green spencer. Her inevitable plumes waved white flags above a lavender hat. Her suppressed anger assaulted him. He wondered if Lady Greenwood was aware of the call.

"You will have to take a hansom. I am using the coach this morning."

"A hansom? You expect me to call on Lady Greenwood in a hansom? Why do you have to have the coach on this particular morning?"

"Because it is my coach, and I am going out. Take a hackney if you prefer it."

"I prefer to look as if we had sufficient funds to keep two carriages. I do not know why we do not. Mr. Darcy has at least two at his disposal."

"Mr. Darcy's coaches are not my concern. I am taking the coach, Caroline, and that is the end of the discussion."

Bingley saw her face darken and waited for the explosion. The servants had wisely chosen to wait just out of sight unless summoned.

He was to collect Darcy and call on the Gardiners with the expectation that Jane Bennet would be there. He refused to allow his sister to upset him; the prospect of seeing his angel again after all that had occurred was causing enough anxiety.

"You are chasing after that woman again, are you not? As if the first time was not humiliating enough. I will not have it, Charles! You have plenty of other choices ..."

She was growing shrill, the words grating on his already exacerbated nerves. Bingley raised his voice more than was his habit, not caring at the moment if the servants heard him.

"I have had enough of your interference, Caroline. This is my business, not yours. I intend to do what will make me happy and hopefully make Miss Bennet happy without reference to your needs, wants, likes or dislikes."

He called the butler who brought his outerwear. He was pulling on his gloves before she found her voice. "You want to ruin me, ruin us, for some country nobody you have not seen in years. How can you do this to me!"

"I will not continue this conversation, if that is what it is, at this time or in the entry hall. Go out or stay home, it is of no difference to me."

Mr. Hastings held the door for him. The coach waited in the driveway. Bingley put his hat on and went out, Caroline's furious face imprinted on his consciousness.

He found Darcy ready and the coach proceeded through the quieter streets of Mayfair eastward to the thronging crowds of vehicles and pedestrians near the docks. The passing scene was of no interest to Bingley. He only thought of the interview to come; the result would make or destroy the rest of his life.

Darcy noted that his friend could not control his nervous expectation. He tugged at his cuffs, tapped his fingers against his knees, shuffled his feet, and finally tugged at his cravat as if it choked him.

"One would think that was a noose around your neck, Charles."

Bingley looked at his friend sharply and then subsided with a cha-grined expression. "I am sorry, Darcy, but I do not know exactly what to expect and that has me discomposed."

"I can well understand your feelings, however arriving with your clothing in disarray will hardly help your reception."

Bingley closed his eyes and nodded. Looking down he said, "Caroline knows about Miss Bennet. She must have found out that I saw Miss Elizabeth and realized I would not rest until I was allowed to meet with her sister. I had a sort of row with her this morning. She tried to stop me leaving the house. I was more abrupt with her than usual, but I am tired of her constant attempts to run my life." At Darcy's raised brow he sighed. It was not easy to break old hab-its. "She kept the news of Mrs. Bennet's passing from me for several months. I do not know how she found out, she disdained making friends in Hertfordshire. I doubt it was in any London paper."

Darcy did not respond. Caroline probably had engaged someone local to keep her informed of the Bennets' affairs, it was the sort of scheme she would employ. They proceeded with the motion of the Thames a constant restless presence flowing toward the sea. After nearly a half hour that seemed much longer, the coach turned into Gracechurch Street. They passed homes of two and three stories with well-kept yards behind neat fences. The coach finally pulled up to the curb before a gray stone home with green painted door and shutters. Flowers bloomed in circular brick beds on either side of a flagged walkway. It showed pride and prosperity. It was not, Darcy thought, what he expected.

# CHAPTER ELEVEN

April 1814
Gardiner Residence, London

His footman opened the coach door. Darcy saw Bingley gather himself and climb out. Darcy followed him, standing on the sidewalk while the younger man hesitated, one hand on the gate. Elizabeth was most probably inside with her sister. He dreaded the encounter, knowing it could only intensify his longing while reminding him nothing would come of seeing her again but more pain. Briefly he considered walking to the park they had passed several blocks away while Bingley called, rejecting the idea immediately. He had come to support his friend, it would be a betrayal to leave now.

A butler answered Bingley's knock. There was no sign of anyone watching from a window Darcy noted, unlike the Bennet home at Longbourn. Combined with the respectability of the neighborhood it was encouraging of a more dignified meeting than he had expected. The interior continued the impression of the outside. The polished floor of the entry caught muted gleams of light from two side windows. A strip of carpet centered the stairs rising to the upper floors. On the right a small table held a silver tray and a vase of tulips so yellow they might have been made of sunlight. On the wall to the right a painting caught Darcy's eye.

"That is a handsome scene," he noted as the butler took his outerwear. The man glanced at the painting.

"If you have ever been to the Peak District in Derbyshire, sir, you will recognize it as Dove Dale. The mistress is from that area."

It was perhaps more than a well-trained servant should have said, but Darcy was glad for the information. *What a strange coincidence,* Darcy thought as he proffered his card. The butler placed both calling cards on the tray and indicated the gentlemen should follow him. The three ladies waiting in the drawing room rose as the men entered. Bingley bowed to the older woman and indicated Darcy.

"Good morning, Mrs. Gardiner. May I present my friend, Mr. Darcy of Pemberley in Derbyshire?"

She curtsied to both gentlemen. "Good morning, Mr. Bingley, Mr. Darcy. I know you are both acquainted with my nieces,. Miss Bennet and Miss Elizabeth Bennet."

Darcy felt his body stiffening as if to repel a blow. Elizabeth straightened from her curtsey and for a moment their eyes met. Darcy held himself rigidly in check. She had lost the lovely color of her days in Hertfordshire when she walked out every day. Her face showed the grief she had endured, the skin lying close over her fine bones. She had never been as full-bodied as her sisters, now she was thin, her mourning dress falling loosely around her in spite of obvious adjustments to the fit. But it was her eyes, her wonderful eyes, that affected Darcy most. Bingley had been right; they were old. She had lost her joy in life.

Bingley greeted her with restraint and turned to Jane. She sat down on the far end of the sofa she shared with Elizabeth. It was covered in a lovely lilac jacquard with a white pattern. Against such a backdrop Jane's black dress emphasized her startling pale beauty. After a short hesitation, Bingley took a chair across from her. Darcy seated himself near the end of the sofa where Elizabeth had resumed her former place. She did not seem uncomfortable in his presence, only withdrawn. Darcy wondered if she blamed him for Bingley's precipitous departure from Netherfield. He must find something to say, simply sitting in her presence was too disturbing without words to fill the time.

"I am profoundly sorry for your loss, Miss Elizabeth. I did not know of either your mother's or father's passing until Bingley told me. Losing a parent is a terrible event."

"Thank you, Mr. Darcy. I recall you lost both of your parents at a young age."

"Yes. My mother when I was sixteen, my father at two-and-twenty. With my father's passing I had Pemberley to manage and my sister to care for. In a way that made it easier as I could not dwell on his loss so completely."

Elizabeth did not respond. She kept her eyes on her hands folded in her lap. It was strange to be talking to Mr. Darcy again after so long, as if they had just parted. She remembered the night of the Netherfield ball, her confusion and uncertainty at his revelations about Wickham's character. Was he thinking of that night as well? What poor use she had made of the information! But would it really have made any difference in the end? Her mother would have waved away her concerns, and her father…her father laughed at her for thinking any man in need of money might seduce poor, silly Lydia. Elizabeth realized her aunt was speaking to Mr. Darcy and attended the conversation with a guilty start. His deep voice, so well remembered, sent a throb of response through her chest. He was as he had been, she thought. She was not.

Mrs. Gardiner was talking of Lambton where she had spent her childhood. She had seen Lady Anne in the village from time to time and admired her kindness very much. Darcy made appropriate responses. He glanced at Bingley when Mrs. Gardiner rose to ring for tea. His friend and Miss Bennet sat in nearly mirrored attitudes, bent forward, not looking at each other, Bingley's voice a penitent murmur. Before he could look away, Bingley straightened. He blurted out something that caused Jane to blush. Elizabeth frowned, then sighed.

At that moment, Darcy vowed to assist his friend by every means in his power to court Miss Bennet. If she accepted Bingley and they wed it would benefit Elizabeth nearly as much as her sister. He wondered if that was why Elizabeth seemed less than happy at this reconnection. Did she doubt Bingley's constancy, as well she might, or was it on her own account? She would not want to be seen as using her sister's marriage to improve her own situation. Darcy knew he had to find out her feelings on the matter before it went much further. If she spoke against Bingley, Miss Bennet might listen, leaving both men bereft.

Tea arrived and Darcy took a cup. He looked up in surprise at the robust flavor to see Elizabeth's lips twitch. "It is a new blend from Mr. Porter's shop." Mrs. Gardiner sipped her own tea, indicating the two pots on the tray. "My nieces and I tried it last week when Mr. Porter brought some samples of new blends. I thought gentlemen would like it. I prefer a milder taste, but Lizzy has adopted it."

"Porter's Tea and Coffee?" Bingley finally realized he should join the general discussion. "Caroline buys a special blend from him. It is too flowery for my taste. This is quite good."

"We are visiting his shop to tour the blending facility in a few days." Elizabeth set her cup down and placed a small cake from the tray on her plate. "I have no doubt it will be very interesting. I shall have questions for Mr. Porter."

"He is a family friend," Mrs. Gardiner added. "We have known him since before his wife died. He puts a great deal of time into his business. It is a shame he has not remarried. He is a kind man who would make a very respectable husband."

Darcy saw Bingley glance at Jane and swallow hard. She seemed to have regained any composure the visit may have robbed her of. With a sudden chill, Darcy wondered if Mr. Porter might be attracted to Elizabeth. *If she marries into trade she will be lost to any status of gentility. It must not happen.*

*And why not?* his rational mind asked. She would be safe, well cared for, perhaps even happy. Did he really want to deny her that? The image of her with another man tore at his mind. Darcy felt her eyes on him and looked up. The cool, aloof mask he habitually wore snapped into place like the visor on a medieval helmet.

Elizabeth watched him quizzically, her head a little on one side, a gesture he remembered well. His mouth was dry, he took another sip of the tea, which had suddenly turned bitter on his tongue.

"More tea, Mr. Darcy?"

"No, thank you." Darcy set his cup aside. "I have had sufficient."

The gentlemen stayed another few minutes and then departed after expressing their appreciation to Mrs. Gardiner. Alone with her nieces, she surveyed them with some satisfaction.

"That went well, I thought. Jane, what are your feelings after seeing Mr. Bingley?"

Jane's color made the question superfluous. "He is not as he was in Hertfordshire. He seems more thoughtful. I believe he did not mean to harm me when he left, although he admits his weakness in listening to his sisters. He has asked nothing of me except to allow him to see me again with any chaperones I choose. He indicated he would welcome Lizzy's presence if she agreed."

"And where would you meet?"

"Here, if you and uncle have no objection? I—do not like to ask him to call at Meadow Lane, even though Lizzy would be there."

Mrs. Gardiner rang for the maid to remove the tea things. "I agree. It is best for now to keep any contact on neutral ground. I do not expect Edward to object, but I will ask him just to be sure. I think he rather likes Mr. Bingley."

Elizabeth kept her reservations to herself. At present Mr. Bingley seemed changed from the heedless young man she had met in Hertfordshire. How permanent the changes were in the face of his sisters' certain opposition was still unknown. If necessary she would intervene to try and save Jane from being hurt once again.

The post came while they waited for Mr. Gardiner. The butler brought in a letter for his mistress with Mr. Clarke's direction. Mrs. Gardiner opened the missive quickly and scanned the contents, a smile suffusing her face.

"Mary has had her baby, a boy! Both are doing well. He is to be called Stephen Thomas after both of his grandfathers. Oh this is wonderful news. Mary was so sick at first, but she recovered and now has a son. I shall write our congratulations. I know you will wish to do the same."

The ladies spoke of Mary and the baby until Mr. Gardiner arrived, in good time for dinner. He was pleased with Mary's news and the chosen names. The visit by the two gentlemen was not discussed. Mrs. Gardiner would speak to her husband later when they were alone. After the ragoût and the crimp cod in oyster sauce had been served and eaten, the entrée arrived and conversation turned to the sisters' living arrangements.

"The lease on the house expires at the end of this month," Elizabeth addressed her uncle after a glance at Jane. "We do not know if the landlord will want a new lease or how much the monthly rent might rise if he does. We have talked of perhaps moving to rooms or a flat somewhere closer to the City. We hoped you might advise us, uncle."

Mr. Gardiner met his wife's gaze. She gave a very slight shake of her head and he replied with an equally slight nod. "Are you determined to move at this time?"

Elizabeth hesitated. If Jane married, she would be alone and a house was a burden she did not want to assume. "Not determined, we are only discussing the options. Neither of us wants to continue in a house with more space than we can use. We believe we can prevail on our maid to accompany us, and arrange for a full-time housekeeper and cook, who might live in. We greatly value your opinion and your experience in such matters. Papa...Papa told me at the end to consult you with any problems we might have."

Her uncle's raised eyebrows told her he was surprised by her father's advice, however he thought for several minutes before replying. "Let me speak to the landlord. He may be willing to allow you to stay on a month-to-month basis for now. Most landlords like to retain good tenants if they can. I have his name and direction at the office, I will contact him and let you know what I find out."

Elizabeth and Jane thanked him and finished their meal conversing on the usual table subjects. Both of the Gardiners were thinking the same thing; if Jane married, whether Mr. Bingley or some other suitor, would Elizabeth live with her? Neither knew Elizabeth's fierce determination never to be a burden to her sister. She only hoped her uncle would not put impediments in her way.

May 1814
Darcy House, London

"We have received an invitation from Caroline Bingley to a dinner at Hephaestus House the day after tomorrow."

Georgiana looked up from her tea cup to her brother who had been sorting the post. He held an invitation on heavy cream paper with a deckled edge. She could not see the script however she recognized the invitations Caroline always used. Georgiana set her cup down and watched Darcy's expression. She was not particularly friendly with Mr. Bingley's younger sister. Georgiana knew perfectly well that in Caroline's eyes she was merely a conduit to her brother.

"Do you wish to go?" she asked carefully.

"If we have no other engagements that evening. I can go alone if you do not wish to attend."

Georgiana considered his offer. William was aware that she was not partial to Miss Bingley and approved her keeping a distance from Bingley's sister. Her brother and Mr. Bingley were best friends, however, which posed a problem in social situations.

"Mr. Bingley has located Miss Bennet." Darcy had told her briefly of their call on the Gardiners. "Do you think she and Miss Elizabeth Bennet will be at the dinner?"

Darcy wanted to say, *Not if Caroline has anything to say about it.* He temporized instead. "The invitation is from Miss Bingley. As it is apparently her dinner, I doubt very much if they will be invited. They are in half-mourning for their father, and they would not know most of the guests."

"I suppose we both ought to attend." Georgiana reached for the invitation Darcy held out to her. "I shall write our acceptance."

"Thank you."

He sipped his coffee, watching his sister rise and leave the room after a brief curtsey. Georgiana moved with the confidence of a woman rather than the uncertain dignity of a girl. Inevitably she would marry, and that sent a hot wave of anger and apprehension twisting Darcy's stomach. She did not know. she must never know, of the threat he had protected her from for so long. The incident with Sir Frederick was only a shadow of the scandal they faced if he failed.

She still seemed troubled, he thought. He meant to call on the viscount today and ensure that no rumors were started by Lady Tennerley. He already had the means to stop a campaign against Georgiana and Lady Matlock. Just the threat ought to be enough if the viscount was at all reasonable.

Darcy found that gentleman in the lounge at White's. He looked up as the younger man approached but did not rise from the heavy chair he occupied. The corner where he waited was a little distant from other occupants. The lamps were lit as the room had no windows. They cast shadows over the viscount's gaunt form, absorbed by his fine wool suit so that only his white cravat caught the edges of light. He looked up at Darcy from beneath shaggy gray brows and indicated the companion chair with a flick of his hand.

"Let us forgo the preliminaries, Mr. Darcy. If you have come to advise me you want satisfaction from my son, I must tell you he is no longer in England."

Darcy took the chair so their meeting would not draw undue attention. The viscount's voice had a rusty quality, as if he had been overusing it. He looked tired, Darcy noted. Perhaps he had spent the past day arguing with his wife.

"I have come to ensure that no tales or rumors are started that implicate my sister in impropriety. Lady Tennerley has already called on my aunt, Lady Matlock, and indicated her displeasure with Miss Darcy over the incident at your estate two days ago."

Viscount Tennerley ran a long, narrow hand over his receding hairline. He said after several moments, "I have already spoken to Lady Tennerley about the matter. There will be no more calls, and no rumors. I own an estate in Ireland where I breed some of my racing stable. I have sent Frederick there for the indefinite future. My steward is a local man, he has my instructions and he will carry them out. I have also spoken to my nephew Giles, who informed me of the situation. I trust this satisfies any concerns you have."

"At present." A waiter appeared with a tray holding a bottle of port and two glasses. Viscount Tennerley took a glass and gestured to the second glass. Darcy shook his head. When the man left, he said, "I visited the Jockey Club yesterday. I spoke to several members of my acquaintance and obtained the information that Sir Frederick is in debt to at least the amount of ten thousand pounds. I can easily purchase those and any other vowels he has outstanding. I will do so, and call them, if a whisper arises against Miss Darcy."

The viscount realized the threat was not a bluff. Darcy could afford to buy the majority of his son's IOUs, perhaps all of them. Viscount Tennerley drank his port in two swallows. "I give you my assurance, Mr. Darcy, that will not be necessary."

His tone was a dismissal. Darcy rose to leave. Viscount Tennerley poured himself another glass of port before he looked up at Darcy's tall figure. He said as if speaking to himself, "It is not easy raising a son who knows he is the only viable heir. I have not done well at it. Perhaps a stay in Ireland will accomplish what I have not."

Darcy left him with a formal bow. He believed the threat was enough to suppress Lady Tennerley's gossip, however he had already set in motion the purchase of Sir Frederick's most pressing debts in the event the viscount had no more control over his wife than he did over his son.

May 1814
Darcy House, London

Darcy arrived home to find Richard Fitzwilliam occupying a chair in his study and enjoying a glass of old brandy. "You," he raised his glass, "look like a thundercloud that just rained on someone's picnic."

"In a manner of speaking. Do make yourself at home."

Richard's grin followed his cousin to the sidebar where Darcy poured himself his usual modest brandy. He joined Richard and sat in the companion chair, sipping his drink.

"I found out what was bothering Georgie. A young scapegrace named Sir Frederick Hawes-Brent, the son of Viscount Tennerley. I have, I hope, taken care of it."

Richard sat back. "Tell me all, cousin."

Darcy told him. When he finished, Richard was scowling. "The little cur needs a good hiding. I suppose your way is less public and apparently effective. How is my little bird now?"

"She seems to be well, although I wonder if the whole situation has had an effect on her feelings about the Season."

"If it has, she will get over it. She is a sensitive lady. I am glad to know it was no worse, thanks to this Giles Worthington. Have you met him?"

"No." Darcy did not elaborate. "What are you doing in London? I thought you were at Rosings Park. Is Anne well?"

"She is doing quite well, although I intend to consult Sir Edgar before I return."

"How is our aunt behaving?"

"Badly, but discreetly. She knows I will do what I say. I have left strict instructions that she is not to be admitted to the house while I am gone. She does not like it, which bothers me not at all. If she puts a toe in the door, she will start trying to take over. Anne does not need the agitation."

"So you are here to consult Sir Edgar Crane. It seems a long way to go when you might have written."

"I had to see to some minor details of resigning my commission. If Boney pops up again I do not want to be called away."

"You think he will?"

Richard shrugged. "He is a dictator and his thirst for power is insatiable. Men like that do not give up easily." He finished his brandy and waved away Darcy's offer of a refill. "Dealing with the War Office sober is difficult enough. Drunk it is impossible, if more pleasant."

Darcy's lips turned up at the corners. He took another swallow of his brandy before Richard said, "I know where Miss Elizabeth and her sister live. A leased cottage on Meadow Lane. The area is not fully built up yet although it probably will be in another year or two. It is not a bad neighborhood, mostly older people. St. Giles rookery is not close enough to cause a major problem. They have a housekeeper who also cooks—she comes in six days a week—and a young maid who is devoted to them, especially Miss Elizabeth. They are not well off, but comfortable enough."

"Thank you for the information. It helps to know they are at least living at some level of gentility." Darcy finished his drink and set the glass down on the small Chippendale table between them. "Nothing on Wickham?"

"No. I have come to doubt that the militia officer my man saw was he. There has been no other sightings and the reward for his capture as a deserter is unclaimed."

Darcy had drifted into a brooding silence. Richard watched his cousin closely, wondering at the real reason for his obsession with his former friend. He said experimentally, "He may never be found, you know. He may have left England for the Americas or some other place where he can start his nefarious activities anew."

Darcy gave a low growl that was almost animal in nature. "The (he used an obscene epithet) is here, somewhere."

Richard never pried into Darcy's personal affairs, however his cousin's reaction was so extreme he leaned forward in concern. Darcy rarely swore, and never in those terms.

"Why do you think so, Will?"

*I have trusted Richard with so much, I can trust him with this. The burden is growing too heavy to carry alone, and he is Georgie's co-guardian. He has a right to know.*

Darcy closed his eyes for a moment. He did not look at Richard, his voice emotionless. "It began the day of my father's death." Only Darcy's rigid posture as he spoke told his cousin how closely he held himself in check. He reached his search for the letter before anger began to seep into his narrative, his hands clenching the arms of his chair.

"I spoke to Mrs. Reynolds and Mr. Niles, no one had been near the desk. When I found no sign of the letter I though my father may have destroyed it and forgotten. Wickham was not happy with the £1,000 father left him in his will. He was equally disdainful of the Kympton living, declaring—with more truth than usual—that he had no ambition to be a 'bowing and scraping' dependent. I gave him £3,000 in lieu of the living and he signed a waiver releasing any claim on the living. That was all I heard from him for two years."

Unable to sit still any longer, Darcy jumped up and began to pace from the fireplace to the windows. Richard sat forward. He knew motion was his cousin's response to distress of any kind. "He wanted more, I assume."

Darcy halted and faced Richard. "He wanted money. One thousand pounds. Every month. He had the letter."

Richard drew a hissing breath. "Did you see it?"

"He would never get that close to me. He quoted the beginning. It was from Mother to John Wickham. It...it supposedly concerned the child she was carrying: Georgiana."

"My God." Richard felt stunned. He watched Darcy throw himself into the chair, his head in his hands. When he could control his voice, Richard leaned over and put a hand on his cousin's shoulder. "How much has he bled you for?"

"I cleared his debts at the time and gave him £100. Since then he has not pressed me and there is only one reason. He is waiting for Georgiana to become betrothed before he issues his ultimatum. I should not be surprised if he wants part of Pemberley. He used to say father ought to have adopted him!"

For a time both men sat in silence. At last Richard rose, went to the sidebar and poured two more brandies. Darcy took his without looking at it and drank a swallow. His throat felt constricted from the narrative. Richard drank slowly, contemplating everything he had heard. He felt a small twist of resentment that he had not been taken into Darcy's confidence earlier, but he understood that his cousin was loath to share his responsibilities or problems, and he had been away so much of the time at war.

"He must be found."

Richard took another swallow of his brandy and set the glass aside. After that first swallow Darcy had not touched his drink. He put the glass down, feeling drained.

"You have had men looking for two years. There has been no sign of him. He may be here in London, or he may be in Scotland, waiting for the announcement. It does not matter. He will have to come out to be paid, I will not give him another ha'penny until I have that letter in my hands."

"Do you really believe," Richard was reluctant, but he knew it must be asked, "that aunt Anne could have engaged in a—liaison with your father's steward?"

Darcy ran a hand through his hair. "I remember she spent much time with him while father was in London. We had two bad harvests and then something went amiss with one of his major investments. He had to stay in Town for several months with only a short trip or two to Pemberley. I was not aware of it then, but she was with child. He asked

John to look after her. I was eleven and not wise in the ways of men and women, but they seemed proper in their interactions." He seemed to look into the past, shaking his head. "I cannot believe my mother would abandon the propriety and decency that were so deep a part of her nature for any man. She loved my father to distraction. And he certainly would not have tolerated a man who seduced his wife, it would have been the ultimate betrayal. John Wickham was not like his son."

Richard felt a surge of red fury he had only before felt on the battlefield. His war-hardened sensibilities told him Wickham must be found, and not by Darcy. His cousin was incapable of doing what had to be done to stop the torment Wickham had inflicted on him for so long.

"If you add another £500 to the reward we may find someone willing to risk turning him in. I will talk to some of my former associates. One of them might know someone with connections in St. Giles or Whitechapel. If he is there, we may get lucky. If he is in Scotland, we will have to wait for him to come out."

Drained, Darcy nodded. "As much as it takes. I cannot have Georgiana threatened with disgrace for the rest of her life."

Richard almost spoke, but thought better of it. Georgiana's betrothal would bring Wickham out—but so would Darcy's. Later, perhaps, if nothing worked out to find Wickham, he might suggest it. For the moment it was better left alone.

May 1814
Hephaestus House, London

Caroline Bingley stopped inside the doorway of the dining room feeling happier than she had for several days. When Caroline felt happy it was usually because someone else was feeling unhappy. Everything was in perfect order for her dinner party. Silverware caught the candlelight in shifting gleams; the china, crystal glasses, table linens were without fault. Flowers scented the air from Wedgewood vases at either end of the sideboard and in the center of the table. Caroline was known as a skilled hostess, a reputation she encouraged. It was not, however, the perfection of the dining room or the entire house. Caroline was happy because she had not been forced to invite Jane and Elizabeth Bennet.

Caroline entered the breakfast parlor the morning she meant to send out invitations to find her brother Charles sitting over a last cup of coffee, *The Times* in an untidy heap next to his plate. He looked up at her over the rim of his cup with an expression she saw all too often of late—a mixture of impatience and annoyance.

"Good morning, Charles."

Caroline waited until the footman came and held her chair, something her brother could easily have done. She ordered tea and toast and watched Bingley set his cup carefully in the saucer so he could fold *The Times*. Caroline preferred the *Morning Post* for its emphasis on society news. It waited next to her plate but she was not ready to enjoy it yet.

"I am going to send out the dinner invitations today." Her breakfast arrived and she waved the footman away imperiously. "I suppose I am to invite Miss Bennet and her sister?"

"No," Bingley replied. He stood up. "They are in half-mourning, however I think it best if you keep your guest list to your friends."

He started for the door when Caroline's surprised voice halted him. "You do not want them here?"

"Not at this time or for your reasons."

"I have no reasons, Charles. You are becoming positively rude."

"I trust the truth is not rude. You do not like either lady, and please do not tell me that you are interested in what pleases me." He turned away. "I shall be in my study if anyone has need of me."

With a smirk of satisfaction Caroline returned to the present. Her guests were due to arrive any minute. She had placed Mr. Darcy on her left and Sir Eldridge Bromley, baronet, on her right. She was determined to monopolize Darcy for the entire meal. Lady Addington was next to Darcy and Mrs. Cynthia Callforth next to Sir Eldridge. Mrs. Callforth was in her fifth decade, a widow and noted society matron with definite ideas of class distinction, and a bosom that preceded her like the prow of a frigate. Mr. Stanford, MP, sat between Lady Addington and Miss Lambert. Caroline put Mr. Burkhalter beside Georgiana who was placed on Bingley's left with Miss Lambert on his right.

After the third course she looked down the table to where Charles Bingley politely listened to Miss Lambert discussing the weather. Lady Addington seemed amused by something, probably not her dinner partner, whose main topic of conversation had been the repairs to the family mansion and the outrageous cost of labor and materials. He had partaken liberally of the wines served with each course, discoursing on vintages and vintners, until his appreciation for the fruit of the vine left him barely able to get an intelligible word out. Sir Eldridge's estate was in the Cotswolds where he ran Cotswold sheep, a popular breed for over a century and one he could not commend enough, when he was not despairing of the wool market.

Darcy was not faring particularly well. The Bingley chef was skilled and Miss Bingley always set an excellent table, especially if one appreciated French cooking. In order to avoid responding to Miss Bingley's effusive compliments and dreary complaints, Darcy's usual procedure was to praise one or more of the main dishes at the beginning of each course; at the moment his choices were la poularde à la Montmorencie and les côtelettes d'Agneau saut s. He was then free to let most of Miss Bingley's discourse—for one could not call it conversation—pass over him with only the occasional noncommittal response needed.

He employed this free time imagining what he would have talked of with Elizabeth had she been his dinner partner. She would have given him a lively and interesting recounting of her visit to Porter's tea blending facility. They would speak of the various teas and the far places where tea grew, and the cultures of those places. It would have been delightful, compared with Miss Bingley's dull spate of self-serving prattle.

After two hours of listening to Caroline Bingley's fawning compliments, Sir Eldridge's sheep and Mrs. Callforth's social commentary, Darcy began to feel even his rigid self-control eroding. He was not a man who would ever engage in rude behavior to a lady, even one as tempting as Caroline Bingley. After her latest suggestions that Darcy take her brother to his tailor, and encourage him to frequent Angelo's Fencing Academy rather than Gentleman Jim Jackson's boxing saloon, he made his usual noncommittal verbal response and silently answered her as he wished to.

*Tell me, Miss Bingley, do you really believe spending dinner listening to you disparage your brother, my best friend, endears you to me? You treat him as if he were a difficult youth instead of a grown man. He dresses as fashionably as any man of my acquaintance and his entertainments are the same as most men, including myself. Why should I encourage him to fence more at Angelo's? Are you planning to drag him into a duel? If you are...*

Miss Bingley, unaware of this internal dialog, dipped her head toward him so suddenly only superb reflexes saved Darcy from one of the feathers wobbling in her coiffure striking him in the eye. Completely unaware, Miss Bingley dropped her voice to a husky whisper.

"You know Charles is running after Jane Bennet again."

Since it was a statement rather than a question, Darcy did not bother to reply. He had expected Miss Bingley would at some time during the evening bring up the subject. Before Darcy was able to indicate to his hostess that he considered her brother capable of choosing a wife without his interference, Miss Lambert's voice traveled along the board in a trill of self-satisfaction.

"Have you heard the new gossip about Viscount Tennerley?"

Darcy saw Georgiana stiffen. He prepared to rise, but Miss Lambert, having gathered the attention of the guests, was not about to be silenced.

"Apparently, the viscount sent his son to Ireland over some peccadillo with a woman. His wife tried to accompany her son, but the viscount locked her away at their estate in Dorset. She escaped and bribed a fishing boat captain to take her to Dublin. Can you believe it?"

While Miss Lambert still basked in the attention of the diners, Lady Addington's voice cut sharply through her satisfaction. "No, and neither should you. Viscountess Tennerley is at the family estate in Dorset. She was not locked away, as you so dramatically put it, she removed there voluntarily. Viscount Tennerley sent his son to Ireland to learn more about the responsibilities of managing an estate, without the distractions of London, and about time in my opinion."

"These young people today," began Mrs. Callforth, but Darcy had long since ceased to listen to her.

Georgiana looked pale, he thought, grateful for Lady Addington's intervention. His sister had returned to conversing with Mr. Burkhalter with a poise Darcy admired. He silently cursed the nattering gossips of the *ton* who gleefully spread falsehoods and speculation as fact. Darcy realized Miss Lambert was attempting unsuccessfully to hide her vexation. Her aunt was wealthy and old, she did not intend to offend the lady if it could be avoided, no matter how annoying her old-fashioned morality.

"Too many of the wrong sort calling themselves ladies and gentlemen these days." Mrs. Callforth leaned her bosom dangerously close to the apricot glacé. "When my husband was alive…"

"Oh, we met some supposed ladies the other day when my aunt and I went shopping. They seemed quite common to me. They were with their aunt, whose husband owns the warehouses. My aunt knows such ordinary people."

Lady Addington surveyed her niece's studied expression of innocence with an inward anger she was too well bred to let show. She said after a moment, "I met the young ladies as well, very pleasant, well-mannered ladies of gentle birth. I have known their aunt for over a year. Mrs. Gardiner gives more of her time to charitable works than most of the ladies of the *ton* and with greater success. Her nieces were obviously in mourning, so could not dress fashionably. Had they been able to do so, you would have been quite amazed."

It took a moment for Bingley to realize that Miss Lambert had been disparaging Jane and Elizabeth Bennet. He paled, turned red, and reached for his wine glass. Beside Darcy, Miss Bingley smirked.

"I see Miss Lambert is of my opinion."

"She would be," Darcy coldly responded.

He spent the remainder of the meal speaking quietly to Lady Addington and ignoring Miss Bingley's attempts to engage his attention. When the gentlemen rejoined the ladies after port, cigars and more about sheep from Sir Eldridge, Darcy was not surprised that Georgiana pleaded a headache and they were able to leave early. In the coach on the short ride home, she was silent for most of the way, wrapped in thought. At last she raised her head to look fully at her brother, her face earnest in the dim glow of the street lamps.

"William, I wish to meet Miss Bennet, and Miss Elizabeth. Please, do not refuse. If Mr. Bingley marries Miss Bennet she will need friends to support her. Miss Lambert is representative of the attitude of most fashionable ladies. They reject anyone who does not meet their standards of wealth or fashion. I do not want that to happen to her. She and Miss Elizabeth have suffered enough pain without adding the *ton's* gossips to their burden."

The coach pulled into the drive of Darcy House before Darcy answered her. He was torn between discouraging her from an acquaintance with Elizabeth for reasons he did not want to examine too closely, and the benefit her assistance would provide both sisters. Georgiana was correct, however; just as with Bingley and himself, Miss Bennet would be rejected by the majority of the upper social classes unless she had a friend who was fully accepted. He hoped he was not making a bad decision,

"I will see what can be arranged," he said.

Darcy climbed out of the coach and extended his hand to his

sister. She stepped out and stood beside him in the white wash of moonlight. "Thank you, William."

Darcy tucked her hand into the crook of his elbow. Once inside they continued upstairs to the family wing together. As they climbed the second flight, Darcy said, "How did you get on with Mr. Burkhalter?"

Georgiana smiled with amusement. "I am sure Miss Bingley sat him next to me so Miss Lambert could impress Mr. Bingley."

"She certainly accomplished that," Darcy grinned. "What did you speak of?"

"Actually he was quite interesting. His pastime is ancient history. He went to Egypt last year to look at the pyramids and some ruins at a place called Thebes. I was not bored at all. Much better than all those sheep!"

Darcy laughed, bade her goodnight and continued on to his chambers.

The next morning's post brought a note from Richard Fitzwilliam. Darcy read it with a frown marring his brow.

*Rosings Park, Kent*
*May 14, 1814*

> *Cousin,*
> *I returned home to find that our aunt had stormed the citadel. She forced her way into the house and attacked one of the under-footmen with her cane, which has a leaded tip. He is a man of mine who luckily knew how to deflect the blow. Otherwise she might well have committed great bodily harm if not worse. My dear Anne called the other footmen and instructed them to return her mother to the Dower House, in spite of her threats and claims that Rosings Park is hers,*

*not Anne's. I have written to father as well. We will have to find her*
*an establishment somewhere away from Kent, perhaps a house in Bath*
*with appropriate staff. Some of her former cronies have retired there,*
*so she will have friends in place. I will let you know what is decided. I*
*hate to feel forced to act against my own flesh and blood, but I will not*
*have Anne constantly upset.*
*Richard.*

Darcy sighed. He thought of speaking to his uncle and then rejected the idea. He really had nothing of importance to offer. Better
to let Lady Catherine's brother and nephew handle the situation. He
only wondered if removing her to a different location would stop her
harassment. With a shrug Darcy put the note aside. He had other
matters to consider. Bingley wanted to begin his tentative courtship
of Miss Bennet. To that end Darcy was to accompany him to the
Gardiners' the next day and then on an excursion to Twickenham.
The popular area on the Thames some ten miles from Town with
villas and cottages built near the water was a retreat for many upper-
class Londoners. Darcy had suggested a picnic, to which Bingley readily agreed. Darcy had not specified where the picnic was to take place,
and Bingley had not asked, his focus being entirely on Miss Bennet.

## May 1814
## Twickenham, near London

The following day Darcy called for Bingley in his traveling coach,
which was larger and more luxuriously appointed than his friend's
carriage, as Miss Bingley reminded both men at every opportunity.
They proceeded to the Gardiner residence, where after a few minutes of pleasantries the foursome departed on their journey. Darcy
had hardly allowed himself to dwell on Elizabeth's person, let alone
study her, but as the coach left London he could not be unaware
of her presence. She sat across from him, her gaze on the passing

countryside. Bingley and Miss Bennet chatted, comfortable in one another's company and oblivious to their companions.

Darcy watched the play of light and shadow over Elizabeth's face, the perfect oval framed by her black straw bonnet and a stray curl of lustrous ebony hair. She was still pale, he noted, although there was more color to her complexion than before. Her day dress of pine green muslin was plainly cut and trimmed with black lace. She wore black gloves as well. Her eyes sparkled at this mild adventure. Darcy pictured their dark depths, the color of black coffee with glowing flecks of gold and green. He forced himself to pull his gaze away and speak with what normalcy he could manage.

"Have you been to Twickenham before, Miss Elizabeth?"

She turned her eyes briefly to his before responding. "No, Mr. Darcy. I have heard of it. The poet Alexander Pope had a house there and a famous grotto. I do not know if it is available to be toured, but I should love to see it."

Darcy had already arranged for the party to see the grotto with its watercourse, and its walls studded with angular pieces of looking-glass, shells. ores, crystals as well as Bristol and Cornwall diamonds. There was also a stalagmite It was said to resemble an Aladdin's cave. The excitement in Elizabeth's face at the prospect made him glad he had thought of it. She was coming out of the dark night of trouble and loss, he thought. He wanted to assist her into the sunlight as much as he was currently able. Darcy did not allow himself to consider that he was laying the groundwork for more.

With some reluctance, he said, "I am afraid you may be disappointed, Miss Elizabeth. The house was demolished in 1808 when Baroness Howe of Langar purchased it. She rebuilt on the site. The grotto is more or less intact, minus some of its decorations removed by the baroness."

"It is a shame not to leave it as it was designed. however I am certain it will be unusual and interesting."

They arrived in Twickenham after over an hour's drive. The house where Darcy had planned the picnic was a pretty little Italianate villa set back from the water. The white plastered exterior had a round tower at one corner and an arched loggia in front rather more like a porch than the original architecture it resembled. Two tall dark cypress stood sentinel at each side of the façade. The coach followed the graveled drive around the building and stopped near a white plastered and painted stone wall.

"The house was purchased from the estate of an elderly gentleman who died with no known relatives. It is currently undergoing renovation, but I have use of the grounds."

Darcy assisted Elizabeth from the coach as Bingley did the same for Miss Bennet. The two couples walked around the wall while the coach went on to the stables a short distance away in the rear of the property. Before them lay a terrace of terrazzo tiles with apple and pear trees in huge decorated stoneware pots shading various areas. Geraniums filled smaller pots with a profusion of red, orange, pink and white flowers. A lawn reached back toward the end of the garden marked by a small gazebo.

"It is lovely." Elizabeth turned her face up to Darcy with a hint of a sad smile playing over her lips. "The old gentleman must have loved it here."

"I suppose he did. He lived here for many years. Darcy indicated the table and chairs set between two of the trees. "I thought we might have our picnic here, and then see the grotto."

The others readily agreed. Bingley, of course, asked the obvious question. "To whom does the property belong?"

Darcy hesitated only a moment. He could have dissembled, however it crossed his mind that a time might come when he would want Elizabeth to know that the villa belonged to him.

"I own it."

After a short silence, Miss Bennet said, "It is a wonderful summer home. I am sure Miss Darcy will enjoy it greatly."

There was no more discussion and conversation moved along conventional lines until the picnic was served by footmen from a second carriage. Linen and silver appeared, along with crystal goblets.

The table was set while the party admired the view of the river. A cold collation being served, they returned to the terrace and began to eat.

Remembering the dinner party at Bingley's, Darcy regarded Elizabeth as she partook of the food with obvious enjoyment. She glanced up, and seeing his attention focused on her patted her lips with her serviette and smiled.

"How did you enjoy your tour of Mr. Porter's tea blending facility?"

She leaned toward him a little and Darcy felt her presence even more vividly. "It is not as large as I imagined. He only makes blends there for his customers who order them especially, and experiments with new blends like those we sampled at our aunt's. Mr. Porter imports his regular teas and tea blends in large amounts and makes small batches here, as well as packaging the imported tea for sale. I did not know that tea only grew in China until some plants appeared in northern India."

Elizabeth went on to describe the divided frames that held the various teas and grades of tea, the huge kettles where tea was blended with dried flowers, herbs, essences and other additives. Miss Bennet made the comment that the smell, while not individually unpleasant, in the mass was somewhat overwhelming. As Darcy had fantasized at the dinner, they talked of the cultures of China and India, how trade was opened, and the substitution of tea when coffee became too expensive. Darcy watched Elizabeth's eyes glow with interest; it was an echo of the way he remembered her that tightened his throat with regret.

After luncheon they walked along the river and visited the grotto. Even with the alterations after Pope's death, it was still a place unlike any they had ever viewed and the sisters were entranced. Darcy had seen it once before as a child. His memory of it was somewhat hazy and visiting it again as an adult gave him a wider perspective of its utter uniqueness. They returned to the carriage afterward to begin the trip back to London. In the coach the ladies talked of their experience. Darcy was satisfied to listen and put in an occasional word.

Darcy noted that Miss Bennet, while not as physically affected by the family's ordeal, appeared more reserved than previously. She still smiled, but in a more guarded manner. He could not discern if it was because she had grown more distrusting of people or if it was a manifestation of her history with Bingley. Elizabeth showed more animation than Darcy had seen since Hertfordshire, although it was tempered by a stillness he did not entirely understand. As if Elizabeth were listening to some internal voice of caution or uncertainty.

"Pope was right, it is much like a magic lantern performance with the door to the grotto closed."

Miss Bennet looked at her sister in agreement. "We saw a magic lantern performance in Meryton when we were younger. The reflections of the river and everything on it are quite similar."

"Have you ever been to a phantasmagoria?"

Bingley glanced from one sister to the other. Both indicated they had not. "It can be frightening. We went two years ago when a famous showman was in London. Caroline nearly swooned. It has the effect of ghosts hovering over the audience and swooping around, as well as other such effects. I do not know how they accomplish it but it is very real."

Darcy felt it was only courteous to allay Bingley's curiosity. "They project the images on smoke. As it drifts, the figures appear to move and hover in air."

"Is that all? It seems simple enough when one knows the trick."

"Most unexplained phenomena are simple enough when one knows what causes them," Darcy replied dryly.

"I should like to see such a performance." Elizabeth held his gaze for a moment, causing a tightening in Darcy's chest.

Darcy drew a breath and replied, "If there is such a show in London over the holidays I would be pleased to take you and Miss Bennet."

"Perhaps we ought not to take Mr. Bingley," Jane put in with a twinkle, "now that he knows how it is done."

Amid laughter the coach continued on its way. The ladies were deposited at Gracechurch Street, where the Gardiners would see them home, and after a short visit Darcy and Bingley left them there. In the coach, Bingley was silent for most of the way to Mayfair, only turning to his friend as they approached his residence.

"It went well, do you not think, Darcy?"

"Very well."

There was a short silence before Bingley cleared his throat and said, "If I may ask, why did you really purchase the villa? You rarely spend any summers in Town."

Darcy had wondered if his friend would ask the question. He was not a particularly curious man, however some instinct of protection must have stirred at Darcy's admission he owned the house.

"I was contacted by a solicitor for the estate shortly after the old gentleman's death. He was a friend of my grandfather whom I had never met. I remembered the name but had not known he still lived or where he was. He had fallen into near poverty and the house required repair as well as refurbishing. I originally intended to sell it, now I do not know."

Darcy did not inform Bingley that the old gentleman had died without funds sufficient for a proper burial. He was not a man to advertise his charities, even to friends. Bingley seemed satisfied with the explanation. Darcy was not certain he was himself as convinced of his motives. He kept seeing Elizabeth sitting on the terrace in shivering tree shadow, or in the little gazebo with a book in hand, her face concentrated on the page, a loose summer gown draped in soft folds around her.

The coach jolted to a halt, shaking away his fantasy. He watched Bingley depart with more thanks and the coach creaked and clacked into motion.

*How can I go on like this, seeing her so close and unable to speak, to reach out to her? What do I want from her, a sign, a look, a gesture to tell me she would welcome my attentions? It has to stop!*

But Darcy knew in his heart it would not stop until some event happened, some revelation to decide his future and hers, for good or ill.

# CHAPTER TWELVE

May 1814
Meadow Lane, London

"Was the grotto not wonderful?"

Jane brushed down the skirt of her lavender day dress, smiling at her sister. She sat on the sofa with a happy expression on her face that Elizabeth had not seen in far too long. Elizabeth joined her. She had also found the excursion enjoyable and Mr. Darcy's company agreeable, something she had not expected. He had been less reserved and more open; she said as much to her sister, who nodded.

"Mr. Darcy planned it all. Mr. Bingley did not even know he owned property in Twickenham. It is a lovely villa." Her eyes moved around the parlor before she looked down at her hands. "Do you think Mr. Darcy purchased it for his sister?"

Elizabeth considered. "He has indicated in the past that they spend the summers at his estate. It might be part of a dowry I suppose. She will probably marry before long."

"Mr. Bingley told me Miss Darcy was ill over the summer and is only now recovered enough to return to Town. Mr. Darcy is devoted to her. He has been as much father as brother to her since their father died."

"It is admirable of him. He could so easily leave her to the care of servants and live his life as he pleased. He is certainly wealthy enough, as it was noised about when we first met him."

"Charl—Mr. Bingley," Jane colored, "told me Mr. Darcy is worth far more than the income from his estate. He has a number of investments that produce additional funds. As much as twice what was rumored."

Elizabeth considered how little she knew of the man other than the face he showed the world at large. That face had indeed changed in the two years since their ordeal began. The arrogance that repulsed her on their first acquaintance she now understood to be reserve and a lack of exposure to society outside his established element. No doubt he had been taught to think meanly of those whose wealth and position in life did not match his own. Elizabeth wondered about his present acceptance of her aunt and uncle. Perhaps he was only accommodating his friend.

She said as much to Jane, only to have her sister's expression grow thoughtful. "Do you know anything of Mr. Darcy that indicates he would dissemble in that manner?"

Elizabeth was silent for a time. *Disguise of any kind is my abhorrence.* The words returned to her from the past and she sighed. "No, I do not believe he is capable of presenting approval when he does not feel it. He is much less rigid in his opinions than he was in Hertfordshire. He is used to move in the highest circles of wealth and social prominence. The fact that Mr. Bingley is his friend and that Mr. Darcy has accommodated us to the extent he has speaks well for his improvement. What might have caused such a change I cannot imagine."

Elizabeth rang for Nettie to bring tea. While they waited, she contemplated the idea that she might have misjudged Mr. Darcy from the beginning. She had thought him an arrogant and prideful man, and so he had been, but she had not looked beyond that. She had not looked for any depth of character other than his education and intelligence. Now Elizabeth saw that she had dismissed him too easily. He was far more complex, and far more admirable, than she had ever believed. Jane's soft voice broke into her thoughts.

"Indeed, he is not like he was in Hertfordshire. Perhaps it is Mr. Bingley's influence at least in part. Whatever causes him to behave as he has, I am grateful for it."

Tea came and the sisters sat quietly, comfortable in each other's company without the need for conversation. After a time Jane set her cup down and turned to watch Elizabeth. The day was drawing to a close and both sisters were fatigued from the expedition. After hesitating for a short time, Jane gathered her resolve.

"Lizzy, if Mr. Bingley and I should marry will you come and live with us? I should like that so very much."

Elizabeth was not taken entirely by surprise by the question. She knew Jane would be reluctant to leave her alone, even in rooms or a flat. She had contemplated moving in with the couple should they marry and was still in two minds on the subject. Better to dissemble for the time being, she thought, and wait until matters were settled.

"I do not know, dearest. It will depend on circumstances. If you marry, you will want a wedding trip and to assume your life as mistress of Mr. Bingley's home. Perhaps when all of that is accomplished we can revisit the idea. Mr. Bingley has not even proposed yet."

Jane blushed a becoming pink. "He has not, exactly. I think he is a little frightened that I will reject him because of the past. He can be very unsure of himself at times."

"Is that not a good thing? He does not make rash decisions then."

"Sometimes he does not make decisions at all!"

Elizabeth was unused to her sister criticizing anyone, even mildly. It disturbed her because she believed she knew what troubled Jane.

"Does the idea of Miss Bingley's disapprobation bother you greatly?"

Jane's expression took on an air of sadness. "She will never approve of me, or anyone not of the *ton*. I can see that and it does not trouble me overmuch. But she is his sister, Lizzy. A member of his close family. If we marry, her dislike may cause his relatives to take sides, and that can deeply harm a family. I do not want to be the source of such a situation. We have seen what happens when a family is torn apart. I could not in conscience let that happen."

Anger stirred in Elizabeth, roiling in her stomach like a bitter brew. "Will you let a selfish, spoiled woman take away your happiness?"

"I do not want to, but I cannot change her mind. If Mr. Bingley will do something to control her, or at least keep her from open confrontation, she may in time accept a marriage. Otherwise…"

"Otherwise you will give up and let her have her way. Jane, dear one, do you not see that is how she has always manipulated people to get whatever she wants?" Elizabeth reached out and took her sister's cold hands in hers. "Mr. Bingley is in love with you. Are you in love with him?"

Jane's fingers tightened on her sister's. "My heart has never lost its affection for him, even after he fled Hertfordshire. He sought me out, Lizzy, as soon as he knew I was in London. It is just—we have suffered so much rejection, so much turmoil, I could not live in a home where there was bitterness or division."

Elizabeth sought to control her anger and speak quietly. "It is not only your decision, dear, it is his. Perhaps more so than anyone else. Thus far nothing adverse has occurred. Let us wait and see if he offers for you, and if there is any reaction from anyone. One cannot solve problems until they happen."

Jane seemed relieved. She squeezed her sister's hands and rose. "I want to freshen up before dinner. Are you coming?"

"In a few minutes." Elizabeth rang for Nettie to take away the tea things as Jane left the room. *Will there never be an end to the persecution? Jane deserves happiness. Why should Caroline Bingley have the power to ruin her life because of her own ambition?*

Elizabeth felt the old dark stirring in her mind. She forced it into quiescence and went upstairs.

## May 1814
## Darcy House, London

Darcy continued his assistance with Bingley's courtship of Jane Bennet. They visited with her and Elizabeth at Gracechurch Street, dined there and at Darcy House, drove in the country, walked in the small park near the Gardiners'. He was unsettled by the growing affection between Elizabeth and Georgiana. They had taken to one another immediately. Georgiana's shy sensitivity blossomed under the sunlight of Elizabeth's caring nature, wit and sense of humor. With music as a beginning bond they discovered much in each other to admire; soon they behaved as if they were truly sisters.

Disturbed by their intimacy but unwilling to interfere, Darcy watched as Georgiana grew more confident, maturing before his eyes. It was, he ruminated, a two-edged sword. Georgiana's newfound self-assurance made it more likely she would choose a suitor at the little season. He felt as if Elizabeth, by befriending his sister, was driving him further from any thought of marriage.

He had to find Wickham. To that end, Darcy had hired two men through the steward on his Scottish estate in an attempt to track the miscreant in the event he was still over the border. He had a sketch copy of an old miniature of Wickham made for their use, however the effort proved as futile as every other effort to discover where Wickham had gone. It had been too long for memory to place him at Gretna Green, something Darcy anticipated. Neither was there word of him in Edinburgh, or any other city of size, or along the border where an Englishman would not be as noticeable. He threw the latest report aside and determined to write and call off the hunt in Scotland.

*Perhaps Richard was correct. Perhaps he has left England for some other place. But he will be watching the London papers for any news of a betrothal to come out of his rat hole and accost me. There is nothing for it but to wait.*

His next correspondence was a note from his cousin. Darcy opened it with some curiosity as to what had transpired since the last communication.

*Rosings Park, Kent*
*Cousin,*
*Our esteemed aunt is presently settling in a house I have leased for her*
*in Bath. She will not keep a carriage, but there is ample transporta-*
*tion and her friends will undoubtedly assist her. Her maid declined*
*to go, I believe with much relief, and is now employed in the manor*
*house. I arranged for her butler to accompany her, and hired a new*
*housekeeper and servants in Bath. How long they will remain in her*
*employ is another story. She will have her usual funds from the interest*
*on Sir Lewis' trust and any other money she may need for unforeseen*
*expenses, paid, I am happy to say, by Father's accountant.*

*Anne tried to say goodbye to her mother, only to be rejected with a*
*diatribe on her lack of respect and daughterly obedience. She insisted*
*on seeing Lady C alone, and came through the ordeal better than I*
*expected. I believe the chains have finally been severed.*

*We will not come to Town for the little season as neither of us has a*
*taste for the* ton's *pleasures or company, however we plan to spend the*
*holidays at Janus House, and look forward to seeing you and Georgie*
*if you are in Town.*
*With our best wishes,*
*Yrs. etc.,*
*Richard*

Having a vengeful Lady Catherine removed from Rosings was not
ideal, Darcy thought, but at least it removed a source of disruption
from a delicate situation. Something else had begun to prey on his
mind. He received letters almost daily from Mr. Standish, his steward
at Pemberley, asking for instructions on matters the steward could
not handle himself. It was past time he journeyed to his estate and
took up the vital business of running it. It was unfair to linger in Town
when those who depended on him for their livelihood needed his
personal supervision. To that end he called on Bingley, only to find
he had gone out to his club.

Bingley was seated in the dining room with a glass of wine and the remains of a plate of veal chops, only a small amount of which he had eaten. He looked up as Darcy approached, his countenance lightening.

"Sit down, Darcy. Let me order you lunch."

"No lunch, I thank you. I will have a glass of port with you."

Bingley signaled the waiter. In a matter of several minutes the port sat before Darcy, and Bingley had refreshed his own glass of Cabernet from the bottle on the table. He pushed the plate of food aside and took a rather large sip of the wine. He looked troubled, unusual for a man who was generally good-humored.

Darcy sampled his port. "Is there a problem with Miss Bennet? I thought you were getting on quite well."

"We seem to be. She is not as open as she was, and I can well understand her reasons after my behavior in Hertfordshire. But it is not Miss Bennet who troubles the waters—it is Miss Bingley. Caroline will not leave it alone. She nags and pouts and snarls at any thought that I am courting Miss Bennet. I have tried to reason with her, with results you can well imagine. I have tried ignoring her, which only inflames her." Bingley finished his wine in a gulp and poured more. "I have told her flatly that it is not her business whom I marry, and to leave off her interfering. Nothing avails. I am becoming afraid she may divulge the old scandal, although she knows perfectly well it would harm her as much or more than it would me. I do not know what to do."

Images of his aunt Lady Catherine filled Darcy's mind. "Is she not to reach the age shortly where she will inherit the money from your father's will?"

"Several months, yes."

"Can you convince her to set up her own establishment, perhaps somewhere near London or on the seacoast?"

"I do not know. There is no guarantee she would behave any better on her own than she does now."

"But she would not inhabit the same house to which you will

bring your wife. Perhaps the independence will occupy her time and energy and she will not need to interfere in your affairs."

Darcy doubted the words even as he spoke them, but he had nothing else to offer. Bingley considered his wine pensively. At last he shrugged. "It is worth a try. I do not want Jane—Miss Bennet to feel any doubts about her precedence in my life. If she feels marrying me will cause a rift in my family I know she will decline my offer. I could not bear that."

Darcy steeled himself. "Bingley, I looked you up today to tell you that I must return to Pemberley. The summer harvest is upon us, and there are decisions to be made that require my personal attendance. I have done what I can to assist you in your courtship, but my own responsibilities weigh heavier and heavier. I cannot stay in Town. Also, Georgiana does not do well in the heat. If she is to return in the fall for the little season, she will require time to rest and regain her equilibrium."

Bingley was immediately apologetic. "Of course. I have taken up an inordinate amount of your time, and I am sorry. You have been a true friend to assist me and I appreciate it more than I can say."

"Not at all." Darcy felt some embarrassment at the praise, as he had used Bingley's pursuit of Jane Bennet in part to spend time with Elizabeth. "Write me if there is any news. I shall return in late August or early September."

They shook hands and Darcy left his friend contemplating the empty wine bottle before he called the waiter and ordered another.

## July 1814
## Lady Addington's Home, London

"I am so glad you ladies were able to attend this evening."

Lady Addington greeted Mrs. Gardiner and the Bennet sisters in the foyer of her town home, a neo-classic Georgian mansion in Mayfair, not far from Darcy House. Elizabeth looked around the foyer as they exchanged pleasantries with their hostess. She could not but admire the restrained luxury of the space with its unembellished Doric columns and ironwork lantern suspended from the coffered ceiling, the candles enclosed in glass to protect them from draughts. A round skylight, dark now but no less impressive, emphasized the cantilevered staircase.

Lady Addington saw her study of the stairs and smiled. "Very light, are they not? One wonders at first if they will not collapse under one. They are cantilevered off the wall, and quite sturdy. We have not lost a guest in fifty years."

Elizabeth felt her face grow warm. "They are lovely."

Lady Addington motioned the butler. "Johnson, please convey my guests to the music room. Ladies, I hope you will enjoy the program."

"I am sure we shall," Mrs. Gardiner replied.

They found the music room to be as grand as the rest of the house. Chairs covered in blue silk shone in the candlelight, set out facing a small dais where a quartet of musicians set up their stands and instruments. In addition to the usual rows of chairs, several sofas had been placed against the wall panels. The three ladies occupied one of them; a number of other guests had taken seats already in anticipation of the entertainment. Jane suddenly sucked in her breath. Startled, Elizabeth looked at her sister to find her gaze fixed on a gentleman and lady sitting together near the rear of the room.

Recognition dawned on Elizabeth and she reached out and touched Jane's arm. "Mr. and Mrs. Hurst are in attendance," she murmured to her aunt. "The lady in pink velvet near the back."

Mrs. Gardiner looked casually in the direction and dipped her head to speak in a soft voice. "She looks as if she has been ill. Jane told me Mr. Bingley's older sister had a child in January, and has been recovering over the spring."

There was a mild stir at the doors that caught their attention. Elizabeth heard a too familiar voice, her hands clenching in the fabric of her dress. Miss Lambert and Miss Bingley entered arm in arm.

She looked around the room expectantly. Fortunately her gaze fell on her sister before she saw the Bennets and their aunt. She made her way to the Hursts as Elizabeth watched, an expression of exaggerated surprise on her sharp features.

Elizabeth was too far away to hear anything that was said as the Hursts rose. Louisa curtsied to her sister and Miss Lambert while Hurst bowed. Miss Lambert and Caroline Bingley reciprocated. The formalities observed, Louisa sat down again while her husband remained standing in what Elizabeth could only think of as a protective attitude. Any conversation was brief. Miss Bingley spoke and her sister replied, her pale face expressionless. Her husband shifted his heavy shoulders but did not respond. With a self-satisfied smirk, Miss Bingley and her new friend walked away to find seats toward the front of the room. Mrs. Gardiner's voice interrupted her thoughts.

"I wonder what that was all about? They did not greet each other with any degree of sisterly affection."

Her curiosity mirrored Elizabeth's. Overhearing her aunt's words, Jane said softly, "Mr. Bingley told me Miss Bingley has been trying to get her sister to attend society functions with her, but Mrs. Hurst has not felt well enough to be out in society. Miss Bingley may have been surprised to see her here."

The expression on Caroline Bingley's face when she saw her sister returned to Elizabeth: surprised, but not happy. It came to her that Louisa Hurst had always been a follower. She had let her younger sister take the lead in their relationship. The addition of a child and her ill health after the birth had detached her from Caroline Bingley's control, and Caroline did not like the situation. Apparently Mr. Hurst stood firmly on his wife's side. It was the sort of observation of people one knew that had so fascinated Elizabeth in the past.

The music began and the room quieted. It was Haydn's string quartet in D minor played brilliantly by four men who knew each other so well they worked as a single unit. Elizabeth relaxed into the enchanting sounds, letting them pour over her in a soothing stream. They finished to applause and surrendered the stage to a harpsichordist who performed several pieces by Pleyel and Mozart. The violinist from the quartet then returned to play a piece by an obscure Italian composer named Vivaldi. The music was lively and complex and Elizabeth thought she would love to hear more of his work. The quartet finished the program with Beethoven's string quartet in C minor.

When the performances were over everyone rose and moved slowly to the refreshment tables. Elizabeth took a cup of punch and a small cake and slipped out of the mild confusion. She did not see her aunt, but Jane joined her and together they returned to the sofa they had occupied during the concert. Not knowing anyone, they had no interest in remaining longer than courtesy dictated. Elizabeth discovered her aunt in conversation with Lady Addington. She was about to suggest they join her when she felt a presence and looked up to find Miss Bingley standing next to her. Both sisters rose after setting their cups and plates on a low table to the side. Miss Bingley did not curtsey. She stared at Jane with disdain, her lips curling in a contemptuous sneer. Her voice hissed with malice.

"I suppose you think mingling with those above your station means you are accepted? Do not deceive yourselves. You will never be part of the upper levels of society. You are nothing but country dirt. Leave my brother alone and return to the pigsty you came from."

"Miss Bennet, Miss Elizabeth, it is good to see you again."

Elizabeth had been so focused on Miss Bingley she had not noticed the approach of the Hursts. Miss Bingley startled at her sister's voice and stepped aside, glaring at her. Louisa curtsied to the sisters and her husband bowed as they returned the courtesy. Tense, Elizabeth waited for whatever came next, but Louisa Hurst was smiling politely.

"I hope you are both well? I have not been in society for some time, however I could not resist Lady Addington's invitation. I do so love music."

"As do we," Elizabeth replied. "I recall how beautifully you played at Netherfield. It was quite professional."

"Louisa, what are you doing?" Caroline turned on her sister, her face flushed and her hands claws at her sides. "Are you mad? How dare you...."

"I am not the one who is mad, Caroline. I shall speak to whomever I please. I suggest you withdraw before you cause a scene that will not be taken well by our hostess."

"Traitor!" Miss Bingley swung to the Bennets. "You will never be part of society, I shall see to it."

"Marrying the Prince Regent, are you?" Hurst drawled. "Setting the social standards?"

Shaking with fury, Caroline turned on her heel and stomped away. Hurst shook his head. "One of these days that woman will go too far. Back to Newcastle, I hope."

His wife could barely hide her smile. Jane looked pained, but Louisa impulsively took her hand. "Do not listen to Caroline. She likes to have things her own way, but a disappointment now and then is good for her." She glanced at her husband. "Come and have tea with me tomorrow afternoon? You will be most welcome."

"Thank you," Elizabeth answered after a swift glance at Jane. "We would like that very much."

The Hursts left them and they made their way to their aunt and Lady Addington. The noblewoman's eyes followed the Hursts for a moment and then switched to where Caroline Bingley sat in close conversation with her niece.

"I dislike speaking ill of anyone," she said quietly, "but that woman is trouble." She smiled at Elizabeth and Jane. "I hope you enjoyed the music. I find Haydn delightful."

Lady Addington found her niece in the drawing room after her guests had all departed, lounging decoratively on a chaise. She sat rather heavily on a chair across from Miss Lambert, who wore a smile that told her aunt she had indulged in more wine than a lady ought.

"I am surprised at your attachment to Miss Bingley. I would not think her someone you would choose for a friend."

"She thinks we are friends." Miss Lambert smirked in an unpleasant fashion. "She is only amusement. Miss Benton-Glass and I laugh heartily at her pretensions. Did you know she believes Mr. Darcy, of all people, is going to marry her? Just because her boring brother is his best friend."

Miss Lambert snickered. Lady Addington's brow darkened, she sat back and contemplated her niece with disapproval. "You can find other amusements I am certain. Miss Bingley is not a suitable subject for your questionable humor. And what is wrong with her brother? I like Mr. Bingley."

"He is boring, boring, boring. He never does anything exciting or dangerous. And their money comes from *trade*. I would not have him as a gift with a pound of Porter's tea."

Lady Addington's countenance grew cold. "You are quite vulgar tonight, my dear. I do not approve. If Miss Bingley is not your friend, drop her, quietly, and find someone more to your liking. I will not have it said that anyone in my house treats a fellow human being like a pantomime character. Is that understood?"

Miss Lambert sat up, her face sullen. "Yes, Aunt."

She rose and left the room without the courtesy of a "good night." Lady Addington sat without moving for a time, and then sighed. *I had hoped to find Ethel improved but it seems she is even more crass and rude than she was as a child. I shall have to write my sister to call her home. The Bennets have enough problems without Miss Bingley adding to them and Ethel encouraging her. And I like those young ladies.*

Determined on her course, Lady Addington rose and went to bed.

## July 1814
## Hurst Town House, London

Unlike Hephaestus House, which had been decorated by Miss Bingley, the Hurst home was fashionable without ostentation. The white marble tiles of the entryway had small black diamond tiles at the joined corners, below walls painted a dark green and hung with seascapes. Elizabeth and Jane were shown up a marble staircase with a decorative iron balustrade to Louisa Hurst's private parlor. She rose to greet them, handing her baby to the waiting nurse.

"I am happy you came," she said as they sat down. "This is our son, Daniel Miles Hurst. We decided to name him after Mr. Hurst's grandfather as Charles may want to use our father's name if he eventually has a son."

Elizabeth saw the love in her hostess' face as she looked at her son. Jane immediately drew to the baby and at a nod from his mother, took him from the nurse. "He is a lovely child," she said as she rocked him gently in her arms. "He will be a fine man someday."

"I trust so." Louisa asked the nurse to take the baby, and she departed leaving the ladies alone. "Mr. Hurst's estate is not large, but it is prosperous. It will make a proper legacy for our son."

She rang for tea and reseated herself. In the clear light falling from the windows, Louisa looked thinner than Elizabeth remembered her from Hertfordshire. Without cosmetics there was a pallor to her skin that spoke of illness and suffering.

"I trust you are feeling better, Mrs. Hurst?"

"I am slowly regaining my strength, I thank you. And please call me Louisa. We have known each other for some time, and I am tired of the formalities."

"Thank you, Louisa. And I would like it very much if you called me Elizabeth."

The tea came with tarts and biscuits. When the three women were settled again, Louisa seemed to gather herself before she spoke. "I asked you for tea today in part because I wanted to clarify something. When we were first at Netherfield Park I was happy. It was peaceful and there were no demands on me as Caroline insisted on acting as Charles' hostess. It was only when we noticed his particular attention to you, Jane, that everything changed." Louisa sipped her tea, giving herself time to find the words she wanted. "Our father always insisted that we must all marry into the gentry, and as high as we could manage. He liked Mr. Hurst and I was pleased with the match. Charles is unpretentious, I thought he might find a wife among the lower levels of the *ton*. It was only Caroline who imagined herself wed to a man of either noble blood or great wealth or both."

"She was never happy with Mr. Bingley seeking my company," Jane said sadly. "It bothered me, however there was nothing I could do except reject him completely, and I found myself unable to act in that manner."

"Caroline refused to let it drop. She can be cruel when balked, and Charles has never been able to deal with her. He was trained in business and finance by our father, he went to university, but Caroline has intimidated him since childhood. Somehow he could not break away."

"And now?" Elizabeth asked. She hoped the question was not offensive, but it was imperative they have Louisa's opinion on the subject.

"He has grown stronger. I made a terrible mistake in agreeing with Caroline that you seemed to have no particular regard for our brother. I do not know whether I wished to believe it, or if it was not the sort of reaction to him I was used to see from society ladies. I helped Caroline break his heart, and I am deeply sorry for my actions, and very glad that he has found you again."

Elizabeth felt cold. She rubbed her hands together to warm them. She forced herself to speak normally in spite of her apprehension. "Did Mr. Darcy encourage Mr. Bingley to return to London and stay here?"

"Not in so many words. It would be more accurate to say he did not discourage Charles. None of us knew of Mrs. Bennet's passing until last summer when Charles determined he would return to Netherfield. Somehow Caroline found out and told him. I believe you know the result."

"She was angry with you last night." Jane looked distressed. "I am so sorry if my presence caused you pain."

For the first time Louisa smiled with genuine humor. "You caused nothing, Jane. Caroline is her own worst enemy. She and I have grown apart in the past year for reasons that have nothing to do with you or Charles." It was only a small fib, she forgave herself immediately. "Mr. Hurst and I are leaving for his estate in several days. We intend to stay there the rest of the summer and fall. I do not know if we will return for the holidays or not. It is close enough that Mr. Hurst can travel to London when he needs to, and I will be able to rest without interference."

She did not say interference from whom. She did not have to. Elizabeth wondered how a sister could be so callous as to harass this delicate woman who was obviously not in good health.

"I have always found the country healing. I am sure you will feel much better there."

They spoke no more of the past, it was not a comfortable subject for any of them. When Elizabeth and Jane rose to go, Louisa walked with them to the front door. She waited until they had put on their bonnets and gloves before handing Jane a visiting card with her name engraved on the pale cream surface.

"Call on Lady Abercroft one day soon. I have written an introduction on the back of my card. She is a friend of Lady Addington. You will like her." She smiled, a little sadly. "I am happy to have had this time to talk. I hope one day soon we may share a closer relationship."

Impulsively, Jane hugged her. "Thank you, Louisa. It is my hope too."

Elizabeth accompanied her sister to their uncle's carriage. She was still not entirely easy with Mrs. Hurst's proffered friendship as it might rest only on a temporary division with her sister. Jane watched her as they rattled over the cobbled streets, the sound of street vendors and other vehicles accompanying them.

"You do not trust her." Jane did not sound upset, only curious.

"I do not know. I am sorry, dearest, it is just that I have learned how deceptive people can be. She seems sincere. For the moment I will take her at her word."

Jane sat back against the squab, serenity returning. "Daniel is a lovely baby. I think sometimes motherhood changes our perspective. And our priorities."

Elizabeth did not disagree with her..

## July 1814
## Hephaestus House, London

"Well, dear sister, how was your tea party?"

Caroline Bingley's voice was honey sweet; it did not deceive Louisa for a moment.

"Enjoyable. Where is Charles, I was told he is at home?"

"I am sure one of the servants has gone to fetch him. He is out so often of late I am never sure when he is here. He spends most of his time in Cheapside." She spat the word, her lip curling. "Think how cozy it will be when he has married that tainted hussy and her relatives in *trade* visit you. I am sure your friends will be vastly amused."

Louisa seated herself in a carved and gilded chair. Its silk brocade pattern of orange and green clashed with the soft lilac muslin of her day dress. There was hardly any furniture in the drawing room that did not. Sunlight slithered in around the drawn drapes; the air was thick and stuffy. Louisa felt as if a small Indian boy in a turban should be standing behind her, cooling her with an enormous feather fan like drawings she had seen of oriental courts.

"I came to say goodbye to my brother, not listen to another harangue from you. We are leaving for Nordfel tomorrow. I shall probably not see either of you for some time."

"Running away so I must handle everything. I do not know why I ever considered you an ally in saving this family!"

Exasperation laced Louisa's words. "Whom exactly are you saving, Caro, and from what? Jane Bennet may not be at the top level of the *ton*, but what has the cream of society ever done but laugh at us? Oh, they pretend to accept us, conditionally, but only because Mr. Darcy and Charles are good friends. We are nothing to them but interlopers whose wealth came from the detested *trade*."

"You can say that because you managed to catch a man with property. I will have a man so rich and powerful no one will dare laugh at me. If Charles would come to his senses and marry someone like Miss Lambert or Lady Crevwall's daughter, we would have a firmer place in the upper ranks. That reminds me—did you ask Lady Addington to send her niece away?"

"Her niece?" Louisa was genuinely puzzled. "Who is her niece?"

"Miss Lambert, the lady I came to the musical evening with."

Louisa stared at her sister as if she had taken leave of whatever rationality remained to her. "I do not even know Miss Lambert, and I would never presume to interfere in a family not my own. What has come over you, Caro?"

"The realization that I cannot trust you. You are on their side now. You want Charles to marry Jane Bennet no matter what damage it does to our standing in society."

Louisa rose and moved toward the door. "I have heard enough. Do as you will, in the end you will only harm yourself. Please tell Charles that I will be at home until ten tomorrow morning."

"No need, Louisa. I am sorry I was delayed, but it seems I have arrived at an appropriate time."

From the doorway Charles looked over Louisa's head at Caroline. She put on her superior expression only to find it did not affect him. "I suppose there will be another lecture on family unity."

"No, Caroline, no lectures. I will deal with you in another way." He took Louisa's hands and kissed her cheek. "I intended to call on you today to wish you and Miles a safe journey and a pleasant rest at Nordfel. Will you be returning for the holidays?"

"I do not know." Without looking at Caroline, Louisa gave the impression that she did not want to say more in her sister's presence. "I shall write to you once we are settled."

"Excellent." Still holding her hand, Bingley walked her into the entry.

"Take care, Charles," Louisa murmured when they were alone. "Caro is determined to stop you from marrying Jane Bennet." She raised her face to her brother in consternation. "Jane is in love with you. For your own happiness, do not let her go again."

"I shall not, Louisa, I promise."

He smiled down at her, at last drawing a smile in return. A maid brought her bonnet, gloves and parasol. Bingley saw her to her carriage. When he returned inside his face was grim. He went directly to his study and locked the door. For the next half hour he occupied himself writing to his attorney and accountant.

# CHAPTER THIRTEEN

July 1814
Gracechurch Street, London

Elizabeth followed at a short distance as Jane and Mr. Bingley walked along the brick path through the little park. Rose bushes bloomed in a pattern of red, pink and white; their scent warmed by the sun filled her with memories of the gardens at Longbourn. For the first time she did not suppress the images, but allowed them to fill her with a sense of who she was and who she had been. The grief for her parents would always be with her, but it no longer dominated her thoughts. She had no doubt Jane would marry soon, and she then had decisions to make for her own life.

Mr. Bingley had obviously dressed with exceptional care today, His fawn trousers and green tweed coat were new and expertly tailored. Elizabeth smiled to herself. She had noted her sister's careful toilette as well; Nettie had put Jane's hair up in a simple style with small curls framing her face. Her deep blue silk day dress, although no longer new, enhanced her cerulean eyes and soft pink-tinted complexion. Even her straw bonnet sported new pink satin ribbons.

*If he does not propose today, I shall lose hope of him.*

Water from a central fountain tinkled like a harpsicord. Elizabeth noted that the couple's steps had slowed to a near halt and she stopped to admire a stand of day lilies. Bingley's head was bent to Jane, he was speaking rapidly before he suddenly halted, staring into Jane's eyes. She dropped her gaze for a dozen heartbeats, and then raised her face to him with a trembling smile. Elizabeth did not have to hear the single word her sister spoke to know that the betrothal was sealed.

Elizabeth hurried to them, unable to repress her smile. Bingley looked at her, looked at Jane and blushed to his hair roots. Jane embraced her sister without words. Elizabeth shook Mr. Bingley's hand and spoke her congratulations. Their mutual happiness reassured her. The only shadow was Caroline Bingley's reaction and what she might attempt, even now, to separate them.

As if reading her reservations, Bingley's mien grew sober. "I should tell you both I gave Caroline an ultimatum this morning. That is why I could not call for the past two days, I was engaged in settling her inheritance on her and securing her a separate establishment. Two, actually. She can either live here in London, or at Scarborough, where our mother lives. I will tolerate her in my home no longer."

"Oh, Mr. Bingley, I never wanted to come between you and your sister." Jane's distress caused him to take her hand with a shake of his head.

"You have done nothing of the sort," he reassured her. "Caroline has grown more extreme in her actions over the past year. I do not understand why, perhaps because she is frustrated by Darcy's indifference, or because she feels her power over Louisa and myself has ended. She has always been strong in her opinions and inclined to impose her will on others. I sometimes think she might have been happier had she been a man. This breach has been caused by her inability to accept that she can only manage her own life, not mine or Louisa's. Now," his grin warmed Elizabeth, "shall we return to the Gardiners' and relieve your aunt's suspense?"

## August 1814
## Pemberley, Derbyshire

Darcy looked over the scrawled note with exasperation. "Good Lord, Charles, did not a governess or tutor teach you penmanship?"

The words on the page were just decipherable on careful study. Miss Bennet had accepted Bingley's hand in marriage. The wedding was scheduled for December 15th at the Gardiners' church. Darcy felt a certain relief on his friend's behalf. Once it was agreed, there was only the ceremony to get through and Bingley could settle down with his angel. Darcy wondered if Elizabeth intended to live with her sister and brother-by-marriage. Undoubtedly they would ask her to do so; if she agreed, he thought, it removed his concern over her care. Bingley would not let anything happen to her. And her sister's status would put her at the fringes of his own social circle. He would have the continuing pain of seeing her frequently as Bingley's sister-by-marriage. If she married, as she might well do, his life would become a long dark road he must always travel alone.

Necessity forced Darcy to concentrate on the harvest and plans for the winter planting, putting Elizabeth from his mind by sheer force of will. If Georgiana noticed his abstraction, she did not speak of it, for which he was grateful. He rode out with his steward to speak to his tenants and survey the land, make decisions on crop rotations, on improvements and what timber was to be thinned, on the sale of the wool clip to a mill he owned an interest in. He met with Mrs. Reynolds on household repairs and renovations and Mr. Niles on staffing. He met with the head gardener and the head groom. He was kept as busy as any responsible landowner at a time when plans for the coming winter and spring must be made.

And still Elizabeth was there. One night he found himself alone in his bed chamber, restless and unable to sleep as on most nights. On impulse he took up a candle and went to the door separating his room from a small sitting room and mistress' dressing room. Darcy crossed the sitting room, after a moment's uncertainty his hand fell on the doorknob of the dressing room. For several minutes he stood unmoving, not knowing why he hesitated or what called him to his mother's chambers, unused since her death over a decade before.

When he entered the dressing room he was immediately drawn

back to childhood. His mother had been a beautiful woman; he loved to watch her at her dressing bench, her maid brushing out and piling up her golden hair, fastening a necklace or pendant around her slim white throat. When she stood, her gown fell around her in folds of radiant silk or velvet or rich brocade. She looked like a queen, proud and delicate and full of wonder.

Reality reclaimed Darcy. The room was cold and empty. He found himself striding to the door of the bedchamber beyond. The rooms were cleaned several times a year, but nothing could remove the musty, gray smell of disuse. Sheets covered the furniture. The bed was stripped, bed curtains and drapes hung limp with age. The blue and rose that were his mother's favorite colors had faded on walls and carpet. It had the feel of a tomb or a memorial kept exactly as it had been when she lived. Darcy returned to his own rooms, closing the door behind him. Before they left for London, he wanted one more consultation with Mrs. Reynolds.

The night before their departure as they sat at dinner in the small dining room, Darcy watched Georgiana unobtrusively. She had spent the day directing the packing of her trunks and visiting her favorite places in the gardens. Mrs. Annesley had asked for a tray in her room, leaving brother and sister to each other's company. While they finished their summer soup, Darcy ventured a comment.

"Are you ready to return to London and the little season?"

Georgiana looked at him. When she responded her voice was thoughtful. "Ready? Yes. I know it must be."

"But you are not happy."

"Not happy, only resigned. I know there are worthy men, and you will not let me go wrong in my choice of husband. But when I marry, Pemberley will no longer be my home. Oh," she stopped his half-spoken protest with a smile, "I know my husband and I will always be welcome here, but you are aware it is not the same. Still, I think I should like to have my own home and family." Her lips turned up mischievously. "How will you like being 'uncle Fitzwilliam' to my children?"

Darcy returned her smile, trying not to show the sadness he felt. Georgiana was correct, she would have a new home, and while Pemberley would always be open to her, it would never be the same. The house would echo with the memories of quiet dinners, of riding over the estate, most especially with the sound of her brilliant performance on the pianoforte. For a moment he selfishly wished she not marry. But Darcy dismissed the thought as unworthy. His mind ran to Wickham. If she chose a suitor the betrothal must be handled very carefully. All of that could wait until they reached Town.

They finished the meal in mild conversation about their itinerary and what they might do once they reached London. Georgiana excused herself early to get as much sleep as possible before an early start. When she said good night, she leaned and kissed his cheek.

"You are the best brother any lady could ever have."

The soft words lingered in his mind like a blessing. *I will protect her at whatever cost. She is all I have, and all I am ever likely to have.*

## August 1814
## Hephaestus House, London

They reached Darcy House three days later, having taken the journey in easy stages. Georgiana stayed in her rooms until dinner, but Darcy was anxious to see Bingley and discover the state of his betrothal to Miss Bennet. He was at home when Darcy called and welcomed his friend to the small terrace at the rear of the house. The oppressive heat was only slightly mitigated by shade from an old elm and the plashing of the fountain. Darcy accepted a glass of wine punch, still chilled from the basement cold room, and took the chair his friend indicated with a wave of his hand.

"It has been like a dream," Bingley told him. "A good dream."

"Is Caroline resigned to the situation?"

Darcy sipped his drink and watched the play of emotions flicker across the younger man's face. Bingley was a terrible card player, he could never keep countenance whether his hand was good or bad.

"She no longer resides here. I rented her a row house in Meridian Square and transferred her inheritance to her management. I have not heard from her since then. She drove the Hursts to his estate, not that the country is not more pleasant at this time of year, but it is difficult for Louisa to travel, and there is the baby to consider. I do not know what has come over her, Darcy. She has always been selfish and frequently unreasonable, but she was positively—" he finished the sentence with a grimace.

"Out of control?"

"Very much so. Jane did not tell me, but I heard from Louisa that at Lady Addington's musical evening she insulted the Bennet sisters in language so offensive I was truly shocked."

Darcy felt a moment's sympathy for his friend. He knew Bingley was fond of Caroline, however he had made the right decision and Darcy told him so. "You cannot have a house divided between your wife and your sister. If Miss Bingley wants a reconciliation she will have to make the first overture."

Bingley shook his head. "I cannot see that happening at any time in the near future. Perhaps when Jane and I have been married for a time, she will realize I am happy and behave as she ought."

Darcy made no reply. He was not sanguine on the idea of Caroline Bingley admitting she was wrong about her brother's choice of wife or anything else. Instead he said, "I know Miss Bennet and Miss Elizabeth cannot attend balls or parties at this time, however there are other entertainments they might enjoy without impropriety. I received word of a private gallery showing, new artists just gaining reputations. If you would like to go, I shall arrange it."

The matter was settled and the men parted in mutual agreement. The gallery show was a success. After much urging from Bingley, Jane picked out a painting of a landscape of autumn trees and fallow fields for the morning room at Hephaestus House. He insisted he meant to redecorate and wanted Miss Bennet's taste to prevail. Darcy saw that Elizabeth admired a painting of Dove Dale similar to the one he had seen at the Gardiners', and made a mental note to purchase it and put it aside. He could not give it to her now, but perhaps one day ...

There was a lecture on art by J.M.W. Turner, whose Cockney accent amused Bingley and intrigued Elizabeth. Darcy informed her that Turner had been born in London and refused to live anywhere else, or lose his native accent, although he traveled extensively on the Continent. They retired to Hephaestus House afterward for tea and to discuss the lecture. Bingley and Jane rapidly entered into a quiet conversation having nothing to do with art. Darcy sat in a chair at the end of the sofa where Elizabeth had settled with her tea and a slice of cake. They were soon engaged in comparing opinions on landscape art and the relative merits of John Constable and Turner.

"I have seen a depiction of Turner's oil *Fishermen at Sea.* It is almost terrifying."

Elizabeth leaned a little toward Darcy, causing his pulse rate to increase. He was aware of every nuance of her face, how her eyes glowed with animation, the stray curl escaped from her coiffure to lie like a strand of silk on her neck. It was a struggle to keep his hand from reaching out to touch it. He sipped his tea, his mouth suddenly dry.

"I saw it at the Royal Academy show. It is even more spectacular when you stand before it. One can feel the danger of the surging waves, and the trees on the low peninsula in the background only intensify the isolation of the small boats."

Elizabeth set her plate aside. She folded her delicate hands around her cup, seeking words to explain what she felt. "It is the moon, partially obscured by the black clouds, the entire scene surrounded by darkness and the small white birds flying, like the souls of lost sailors. The painting speaks like a poem."

"He has been influenced by Cozens and the Welsh landscape artist Richard Wilson. It has broadened his outlook. I believe Turner has not yet approached his potential."

"I hope one day to see some of his works in person. My father had several parts of his *Liber Studiorum* in his library. He intended to purchase more but—it was not possible."

The momentary sadness in her expressive eyes hardened into a lump beneath his breastbone. "Surely he kept his library?"

Elizabeth finished her tea before she answered. "No. It was sold through a broker shortly before we came to London. He only kept a few favorites that were not worth enough to sell, and two of the most valuable in the event we needed money for an emergency."

"The Shakespeare First Folio and the Chaucer."

Elizabeth met his steady gaze wondering at their suddenly veiled look. "Yes. He showed them to you, I know. I only hope whoever bought his books will treat them with the care they deserve."

Darcy could not bring himself to speak. He put his cup carefully on the tea tray not wishing to let Elizabeth see his agitation. He wanted to reassure her, however he was not sure of her reaction to what he must tell her. Swallowing past a dry throat, Darcy gathered his resolve.

"They are already being cared for with the respect they deserve. They are in my library at Pemberley. I did not know when the broker wrote me to whom the library belonged to, but the titles were intriguing and I purchased them on his word that the price was fair."

There was no way to say that if he had known, he would have raised his offer. Elizabeth stared at him, unable to assimilate the information. At length she found her voice, careful to keep the words unemotional.

"You did not notice the bookplates?"

"I have not seen them. I was in Scotland at the time. The broker keeps watch for any volumes I might want to acquire when they come into his hands and gives me first refusal." Darcy did not know what else to say.

Sensing his discomfort, Elizabeth said, "I am glad they went to you, Mr. Darcy. It relieves my mind on their disposal."

*This is my fault as well. His books were his children. It might have been wrong of him, but so they were. Losing them would have caused him great pain, and I could have stopped it, stopped the family's descent into shame and degradation. How can I even hope that Elizabeth might forgive me?*

"Mr. Darcy? I hope you do not regret buying my father's library? I can think of no one I would rather have it."

Darcy's breath quivered as he drew it in. Before he was able to find a response, Jane called softly to her sister. "Lizzy, we should be leaving. Mr. Bingley has offered to send us in his carriage."

She sounded tentative and Elizabeth hurried to reassure her. "That is very kind of you, Mr. Bingley. Thank you."

Bingley beamed. Darcy felt a pang of jealousy. Bingley did not yet know where his fiancée and her sister lived, while he was aware of their location and could not say so. They all rose and Bingley sent for the carriage to be brought around. In the entry, Bingley and Jane said quiet goodbyes. Elizabeth turned to Darcy, the corners of her mouth lifting in a way that caught at his heart.

"I have missed our discussions, Mr. Darcy. Thank you for a most enjoyable afternoon."

He bowed over her hand, the feel of its small weight as if he held his own heart in his grasp. "I hope we shall have many more enjoyable times together, Miss Elizabeth."

Darcy released her hand and offered her his arm to the carriage. When the door closed behind both ladies, he turned abruptly and reentered the house.

## September 1814
## Meadow Lane, London

Jane sat at the dressing table, brushing out her hair before plaiting it for the night. In the mirror she saw Elizabeth standing at the open window, the night breeze wafting her light robe around her. She seemed wrapped in a stillness that Jane realized was an illusion.

The sudden liquid trill of a night bird broke whatever spell held Elizabeth. She turned to the room and sat on the bed.

"What is troubling you, Lizzy?"

Jane finished her plait, tied a ribbon around the end, and joined her sister on the bed. Elizabeth took so long to respond that Jane wondered if she had even heard the question.

"I am not troubled, only confused. We have spent much time with Mr. Bingley and Mr. Darcy, more than I would once have thought possible. Now that you are betrothed it is perfectly proper that your fiancé court you, but why does Mr. Darcy continue to attend us? You do not need two chaperones. And yet, he persists, almost as if..."

Elizabeth did not go on. Jane held her sister's hand as she had done since childhood. "I believe he finds your company enjoyable. You do not simper and flatter, and you have interests wider than the majority of young ladies. I nearly went to sleep at Mr. Soane's talk on neoclassical architecture, but the two of you discussed styles of building all the way through dinner."

"And the English architectural gardens through coffee afterward."

"And Capability Brown."

Both sisters were laughing. Elizabeth sobered first, she squeezed Jane's hand, her gaze on the small carpet covering the center of the bedroom. "Mr. Darcy is a fascinating man. His knowledge is wide and his understanding superior. When we talk, he listens to me, he never implies that my opinions are inferior or unimportant. When we do not see him for several days, I find myself—missing his company."

Jane grew very serious. She watched Elizabeth's profile in the yellow glow of the candle lamp. "Lizzy, are you—becoming fond of Mr. Darcy?"

Elizabeth rose suddenly. She returned to the window, shadows painting her slim form in grays. "I cannot, Jane. I dare not! I know as Mr. Bingley's friend we will see one another occasionally as friends, but that is all it can ever be."

The desperation beneath the words struck at her sister's heart. "I know it is difficult in our situation to hope for love. I am aware every day of how fortunate I am to have found Mr. Bingley. I do not think Mr. Darcy would purposely deceive you, he may simply want the conversation you offer. Have you any indication that he—he feels more for you than a friend?"

Elizabeth's head lowered until her forehead rested on the cool glass panes. "Not in words. Sometimes, when he looks at me and he thinks I am not aware of his scrutiny, I see something in his eyes, an intensity, as if he wants to say or do something he knows he cannot. Oh," she swung around, and Jane saw tears glistening unshed in Elizabeth's eyes, "I sound like a heroine in a novel. It is hopeless. I shall simply treat him as any other acquaintance. When you are married, he will return to his own circle and we will see him only on occasion. It is far better that way."

Jane blew out the candle and they went to bed. Neither slept for a time, each filled with their separate thoughts. At last Jane slipped into slumber, but Elizabeth lay silently awake beside her, the darkness filled with a face of male beauty dominated by dark eyes that reached into her heart and left only desolation.

The following morning when Nettie brought in the post, there was a note from their aunt Gardiner. Elizabeth opened it and read it quickly.

"We are invited to tea at Lady Addington's today with aunt Margaret. She will call for us at one o'clock."

"Lady Addington has been most kind to include us with our aunt in her musical evenings. I am sorry she felt it necessary to send her niece away."

"If it were up to you, dear Jane, no one would ever be held accountable for their behavior."

"That is not true, Lizzy. Some sins require repentance and

whatever reparation can be made. But foolishness does not need such harsh measures. We only met her once, and her actions were socially acceptable."

"Socially acceptable, perhaps, but certainly not courteous in my view. In any case, Lady Addington knows Miss Lambert far better than do we and it was her decision. Now, what will you wear today? Your new purple muslin, or the blue silk?"

## September 1814
## Lady Addington's Home, London

They had tea in Lady Addington's private sitting room on the second floor. Lady Addington rose from a gold silk settee as the three women were announced by the butler. The greetings and curtsies observed, she indicated they should be seated. Elizabeth paused to appreciate a vase of white roses on a pillar between a pair of narrow windows. Their fragrance was exquisite. She sat down next to Jane on the settee Lady Addington had left for a chair, her glance still turning to the bouquet.

"You have a particular liking for roses, Miss Elizabeth?"

Elizabeth felt her face warm with embarrassment. "Forgive me, Lady Addington, I cannot help but marvel at the perfection of those roses. There is not a spot of any color on them. And the odor is intoxicating."

"It comes of having an excellent gardener, and a small glass house. I refuse to live without flowers, even in the middle of London. But, then, you come from the country, do you not? It must be a great contrast to move to a city the size and enterprise of London."

A small *frisson* of disquiet slid over Elizabeth. Cautiously she said, "Yes. I miss the long walks I used to take."

"And knowing one's neighbors."

"That is not always easy in the city." Mrs. Gardiner sounded undisturbed. "Unfortunately it is not always easy in the country either."

"In the sense of deep knowledge, you are correct. However, one has more leisure to spend time with one's neighbors rather than the odd meeting at a soirée or dinner party, or a short morning call. I am not one for the salons of some of my acquaintances. I prefer conversation to gossip, especially the sort of gossip the ladies of the *ton* prefer."

"Gossip can only be hurtful," Jane said in her soft voice. "So often it is untrue, or a gross exaggeration of the truth. And it can do great damage."

"To the innocent, yes, it can. Among the *ton* it is more a cruel game. Every fortnight a new victim, who is quickly submerged in the next round of scandal. My niece, unfortunately, enjoys the game. She has returned to London, and has renewed her acquaintance with Miss Bingley."

Elizabeth looked immediately at her sister. Jane sat frozen, blanched; Mrs. Gardiner stiffened, however Lady Addington rang for tea and resumed her seat with a sympathetic smile at the sisters.

"I am not trying to alarm you. I have made it very clear to Miss Lambert that any attempt to assist Miss Bingley in causing trouble for you will result in my extreme displeasure. I thought you ought to be made aware of the situation as you might not hear of it otherwise."

Jane's hands trembled. Elizabeth touched her arm, meeting Lady Addington's wise eyes. "Thank you, my lady. It was generous of you."

Mrs. Gardiner smiled. "Yes, Isobel, I appreciate your assistance and your candor."

Lady Addington still watched Elizabeth. "There is something of old Eve in every woman. Just because a woman succumbs to it, does not mean she is an evil person. Nor are her relations."

The tea came, easing whatever tension remained in the room. Mrs. Gardiner and Lady Addington discussed mutual acquaintances and their charity projects, giving Jane and Elizabeth time to recapture their composure. On their way back to Meadow Lane, Mrs. Gardiner was thoughtful. The rattle of wheels over cobblestones and cries of street vendors gave way to less active streets. At last as they passed Sloane Square, she sighed.

"Lady Addington may stop her niece from spreading rumors, but if Miss Bingley has confided even a general idea of the scandal to an outsider, she may be desperate enough to go farther as the wedding approaches. Once you are married, it will be of little consequence."

Anger boiled in Elizabeth's chest making it difficult to draw a full breath. "I had known her lacking in principle, but not thought her so lacking in affection for her brother as to spread a story that can only harm him, and herself."

"She is not discreet," Jane stared at her hands clasped on her reticule, "but I did think she had a greater desire to preserve her own status."

"Hatred and arrogance are dangerous partners." Mrs. Gardiner's voice reflected her concern; it also was more determined than her nieces were accustomed to. "Jane, I will make an appointment with Mrs. White for her to create your wedding gown. You and Lizzy can spend the day tomorrow with me, we will look at the silks in your uncle's warehouses for a suitable fabric. You need not wear dark colors after the fifth, the wedding can be moved up to a date as near that as possible. Mr. Bingley will be able to secure a special license so no banns need be read. You can see my modiste for several dresses and gowns as a partial trousseau, and have others made after you are married. Does that sound acceptable to you, my dears?"

Jane looked to Elizabeth. "It sounds the best course of action, aunt. I am sure Mr. Bingley will agree."

"Yes." Elizabeth felt suddenly bereft. The emotion was so unexpected she was stunned by its intensity. She had to take several breaths before she regained her self-control. She forced a smile hoping it appeared normal. "That seems the best course."

Her aunt was not fooled, and resolved to speak to Jane privately about the possibility of Elizabeth living with her and Mr. Bingley after their wedding. It was unlike Elizabeth to withdraw from change;

however, this was not the Elizabeth of Longbourn and Meryton. Damage had been done, perhaps irreparable damage. Mrs. Gardiner felt it imperative on her to help her niece adjust to the marriage—and therefore loss—of her dearest sister's constant companionship, the only sister still within her circle of immediate family. She knew she might meet resistance, for Elizabeth was even more fiercely independent than before. She would have to deal with it if and when it came.

## October 1814
## Darcy House, London

The sound of music and feminine laughter drew Darcy to the music room at Darcy House. He had just come from a meeting with his accountant about an investment he had not yet decided whether to keep or sell, and the sounds had an additional appeal to his sober mood. He halted at the door, a silver laugh ringing through his nerves like a peal of Christmas bells. Her voice came then, and he leaned momentarily against the doorframe, desperately seeking a calm he did not feel.

"Listen, Georgiana—can you not hear the sound of Herr Mozart turning in his grave? Or perhaps it is only your beautiful pianoforte complaining at this abuse."

Georgiana's light tones responded in a terrible French accent. "Ah, mademoiselle, you 'it the keys zo hard, zey 'av not attack you, w'y you attack zem?"

The two melded in more laughter. A light, happy piece began; Darcy knew it for a duet Georgiana had learned some years previously. When the second player joined in, the sound was much as he remembered it being played by Georgiana and their mother. He stepped into the room, motioning Mrs. Annesley to remain seated and quiet. Darcy slipped into a chair to listen. When the music ended, Georgiana smiled widely at Elizabeth.

"You see? It is only lack of practice. You play quite well considering you have not had access to a pianoforte in some time. I am convinced I could not live without my music."

"Perhaps I shall have access to one after my sister marries. There is one at Hephaestus House."

'It is quite a good one, too. I have played on it a number of times."

Darcy saw Mrs. Annesley murmur something, and both ladies stood up and turned as he came to his feet. "That was delightful, Georgiana, Miss Elizabeth. Are you calling alone today?"

"Good afternoon, Mr. Darcy. Yes, my sister is with our aunt, ordering some gowns for her trousseau. Miss Darcy was kind enough to send an invitation to luncheon, so I came alone."

"We have had such a lovely time, Fitzwilliam. Miss Elizabeth plays and sings with such spirit."

"I know," Darcy's lips turned up at the memory, "I have heard her before. She has great feeling for the true meaning of the music."

Elizabeth colored. "Praise from Caesar."

Georgiana laughed. She said, "I am glad you are home in time to join us for luncheon, Brother. One man to three women ought to be the right number."

Darcy excused himself to wash and freshen his clothing. He returned in time to take Elizabeth in to the breakfast parlor they used when the size of the formal dining room was not needed. A cold collation had been laid out on the sideboard. Two footmen stood ready to serve the raised game pie, cutlets and peas, crème chicken, piped ham and salads. They poured wine as well, all under the watchful eye of Mr. Burgess. By the time the dessert course was introduced, Elizabeth was not sure she could hold any more. She tried a poached pear and one of the biscuits before stopping.

*If I keep eating like this, I shall have to have all my gowns let out!*

Darcy seemed to read her thoughts. "You will need a walk after this."

"Oh, I should love one. I do miss the long rambles I was accustomed to."

"Hyde Park is only a short distance. We can walk there. If Georgiana does not wish to join us, I will have one of the maids come."

Georgiana declined and Mrs. Annesley was not a great walker, so in the end one of the upstairs maids accompanied the couple, keeping a discreet distance behind them. Darcy shortened his stride as Elizabeth was walking more slowly than usual. When they had covered a little distance along an elm-shaded walk she raised her head so that Darcy was just able to see her profile within the shelter of her bonnet brim.

"Thank you for slowing, Mr. Darcy. We shall lose the maid if we walk at our usual pace."

Darcy felt comfortable enough to say, "Would that be so disastrous?"

"If we are seen by anyone you know, it could cause talk."

The seriousness of her words told him how damaged she had been by gossip; he began to apologize when she looked up at him, stopping his words and his breath.

"Please do not apologize, Mr. Darcy. I am, perhaps, over-cautious. I do not want you to have cause to regret your kindness to Jane and myself."

"I could never regret anything that assists either of you."

It was all he dared say. Elizabeth returned to surveying the park. A shiver of light from the Serpentine echoed the breeze swaying the branches of the trees. Lawns spread away in green undulations with benches here and there, showing like pale monuments to the sedentary. A leaf hung from one of the elms, half torn off its stem. She pulled it free and turned it in slim gloved fingers. The gloves were new, Darcy saw, cloth rather than kid and not of the best quality. He had seen her gray silk gown before, edged with black lace at neck and sleeves. Soon she would be able to wear the vibrant colors that brought out her dark beauty.

*I would dress you in the finest silks and velvets, the best quality gloves and hand-made slippers. It is only what you deserve, my beautiful Elizabeth.*

But she was not his Elizabeth. Pain seared his chest. Darcy found her eyes on his face and smoothed his features, but she had seen— something. Had he unwittingly revealed too much of his thoughts?

Elizabeth turned the leaf in her hand, contemplating its serrated edges. She stopped and took her hand from his arm. Elizabeth broke off a leaf from a shrub beside the walk and held them up together. Although both were of about the same size and shape the contrast was obvious.

"If one only looks at the mass of a tree or shrub, one sees the color and shape and nothing more. In the mass, they all fade into sameness. But when one looks at individual leaves, one can instantly see that they are very different. They may look well together, but they can never be other than companions."

Elizabeth dropped the leaves beside the walk. Darcy said with some harshness, "People are not leaves. Differences are more artificial than natural, whatever the social prophets say. I have come to believe class is more a matter of economics than nature. Was your father any less a gentleman than mine because he was not born the master of a large estate, or the son of a nobleman?"

"Most would say so. It does not matter, Mr. Darcy, what you believe or I believe. We still must live with the rules the majority adhere to and enforce on all of us. To do otherwise brings only misery." Elizabeth felt her anger fade into an aching emptiness. She turned back the way they had come, "Please let us return to Darcy House. My aunt is sending the carriage for me at three."

It was no use, Darcy thought. Better to walk away and let her go. His brain fought to compel his treacherous heart's obedience, but the battle was lost before it began.

Darcy escorted Elizabeth in silence. In the entry, Mr. Burgess approached as a footman took their outerwear.

"Excuse me, Mr. Darcy, but Lady Fitzwilliam has called unexpectedly. She is in the drawing room with Miss Darcy."

With a brief thanks, Darcy offered Elizabeth his arm. She did not take it immediately, her gaze traveling toward the open door farther down the hall. Darcy took her hand and placed it on his arm, ending any protest. Elizabeth's chin rose. She had as well meet his aunt now and have it over with.

In the drawing room Lady Eleanor sat across from Georgiana with a cup of tea, the two chatting amiably about a ball Georgiana was to attend in two days' time. She looked up at their entrance, taking in Elizabeth at a glance and smiling at Darcy. Georgiana rose and curtsied as her brother bowed to his aunt. The older woman set aside her cup and rose as well.

"I have been hearing about Georgiana's new friend. Please introduce me."

Darcy took a much-needed breath and said, "Lady Fitzwilliam, Countess of Matlock, may I present to your acquaintance Miss Elizabeth Bennet."

Elizabeth made a perfect curtsey, silently blessing her mother for teaching her daughters as girls what was due gentry and what was due the nobility. Lady Matlock noted Elizabeth's demeanor and nodded.

"I am pleased to meet you, Miss Elizabeth."

"It is an honor, my lady."

They were seated and Georgiana poured tea for her brother and Elizabeth. Lady Matlock watched Elizabeth's movements without seeming to, a trick she had learned long since. The wife of an earl and an astute hostess, Lady Matlock rarely failed to learn what she wished without intrusive questions.

"I see you are in half-mourning. My condolences on your loss."

"Thank you, my lady." Elizabeth sipped her tea. Darcy thought she was taking Lady Eleanor's measure as thoroughly as his aunt was taking hers, and suppressed a smile.

"I believe your sister is to marry my nephew's friend Mr. Bingley. Has a date been set?"

"The fifteenth of December. We shall be out of mourning by then. We met Mr. Bingley several years ago in Hertfordshire, and renewed the acquaintance last spring."

"You met my nephew then too?"

Elizabeth's voice was courteous but not subservient. "Yes, my lady. My late father's estate bordered Mr. Bingley's leased property."

*We are gently born and Mr. Bingley only leased land. It is not exactly sparring, only a subtle reminder that Elizabeth will not be looked down on by anyone, whatever she may say.*

Darcy hid a smile in his teacup.

The Gardiners' carriage arrived promptly at three o'clock. Elizabeth thanked her hostess and took proper leave of Lady Matlock. Darcy walked Elizabeth out and handed her into the vehicle. He returned to find his aunt waiting for him with a bland face that did not deceive him for a moment. With friends and relations Darcy's aunt was the soul of tact, however with close family she was known to speak her mind with the frankness Lady Catherine always claimed for herself.

Georgiana had gone, no doubt at Lady Eleanor's suggestion. She folded her hands in the lap of her iris gray gown and appraised her nephew with a raised brow.

"So, Darcy, you have known Miss Elizabeth Bennet for three years. That was about the time you returned from Mr. Bingley's estate and disappeared."

"I did not disappear. I was at my estate in Scotland."

"Where no one could reach you without sending a search party."

It was no use. Lady Eleanor saw through prevarication and refused to accept it. Darcy sat back in his chair to consider what he would and would not reveal. Certainly not the situation with Wickham. As for the rest, what did it matter if his aunt knew? The admission would go no further.

"I found myself falling in love with a young woman of impeccable character and gentility, but without fortune or connections, and with a mother and younger sisters who were vulgar in the extreme. There were also relatives in trade, although I have since met them and they would be at home in any drawing room. I knew the resistance I would face from family and friends if I tried to court the lady. I have Georgiana to protect from the viciousness of the *ton*, and the expectations of my position to fulfill. In short, I ran away."

"And now you have run back."

Darcy sat silent. He drew a breath through his nose and forced the tension out of his shoulders. "Bingley accidentally met Miss Elizabeth near Sloane Square. Her mother and father had both died, two of her sisters married. Miss Elizabeth lives with her elder sister in a small house leased by their late father. There is a live-in maid and a housekeeper who comes in six days a week."

"And her sister?"

Darcy wondered how to answer. He did not really know Jane Bennet, except for her close connection to Elizabeth and her outward characteristics. Better not to speculate. "She is a very beautiful woman, with a serene nature somewhat darkened by the loss of their parents. Mr. Bingley wanted to marry Miss Bennet after they first met, but his sisters managed to convince him she was only after his fortune, which was not true. When he learned the Bennets lived in Town he found their uncle in trade and renewed his courtship. They are to be married as soon as their half-mourning ends in December."

"So." Lady Eleanor tipped her head a little to one side. The gesture reminded him briefly of Elizabeth, although this formidable woman wielded more power privately and in society than most duchesses. "That is the reason you have avoided the Season for three years, and refused to choose a wife with wealth and connections."

"In part. I have also been concerned about Georgiana, with good cause as it turned out."

"In one instance, yes. She told me today she plans to be married by next summer."

Darcy sat up straighter. "That is news to me."

"Perhaps she feels she is holding you back by requiring your guardianship?"

Darcy contemplated the idea, and did not entirely reject it. "No,

I do not think so. She has matured greatly in the past few months. I think she is ready to marry. So long as she chooses well, I have no objection."

Lady Eleanor studied her nephew for a time. "There is something you are not telling me, William, but I shall not press you. The Season is effectively over. Next week I will give a small dinner party and issue invitations to both Miss Bennets and Mr. Bingley. It will be just family and a few close friends. Mr. Bingley has dined with us before, as have his sisters. I understand the Hursts have retired to the country for an indefinite stay, and Miss Bingley is living with a companion, apart from her brother."

She watched Darcy's reaction casually. He took care to let her see no particular response. "Which friends?"

"Lady Addington. She is always an agreeable dinner guest. Mr. and Mrs. Bergman-Rayles; Sir Eugene Samuelson; Baron and Baroness Rathbone; Sir Craymore and Lady Fortesque. You and Georgiana, and Brentmore and Adele, of course. We will be short one gentleman, but it hardly signifies."

"Of course."

Lady Eleanor's lips twitched at his tone. "I will not throw the Bennets to the lions, William, I promise. Although I suspect any lion that encountered Miss Elizabeth would come out second best. Now, if you will please have my coach brought around, it is time I returned home. It has been a most enlightening afternoon."

Darcy saw her off. He could not help wondering if he had just opened Pandora's box.

# CHAPTER FOURTEEN

October 1814
Bond Street, London

Mrs. Gardiner, Jane and Elizabeth found Madame Colette's shop less busy than they had anticipated, allowing Jane to proceed with the fittings for her new gowns without the anticipated wait. Elizabeth stayed in the small room where the fittings were accomplished until her sister was swathed in silk and prickling with pins like some fashionable hedgehog. She emerged to see a familiar face looking through a display of handkerchiefs. At Elizabeth's greeting Georgiana Darcy immediately left the search to meet her friend. Elizabeth became aware the younger woman's movements were nervous, her face reflecting a sleepless night. She curtsied quickly and took Georgiana's hand in concern.

"Is something wrong, Georgiana?" Elizabeth drew the girl closer to her so any shop assistant who watched them would only see a conversation between friends.

A swift breath and Georgiana held tightly to Elizabeth's hand for a moment before regaining her self-control. "I need to speak to you, Elizabeth, alone. I have not had the opportunity, there are always people nearby at Darcy House, and while the servants would never eavesdrop, I would rather we were somewhere no one knows or cares what we discuss."

"It is that serious?"

Georgiana nodded. "Can you leave for a few minutes? Hatchard's bookshop is just a short way past the corner on Piccadilly. We can talk there."

Intrigued and a little alarmed, Elizabeth went to find her aunt. She returned and the two young ladies walked the short distance to the renowned book store. Once inside, Georgiana led her friend to a quiet corner on the second floor. Soft light from the windows limned them in pastel shades. Elizabeth waited for her friend to speak, the words taking unusual time to form.

"I do not know where to begin. There is a young gentleman I have—grown fond of. He rendered me a great service a year ago, but I have not seen him since. I...he...oh, Elizabeth, I have never felt this way about any of the men I have met who wish to court me, but he—my brother—I am afraid William will not approve! The gentleman is not wealthy or socially prominent, and he has never said anything of courtship to me, but I know in my heart he feels the same way about me that I feel about him. I do not know what to do!"

The spate of words ended. Georgiana was breathing rapidly, her hands trembling. Elizabeth took them in hers and waited until the girl calmed enough to understand what she needed to say. "My dear, you must talk to your brother. Does he know of the service this gentleman rendered you?"

"Yes. But he has never asked to meet Gil...the gentleman. And Fitzwilliam has reason to dislike the gentleman's relations."

"That may make the situation more difficult. However, I have found that your brother is less rigid in his opinions than I once believed, and I know he loves you very much. If your gentleman is honorable, his social situation may not be as important as you think."

Georgiana's face regained a little of its color. "Do you think so, Elizabeth? I never want to disappoint William, he has always been so good to me. And there is my aunt Eleanor, she expects me to marry very well. She sponsored me my first Season, I would not want her to reject my choice."

Elizabeth felt a splinter of resentment prick her mind. "I do not think your aunt's expectations ought to take precedence over your happiness. *You* are the one marrying. Only you should choose your future husband."

"It is not always that easy."

Georgiana sounded sad. Elizabeth put a hand on her arm in comfort. "I understand, better than you know. But you must at least try to choose a man you admire and respect, not someone whose only recommendation is his money or his title."

"You are right, Elizabeth." Georgiana assayed a small smile. "I have struggled with this situation for over a year. It is time to bring it to an end. I shall speak to my brother this evening. Thank you, dear Elizabeth, for listening to me."

"I will always listen, Georgiana. That is what friends do."

They left Hatchard's together, strolling back silently past shop windows displaying luxury goods. Jane's fittings were just over when they reached Madame Colette's. Mrs. Gardiner came out of the small room while Jane was helped to dress by a shop assistant, and exchanged curtsies with Georgiana.

"It is lovely to see you, Miss Darcy. How are you keeping? Your family is well, I hope?" Georgiana answered in the affirmative. Mrs. Gardiner turned to Elizabeth. "You did not find anything to your liking at Hatchard's, Lizzy?"

Knowing her aunt's perceptive intelligence, Elizabeth decided to tell a portion of the truth. "We were talking and I am afraid I did not really look at the offerings."

"Well, Hatchard's will be there when you are less distracted. I have sent for the carriage, we need to return home, your uncle will be there for luncheon. If you will excuse us, Miss Darcy?"

Georgiana answered appropriately. Jane joined them, a little flushed, tying the ribbons of her bonnet. She greeted Georgiana and settled her spencer more comfortably.

"I have been standing so long without moving it will be a comfort to sit down for the ride back to Gracechurch Street."

They discussed the rigors of fittings until Mrs. Gardiner's footman appeared at the door of the shop to indicate the carriage was outside. As they parted, Georgiana lowered her voice so only Elizabeth would hear her.

"I shall let you know what happens."

"I would appreciate that very much."

Not only for Georgiana, but for her own understanding of how honest Mr. Darcy's sentiments regarding social differences were.

Mr. Gardiner was at home when they arrived in Cheapside. They refreshed themselves and sat down to luncheon. During the second course Mr. Gardiner turned to Jane with a smile Elizabeth could only think of as fatherly.

"Is Mr. Bingley agreeable to being married at our parish church, my dear?"

Jane put down her fork and looked to her aunt before replying. "I should like to be married from here, if that is acceptable to you and aunt? Mr. Bingley attends his parish church, however he is agreeable to wherever I choose."

"I hope he is always so accommodating," their aunt said with a smile extended to her husband. "I certainly have no objection. Do you wish to have the wedding breakfast here? We have room for a fair number of guests."

Jane hesitated. "I do not know how many people will attend the wedding. Mr. Bingley has friends in trade and also some members of the *ton*, although none as highly placed as Mr. Darcy. They will not all be invited to the breakfast, of course. He has a full staff at Hephaestus House, but no hostess since Miss Bingley's departure. If you would be willing to organize the wedding breakfast, it could be held there."

Mrs. Gardiner glanced at her husband who gave a small nod. "I shall speak to Mr. Bingley the next time he calls on you. You do not think his sister..?"

Jane's expression grew sad. "No. She has cut herself off from him and her elder sister. I wish it was not so, but Mr. Bingley thinks she will eventually regret her actions."

They finished luncheon and Mr. Gardiner returned to his office. After another half hour Jane was obviously growing fatigued and Mrs. Gardiner called for the carriage. The driver was skilled and easily set them into the flow of traffic along the street. They passed the corner without anyone, including the driver, noticing as a hansom cab inserted itself in the line of vehicles behind them. It followed as far as Meadow Lane before turning into a cross-street and disappearing. The passenger had made a mental note of the house where the carriage stopped, smiling in satisfaction. The whereabouts of the Bennet sisters was no longer a mystery to someone.

## October 1814
## Darcy House, London

Darcy laid his serviette beside his plate and watched Georgiana push the tattered remains of her raspberry tart around the Wedgewood dish one last time. She indicated to the footman in attendance to clear the table but did not rise. Darcy knew she was gathering herself to speak to him on a subject of importance. Her reluctance made it imperative he allow her to address the matter in her own time.

At last she rose and faced him. "May I speak to you privately, Brother?"

"Of course. Would you like to go to my study, or will the drawing room be suitable?"

"The drawing room will be fine."

He offered her his arm. The drawing room was empty; a fire burned in the large hearth, warming the air from the icy wind that snuffled at draped windows. A serene room, it was organized to facilitate conversation, both in larger groups and more intimate interactions. Georgiana seated herself on a settee and straightened her skirts, her hands fussing with the silk in a way that told Darcy she was more agitated than she appeared.

Darcy took a chair across from her, close enough to offer comfort if it were needed. After several minutes she looked up and met his eyes. "I have met a gentleman whom I wish to marry. I have known him for over a year. He is not wealthy and his only connection of note is a man with whom you do not have a friendly acquaintance. In short, he is not suitable according to what has always been expected when I marry."

"May I know his name?"

Again Georgiana hesitated. Darcy could see in her face she had gone so far there was no turning back. "Mr. Giles Worthington."

It took a moment before the name came into focus in Darcy's mind. "The gentleman who rescued you from…"

"From a marriage that would have been torture, yes. He has not approached you, or me, because he understands my position, and he will not do anything to cause me embarrassment or discomfort. Last summer…"

"Yes?" It was gentle encouragement. Darcy kept his voice low and calm. "You saw him at various functions I imagine."

"I did. His cousin was always bringing him to social events, and then using him as some sort of—of jest. It was one of the things I disliked most about Sir Frederick. We did talk, however, and I know him to be honest and a good man."

"Who are his people?"

Georgiana obviously felt more at east now the first difficult part of the conversation was past. She did not want to tell her brother she had spoken to Elizabeth before informing him. Not at this time. Darcy wanted to do nothing to distress her. He remembered Richard's statement that she would confide in him eventually. This, then, was the burden his sister had carried for more than a year. Its parallel to his own feelings for Elizabeth Bennet stunned him.

"His father is Eustace Worthington, he is a mathematician and former fellow of the university. Mr. Worthington's mother passed when he was twelve, and his father never remarried. You know of the Tennerleys. The elder Mr. Worthington owns a small estate in Cornwall. He is very interested in the work of Mr. Watt and Mr. Trevithick in steam engines. We did not talk much of his family, especially after—what happened. I only saw him once more, at a musical evening."

Darcy did not want to upset Georgiana, however there was one question he had to ask. "Is Mr. Worthington fully engaged in the family estate, or does he have some other means of support?"

Although he had asked the question with as little emphasis as possible, his sister stiffened. "His passion is steam power. Mr. Worthington sees it as a revolution in manufacturing and transport. He has a degree in engineering and has studied with Thomas Hatfield who is a friend of his father."

The words came out in a rush. Georgiana fell silent, her eyes on her hands, now still in her lap. On some level it had not been a total surprise to Darcy. Her reluctance to consider the gentlemen who showed an interest in a courtship, her evasion of the Season and little seasons, her withdrawal and continuing melancholy ought to have told him that it was her heart involved rather than any fear of commitment. Thomas Hatfield was a well-known and respected designer of steam engines with a reputation for refusing to compromise his principles.

"An engineer is not a tradesman." Darcy watched Georgiana's face carefully, not wanting her to see the comment as a condemnation. "But even though he may be born a gentleman, he works for those in trade. It is a fine line, many people would call the occupation a craft. It is also a business. It falls into the gray area of social status, much as attorneys and bankers."

Georgiana raised her head. "I do not care, Fitzwilliam. I know my choice will disappoint my family, but I cannot wed a man I have no respect or affection for. I…I do not want you to be angry with me. You have done so much to protect me, to make my life full and happy, it would pain me beyond telling if you disapproved of my husband."

"But it would not stop you?"

Georgiana met his gaze directly. "No, my dearest brother, it will not. Only if he rejects me."

Darcy felt the need to reassure her without committing himself. "I want to meet Mr. Worthington. I will arrange it in a small social setting. Is that acceptable?"

"Yes. Thank you."

Georgiana rose, said goodnight and left Darcy alone. He heard her footsteps echo softly along the hall, poured himself a brandy and stood quietly by the fire listening to the harsh purr of burning coal. Its rubescent glow added to the warmth of the dark red patterned rug and turned the tawny upholstery on the nearby chairs to glowing amber. He had a decision to make, one that affected his sister's future and perhaps his own. He wished he were able to discuss this with Elizabeth. She would know better than he the results of what some would see as a misalliance. That was not possible, not now, perhaps not ever. He was afraid the subject might be too personal for her—and for him.

Darcy drank the brandy slowly. In his study he wrote his aunt a note, before finally going up to his own chambers and the long night ahead.

## October 1814
## Matlock House, London

Lord Henry and Lady Matlock greeted their guests in the entry of their town home, now lit with gas lamps. For the moment it was only the outside entrance and the hall, but eventually the earl intended to illuminate the entire house. He considered himself a progressive man in spite of the fact his wife preferred the softer candlelight. Candles might not explode, but they caused fires and the gas light, while a bit hard, let a man see where he was going without straining his eyes.

Lady Eleanor awaited the arrival of the Bennet sisters with some anticipation. Her nephew had been long enough about marrying, if this was his choice she was willing to accept it. Miss Elizabeth Bennet was a lady, if a rather impoverished one compared to the upper levels of the *ton*. She had not been wealthy herself when the then-viscount Brentmore approached her father. Her father would have consented to the match whatever her feelings. She had been lucky, she reflected, that Henry was a good man and respected her, even if his older sister did not.

*At least Richard has finally removed Catherine's claws from Anne and Rosings. I do not know how she does at Bath, nor do I care, so long as she troubles the family no longer.*

The first carriage arrived, and Lady Eleanor took up her duties as hostess. The guests were conducted to the drawing room where drinks were served and conversations begun. Bingley introduced Elizabeth and Jane to several of the attendees and Lady Addington took both sisters with her to meet the others. Bingley knew Sir John Rathbone from other social occasions and a mutual interest in steam power. They soon settled themselves not far from the ladies and took up a discussion of the latest advances in Trevithick's Cornish engine. Lady Rathbone patted her husband's arm and made her way to the small group of ladies seated close to the fireplace. Lady Addington greeted her warmly, made room for her on the sofa she occupied with Elizabeth and drew her immediately unto a discussion of travel to the Continent now that the war was over.

Darcy and Georgiana followed a few minutes later. Georgiana had taken particular care in her toilette, Darcy noted. She wore a sea green silk gown in a classic rather than fashionable design, her blonde hair put up in braids and a twist with several long curls hanging over her shoulder. She wore a pearl necklace that had been their mother's and pearl earrings, no other jewelry. She looked, Darcy thought, heartbreakingly innocent. Lord and Lady Matlock greeted them in the entry. Darcy saw his own feelings reflected in his aunt's swift glance.

The remaining dinner guests arrived and were settled in the drawing room. In the entry the Matlocks waited with some impatience for their eldest son and his wife.

"Late as usual," Lord Henry grumbled. "Why Chadwick ever married that French tart…"

"Henry, please. She is the mother of our grandsons and granddaughter. I find her difficult as well, but calling her a tart is untrue as well as unkind. She is more of an overly decorated confection. All appearance and no substance."

Her husband grinned. "True. But she causes trouble nonetheless. She…"

The butler indicated that the viscount and viscountess had arrived, and Lord Henry fell silent. The courtesies over, both couples repaired to the drawing room where Lord Brentmore immediately sought out a tray of drinks and his wife an audience. Her eyes scanned the ladies as she sauntered across the room. They narrowed as she took in Jane Bennet before she noticed the betrothal ring on her left hand. That left the other lady sitting next to Lady Addington. She was not particularly pretty, Adele decided, but she had a look of independence in her posture and bearing that lifted the viscountess' nose higher in the air.

Darcy and Georgiana entered the drawing room to the sound of Lady Addington's laughter. She looked up as they came in, amusement still in her wise eyes. She was talking to Elizabeth. Georgiana felt the muscles of her brother's arm harden under her hand and followed his sight to her friend as Elizabeth rose. They greeted Lady Addington before Georgiana took Elizabeth's hands. She did not have to speak, her demeanor told Elizabeth that she had spoken to her brother with success.

Bingley and Lord Rathbone were still engaged in a discussion of steam power. Lady Rathbone kept an eye on her husband with the tolerance of a long-married and loving spouse while she talked knitting with Jane. Georgiana curtsied and took a chair across from her, next to Lady Fortesque, who patted her hand and motioned a footman carrying a tray of drinks to them.

"You and your brother have divided the attributes of your dear mother. You have her beauty and poise, and he has her independent attitude."

"I hope I am learning to be more independent as I mature." Georgiana accepted a glass of sherry, settling into her seat.

Elizabeth shook her head at the footman, replacing her empty glass on the tray. Her eyes twinkled. "If a little learning is a dangerous thing, I wonder if a great deal of learning is more or less dangerous?"

"I believe the warning is against less rather than more. The danger is in knowing too little, rather than too much."

Darcy stopped beside Elizabeth's end of a brocade settee. She looked up at him; Darcy felt his heartbeat quicken, he had to make a conscious effort to control his breathing. He seated himself in a chair next to her. She wore the iris gray silk, its black lace setting off the pale cream of her skin and dark curls swept up in a simple coiffure interlaced with black ribbon. Her beauty made his throat hurt. Her silver voice reached into his mind and held him spellbound.

"And so gentlemen with a university education are more able to control their lives than those who are only taught what they need to know to survive?"

Darcy made an effort to reply impassively. "More able to live a full life, perhaps."

"Learning promotes independence, then?"

"After a fashion. Some men at university train for a profession, some follow an interest. It is a matter of mental discipline in either case, of applying logic and reason to factual information. I believe that process improves life in general."

Elizabeth did not take her gaze from Darcy. "No wonder women are not allowed an advanced education."

Lady Addington raised a brow at Darcy as well. "Do you think meanly of women's ability to accomplish a higher education?"

His gaze on Elizabeth, he said, "I would never presume to speculate on women in general."

"Wise man," Lady Addington approved wryly.

The corners of Elizabeth's lush mouth turned up in a way that caused Darcy to wish they were alone. Darcy almost groaned. "I had forgotten your tendency to entrapment. I shall be wrong whatever I say."

Bingley and Lord Rathbone still engaged in their discussion, however Lady Rathbone and Jane were now attending to the exchange between Elizabeth and Darcy. Georgiana watched her brother anxiously, unused to the verbal fencing and a little unsure if it was proper.

"Not if you speak what you truly think."

"Very well." Darcy gathered himself for the fray, wondering if Elizabeth was testing him in some manner. "No doubt some women, if offered a university education, would act as some men do. They would get through the courses with as little effort as possible just to say they had accomplished it. Those who truly desired knowledge would put in great effort and succeed at whatever they studied."

"So you do not think it a matter of gender but of the desire and ability to learn?" Lady Addington watched the mischief in Elizabeth's eyes take on a more serious shadow.

"I think it is the individual, rather than gender. Some women educate themselves because of a love of knowledge, others are content to know only what they need to make their lives comfortable. Now I have committed myself, Heaven help me."

"But if women were educated equally with men, would it not destroy society?" A little alarmed at her boldness in entering the conversation, Georgiana dropped he gaze and fell silent.

"You think we would rebel, like the women in the Greek play?" Lady Rathbone joined the fray with quiet relish.

Mrs. Addington raised a brow at Darcy. "The American president Jefferson said, 'A little rebellion now and then is a good thing.' I believe from his point of view he was proven right, although the statement was some time after the fact. Perhaps it is time for another sort of revolution."

Elizabeth leaned forward, serious now. "Society has made marriage the only honorable provision for women of small fortune, even those with an education beyond household matters. Sadly I do not believe most women today would take up an advanced education if they were afforded the opportunity."

"You think meanly of your sex, Miss Elizabeth?"

Elizabeth smiled a little sadly at Lady Fortesque's question. "I think society must change before women gain not only the right to an education such as we speak of, but a desire for it strong enough to topple the pillars of prejudice and tradition. That may take a very long time, but I believe it will come eventually."

"As a matter of fact," Mrs. Fortesque began, only to be interrupted by Lady Chadwick.

"Women changing society. What a novel concept."

None of the group had noticed Adele Fitzwilliam enter the room, or approach them. Darcy turned an austere face to the viscountess as he rose to introduce Jane and Elizabeth. "We were discussing higher education for women."

Lady Brentmore gestured expansively. "What is all of that dismal learning to a woman? Education is for gentlemen. Women must get what they want by using what beauty they were born with. What do they care for the intellect? They are made to be wives and mothers, nothing more."

" 'Woman was created to be the toy of man'," Darcy quoted.

Adele smiled on him graciously. "Exactly, Mr. Darcy."

Sensing a trap for the viscountess, Lady Addington watched Elizabeth, who looked as if she knew exactly from whom the quote came. "Whom are you quoting, Fitzwilliam?"

"Mrs. Wollstonecraft. I believe she was employing sarcasm at the time."

The viscountess frowned, uncertain if she had just been insulted by a male she admired and wanted to admire her. Elizabeth held her tongue with an effort. He realized she did not want to create a scene, as much for Jane's sake as for propriety. As usual when conflict threatened, Jane tried to diffuse the sudden tension.

"That is a lovely pendant, my lady. It is a pigeon's blood ruby, is it not?"

Adele shrugged, distracted. "It is an old family piece. I am not *bijoutìere*, I only know it is beautiful."

"Rubies are so lovely." Jane kept her smile, ignoring the tone of the older woman's words.

"They are for ladies." The hauteur of the statement caused Elizabeth to bristle. The viscountess left no doubt she did not include the Bennets in that definition. She glanced at Jane's hands. "You are engaged, yes? What a nice little ring. So appropriate."

The viscountess gestured dismissively, the light gloving her hands in facets of gemmed color from her several rings and bracelets.

"Thank you, my lady." Jane glanced at Bingley who had risen along with Lord Rathbone at Adele's intrusion. He smiled at his fiancée, his words so inoffensive even the viscountess could not quarrel with them.

"I am afraid the ring is only temporary. My grandmother's sapphire and diamond wedding ring is being reset for Miss Bennet. It, too, is a family piece."

"How romantic." Adele noticed the approach of her mother-by-marriage and drifted away toward the other guests, giving the gentlemen the opportunity to admire her figure in motion.

"If that pendant is antique French," Lady Addington muttered, "then so am I." She watched the viscountess' progress for several moments. "I am an old lady with a wicked tongue. And I am not repentant."

Lady Matlock came up at that point, smiling at the group. "Dinner will be announced in a few minutes. Darcy, will you take Miss Elizabeth in?" She made a little inclination of her head toward the hall.

"It will be my pleasure."

He turned so he could watch the doorway. Georgiana caught her breath as a tall, dark-haired young gentleman entered. The butler announced, "Mr. Giles Worthington."

Georgiana remained utterly still as Giles entered the drawing room. Then she rose and took her brother's arm, her hand trembling. Darcy put his free hand over hers in reassurance as he conducted her to meet the newcomer. Giles had stopped just inside the doorway. He looked perfectly self-possessed except for the tension in his shoulders. Darcy felt Georgiana draw away from him as they met and released her.

"Mr. Worthington, it is good to see you again." She curtsied to his formal bow.

"Miss Darcy. I hope you are well?"

"Yes, quite well."

It never ceased to amaze Darcy how a woman could put so much meaning into so commonplace a thing as a conventional greeting, If he had not known their history he would have thought nothing of the waver in her voice.

"Will you introduce me to your friend?"

Georgiana swallowed. "Mr. Fitzwilliam Darcy of Pemberley in Derbyshire, may I present to your acquaintance Mr. Giles Worthington of High Coombe Farm, Cornwall."

"Mr. Worthington, I am pleased to make your acquaintance."

"It is an honor to meet you, sir."

His bow was proper but in no way subservient. Taking his measure, Darcy said, "I understand your father is Mr. Eustace Worthington, the mathematician."

"Yes, sir."

"I remember the name from university, although I was not a student of his. He has a well-deserved reputation for brilliance in his field."

"Thank you, Mr. Darcy. My father is retired now to his estate in

Cornwall where he follows his passion for mechanical engines. It is a mathematical science that has long attracted him."

"He believes they will take on even more importance in manufacturing?"

"And other areas of society including transportation."

"The Cornish engine?"

"And improvements to it."

"You do not follow his profession as an academic?"

"No. I am engaged in building a career as a designer of more compact and efficient steam-powered engines."

For the first time Darcy heard something defensive in Giles' voice. Georgiana moved beside him, only a small shift in her weight, as if she wished to stand beside Mr. Worthington. "Are you engaged in any projects?"

"I presently work independently. I am working on plans for a new high pressure engine small enough to be used for transport applications. I shall be applying for a patent when it has been tested."

Darcy knew of the development currently going on in cloth manufacturing. It was a growing segment of the production of exported goods as well as internal sales. Before he was able to comment, Georgiana suddenly spoke.

"Please let me introduce you to my friends, Mr. Worthington."

Giles' eyes softened in a way that required no explanation. "Of course, Miss Darcy. If Mr. Darcy has no objection?"

"None." Darcy watched his sister take Giles' arm and conduct him to the Bennets and the others.

A dozen thoughts and emotions fought for precedence in his mind. She had made her choice, apparently choosing a man who felt deeply for her as well, but it was not that simple. There was the family to consider; their expectations would predispose them to reject the match. There was the matter of income, of protecting her dowry, although Darcy did not believe the man was a fortune hunter. He could easily have taken advantage of his actions the summer before had he wanted to. There was the wrench of letting his sister go to another man's care after so many years of watching over her. And there was Wickham.

"Feeling a little fatherly, Fitzwilliam?"

His aunt's voice sounded both sympathetic and amused. He saw that she was watching Georgiana in a speculative fashion.

"I am afraid so."

"Well, it is only to be expected. When you requested I invite the young man I thought I had heard his name before. Georgiana told us of him after the incident with Sir Frederick. It is a shame their fathers do not get on well. Viscount Tennerley could be of assistance if the families were closer."

"I wonder if Mr. Worthington would accept assistance if it were offered?"

Lady Matlock shrugged. "There's no money, of course, or not much. The estate is small, it came to Worthington senior through his marriage. As you may have surmised, Mrs. Worthington was Viscount Tennerley's sister. The family did not approve of her choice."

He could not help thinking that the situation might be in the process of repeating itself. Darcy thought it time to change the subject.

"Where is my uncle?"

"He received a visitor a few minutes ago. He will join us shortly."

Darcy recognized his aunt's attempt to minimize the earl's absence. It was unlike him to leave guests unless some problem occurred in the House. He said as much, only to watch his aunt's face turn momentarily bitter.

"Not that house."

The subject of their discussion entered the room at that point, and Lady Matlock went to her husband, leaving Darcy puzzled. They spoke briefly, the earl nodding in response to his wife's words. His gaze fixed on his eldest son with a momentary scowl before he gestured to the butler, who waited in the hall.

"Dinner is served."

Darcy took Elizabeth in to dinner. Her hand rested small and light on his arm, the scent of lavender she wore intoxicated his senses. He knew current societal standards would not find her beautiful, but in his eyes she was the loveliest woman he had ever known. He wanted her there on his arm for the rest of their lives, and damn what society thought. Georgiana's soft voice came to him from behind them as they entered the dining room, only the sound, and a quiet male voice answering her. Darcy felt like a man who steps into shallow water and finds it suddenly deep enough to drown him.

As it was a party of friends and relatives precedence was only loosely observed. Lord Henry took Lady Addington in, followed by Lord Rathbone and Lady Eleanor. The rest sorted themselves out as they had been requested. Darcy found himself between Elizabeth and Mrs. Bergman-Rayles, who continued a conversation with Sir Eustace Samuelson regarding the renovation of his town home. Darcy was not sorry to be able to devote the meal to conversing primarily with Elizabeth. Mr. Worthington was seated farther down the table next to Georgiana, with Lady Addington on his other side. That was his aunt's doing, Darcy knew. If there was anything to find out about the man, that wise old lady was sure to snaffle it out.

Amid the spotless linen and shining flatware, crystal goblets and silver candelabra, the diners were surrounded by Pompeiian red walls that glowed against mahogany chairs, sideboard and side tables. A portrait of the countess' mother in a gilt frame graced an end wall between tall windows draped in fringed silk damask of a deep gold hue. Elizabeth turned her head to Darcy as he took his seat next to her.

"This is a most beautiful room. The colors are bold, but the effect is warm and comforting."

"My aunt redecorated most of the rooms after Lord Henry became earl. She updates them occasionally, keeping to the classic rather than the modern taste."

"I expect Pemberley is much the same?"

Darcy told her of Pemberley; of his mother's love for the gardens, especially the rose garden, of the renovations that had already been accomplished, and those he planned for the future including an enlargement of the glasshouses. Mrs. Bergman-Rayles, who possessed a strong interest in decorating, offered a few suggestions and the name of a decorator she used extensively. From interiors the subject transmuted naturally to gardens and then exteriors in general.

"I loved the terrace at the Twickenham house." Elizabeth spoke softly so her dinner partner did not overhear the comment. "I have never seen any other so lovely."

"I was impressed with it myself when I first viewed the house." Darcy took a sip of his wine to hide the shadow of guilt and longing in his eyes.

"You might put in such a terrace at Pemberley if you have a place for it."

Controlling a sudden bitterness, Darcy said neutrally "I have nothing but space."

The dinner continued. Altogether they passed a pleasant time. On her far side Sir Eustace, perhaps overloaded with advice on paint, wallpaper and furnishings, turned to Mr. Bingley across from him for more manly conversation.

It was only when the ladies retired and footmen brought out the decanters of port and brandy with boxes of cigars that Darcy realized Lord Henry and his eldest son were both absent. Bingley approached him, glass in hand, untouched. He seemed vexed and a little embarrassed. He sipped the wine as if his throat was dry before setting the glass down.

"I apologize for bringing this up now, Darcy, but I will have to make a decision shortly. I have not heard from Caroline since she moved to the house in Meridian Square, but my accountant advised me this morning that she has asked for a £1,000 advance. How in Heaven's name can my sister have acquired such a debt?"

Darcy felt a familiar frustration at the quandary his friend was in. He answered cautiously not wanting to sound judgmental. "Caroline has always been extravagant. Perhaps she decided to redecorate the rooms and got in deeper than she expected."

"One thousand pounds deeper? No, Darcy, something is wrong. I need to find out what she has done without contacting her directly."

"And then?"

Bingley was silent for several moments. "It will have to come from her principal. She cannot repay such a sum from the interest, she needs that just to live on. And I will not give her the money. She knew when she moved out that she must handle her own funds. My accountant is ready to help her, but she has not requested assistance, until now."

There was more Bingley wanted to say. Darcy sipped his own drink and waited. His friend gathered himself, picked up his glass and then put it down again.

"I was speaking to Sir Eustace Samuelson during dinner. He is a widower and wishes to remarry, but not, in his words, 'one of those sugar confections of a debutante'. He is not young or a pink of the *ton*, but he is a baronet with a home in London and an estate in Berkshire. He wants, he says, a woman with spirit, and requires only enough dowry to 'sweeten the pot'. I am debating introducing him to Caroline. If they suited it could solve several problems."

Interested, Darcy considered. "How would you introduce them if you have no contact with your sister?"

"When my accountant refuses to advance her the money, she will come to me. I shall tell her she cannot have the money, and if her dowry is lessened by much more, she will be lucky to ever marry. She is five-and-twenty, I ought to have done this long ago." Bingley finished his port in one swallow. "I wish you would marry, Darcy, and end her obsession that you will offer for her."

His voice bordered on anger, but Darcy knew it was not directed at him. "Caroline's marriage seems an option that would do well for all of you. Let me know if I can be of any assistance."

Bingley nodded. He moved to the far end of the table where the gentlemen were debating the relative merits of Cuban and Philippine tobacco for cigars. Darcy felt some optimism that his friend had finally conquered his natural instinct to protect his sister, a need he could understand even in Miss Bingley's case.

Bingley had barely joined the group of men when he was nearly knocked down by Lord Brentmore, who cannoned into the room in what Darcy recognized was a blind rage. The viscount muttered a quick apology, went to the table and seized a glass and the nearest decanter. The first glass went down in two gulps. He was lifting the decanter once more when Darcy took the cut glass container from him.

"Do you mind?" Darcy said it politely, just loud enough to be heard by the other gentlemen who had taken a guarded interest. With a hand on his cousin's arm he growled, "Get hold of yourself, Edmund. Do you really want speculation on your personal problems bandied about White's tomorrow?"

Edmund Fitzwilliam let his shoulders slump. Darcy refilled both glasses with a small amount of port and replaced the decanter. "Adele," her husband grated, "has been gambling again. She took that pendant she is wearing in lieu of a £2,000 wager when Lady Hatterfield could not pay in I.O.U.. Father is livid. You know how he feels about gambling, especially women gambling. It is not only the money she wastes, in this case it is potentially political. He is in sensitive negotiations regarding the war with America. Lord Hatterfield is somehow important to whatever is being discussed. A scandal now…"

The viscount downed his drink with a muttered "I need something stronger."

Darcy set his glass on the table. It was not like his cousin to lose control over a domestic problem, something more important must be at stake. Edmund had said "again." Not for the first time, Darcy silently questioned his cousin's choice of wife.

"What do you intend to do?"

The viscount had regained control of himself. He shook his head. "What can I do? Telling Adele to stop anything is useless. There has to be some sort of coercion or she simply continues until she grows bored. The ladies she plays cards with gamble for high stakes. What concerns me most is that they have lately brought in ladies who are not usually part of their circle. If any of them decide to expose the games it could become public knowledge. And you know what that means."

"Yes." Darcy did indeed know. "The public euphoria over Napoleon's defeat is subsiding. Our European allies are putting pressure on the government to field all of our military and naval forces to end this war with America."

Neither man spoke of the recent reversals England had suffered both at sea and on land, and news had not yet reached England of their loss at the Battle of Baltimore. It was proof, if such were needed, that the Americans had no intention of giving up.

"And that means an increased drain on the economy. Prices have already risen for the majority of the population, we will have bread riots and worse if it goes much farther. Not to mention the beer flood in St. Giles. Eight people dead, and who knows how much will be needed to pay for the damages. Damn it, there is enough trouble right now without having to deal with a wife who thinks of nothing but her own amusement!"

Edmund straightened, composed his face and left the dining room with the other men to rejoin the ladies in the drawing room. Darcy would have followed except Mr. Worthington had waited near the door. Darcy stopped but did not speak, allowing the younger man to initiate the conversation.

"Mr. Darcy, as I know you are aware, we must speak. This is neither the time nor place. If I might call on you at your convenience, perhaps in the next few days?"

Darcy found himself more and more impressed by Mr. Worthington. He was direct without any aggression, polite without servility. They did indeed have to talk, and with Georgiana unaware of the meeting.

"Call on me at eleven o'clock tomorrow morning. Miss Darcy practices her music in the morning, she need not know you have called."

"Thank you, sir."

Mr. Worthington stepped back and followed Darcy silently to the drawing room.

# CHAPTER FIFTEEN

October 1814
Meadow Lane, London

M r. Bingley took Elizabeth and Jane home after the dinner. He escorted them to their door but declined to come in. It was a neighborhood where anyone hearing a carriage stop at night would be inquisitive. He did not want to cause talk, returning to his conveyance as soon as the door closed and driving away.

*One day soon we will return to Hephaestus House from such events and I will not have to leave you, my angel.*

His thoughts strayed to other pleasures of marriage which occupied him for the ride home.

There had been little conversation on the way to Meadow Lane. Bingley was content to sit across from the sisters and speak quietly to Jane of the evening while Elizabeth sat silently staring at the curtained window. Her face was a pale, indistinct blur in the reflected glow through the sidelights, shadowed by the hood of her cloak. She had enjoyed her initial exchange with Mr. Darcy. It was so like their discussions—she refused to call them debates—after they first met that she could almost believe nothing between them had changed.

*He has learned to tease, at least a little. His manners have softened. He is still a proud man, but he has lost the arrogant disregard for other people I saw in Hertfordshire. He has made it his task to assist Mr. Bingley in courting Jane when he could so easily have distanced himself from what most of his class would consider a disgraceful match.*

What his family, except for Georgiana, would still consider a disgraceful match had it been Mr. Darcy who wished to marry Jane. Elizabeth jerked her thoughts away from the implication. It could never be, she was well aware it could never be. Mr. Darcy must marry where status and wealth brought a wife his family would accept, a wife with bloodlines similar to his own, with all the attributes of someone trained from childhood to act as mistress of a great estate. No, it could never be. To think of it was only to torture herself needlessly. And yet she read in those dark depthless eyes something new, something that both compelled and frightened her.

*What does he want from me? He knows we cannot marry, he made that clear some time ago. I cannot believe he would consider any other relationship. He is a gentleman, he would never...*

Elizabeth's face heated in the dark. She was grateful to realize they had reached the house in Meadow Lane as the carriage slowed. Once inside, Jane went up immediately to get ready for bed, but Elizabeth lingered in the parlor. She still had not made a decision as to her living arrangements once Jane wed. Now that Miss Bingley was no longer resident at Hephaestus House there was no problem with her living there except for her concerns about the couple's privacy. She supposed Jane might want her to accompany them on their wedding trip as it was traditional for a female relative to do. Once they returned, Elizabeth felt reluctant to remain with them until they had time to become accustomed to living together. Perhaps she might stay in Meadow Lane for a month or two and then make a decision.

Jane was already in bed when Nettie helped Elizabeth undress and put on her nightgown. She brushed out Elizabeth's hair and plaited it, hiding a yawn with a cough. Elizabeth dismissed her and blew out the candle. She felt restless and dissatisfied. She had no direction, and when Jane married, no real purpose. Elizabeth knew there was now enough money to live comfortably without depending on anyone else, especially her new brother-by-marriage. Her thoughts turned briefly to Mr. Porter, and as quickly away. Elizabeth realized her uncle and aunt expected her to marry. They would encourage her to live with the Bingleys so she might meet eligible men who did not require a large dowry or great connections.

Elizabeth had said as much earlier in the evening. The only respectable life for a lady of small fortune was marriage. Yet the idea of picking a husband like an apple—not too large or too small, too green or too ripe, no visible imperfections—left her hollow. Elizabeth knew she could never be happy or respectable unless her partner in life was her superior in knowledge and understanding. Nor could she accept the role of compliant wife with no interest in anything but her home and children. She must always be able to learn, to grow, to use her brain, and her husband must understand and encourage her thirst for knowledge.

Elizabeth crossed the room with its vague shapes and moved the drapes on the window enough to look out into the yard. The black outline of the old stable seemed to sag a little on the lucent purple of the sky. A few clouds hung loosely at the horizon, gray and undefined. She closed the drapes against a chill draft and got into bed, Jane's soft breathing assuring her of her sister's deep sleep. Elizabeth settled carefully so as not to disturb her. She tried to sleep, but the night held no rest for her. Her dreams were of soft black curls and dark eyes, ever turning away from her.

## October 1814
## Darcy House, London

The morning after the Matlock dinner party found Darcy in the masculine sanctuary of his study. A fire burned in the hearth, for the weather had turned cold and snow threatened. He sat behind the massive desk in his large leather chair, the early post sorted into neat stacks before him. He had intended to devote the time between breakfast and his appointment with Mr. Worthington to dealing with the less important matters. Instead, Darcy could not settle his mind to business.

He knew Georgiana was determined in her choice and could not be swayed. He knew Worthington was a gentleman by birth and nature. While a designer of steam engines was not a tradesman, the profession walked the invisible line dividing craftsman or artisan from men of independent fortune. Men like Watt, Trevithick and Fulton were paragons, universally admired for their achievements. But they were also supported by patrons or government funding. And Mr. Worthington, however great his talent, was far from achieving such a status.

The hall clock struck eleven. Mr. Burgess tapped on the door and brought in a silver salver with a calling card. Darcy took it, straightening in his chair. It was of moderate quality, simply printed: Giles Worthington, High Coombe Farm, Cornwall. The young man followed, bowing as Darcy rose. Darcy returned his bow with an inclination of his head and gestured to one of the chairs in front of the desk. He did not offer Worthington a drink, nor did the young man seem to expect any special courtesy. He took the chair and Darcy resumed his seat, folding his hands on the leather writing pad.

"Before anything else is said, Mr. Darcy," Worthington began, "I wish to thank you for seeing me. I understand how easily you could have refused."

"I am not one to ignore a situation as important to my sister's future as this appears to be."

Darcy watched Worthington's face. The man was not as calm as he appeared. His hands resting on his thighs were curled as if they would form fists, but his voice was even.

"Miss Darcy is a lovely, accomplished, gentle young lady. To her credit, she is not familiar with the less savory side of life in the *ton*. I can readily understand how she might be taken in by a fortune hunter if he convinced her he felt true affection for her. And I also understand your reluctance to trust my motives as I am not wealthy or socially prominent."

Darcy recognized the sincerity of the words but he remained wary. "Since you appreciate my reservations, Mr. Worthington, perhaps you will tell me what your intentions are?"

"Honorable, I assure you." For the first time a hint of wry humor colored Worthington's voice. It was gone in an instant. "I am requesting the privilege of calling on Miss Darcy, nothing more for the present. I have a career to build and that takes time. At present I cannot think of marriage, and if it should prove that Miss Darcy finds a gentleman she prefers, I do not want to obligate her in any way."

"That is admirable, Mr. Worthington." Darcy kept any shadow of sarcasm out of his voice. "She does, however, have a considerable dowry and connections that could advance your career if you married."

Worthington's face hardened. He was still polite, Darcy noted, but beneath his controlled exterior the statement had stirred anger. "I shall succeed or fail on my own merits, Mr. Darcy, not on my wife's money and social status. If you believe differently, set whatever time limit or conditions you choose."

"Or I may simply refuse you."

Darcy saw the young man's chest heave with a quick breath. "Yes, sir, you may. So long as you understand that I do not promise to go quietly away."

Darcy rang for the butler. Worthington half rose and was waved back into the chair. Mr. Burgess was requested to send in coffee. When it came and both men had a cup, Darcy sat back.

"Tell me about the engine you are designing."

## October 1814
## Hephaestus House, London

Bingley did not have long to wait for the predicted visit from his sister. She appeared at Hephaestus House two days after the Matlock dinner party, sending in her card like any other visitor. In his study,

Bingley looked at the card, sighed, and asked that she be shown in. If he expected an angry outburst, the frightened woman who took a chair before his desk was more of a shock than he admitted to himself.

"Good morning, Caroline. You are well, I hope?"

"I...no, Charles, I am—I am not ill, but I...I am in trouble."

"The thousand-pound advance you requested."

"Yes. I have to have the money, Charles, please! I owe someone who can cause me to lose whatever status I have with the *ton*!"

The desperation in her voice was real. Bingley hardened his resolve, poured a small quantity of port from the sidebar and put the glass in her hands. "Drink that, slowly, and tell me whom you owe and how you came to borrow such a sum."

Caroline sipped the wine, made a face and set the glass on the desk. "I did not borrow it. I...oh, Charles, I lost it playing cards." She would not raise her eyes or she might have seen the disgust that crossed his face.

"Gambling."

"Yes. It was just card games at first, Miss Lambert took me to an afternoon party and it seemed harmless. We have played for so much a point before within the family, and it was no higher than some of those games. Then there was another afternoon and another, and the stakes got higher and higher and I could not be seen as someone who was afraid to lose and then—"

"And then the stakes became so high that ladies were losing hundreds of pounds and you found yourself in debt and unable to pay."

She nodded, her head bowed. Charles expelled a pent breath. "Whom do you owe the money?"

"Lady Clelland." The name was barely audible.

"I shall see that she is paid. The funds will come out of the principal of your investments. That will reduce your dowry, you understand that?"

She looked up then, startled. "My dowry?"

"Yes, Caroline. You understood when you took over management

236

of your money that I was no longer obligated to pay your debts, and certainly not a gambling debt, which are legally uncollectable. You had better marry soon before you waste any more of your funds."

"But—but the little season is over, and I have not been invited to any affair where gentlemen are present. How can I meet eligible men now?"

Bingley was relieved that she did not mention Darcy. Perhaps she had finally gotten over her fantasy of his eventual proposal. Unsure of how long her penitent mood would last, he went on quickly.

"I met a gentleman at a dinner party the other night, Sir Eustace Samuelson. He is a baronet and a widower who would like to remarry. He has no interest in the debutantes of the *ton*, and he does not require a large dowry or significant connections. He is not young and he is not a beau, but he seems a good-hearted fellow. If you wish to meet him, I will arrange for both of you to be invited to one of Lady Addington's musical evenings."

She essayed a weak smile. "I would be Lady Samuelson."

"You would. And that puts you on a social par with Lady Clelland, whose husband is also a baronet."

Caroline clasped her hands in her lap. "Thank you, Charles. I should like to meet Sir Eustace."

It may have been generosity or coercion, but Bingley added, "If you marry, I shall increase your dowry by £1,000 as a wedding gift. And you may marry from Hephaestus House."

## November 1814
## Darcy House, London

"How is your wedding dress progressing?"

Georgiana Darcy poured out tea for the Bennet sisters and passed the tray of biscuits, tarts and slices of cake. They were in her private parlor on the first floor of the mansion, warmed by a fire in the hearth against the blowing snow outside. The room was a mélange of soft colors, from light apricot walls to jonquil yellow upholstery. The patterned drapes with a soft green and apricot design had been drawn against the howl of the wind. It was a room for female conversation and friendship.

"Mrs. White has it nearly ready." Jane sipped her tea with a thoughtful expression. "I can hardly believe the wedding is only a little over a month away."

"I hope there is not a problem?"

Jane smiled at Georgiana. "No, it is just—oh, it sounds silly, but I want to give Mr. Bingley a wedding gift, and I cannot think of anything appropriate."

"Jane does such beautiful needlework, I have suggested handkerchiefs with both their initials embroidered on them, but she does not think that a suitable wedding gift."

There was no resentment in Elizabeth's words. She understood her sister's desire to give her fiancé a memorable wedding present, but while they were not poor, with the trousseau and Mrs. White's charge for the wedding gown, an expensive gift was out of the question.

"If it was his birthday, Lizzy, it would be perfectly suitable, but this is our wedding. I want to give Mr. Bingley something memorable."

Georgiana sipped her tea in contemplation. She set the cup aside and folded her hands in her lap. "What about a miniature of yourself that he can carry with him when he is away from home?"

Both sisters stared at her, speaking over each other.

"What a wonderful idea!"

"A miniature would be perfect, but are they not very expensive?"

Georgiana smiled complacently. "Not if you have a friend who paints and would love to do a miniature of you. Excuse me for a moment."

She left the room to her guests, both contemplating whether they could afford a professional painting. Georgiana returned with a small oval frame she handed to Jane. "I did that of Fitzwilliam last year. I take it with me everywhere so that he is always with me."

Jane held the little portrait so that her sister could see it. It was a wonderful likeness, the dark curls and bold face with its impenetrable eyes. Elizabeth's fingers tingled with the urge to hold the painting; if it were hers she would never let it out of her sight. She sat straighter. Jane returned it to Georgiana with an awed countenance.

"It is a wonderful portrait, Georgiana. But I cannot ask you to go to so much trouble—"

"It is no trouble at all. I love to paint, I have done several paintings of the gardens at Pemberley, but this is my first attempt at a portrait, so I will not promise perfection. Seriously, Jane, I would love to do a miniature for Mr. Bingley's wedding gift."

"I cannot think of a better solution, Jane." Elizabeth's gaze fell on the miniature then she purposely looked away. "It will be the perfect gift."

"Then it is settled." Georgiana refreshed their tea. "I will make some sketches before you go and you can sit for me the next time you visit. It will be such great fun."

Jane's face glowed with happiness as she thanked their friend. For Elizabeth, although she was happy for Jane and grateful to Georgiana, it was one more reminder that in a little more than a month, for the first time in her life she would be alone.

"Was it not most generous of Georgiana to offer to paint the miniature?"

"Most generous."

The carriage rattled and jingled over the cobbles to an accompaniment of vendors' cries. Elizabeth had become so accustomed to the noise she no longer heard it except as a rise and fall of strident voices.

*How could I have let myself feel such an attraction to a man I can never have? I long for his presence, his conversation, I cannot cast him from my mind or my dreams. He has been so kind to Jane, I can hardly refuse to see him, Jane would wonder at my reasons. As soon as the wedding is over, I must separate myself from him, even if it means seeing less of Jane and Mr. Bingley. Perhaps I can go away for a while, anywhere he will not be.*

"Is something wrong, Lizzy?"

Jane's concerned voice broke her thoughts. Elizabeth forced a smile. "I was just thinking about the wedding."

"I am the one who is supposed to worry about that!"

Jane's laugh restored her but in the back of her mind Elizabeth determined to speak to her uncle about a place where she might at least temporarily find peace. The carriage turned into the driveway on Meadow Lane and a hansom passed sedately by and continued on. It was not unusual to see a hansom or even a hackney go by and the wind drove the sisters into the house without noticing its presence.

## November 1814
## Darcy House, London

"I am glad you were able to come today. The storm has closed a good many streets in and around London."

Settled on the sofa in the drawing room, Elizabeth experienced a spreading warmth at the deep timbre of Darcy's voice. "I do not think I could have gone another day without leaving the house, if only to walk."

"Better to ride, especially as it is still so cold. It will freeze tonight I warrant."

Bingley sat across from Jane, his eyes never leaving her pink face. Darcy made a small gesture with one hand as if putting aside such concerns. "I have no doubt it will be a hard winter. According to Mrs. Reynolds the walnut trees at Pemberley dropped their crop early."

"Does she prognosticate the weather by the fall of walnuts?"

Bingley was smiling rather foolishly. Elizabeth glanced at Darcy. He took his friend's mood in stride.

"When the walnuts and other winter nuts drop their crops early, it is a sign that the weather will turn cold earlier than usual. Take that as the experience of a lifelong farmer."

"That is what my father always said as well. He seemed to be right, although he did not know why it was so."

"I like a good chestnut stuffing for the Christmas goose," Bingley said.

Darcy grinned but made no comment, which caused Elizabeth to giggle.

"What?"

Bingley did not sound offended, only puzzled, and Jane quirked a brow at her sister.

"I was just wondering which goose you were stuffing, the one on the board or at the table?"

Elizabeth would never have assayed such a jest at Netherfield, but she had learned her brother-to-be did not take offense where none was intended.

"Just for that," Bingley rose, "I am going to ask Miss Bennet to sit in the music room with me, as Mrs. Annesley is there to act as chaperone."

He took Jane's hand and helped her to her feet. Jane was smiling at the ploy. Elizabeth looked a question at Darcy as they departed. "Mrs. Annesley?"

"Georgiana is with our aunt at Matlock House this afternoon. I hope she does not say too much before anything is settled."

"Forgive me if I am intruding on private matters, but I do not understand."

Darcy drew a long breath, let it out and looked at his hands resting on his thighs. "I have given permission for a young gentleman to call on my sister. His father is a minor landowner and his uncle is a viscount, one for whom I hold no particular respect. He is beginning a career designing steam engines. He has said that he cannot marry for some time, and does not want to obligate Georgiana with a betrothal. He is a man of honor who did her a great service last summer. However, there are problems."

"Your family."

Elizabeth hoped no bitterness colored her words. If there was, Darcy did not appear to hear it.

"Yes. There have long been certain expectations for Georgiana when she marries."

"As there are for you," Elizabeth murmured.

Silence held for a heartbeat before he continued. "Yes. An engineer is not a tradesman, however he designs engines and perhaps equipment used in trade. Unless he achieves the level of a Watt or Trevithick he is always obligated to the control of whomever employs him."

"In other words, however skilled or talented he may be, an engineer must still accept money for his work. He is never entirely his own man."

"Exactly. Georgiana has made up her mind that this is the man she will marry. I have said in the past that I will not force her to marry against her will. I may have to say as well that I will not try to force her to give up a gentleman against her will."

"You would do that for her? Stand against your family so she may be happy?"

"It seems so." His tone was wry, but the words were firm with purpose. "She is my sister. Why would I want anything but happiness in marriage for her?"

Elizabeth did not answer. He would stand against his relatives to ensure Georgiana's happiness, but not his own. Or perhaps duty was his idea of happiness. To be respected, even revered, rather than loved. He was the last of the Darcys, the continuation of an ancient line depended on his sons. Why would he not choose that heavy responsibility rather than his own personal felicity?

"Elizabeth?"

Darcy leaned toward her, his expression questioning. Elizabeth made her mouth smile in spite of the emptiness hollowing her chest.

"Forgive me. I was thinking of the weight that rests on you for Georgiana's future."

"She has taken that into her own hands. Our aunt already knows about the incident last summer so it will not come as a complete shock. My uncle is a different matter."

Darcy turned over in his mind telling Elizabeth about Sir Frederick and decided she was completely trustworthy. In concise sentences he relayed the facts. Elizabeth was more shocked than he expected.

."That is why his father sent him away."

"Yes. His wife was threatening to create scandal and ruin Georgiana. He knew if he did not do something, I would." Darcy's face turned grim. "I have financial connections that are not common knowledge. It is possible to ruin any man if he is already in debt."

Elizabeth was perhaps more shocked by Darcy's statement than by the act that had engendered it. It was a side of him she had not seen before, hard, unforgiving. Even though it was in defense of his sister it showed her a man capable of acting with cold purpose to achieve his ends. She found she had folded her arms around herself protectively and allowed them to fall back in her lap.

"Apparently it was not necessary."

"Fortunately not." The subject seemed to upset her. Darcy determined to change the conversation to something less personal. "Have you read Walter Scott's *Waverley*?"

"Not yet. I believe it was published earlier this year and sold out immediately."

"I have a copy I will loan you if you like?"

Elizabeth smiled with pleasure. "I would like that very much."

"I think you will enjoy it. I found it well written and more complicated than most of the novels I have indulged in. It is a story of conflicting loyalties and shows more tolerance to all classes of people than is usual. Its conclusion is a bit fanciful but satisfying. Perhaps we can discuss it when you have finished the book."

Elizabeth acquiesced and asked if he had read Lord Byron's poetry novel *The Corsair*. Darcy acknowledged he had, although Byron was not a favorite of his. He asked her opinion of the work.

"I have read it is in part biographical. I find his work interesting however as you know, I favor Mr. Wordsworth. I have recently read *The Excursion*."

"And I imagine you felt some sympathy with the Wanderer."

"Indeed. I would love to step out of my house and walk as I used to. But I prefer country roads to public ones."

Literature occupied them until Bingley returned and Mr. Burgess announced nuncheon was served in the dining room. They sat down to cold meats, fruits, cheeses and breads in the beautifully appointed dining room, without Hephaestus House's prevalent atmosphere of too much carving, decoration, pattern, gilt and colors squabbling with each other for precedence.

"Jane will redecorate our homes after we are married." Bingley waved a hand that encompassed the room as well as the house in general. "We both admire Darcy House." He smiled at his fiancée, who pinked prettily. "I believe our tastes in décor are much alike and quite a bit simpler."

"Have you heard from Miss Bingley?"

Elizabeth knew Jane was concerned for Caroline in spite of her attempts to stop the engagement. Bingley glanced at Darcy before he answered.

"She came to see me. She is having trouble managing her finances. It is past time she married. I intend to introduce her to Sir Eustace Samuelson. If they suit, I will encourage the match."

"The gentleman who was at the dinner party at Lady Matlock's?"

"Yes, my angel. He is a solid man of good reputation. Caroline has agreed to the introduction. We shall see what comes of it."

Elizabeth briefly met Darcy's gaze. It was as usual difficult to read, although she thought she saw something of relief in it. Surely he would be pleased to be free of her useless expectations. At least, Elizabeth thought, she was not deceiving herself about his feelings for her. She accepted they could never be more than friends. At her nod a footman poured wine into her glass. Elizabeth took a swallow and her eyes met Darcy's once more. The half-smile faded from her lips, she dropped her gaze immediately. Darcy took a sip of his own wine and concentrated on his meal. The heat that washed through him radiated to her and she felt her hands begin to tremble. Jane's soft voice rescued her.

"I hope Caroline is happy when she marries. It would be sad if she was disappointed in her husband."

"I should worry more about the husband," Bingley said lightly. "She would be Lady Samuelson, a step up in social value at least in her eyes. I suppose I shall have to call her 'my lady'."

His jest allowed the two at the table with agitated emotions to rejoin the flow of conversation. Darcy silently cursed himself for his lack of self-control; Elizabeth was careful for the remainder of the visit to keep her attention on Jane and Bingley and away from Darcy.

In the library of Darcy House, Elizabeth perused the shelves in search of a section of plays she was certain resided there somewhere. She had known her father's library by heart, including certain locked cases that were vulnerable to a skilled hairpin. The Netherfield library had been a jumble of fiction, history, agricultural treatises, memoirs and a few philosophical works, in no particular order. Mr. Darcy's library was the opposite. It was precisely ordered and obviously kept current to new acquisitions, as she had not only found Louisa Stanhope's *Madelina: A Tale Founded on Fact*, which had been out for a time, but a volume on Australia just published the previous month. Elizabeth's problem was a lack of knowledge of the system he used.

"May I find something for you, Miss Elizabeth?"

Elizabeth turned sharply at the sound of Darcy's polite enquiry. It took her only a moment to recover her poise. He stood a little way from her, towering in the flat light from arched windows in the two bays.

"I was looking for plays. I wanted to read *The Platonick Lovers* by Sir William Davenant. Lady Addington said Jane and Mr. Bingley reminded her of two secondary characters."

Darcy looked nonplussed. "Did she?" He moved along the cases and Elizabeth followed. Darcy reached out a long arm and plucked a narrow volume from an upper shelf. "This is an early copy from the 1636 printing. The language is rather old fashioned but quite clear." He handed her the book watching her take it carefully in both hands. "I am afraid it is in part a satire of Plato's notion of platonic love."

"That would not affect me." Elizabeth raised her head and Darcy fought to keep his expression detached. "Philosophy was never an interest of mine, and while my father taught me to read Latin, he was unsuccessful in teaching me to read Greek."

"From lack of desire to learn it, or lack of ability to decipher the alphabet?"

"From lack of application. There were too many other employments I preferred, and Greek poetry and plays have been translated a number of times."

She returned her attention to the slim volume she held. Darcy was unable to take his gaze from the curve of her cheek and the delicate shell of her ear, brushed by a stray onyx curl. His hand was half-way to brushing it behind her ear when she looked at him again. Darcy turned the gesture into pushing a book an inch back into place.

"You said it is a satire?"

"And a tragicomedy and an examination of Plato's idea of platonic love, which was then popular at the royal court of Queen Henrietta Maria. She had been raised in the French court where the notion of courtly love was in vogue."

"Sir William must have been clever if he satirized a movement the queen admired without losing his head."

"Apparently he was. When you have read it, you must tell me what you think of it."

"Of the play, or Platonic love?"

She was teasing now, her eyes sparkling. Darcy felt his chest tighten, he pressed his hands hard to his sides. He wanted to take her in his arms and kiss her into submission before he carried her upstairs to his bed. Instead, he held tightly to his hard-won control. If his voice was strained, he hoped fervently she did not notice.

"Either. Both."

"Courtly love seems to have come from Plato's idea of a loving friendship. My father was a scholar, he was fluent in Greek and read the philosophers in the original language. He explained it to me although I think he left parts of it out. As I said, I have never had an interest in philosophy."

"Why not?" Darcy had his voice under control. "You like to study character I know."

Elizabeth tipped her head a little to one side. "Society changes. People are forever altering. Are you the man you were at eighteen?"

"Essentially, yes. I am. Society changes, human nature does not. However I agree that no one stays the same over a lifetime. And some of the changes are in response to how society itself alters." *At eighteen I would not have considered having a close friendship with a tradesman's son. I would not have considered a minor gentleman's daughter as a wife under any circumstances. I have grown wiser.*

"So a philosophy that seeks to answer all the questions of human behavior is bound to be temporary at best."

"If that is what it does, yes. Plato speaks to various stages of love, and how they develop from what might be called carnal love to a love of the divine."

Elizabeth leaned her shoulder against the bookshelf, contemplating. "I do not think that love can be so easily classified, neatly boxed and put on a shelf. One can love a friend without feeling any desire for him." If she intended the pronoun she gave no indication of it. "There was a long list of elements to a Platonic friendship, I do not remember all of them, but two I found most important were trust and honesty."

"Loyalty, mutual understanding, the ability to freely express oneself without fear of judgment." He was talking to her as he might talk to another man. It was exhilarating, and in their case it was dangerous. "Do you not believe such a friendship is possible?"

"Between close relations it may be. But I do not think anyone ever discloses their deepest thoughts or feelings, it gives away too much of one's soul."

"Is that not what Plato saw as the goal of love, the joining of two souls in search of ultimate truth?"

Elizabeth did not look at him. "Even if he spoke of love, Plato was a man speaking to men. Women have never been included in that rarified plane of existence, even queens. I understand Henrietta Maria absorbing herself in courtly love and other distractions. Queens, like other wives, are not allowed to participate in matters of state business or, I imagine, any other concerns relegated to men."

"My wife will be if that is her choice."

Elizabeth turned away, holding the book against her chest. "She will be a fortunate woman."

Darcy said to keep her from going, "Do you not believe you may marry such a man?"

"I have no intention of marrying."

Elizabeth stopped near the door but did not face him. Darcy followed cautiously, not wanting to drive her away. "Why not? Are you afraid of being subject to the will of a man who will allow you no independence of thought or action? Not all men are tyrants. Surely your uncle is not. Can you not believe in a man who will love you for who you are, not whom he wants you to be?"

"Love has a price. Love always has a price. Friendship may benefit both parties, but love demands its due. I have paid enough, I will pay no more. Thank you for the book."

She was gone on the words. Darcy heard their pain; he also heard an undernote of rage he had never heard before. He would hear it one more time.

## December 1814
## Bond Street, London

"There," Mrs. Gardiner expressed her satisfaction, "your trousseau is finished and will be delivered in two days. All that is left is to pick up a few items at the milliner and everything will be ready for your wedding."

Jane smiled at her aunt's enthusiasm. "I cannot thank you enough, aunt, for overseeing the wedding breakfast. I know it has taken you away from your family more than I would wish."

"I am quite used to being away from home when it is necessary. Nanny is very capable of caring for the children, and we will want a governess for Melissa this year. I expect your uncle will see to a tutor for Ned as well. So I shall be less engaged with day-to-day matters of their education. I am quite enjoying myself."

The doorway of the milliner's shop was a few steps ahead of them when a too familiar form emerged. Caroline Bingley started past them, stopped, and actually smiled.

"Good morning Miss Bennet, Miss Elizabeth, Mrs. Gardiner. I expect you are shopping for Miss Bennet's wedding clothes?"

"For some accessories," Mrs. Gardiner answered politely. Her expression showed none of the wariness she felt. "Will you be able to attend the wedding?"

"Oh, yes, thank you. My fiancée and I will be in attendance. You do know I am engaged to be married?"

"Yes," Jane responded in her soft voice. "Mr. Bingley informed us. Congratulations."

"Thank you. Sir Eustace is a wonderful gentleman, so considerate. We are redecorating his town house on Bremen Mews. Such a beautiful home! And of course there is his estate in Berkshire. I cannot wait to see it."

"I wish you every happiness," Jane said sincerely.

"Oh, I shall be quite happy. I shall have to have new visiting cards printed, of course: Lady Caroline Samuelson."

"That will be quite a triumph." Elizabeth kept any sarcasm carefully restrained. "I am sure all of your friends will be pleased for you."

Caroline smiled in condescension. With a few conventional pleasantries she departed. The three ladies continued into the millinery shop. "I do hope she will have a good marriage." Jane stopped to look at a tray of gloves. "Perhaps once there are children Caroline will understand how important family is."

Elizabeth doubted it but did not say so. Mrs. Gardiner was already perusing lace to match the wedding gown; the lace would be placed over Jane's coiffure in the new fashion that was supplanting the traditional wedding bonnet. Jane touched a pair of kidskin gloves wistfully before joining her aunt. When she was absorbed in the lace on display, Elizabeth quietly picked up the gloves and took them to an assistant for purchase. They would make a perfect Christmas gift.

*Let Caroline preen and think herself above others. It is my dearest Jane who will know contentment in marriage and the love of a truly good man.*

Unlike herself. Not for the first time Elizabeth felt a great emptiness fill her. She had fought the growing awareness that her feelings for Mr. Darcy were more than friendship. He was the only man she had ever felt that sort of affection for, and he was as far beyond her as a distant oasis seen from the heat of scorching sands. She must get away before the strain of meeting him simply as a friend overcame her and she betrayed herself.

When Elizabeth spoke to her uncle that evening after dinner, he was less encouraging than she had hoped.

"My dear, winter is not the best time to travel. The roads can be treacherous, and the seaside is not pleasant, sometimes storms make it actually dangerous. We had hoped you would stay through Christmastide. In spring there are many choices of places to visit. I am certain you would enjoy a trip then much more than at present."

Elizabeth acquiesced, whether from a sense of inevitability or for other reasons she did not wish to examine closely. She had begun to feel as if her life had been thrown into a whirlwind, tumbled madly here and there until she only recognized bits and pieces of who she was and who she had been. There was nothing solid, nothing to hold on to. Elizabeth could only push herself through one day after another until she found a way to escape the chaos. It was her only hope.

Somewhere in the depths of her unconscious mind the dark thing stirred from its quiescence.

# CHAPTER SIXTEEN

December 1814
Gardiner Residence, London

"I had a letter from Catherine in the late post."

The three ladies sat in the drawing room after dinner, drinking tea and discussing plans for Jane's wedding. Both sisters knew their aunt was pleased with their younger sister's situation, and would reveal any news from Manchester. She sipped her tea before she continued.

"Mr. Thurgood's factory is doing well. He wants to continue to modernize as soon as it is feasible. He has added another new loom and hired several more workers. He is becoming a fixture in the local community."

"Do they live in the city?"

Mrs. Gardiner reached to refill Jane's cup. "No, a town a short way north called Bury. It is a center of cotton weaving. They have a cottage there, near Mr. Thurgood's business."

"It must be very different from either London or Hertfordshire."

Mrs. Gardiner agreed. "Manchester is a large city, although not nearly as large as London, but there are towns and villages around it that extend north and east, and even south into Cheshire. It may one day rival London as a center of commerce."

Elizabeth refused a second cup of tea setting her cup back on the tray. It was strange to think of their light-hearted sister living in such a place, a wife and one day a mother. Everything had changed for Kitty also, but her life had stabilized with marriage to a man of business. A man with his mind and energies always on his financial affairs, his wife an adjunct rather than a partner in their lives. Elizabeth vowed that was not to be her fate.

"Lizzy? Is something wrong? You are frowning so."

Mrs. Gardiner touched her arm in concern. Elizabeth immediately shook herself free of her personal thoughts to respond. "I am sorry, Aunt, I have a slight headache."

"I think we should return home." Jane replaced her cup. "We can call again when my trousseau arrives."

"Of course." Mrs. Gardiner rang for the butler and requested the carriage. "I imagine you both require a day to rest. The tenth will come before you know it."

Jane laughed a little nervously. Elizabeth was silent. She slept later than usual the next morning. At breakfast Jane watched her sister nibble at a piece of toast, leaving half of it to finish her tea. She had begun to wonder if her wedding was affecting Elizabeth more than she wanted to reveal. Jane knew her sister was happy for her, however the marriage meant major changes not only in her life but in Elizabeth's. They were the last two of five sisters still in close contact. Instead of the family remaining together as one sister after another married, it had been ripped apart by an act of selfish defiance. Two of their sisters had married respectably and were happy in their situations. She was to marry a man she loved dearly. Yet Lizzy, who had always been so independent, so unwilling to surrender her independence, seemed more alone than Jane had ever imagined she might be. And Lydia still hovered over their lives like a vengeful ghost.

In the parlor the two sisters settled to the task of replacing the black lace and ribbons on their half-mourning gowns. Nettie had very carefully removed the trimmings as Jane had shown her. They had bought new lace and ribbon on their shopping trip with their aunt that must now be attached. It was calm, domestic work either could have accomplished from the age of twelve. Instead, as Jane chose a length of lace and began to stitch, she surreptitiously watched Elizabeth sort through their purchases as if she had never seen them before.

"If you cannot find something to match your green silk, perhaps one of the laces I chose will do."

Elizabeth raised her head sharply. She picked up a delicate ivory lace and placed it against the sleeve. "Thank you, dearest, but this is the one I bought for the green. I think it will look well."

"Very well."

Jane put in a few stitches, turning a little to make use of the gray light seeping through the side window. A fire snaffled over coal in the grate, emitting an acrid essence that permeated the room. Nettie had tried to adjust the draft without success.

"Will you stay here after I marry, Lizzy?"

Elizabeth did not look up. "For a short time at least. I have talked to uncle Gardiner about taking rooms, but nothing has been decided. I think I may take a trip in the spring, perhaps to the seaside. We only saw the ocean once when Papa took us to Ramsgate that summer, and I was so young I hardly remember what it was like."

"Charles wants to take me to the Lake District on our wedding trip and then to Scarborough to meet his mother and aunt and cousins. I was hoping you would accompany us. I should like his family to meet you."

"When will you go?"

"Oh, in the late spring or early summer, when the roads improve. Please think about it, Lizzy. We both would love to have you with us."

Elizabeth continued her sewing. After a moment she said, "I will think about it."

If she accompanied Jane and Mr. Bingley on their wedding trip it would inevitably lead to her moving in with them. Elizabeth knew it was what they wanted; was it what she wanted? She would see Mr. Darcy from time to time, attend an occasional soirée or ball where he

was present, perhaps an opera or play. She would see the announcement of his betrothal to a lady of society and attend his wedding with
Mr. Bingley and Jane. Then she would return to her life as a guest in
her sister's home, or leave London for some quiet place in the country where she could make a life of books and walks and dreams.

There was a knock on the front door. Nettie scurried to answer it and
returned with a small package. "This came by messenger for you, madam."

She handed the paper-wrapped box to Jane and reluctantly
turned to leave when Jane said, "You may stay, Nettie. It is my wedding gift for Mr. Bingley."

The paper tore away to reveal a leather case. Elizabeth leaned forward as Jane opened it on a miniature in a silver frame. Nettie caught
her breath. Even Elizabeth, who had seen the completed miniature,
felt a sense of awe.

"Oh, madam," Nettie breathed, "its wonderful."

"It is perfect, dearest. Mr. Bingley will treasure it."

Jane gazed at her image as Georgiana had captured it, held in the
delicate silver frame. "It could not be better if a professional artist
had painted it. Georgiana has a true gift."

She closed the case carefully and set it aside. Nettie remembered
to curtsy before she left them. Jane brushed the tears from her lashes
and smiled. "Oh, Lizzy, I am so happy. It almost frightens me."

"Be happy, dearest. You deserve all the happiness in the world."

Elizabeth picked up her sewing again, her mind a little more at
ease. There was time to make decisions about the future after Jane
was settled. Until then she determined to concentrate on the preparations for the wedding and on her sister's felicity.

## December 1814
## Darcy House, London

Darcy looked up from his silent contemplation of the book in
his lap at the sound of a familiar voice. He was on his feet before

Mr. Burgess tapped at the door, striding to meet his cousin at the threshold.

"Richard! You did not let me know you were coming to Town."

The cousins shook hands cordially as Mr. Burgess closed the door. Darcy indicated the sidebar. "Help yourself, not that you would not anyway. How is Anne?"

"Doing very well. She has improved over the summer, with her mother in Bath. I think she has reached a level of health that she can maintain so long as nothing happens to seriously disturb her."

Darcy refreshed his own drink and returned to his seat before the fire where Richard joined him, taking the companion chair. Darcy felt a lightening of his mood at Richard's appearance. He was reminded of his conversation with Elizabeth about Platonic friendship. Richard was not shy to point out Darcy's perceived shortcomings but he never judged.

"What of Lady Catherine? Is she settled in?"

Richard grimaced. "As I predicted, she has trouble keeping servants now that she is not mistress of an estate on which they depend. I have someone keeping watch on her, however, and if she does anything too outrageous I shall step in. Her friends engage her in social events so she is busier than she used to be. So far she has not requested additional funds, or made any attempt to contact Anne."

"Does that bother Anne?"

"I had thought it might, but apparently not." Richard took a swallow of his drink and stared at the hearthrug. "My only problem with Anne is that she wants a child."

Darcy was silent for several moments. "She must know how dangerous that would be for her."

"She knows but she is adamant that she wishes to give me an heir. Dammit, Wills, I do not want to lose her. She says she feels well enough to carry a child in spite of her condition. One reason we are here is to consult Sir Edgar Crane on the matter. I am hoping he will convince her of the risk not only to herself, but to a child."

"And if he considers it possible?"

"Then she will see an accoucheur for an opinion."

Richard finished the brandy and rose to refill his glass. Darcy watched his cousin with sympathy. Childbirth was a risk women took to provide their husbands with an heir, or because they wanted children, or in the case of the poor because they had no choice. He did not want to lose Anne either; silently he hoped Sir Edgar was able to discourage her. Richard resumed his seat and studied Darcy with a determination to change the subject.

"How is Miss Elizabeth?"

"Soon to be Miss Bennet. Her sister is marrying Bingley on the tenth. I am standing up with him. Indeed, I may have to keep him standing up."

Richard grinned. "Good man, Bingley. I think it will be a happy union. How have you progressed with Miss Elizabeth?"

The silence stretched longer this time. Richard sipped his drink and waited while Darcy swirled what was left of his brandy and said nothing. At last he drank it off in a swallow and put the glass aside.

"We have had discussions of literature and art and history and philosophy. She is amazingly well read and more logical than many men of my acquaintance. I have also been told that she has no intention of marrying. At present we are friends and no more. I do not know if it is because she finds me lacking in some way, or the result of her own parents' marriage and of her sister's defection."

The heavy damask drapes were drawn over the windows but a chill seemed to penetrate the air. Shards of firelight flickered in the glass doors of the bookcases and slid bright fingers over the shafts of silver candelabras.

"Have you proposed?"

"I have not dared." Darcy sounded bitter. "She is damaged in a way I do not understand. I am afraid if I ask her she will refuse, and then I will have to walk away, something I know I cannot do."

"There is no chance," Richard's voice halted, then continued carefully, "of my original idea being accepted?"

"To make her my mistress? It has haunted me like a nightmare I cannot forget. No, Richard, I cannot do that to her. It would be the ultimate insult after what her sister did. She would never forgive me. And I find I no longer want her in that way."

Richard nodded understanding. "Perhaps with a little time, once Miss Bennet is married, she will wish the same for herself."

"I can only hope so."

The two cousins sat in silence for a time each with his own thoughts. Darcy roused first. "Are you staying at Janus House, or with your parents?"

"Mother wanted to spend time with Anne, so we are at Matlock House. I think it best she have family around her as we have been at Rosings since last Christmas. Mother is talking of giving a Twelfth Night ball. Have you and Georgie any plans for the holidays? Where is my little bird anyway?"

"At a musicale at Mrs. Fortesque's. She will be home in an hour or so."

"She is still avoiding marriage, I take it? Perhaps it is something in the air of Town."

Darcy considered telling Richard about Mr. Worthington and rejected the idea for the moment. There would be time when everything was settled. At present the situation was nebulous enough to discourage the confidence, especially since it was Georgiana's secret more than his.

"She will make a choice in time. There is no hurry. She is not yet eighteen."

"I am glad you are not pushing her, Will. She is intelligent, once she gains confidence she will find the right man."

Richard rose and Darcy also stood, walking with his cousin out into the entry. "I am going to invite Bingley and the Bennet sisters and several others to Covent Garden this Friday to see Mozart's *The Marriage of Figaro* with Franchesci singing Figaro. Will you and Anne come?"

"If Mother has nothing else planned, of course." They shook hands again and Richard departed.

Darcy considered returning to his study, rejecting the idea. He went upstairs to his chambers and rang for Martin. When his valet was prepared for bed Darcy put on a robe and sat in a favorite chair in his bedroom, waiting until he heard Georgiana return home before he got into bed. The high canopy over his head filled with darkness as the fire died away to embers. Darcy closed his eyes only to find Elizabeth's face as he had seen it in the library, closed to him in pain and anger.

He knew then he could not wait much longer. He must take the greatest risk of his life for the greatest happiness, or the greatest, irretrievable loss.

## December 1814
## Gardiner Residence, London

"It was good of Mr. Darcy to invite aunt and uncle to join us tonight."

Jane sat still on the dressing bench in the Gardiners' spare bedroom while Elizabeth styled her hair. She was trying a new coiffure Jane had seen in a ladies magazine and while her sister's straight hair was far easier to manage than her own curls, Elizabeth wanted the look to be perfect.

"His cousin Colonel Fitzwilliam—I suppose it is just Mr. Fitzwilliam now—and his wife will be there as well as Lord and Lady Matlock and Georgiana. I believe he has also asked Lady Addington, and Caroline and her fiancé, Sir Eustace."

"I can hardly wait to see what she wears." Jane suppressed a giggle.

"Feathers are always a distinct possibility." The sisters laughed and Elizabeth stepped back. "There. What do you think?"

Jane surveyed her image in the glass. "Oh, Lizzy, will you do my hair for the wedding? This is wonderful!"

"If you wish me to."

Elizabeth began to tidy the dressing table so Jane did not see the pang of sadness she felt. She wanted her sister to marry the man she loved, she wanted above all for Jane to be happy in her choice. It was only the growing isolation Elizabeth felt that clouded her delight for her dearest sister. The trousseau had arrived as promised as well as Elizabeth's bridesmaid dress, been examined and put carefully away. The sisters were to return to the Gardiners' after the opera to stay until tomorrow. Elizabeth was glad they did not have to go back to the house on Meadow Lane so late. Nettie would have a fire lit in the bedroom but it would still be cold and empty. It was too much like the way she would live after Jane married.

A tap at the door brought their aunt's maid into the room. She assisted Elizabeth into the gown laid out on the bed, a new jonquil velvet embroidered at neck, sleeves and hem with gold thread. Elizabeth had allowed herself two new ball gowns, one of which she was holding back for a special occasion. Jane had chosen a silver brocaded Chinese satin in a soft shade of plum. It gave her pale beauty a delicate, ethereal quality.

"Oh, Jane, you look like a princess in a fairy tale. Mr. Bingley will be enchanted."

Jane blushed at her sister's comment. "I feel like a princess in a fairy tale, saved by the handsome prince." She took Elizabeth's hands. "I only wish you find your own prince soon."

"I am not made for fairy tales." Elizabeth squeezed her hands. "Now let us go before our aunt grows vexed with us for being late."

They gathered their cloaks and reticules and left the bedroom together descending the stairs with Jane in the lead. Elizabeth felt weary rather than bitter. *Life is not a fairy tale. My prince will never marry the scullery maid. As soon as the wedding is over he will go back to his own sphere and I shall see little of him. Perhaps after all that is for the best.*

Darcy and Bingley waited for them inside the brilliantly lit theater. The men shook hands with Mr. Gardiner and after an exchange of pleasantries Darcy offered Elizabeth his arm. The Darcy box was on the second tier near the stage. Georgiana, Richard and Anne rose when they entered and Darcy effected the necessary introductions. He had hardly finished when Lady Addington came in. She took Jane's hands and kissed her cheek, bringing a blush to her face; turning to Elizabeth she scanned her pale face before smiling reassurance.

"You look stunning tonight, my dear. Are you familiar with the libretto of the opera?"

They talked of music with Georgiana while the rest of the party arrived, were welcomed by their host, and joined one conversation or another. Richard moved close to Darcy, who was having trouble concentrating on his guests. He wanted nothing more than to stand beside Elizabeth as her husband, to know they would return to Darcy House together, that she would stay with him for all their lives. Richard was watching him without seeming to. Darcy moved to stand beside his cousin so they might converse without being overheard.

"She is lovely," Richard murmured. "I am amazed some gentleman has not offered for her before now."

"Miss Elizabeth does not move in society. As I told you, she says she has no intention of marrying."

"If there is one area where I have more expertise than you, Cousin, it is with women. They have been known to say the opposite of what they think if it suits their purpose."

"Which would be?"

Darcy sounded more annoyed than he intended but Richard ignored his tone. "To hide their true feelings."

Richard returned to his wife, who was speaking to Jane as if they were old friends. Bingley had not left his fiancée's side since she arrived. As usual in her presence he looked as if he could not believe his good fortune. The others of their party had arrived with the exception of Sir Eustace and Caroline. The house lights were dimming when these last guests made their appearance. Sir Eustace apologized for their tardiness while Caroline blamed London's crowded streets for the delay. Jane's glance crossed Elizabeth's; Caroline wore a layered crepe dress the color of chartreuse liqueur adorned with gold sequins, and an orange velvet toque—a green plume of feathers bobbing against her shoulder. Neither sister dared meet the other's eyes again before the opera began.

The box easily seated twelve and more chairs might have been provided if required. Darcy knew his guests well enough to seat those with an interest in enjoying the performance in the front row and on the stage end of the second row. Caroline was seated at the far end of the second row of chairs where she was more easily able to watch the other boxes and whisper comments to her fiancé. Once the opera began Elizabeth was completely absorbed in the performance. The baritone's voice was magnificent; it soared over the audience, compelling even the noisier crowd in the pit to less disruption than usual. At the intermission, Darcy turned to Elizabeth. She was still wrapt in the splendor of the music; she put it aside slowly and smiled at him.

"It is truly the most wonderful music I have ever heard. It makes me wish I spoke Italian."

"Are you familiar with the story?"

"Georgiana explained the libretto. It seems very complicated however I find it easier to follow as I watch it on stage."

"I suppose it could be summarized as 'true love wins out in the end'."

She was silent, not meeting his eyes, not wanting him to see any trace of what she felt. "I suppose so."

"You do not believe it is true?"

"In an opera anything may happen. Life is not like that."

Elizabeth looked up as Caroline approached, smoothing her expression. "Sir Eustace has gone to get me a glass of wine. He is so thoughtful. We are to be married in the spring, so much more romantic than winter weddings I always think." She fanned herself and looked around the other boxes where people were standing in clusters talking and observing other patrons. Darcy had risen. Feeling as if everyone towered over her, Elizabeth also stood. She excused herself and went to speak to Lady Addington who was seated at the end of the row. Lord Matlock had disappeared, no doubt to obtain a drink and speak to any acquaintances he met, leaving Lady Matlock to converse with Jane and Lady Addington.

"That is a lovely gown, Miss Elizabeth," Lady Matlock smiled at her approach.

"Thank you, my lady."

"I can see that you are enjoying Mozart quite as much as my niece. This is one of my favorite operas, and Signor Franchesci is amazing."

Lady Addington glanced toward the stage. "He is certainly an improvement on the last baritone I heard sing Figaro. Of course it was at Bath, so one must take that into account."

"Perhaps he was there to take the waters," Elizabeth suggested.

Lady Addington chuckled. "He did sound rather like he was gargling."

Lady Matlock and Elizabeth chuckled in return. They discussed music until the call for the final acts of the opera. Elizabeth returned to her seat while Lady Matlock watched her thoughtfully. Lady Addington cocked her head to one side considering her friend.

"Am I reading your mind, Eleanor?"

Lady Matlock looked at her. "You have been known to do so."

"He is a fool if he does not marry her. She is exactly what Fitzwilliam needs, hang her status. She is gently born, and the last thing he requires is more money. He needs a wife who will stand up to him, match his wit and pique his interest, not some languid belle with the intelligence of a potato."

Lady Matlock glanced quickly along the row of chairs to where Darcy and Elizabeth were talking, oblivious to anyone else. "She is intelligent, yes, and witty. She is also passionate although she has learned to conceal it. Fitzwilliam had best take care how he approaches her, or he may find depths to Miss Elizabeth that he is totally unprepared for."

At the far end of the row Darcy and Elizabeth were discussing the libretto. Elizabeth said, "It reminds me of Sheridan or Molière with everyone either deceiving or misunderstanding everyone else."

"An apt comparison. The play is based on a play by Beaumarchais that was in part a satire of the French government. With revolution brewing it was banned from production for some time. The satire here is rather more of nobility in general."

Elizabeth leaned a little more toward Darcy, her face alive with interest. He felt his heart speed up; he could have reached out so easily and captured her hand as she gestured.

"I suppose the idea of a servant managing his master is still revolutionary. I am certain your valet would not attempt it."

"Ah, but I am unlikely to find myself in the Count's predicament."

"I agree you are not a man to run after servant girls. But if you grew bored would you neglect your wife?"

"My wife would never bore me."

Their eyes met and held for a heartbeat, two. Elizabeth dropped her gaze, her cheeks coloring a delicate rose. What she might have answered was lost as the intermission ended and the opera began its third act. Darcy knew their conversation had nearly got away from his control. This was not a time or place for more intimate discussion. The wedding was in a few days; he would find ways to speak to her without a chaperone listening to every word.

*It must be soon. I cannot go on with this love consuming me. She is everything I have ever wanted, if I lose her...*

The scene on stage began but Darcy only saw a clear soft profile framed by ebony curls, and forced his attention to the opera he neither saw nor heard.

# CHAPTER SEVENTEEN

December 1814
Hephaestus House, London

W*ith this ring I thee wed; with my body I thee worship; and with all my worldly goods I thee endow.*
The words rang in Darcy's brain as they had since the ceremony in the Gardiners' parish church. It had been torture to stand across the small space from Elizabeth, breathtaking in a pale green sprigged muslin gown, and hear Bingley take the vows Darcy could only hope to take with Elizabeth. Walking back down the aisle with her on his arm behind the newly married couple was worse, a cruel mockery of a wedding that might never occur. She had walked beside him with a stiffness he was not accustomed to in her usually light step, her smile fixed and, he thought, forced. Her attempt to seem happy and unconcerned must have deceived most of the guests; he knew her well enough to see through it.

Now at the wedding breakfast, Darcy watched her with her aunt and uncle and wanted nothing more than to be acknowledged by her.

Elizabeth had suffered her own misery during the ceremony. Jane was radiant in cream silk embroidered with tiny white flowers and trimmed in Brussels lace, a square of lace over her golden hair. Bingley looked as if he might faint. His voice wavered at first, until he spoke the vows that bound him to his love for life when it became strong and sure, causing Darcy mouth to twitch up at the corners. Elizabeth barely heard him. She was aware of his groomsman in every cell of her body, the tall, masterful figure like a constant presence in her mind. When she must take his arm and return down the aisle behind a euphoric Bingley and a sister who seemed to float above the floor, the nearness of Darcy's body was almost more than she could bear. She would never take this walk as his bride. She could never take it as any other man's.

Her gaze went involuntarily to where he stood across the room, and as if she had issued a silent invitation Darcy crossed to where she waited with her aunt and uncle. Mr. Gardiner offered his hand, which Darcy shook. He bowed to Mrs. Gardiner who responded with a curtsey. Elizabeth also curtsied, not meeting his eyes. A footman approached with a tray of drinks. She took a cup of wine punch more for something to occupy her hands than because she wanted it. Darcy obtained a glass of port.

"The wedding breakfast is one of the finest I have ever attended." Darcy indicated the dining room and adjoining drawing room, each decorated with masses of silk ribbons and glasshouse flowers. "You are to be greatly commended, Mrs. Gardiner."

Her cheeks actually pinked at the compliment. "Mr. Bingley has an excellent staff. They have done very well indeed."

"I believe," Mr. Gardiner's eyes twinkled, "they are looking forward to welcoming their new mistress."

Elizabeth automatically turned her gaze to the corner where Miss Bingley was holding alternate court among a small cadre of her friends. Her gown was, of course, in the latest fashion and bore every frill and decoration that could be loaded onto it. Layers of embroidered pink muslin thin enough to read through fell in clouds over a purple satin full underdress with a broad lace band at the hem. Her hair was wound with green ribbons and held in place by ruby clips that matched a ruby necklace and earbobs.

"No feathers?" Elizabeth murmured. "I hardly recognized her."

"Lizzy!" The reproof in Mrs. Gardiner's voice was half-hearted. "She is your sister-by-marriage now."

Elizabeth sipped her punch. Darcy said, "Not all of us can like all our relatives." For which Elizabeth threw him a grateful glance. Their eyes held for a moment before she looked quickly away.

"I understand," he continued after a moment, "that the wedding trip is postponed until spring. Are you spending the holidays with the Bingleys, Miss Elizabeth?"

"I—no, I shall be staying with my aunt and uncle for a short time."

"We will have the holidays with Lizzy and the Bingleys," Mr. Gardiner informed him. "Our specific plans are not fixed yet."

Darcy acknowledged this with a dip of his head. "I am giving a small dinner party on the twenty-third. My sister is sending out invitations. I hope you will be able to attend?"

"We will certainly try." Mrs. Gardiner smiled, just touching Elizabeth's arm, only to have it gently withdrawn.

"I believe I will sample the food, it looks delicious."

Mr. Gardiner offered his wife his arm, and Darcy found himself alone with Elizabeth. "Would you like me to fix you a plate? We can sit at one of the tables. Bingley is from the north as you know, where they do not stand at a wedding breakfast."

He proffered his arm. Elizabeth felt no hunger, her stomach a knot under her breastbone. Still she rested her hand on the fine wool sleeve and allowed him to find a table where they could eat and talk in relative quiet. It was like stepping through a door that should have let one outside only to find oneself in another room with another door, over and over. Was it any harder than it had been all along to sit and talk to this man? She had no more answer to that question than she had a week or a month ago. But soon she would be forced to find an answer. Darcy rejoined her and she smiled as he sat down and searched for a general topic of conversation.

"I can hardly think what I shall be like when my sister marries. A greater wreck than the groom no doubt."

"Is she to marry soon?"

Darcy took a sip of wine. "No. It is simply a prospect I do not look forward to. It is a shame your other sisters could not attend the wedding."

"Mary is unable to travel with her second child due in May. Catherine's husband, Mr. Thurgood, cannot leave his commercial interests at this time."

Jane had received a short letter from Mary with the information that she was having a much harder time with this baby than with Frances. The doctor strongly advised her not to travel, especially in the cold weather. She sent love and congratulations from herself and Mr. Clarke, and the hope they would see each other soon. Catherine was a different matter. Her note expressed conventional good wishes and the short statement that her husband was too busy to leave his business at present. Jane had not expressed disappointment, but Elizabeth felt a simmering resentment. They had been at Meadow Lane looking at the post when both communications arrived.

"Lizzy, Kitty may still feel some guilt over not telling Papa about Lydia's attachment."

"He always believed she knew more than she admitted. How could she not when she and Lydia always had secrets between them?"

Jane considered a moment. "I do not believe she knew of the elopement. That would have been more than Kitty was willing to conceal."

"No," Elizabeth agreed, "but she knew they were meeting secretly. She had to. Lydia could never have kept such a triumph to herself."

"But they were never seen together in Meryton, surely we would have heard of it."

Elizabeth's face was grim. "Yes, if they met openly. I have wondered about that. I do not for a moment think the whole thing was accomplished the sen'night Lydia was in Brighton. She was foolish, but she was enjoying herself too much to race off with Wickham in such a short time."

"You do not think someone …"

Jane's voice trailed off, her face paling in shock. Elizabeth took her sister's hand and squeezed it. "I do not know, dearest. We shall probably never know. Let us put aside the past and concentrate on the future."

Elizabeth returned to the present and she smoothed her expression, however Darcy heard the edge of bitterness in her voice. Apparently one sister had decided to distance herself from her family, or her husband had. It was a shame, but not his concern. A sudden burst of giggling interspersed with hushing noises drew too many eyes to the table where Miss Bingley sat with her fiancé and several other couples. She was flushed, a silly smile on her face. Sir Eustace was speaking to her with a mildly annoyed expression.

"Too much wine punch," Darcy opined.

*Too much wanting to be the center of attention,* Elizabeth thought, but did not say.

They discussed books and plays for a time. The food truly was superb, Elizabeth ate more than she had intended, immersed in their conversation. At last, Darcy seemed hesitant to speak and pushed his plate away.

"Have you been to a pantomime?"

Elizabeth had a momentary vision of a crowded theater, noisy with holiday revelers, of herself and Jane waiting excitedly with the Gardiners for the pantomime to begin. "When Jane and I were younger our aunt and uncle took us to see a holiday pantomime with Grimaldi. He was wonderful. We laughed so hard our sides ached. That was the only time I have been to one."

"Grimaldi is superb. Unfortunately he is not performing at present. However, there is a holiday pantomime at the Theater Royal with a very competent actor. I am taking Georgiana, Colonel Fitzwilliam and Anne Friday evening. Would you do me the honor of attending with us?"

Elizabeth did not respond for several moments. "I—I am not sure it is a good idea…"

"Surely Georgiana and our cousins are sufficient chaperones. I will invite your aunt and uncle if you like."

Elizabeth looked down at her fingers pleating the skirt of her gown. She was no longer a girl; after what she had suffered she felt twice her natural age. It was time to stop depending on her aunt and uncle to keep her reputation intact.

"Yes, I will go with you, thank you. I would very much like to see the performance."

Darcy felt elated. Georgiana and the others were sufficient guarantee of propriety without inhibiting their ability to speak freely. Perhaps at last he could begin to let her know how he felt and what he intended. He looked forward to the night as he had not looked forward to anything for a long time.

On the far side of the room Sir Eustace, having quieted his betrothed's high spirits to a proper level, watched the pair with speculation.

"I wonder if Mrs. Bingley's sister will shortly follow her down the aisle."

Miss Bingley looked up from her ice to follow his gaze. For a moment her mouth pickled before she remembered she was engaged, but it did not completely erase a certain stiffness in her reply.

"Oh, no, no. Mr. Darcy must marry much higher than that. She has a small dowry, but no connections, and relatives in trade."

"Darcy is rich enough to marry whom he pleases. And her sister married to your brother must be a connection of sorts."

Miss Bingley put aside the remains of her ice and tapped her lips with a serviette. Having recently become an advocate of the bird-in-the-hand philosophy she conveniently forgot a five-year quest and responded with a snide little smile.

"I do not think she will ever marry, Sir Eustace. She is too much a blue stocking. Always reading books and contending with gentlemen about subjects a lady ought to know nothing about; politics and such. Mr. Darcy finds her an oddity. When he marries, it will be an heiress, I am sure."

Sir Eustace did not reply and returned to the table at large. He knew jealousy when he heard it, however it did not bother him. Miss Bingley suited him; he wanted a comfortable life and a perceptive wife was not his idea of comfort.

At length guests began to leave. Elizabeth and the Gardiners stayed with Jane as she accepted final congratulations. When the last guest was gone, she hugged Elizabeth with particular intensity.

"My dearest sister, thank you for everything. Your place in my heart will never change. I only wish you may find the happiness I feel with my dear Charles."

Elizabeth determined she would not cry, but she felt the sting of tears on her lashes. "Just be happy, my dearest Jane. I know you shall be."

The Gardiners said their goodbyes and walked out to their carriage. Darcy had just reached his town coach. He bowed but did not come over to them, there was no reason, Elizabeth thought with a small pang of regret, that he should. On the way to Gracechurch Street she was silent, staring out the window. Mrs. Gardiner watched her without comment. She had seen her niece sitting with Mr. Darcy at the breakfast as she had observed his attentions to Elizabeth before. It crossed her mind that her husband might step in and ask the gentleman of his intentions, however she was certain Elizabeth would resent what she saw as interference. He had been careful to follow propriety; unless the situation changed it was better to let matters alone.

## December 1814
## Covent Garden London

The pantomime was on the classic model: Harlequin, Mother Goose, The Three Bears and the Maid with Golden Locks, or The

Three Wishes. The clown was excellent if not the great Grimaldi. When he came on stage as the Fairy Godmother the audience roared. Even Anne Fitzwilliam laughed. Darcy sat next to Elizabeth and watched her when she was absorbed in the action on stage. His first words to her when they were seated in the box had surprised her.

"Tonight we will not discuss literature or philosophy or politics. I want you to be happy. To feel something of the child again. That, I think, is the purpose of the pantomime, to make us all children for a night."

"Does it make you so?"

Her question was serious and he answered it seriously, "In a way, yes. It reminds me that we were all innocent once, and for a short time we can be again."

Elizabeth seemed to relax as the performance progressed. The magical changes in scenery were excellently done and as the action became less fairy tale and more the story of Columbine and her suitors she became lost in the fantasy. When it was over Elizabeth looked at Darcy with some of the brilliance he remembered returned to her eyes.

"Thank you, Mr. Darcy. I do not know when I have enjoyed myself so much."

"Then the evening has been the success I hoped for."

Georgiana came up to them then, smiling happily. "Elizabeth, I have hardly had a chance to speak with you tonight. I was hoping you and Mrs. Gardiner might come to tea tomorrow if you have no other plans?"

"I shall ask my aunt."

Elizabeth wondered if the younger woman wanted to impart some special information to her, or simply liked their conversations when no men were present. Her answer satisfied Georgiana, who joined her cousins as the party moved to exit the theater. Anne held her husband's arm but without her former dependence on assistance in walking. She looked healthier, Darcy thought, than he ever remembered her. Richard, however, seemed quieter than his usual jovial self. Darcy wanted a chance to ask his cousin of Dr. Crane's advice, however this was neither the time nor the place. Perhaps at the dinner on the twenty-third if they did not meet before then.

Darcy returned Elizabeth to Gracechurch Street. He and Georgiana accepted her invitation to come in, finding her relations in the drawing room. The children were in bed, and Mrs. Gardiner rang for tea while their guests talked of the pantomime. Mr. Gardiner kept a quiet eye on his niece and Mr. Darcy. There was nothing to alarm him, only a subtle tension in the gentleman the older man recognized as attraction to Elizabeth. An attraction well under control, he thought. He wondered if his niece felt it as well, or if she had made herself immune to Darcy's admiration. If so, it was sad. Elizabeth was too young and vital to cut herself off from life.

Mr. Gardiner thought of asking her about her relationship with Darcy, but rejected the idea in favor of speaking to his wife. Elizabeth was too independent to accept his concern for her welfare without some resentment. When the Darcys departed, Elizabeth excused herself and went upstairs to bed. Mr. Gardiner moved to sit beside his wife on the sofa, took her hand and smiled a trifle wryly.

"What do you think of Elizabeth and Mr. Darcy, my dear?"

Mrs. Gardiner drew a breath before answering. "I think he wants more than a friendship. I am not sure what Lizzy wants. She has been so deeply hurt, she may not be able to risk more pain if she is wrong about him."

"Well, I suppose all we can do is wait."

"Yes. That is the hardest part, the waiting. Perhaps after the holidays it may come to some resolution."

"She wants to leave London and rest in the country for a time as soon as the weather allows. You have relatives in Lambton, do you think Lizzy might agree to stay with them for a few weeks?"

"What an excellent idea, Edward. I shall write them tomorrow. After all, Pemberley is very close to the village. One never knows how a visit will turn out."

They both smiled at that and went up to bed together.

December 1814
Darcy House, London

Elizabeth had prepared for Mr. Darcy's dinner party with care, wearing a new yellow silk evening dress she considered something of an extravagance. Her aunt's maid put her hair up in a fashionable style that took its curls into account. Elizabeth felt more anticipation than the evening justified, but for once she did not question her reasons.

Darcy House was lit with lamps and candles, gas lights along the street driving the shadows of trees in long banners across the cobbles. Darcy and Georgiana greeted their guests in the entry hall; his sister seemed especially jubilant, her heart-shaped face glowing. She exclaimed over Elizabeth's dress while Darcy voiced a welcome to the Gardiners. He bowed over Elizabeth's hand, his eyes full of their dark fire as they met hers.

"I am glad you could come tonight."

"Thank you."

He released Elizabeth's hand, leaving an impression of heat that ran through her body in a shiver of response. *If the mere touch of his hand can elicit such a feeling, what would it be like to rest in his arms, to be kissed as a man kisses his wife?* Elizabeth put the treacherous thoughts away. She must stop this madness before it consumed her.

Lord and Lady Matlock were already in the drawing room along with Lady Addington and a young man Elizabeth remembered from the Matlock dinner party. Mr. Worthington—no wonder Georgiana was in such high spirits. The Gardiners had no sooner entered the room than Richard Fitzwilliam came in with Anne. She also looked as if she had been given a marvelous present; the former colonel more resembled a man going into battle. Wondering at the strange currents circulating among the guests, Elizabeth greeted Lady Addington who indicated the seat next to her on a sofa.

"How are you, Miss Bennet? Well, I hope."

"Yes, thank you, my lady." Elizabeth looked around the room at the various clumps of guests. "I do not see Viscount Brentmore."

"He and Adele are not in attendance. It seems she and Lord Matlock had what the less sophisticated call a 'blazing row'."

"I am sorry to hear of it." Elizabeth did not elaborate. She was not one for gossip, and although she did not like Lady Brentmore she knew family conflicts usually touched more than two or three members.

"It has been a long time coming. Brentmore has never exercised any control over Adele. She likes to pretend her family were social royalty in France. The truth is, her father was only a minor member of the nobility. Since she married Brentmore, Lord Matlock has supported him. It is an open secret like so many among the *ton*."

Obviously, gratitude was not one of Lady ~~Brentwood's~~ Brentmore's virtues. "It seems foolish to fight with the man who is beneficent to your family."

"One would think so." Lady Addington sighed. "Adele gambles as I am sure you have heard. It has become a large bone of contention between her and Brentmore as well as Lord Matlock. He has threatened to cut her father off if she continues."

Elizabeth sucked in her breath. "Would Lord Matlock do that?"

Lady Addington shrugged. "He has the future to think of. One day she will be Lady Matlock, and Brentmore will sit in the House of Lords. If Brentmore cannot control her, there is potential for damage to the estate as well as a very real chance of scandal. That could be politically disastrous." She glanced across the room to where Richard Fitzwilliam was conversing with Mr. Gardiner and Darcy. "I cannot help but wish Brentmore had been the second son."

Elizabeth could not blame her for the sentiment. She started to reply when Bingley and Jane entered the room with Lady Matlock. The sisters saw one another immediately, Jane hurrying to Elizabeth who rose for an intense hug. Jane curtsied to Lady Addington who smiled widely.

"You are lit from within with love," the lady said.

Jane blushed, her eyes alight. "I am so very happy. My husband is the most wonderful man in the world."

She took a seat between her sister and Lady Addington. "That is a very proper sentiment for a bride." Lady Addington patted her hand. "I am glad you came tonight. It is always good to get away from domesticity for a few hours."

Jane's blush deepened. Elizabeth slipped her arm through her sister's and tactfully changed the subject to Christmas preparations. Georgiana as hostess was keeping an eye on the footmen circulating with drinks and on the general comfort of their guests. Seeing Mr. Worthington standing a little apart, she took his arm and drew him to where Bingley and Lord Matlock stood.

"I do not believe you had an opportunity to speak to Mr. Worthington at the dinner party we all attended, Mr. Bingley. Mr. Worthington shares an enthusiasm of yours."

Lord Matlock looked on with avuncular pride at his niece's composure. Mr. Bingley turned his amiable face on the newcomer with a polite bow which Mr. Worthington returned.

"I should like to hear of it."

Mr. Worthington looked at Georgiana in some surprise. She said, "Mr. Bingley is an advocate for the future of steam power. Mr. Worthington designs steam engines."

"Does he, by Jove?" Bingley was immediately all interest. "I should very much like to hear about it."

"Never replace horses," Lord Matlock observed.

"Certainly not for pleasure or racing." Mr. Worthington agreed. "The army will no doubt depend on them as well. But for transport, steam is the future. Watt, Fulton and Fitch in the States are already working on the idea. Trevithick demonstrated a self-propelling railroad steam engine ten years ago. I believe in ten years, twenty at most, goods will travel all over England by rail."

"Is there not a problem with the rails?"

"Yes," Worthington admitted to Bingley's question. "Steel is too soft and cast iron is too hard. But soon someone will find an answer to the problem. I am not involved in the immediate subject of transport. I design steam-powered engines for manufacturing; weaving, cloth mills, foundries, any enterprise that wants more power with less cost and consistent results."

Lord Matlock looked uncomfortable when the discussion began, but his interest had been caught by the quiet certainty of the young man. Bingley looked more and more excited.

"I understand steam engines allow mills to operate where no large source of water is available. The applications are potentially vast."

"England has always depended on its landholders for the basis of its economy. Are you saying, Mr. Worthington, that the land is no longer of major importance?"

Mr. Worthington gathered his thoughts before he responded. "No, my lord, I am not dismissing farming as a continuing basis for prosperity. But England has grown great on commerce. Anything that promotes commerce is of benefit to the country. Better methods of working the land are important. Better methods of promoting England's goods to the world are also important. If we do not progress, we regress."

"Well said."

Bingley took a sip of his drink. There was a sharpness in his expression that Darcy would have easily recognized. *My friend Darcy is a man of the land,* Bingley mused. *His family has lived on Pemberley estate for hundreds of years. In spite of my father's ambitions of gentility for his son and daughters, he was himself a man of commerce. He meant to buy an estate and learn to run it, but he would never have abandoned an interest in commercial innovations.*

The butler came to the doorway at that moment and looked at Lord Matlock, who nodded.

"Dinner is served."

Darcy took his aunt in to dinner, while Lord Matlock escorted

Lady Addington. Elizabeth felt a small nagging disappointment that she would not sit with him that night; when they were seated however she found that she was between Mr. Worthington and Mr. Bingley, with Georgiana on Mr. Worthington's far side and Jane on Bingley's. Bingley seemed somehow disappointed by the seating arrangement at first, then entered into conversation with her in his pleasant fashion. This lasted for perhaps a quarter hour before his attention strayed to Jane so often Elizabeth took pity on him and began speaking to Mr. Worthington. She found his father's avocation was astronomy and they had an interesting conversation about the new planet Herschel had discovered and what other planets might exist not yet found.

When Georgiana rose to lead the ladies out, Mr. Bingley hardly waited until Elizabeth was out of her chair to lean across to Mr. Worthington. Elizabeth wondered what could be so important that Mr. Bingley's behavior bordered on rudeness in his need to speak to the gentleman. She followed their hostess to the drawing room still pondering his behavior when Lady Addington came up to her with a quizzical expression.

"Your new brother-by-marriage seems to have taken a liking to Mr. Worthington."

"Yes. I do not know what could be of such interest to Mr. Bingley that he was so intent on speaking to Mr. Worthington immediately dinner was finished."

"I have found men are a bit more open with their interests than ladies. You know that Mr. Worthington designs steam-powered machines. Mr. Bingley shares an interest in steam power with Lord Rathbone. I suppose he and Mr. Worthington have that in common."

"I suppose they may."

Elizabeth saw her sister in conversation with Lady Matlock and Anne Fitzwilliam and smiled. Jane's nature was such that she endeared herself to her friends without effort. She was drawn back by Lady Addington's quiet inquiry.

"Are you spending Christmas with the Bingleys or your aunt and uncle?"

"We are all spending the day at our relatives. I have been staying there to give my sister and Mr. Bingley some privacy. As soon as Christmas is over I will return to my house and begin packing. Jane and Mr. Bingley wish me to live with them, but I have not decided yet. I intend to go away for a time in the spring. I am not sure if I will return to London or not."

Elizabeth did not understand why she had confided her plans to Lady Addington, it had simply seemed right to do so. The older lady was silent for a time, a sadness creeping into her expression.

"Time spent away from the familiar can be of great use in settling one's mind and looking at problems from a new perspective, as long as it is not used as an escape. We carry our fears and our conflicts with us wherever we go. Eventually they must be faced."

Her voice was gentle. Elizabeth did not take offense, knowing none was meant. "There has been so much, too much," she clenched her hands in her skirt to keep them from shaking, "I have to think everything out before I can know what I must do."

Although Elizabeth did not feel as if she was making sense, Lady Addington nodded. "Life has put too much on you too young. I hope you will be able to see your way clearly by yourself, but that is not vouchsafed to many of us. Sometimes we need someone to share our pain before we can leave it behind us."

Elizabeth did not answer. She saw in her mind's eye a tall, dark man with burning eyes and a deep rich voice. *He is not the answer! I must do this alone.* But the older woman's words reverberated through her consciousness. She had not told him of her intention to leave London in spite of several opportunities. Why had she not confided in him, were they not friends after all? In her heart Elizabeth knew the answer; she was afraid. Afraid that he would force the issue of his feelings for her, afraid she would respond to him, admit her own feelings for him. It was too dangerous to take that risk. Better to run away if that was what she contemplated, and hope in time the pain would lessen and she might begin to live again.

## December 1814
## Darcy House, London

Fitzwilliam Darcy sat at his desk in the study of Darcy House and pondered how he might see Elizabeth Bennet without singling her out. She had been staying with the Gardiners after the wedding of her sister and Bingley, however he was not sure if she was still there and he was not a close enough friend of her relatives to call on them without some purpose. After the dinner on the twenty-third, he and Georgiana had remained quietly at home until Christmas Day. They attended services at their parish church before repairing to the Matlocks' town home for dinner. Brentmore and Adele were in attendance, speaking to each other only when absolutely necessary. It cast a shadow over the festive meal, and when they left immediately after dinner the rest of the family seemed more relieved than resentful.

Lord Matlock and the others were in the music room when his cousin Richard motioned Darcy to wait a moment in the empty hall. The worry that Darcy noted in his cousin before had grown. He looked almost grim.

"What is the matter, Richard?"

Darcy watched the play of emotion in his cousin's eyes before the former army officer responded in a low voice. "Dr. Crane spoke to me yesterday. I had hoped he would forbid Anne to get with child, but he says she has improved enough that she could sustain a pregnancy if exceptional care were taken for her health. Dammit, Will, I do not want to lose her but she is adamant she wants to provide me an heir. I am at my wits end. I do not know what to do."

Darcy knew this was a highly unusual conversation, one Richard would never have initiated with anyone else, not even his mother. To see a man who had faced a decade of war in such a state over his wife's desire for motherhood was unsettling at best. Richard waited for his cousin's response in tense silence. Darcy considered before speaking. He was poorly equipped to offer advice on the subject, but Richard obviously required a response. He drew in a breath and spoke slowly.

"I take it you cannot reason her out of the idea?"

"No. Anne has a mind of her own I have found, and it is set on having a child."

"Then I see no way around that fact. I love Anne, and I am happy to see her so well settled. All the years she was under our aunt's control must have left her feeling that she would never be able to live a life of her own choosing. Now that she is free, she must want to do the things any other young wife does, including having a child of her own. If Dr. Crane thinks it is possible for her to bear a child, I do not know what you can do except the obvious."

As close as they were, Richard knew Darcy would never want him to discuss intimate details of his marriage. He had tried limiting his time in his wife's bed and found that while she was not an avid partner, she loved him enough to take some joy in their coupling. He had used protection except for the first night, hoping it was enough to keep her from coming with child. That option had been taken from him by Dr. Crane.

"Perhaps in the end, nothing will come of it," Darcy offered when Richard did not respond. "Anne is a year younger than I. That is a little old for childbearing."

Richard shook his head. "You may be right. Her physical condition may preclude a child. I hope so. As much as I want to make her happy, endangering her life is not something I will readily do."

The sound of the pianoforte under Georgiana's perfect control came to them, and they went on before they were missed. In his study, Darcy sat back and contemplated the peaceful room. He always felt at home here amid oak paneling, *terre vert* walls, and built-in bookcases whose glass doors shimmered with the cloudy light from the windows. The fire hummed and hissed in the hearth, taking the chill from the air. He wondered if Georgiana was up yet; he had not broken his fast when he arose, only swallowed a cup of coffee and come immediately to this place where no one was about to disturb him.

At that, Mr. Burgess' tap at the door belied his thoughts. "Mr. Bingley, sir."

Darcy rose as his friend entered, holding out his hand. The two men shook hands and Bingley took one of the two chairs before the fire.

"Do not let the weak sunlight mislead you, Darcy, it is as cold as the devil's heart out there."

They exchanged the usual courtesies before Darcy smiled. Charles was as ebullient as ever, perhaps a bit more so, no doubt the effect of his marriage. "What brings you out today, my friend?"

"My wonderful wife is visiting with her aunt and uncle and Miss Elizabeth. I called because I have an investment proposition I wish to discuss with you."

"Have you broken your fast?"

"Only some hot chocolate and a muffin."

"Hardly enough to sustain a serious financial conversation. I have not eaten yet. Join me for breakfast and then we will talk."

Bingley agreed readily and the two friends repaired to the breakfast parlor, still empty of Georgiana who usually rose a little earlier, but whose regular toilette sent her to breakfast an hour later. A footman served them and they settled to eat, neither man anxious to finish and leave the warm room smelling of fresh coffee and Cook's sweet muffins. At last Darcy finished his final cup of coffee and looked across the table at his friend. Bingley rose with his host and followed Darcy back to the study.

"I need to steal either the receipt for those sweet muffins or your cook," he joked.

Darcy grinned. "Good luck to either, Charles."

In the study they resumed their seats before the fire and Darcy looked across at his friend with a questioning expression. "What is this investment you wish to discuss?"

Bingley took an uncharacteristic time settling himself, which told Darcy he was hesitant to begin. After several minutes Bingley cleared his throat and began in a way Darcy had not anticipated.

"You know Mr. Worthington."

"Yes. He is a friend of Georgiana's."

Bingley brushed an imaginary piece of lint from his trouser leg. "You also know I have a consuming interest in steam power, one I share with Lord Rathbone and several other gentlemen."

"And Mr. Worthington designs steam engines." Darcy was beginning to see a vague outline of Bingley's plans. "You were speaking with him at the dinner the other night."

"I was. I have since spoken to Lord Rathbone, who is interested in my idea." Bingley settled to his narrative, no longer unsure. "My family still owns the original ironmongery started by my grandfather. I have long considered selling it, but it is the origin of my family's wealth and therefore has meaning to me and others. At present a cousin manages it. It does well enough, however in time it will become less profitable as times and methods change."

"You want to convert it in some way—connected to steam power."

Bingley leaned forward. "Exactly. Steam power is transforming industry, especially the milling and weaving of cloth. Mills can now be built where there is no ready supply of running water for mill wheels. And manufacturing is not the only or the greatest application. In the near future, steam will power transportation. In America, Fulton and Livingston have built a steam-powered boat that did the trip from New York City to Albany, the capital of New York, carrying passengers, in thirty-two hours. That is a distance of one hundred and fifty miles. They have since built a steamboat that traveled from Pittsburgh in Pennsylvania to New Orleans in Louisiana, and back."

"I have read about Fulton. He was hired to develop an underwater ship for Napoleon, and did so, with limited success. Luckily for England, Nelson's victory at Trafalgar made further developments unnecessary, and he returned to America."

"America may have Fulton, but we have Trevithick. The Cornish engine is small enough to be used in many other applications than the earlier engines. Darcy, I cannot help the fact that commerce is in my blood. I want to convert my family's old foundry to a plant for the design and manufacture of steam-powered engines. I have no doubt that will eventually include marine craft and railway engines. Mr. Worthington has made improvements to the Trevithick design. He will be managing director. I and Lord Rathbone, and others I hope, will be silent partners. I am meeting with the two of them at my club later today. I hope you will join us, and give me your opinion of the feasibility of the idea."

Darcy sat quietly for a time. He did not disdain investing in commercial ventures, and indeed was a partner in a shipping company with Mr. Gardiner and two other gentlemen. His thoughts were focused on two things: how the success of the venture would affect Georgiana's future should she marry Mr. Worthington, and the inevitable changes in society if Bingley was right and steam power became widely used for transportation. The former he could deal with, the latter was outside his, or anyone's, control.

"I will join you, Charles."

Bingley left Darcy House pleased with himself and the world. His friend was not so sanguine. He was more progressive than the majority of his peers, however he also felt a strong bond to the past. In the last few years reconciling the two had not always been easy. Darcy felt as he returned to his desk that it was to become even harder in the near future.

# Chapter Eighteen

December 1814
Meadow Lane, London

Elizabeth stood in the middle of the parlor and gazed around at the now-familiar furniture. She had paid the monthly rental yesterday and given the landlord notice that she meant to quit the property at the end of next month. There were rooms waiting for her at Hephaestus House whenever she wished to occupy them. Jane assured her that any items she wanted to keep would be stored in the Bingleys' box rooms for as long as needed.

It was another snowy day, the wind howling in the chimney with the sound of a distant wolf. Elizabeth drew her cashmere shawl, a Christmas gift from her aunt and uncle, closer around her and paced to the windows. The rose bushes were pruned back and heavily mulched against the winter cold. In the window boxes the bright geraniums no longer bloomed, covered by straw until spring. A spring she would spend somewhere else.

She did not mourn leaving this place, but she had become used to it over the past two years. It had been intended as a sort of sanctuary, a place to rebuild their lives. Instead, her father had died here and only Jane escaped to a brighter future. Elizabeth pressed her forehead to the icy glass. She felt an emptiness that seemed to stretch out into the future, as if she were lost in a vast gray desert without horizons, lost and alone.

Elizabeth did not stir at a soft tap on the open door. She turned only when Nettie's voice called tentatively, "Miss Bennet?"

Elizabeth straightened and turned to find the little maid watching her from the doorway. "Yes, Nettie?"

The maid entered with an uncertain air. Elizabeth sat on the settee and smiled at her in encouragement. Nettie clutched her apron in both hands. She started to speak, halted, then gathered herself.

"Please, madam, Miss Bennet, Mrs. Hobson says you are going to live with Mrs. Bingley and leave here. I just wondered—that is, if you are, if you—if I…"

Her voice trailed away. Elizabeth felt a sudden warmth for the maid she had not felt since the servants at Longbourn. "Yes, Nettie, I am giving up this house at the end of next month. I am sorry I have not spoken to you and Mrs. Hobson sooner, but my sister's marriage and—other things have interfered. After Lady Matlock's Twelfth Night ball I will be staying with Mr. and Mrs. Bingley for a short time, and then I am going away. My plans are not yet set, however, I would be very happy if you feel you can accompany me as my lady's maid."

Nettie's face had undergone a series of expressions during this speech: sorrow, acceptance, surprise, joy. "Oh, madam, yes, I'd like that ever so much. I've been very happy here, but I'm sure wherever you go makes no difference."

"Excellent. Also, I have a special task for you."

Nettie looked eager rather than cautious. Her enthusiasm was one of the traits Elizabeth liked most about her.

"When I am at the Bingleys', or before if you find time, I want you to pack everything of a personal nature in my—my father's room. There will be very little, only what is in his desk and perhaps the night table. Use the small trunk in the box room with 'T. Bennet' on the lid. I will also make a list of the furniture and household items that will be stored at my sister's. You may have to direct the footmen when they come to transfer them. Now, send Mrs. Hobson to me and I will speak to her."

Nettie bobbed a curtsey and hurried out. Mrs. Hobson was not as difficult about the end of her employment as Elizabeth had expected. The cook nodded when Elizabeth told her of the imminent move, her ruddy face placid.

"I knew how it would be when Miss Bennet married. A young lady doesn't want to rattle around in a house alone, not when she has relatives ready to take her in. My daughter has been after me to give up regular work lately because of my rheumatics. I'll be stayin' with her permanent I suppose."

"I am afraid this is not much notice, however I will pay you an extra month's salary in lieu if that is acceptable?"

"That's very generous of you, madam. Nettie says she's goin' with you. I'm happy for that. She's a good girl and bright as a new sovereign."

With domestic matters settled, Elizabeth allowed her mind to contemplate what she had put off for over a year. With the exception of packing up his clothing for the local parish poor, her father's room had never been cleared out. Elizabeth knew he had brought almost no personal property from Longbourn except his books. The desk in his room, rarely used, had been purchased along with the beds and dining room set. Jane had insisted Elizabeth keep her rocking chair for the time being. Elizabeth also had the dressing table and bench from her old room, but they seemed a part of a distant past to which she was no longer connected.

She would have her uncle Gardiner help her sell everything except several pieces she wanted to keep and her father's books. Eventually Elizabeth could purchase new furniture when she settled on a place to live. She rose and climbed the stairs, meaning to survey her father's room one last time before it was emptied, all material signs of him removed. As she reached the door she stopped. Her heart clutched, squeezing the breath from her lungs. Elizabeth turned, her knees weak, and leaned against the wall. The morning he died was as vivid as if it were today.

When her sight cleared, she went on slowly to the upstairs sitting room and dropped heavily onto the settee. *Not yet. Not now!* A voice deep within whispered, *Not ever.*

"Nettie can clear out anything that is left," Elizabeth said aloud.

She did not want to think about it anymore. When she was ready to leave. There was no hurry. Elizabeth rose and rang for Nettie to bring tea.

## December 1814
## Hephaestus House, London

"Darcy," Bingley came from behind his desk to welcome his friend with a handshake, "I'm happy to see you. What brings you here?"

In reality it had been the hope that Elizabeth was living with the Bingleys. Instead he said, "I wondered how the partnership was progressing."

"Capital. Lord Rathbone has several other gentlemen interested in participating. Once they have been quietly vetted by my attorney, the papers will be drawn up. Sit down, my friend, let me offer you a drink. It does not look like the weather will improve any time soon."

Bingley busied himself pouring two brandies and carrying them to the hearth where Darcy occupied one of the heavy chairs. He took the other and raised his glass in salute. "Here's to the success of our venture."

Both men drank. Darcy had joined the plan and was happy to see that his friend did not propose to accept investors on the basis of their names or relationship to Lord Rathbone. He had done the same before entering into any investment including the one with Mr. Gardiner. He said as much bringing a smile to Bingley's face.

"I am glad to hear it. I suppose it is my early training. My father was a careful man especially where money was concerned. I want this venture to succeed, not only for any profit it may bring, but because it gives new life to my family's heritage. I am taking Jane to Scarborough to meet my mother and cousins in March. I have been trying to persuade Elizabeth to join us. I would like my family to meet her as well."

Darcy's mouth went dry. He took a sip of the brandy before replying. "Is Miss Bennet staying with you now?"

"No, she has returned to..."

"Meadow Lane. Yes, I know where she lives although I have never been there."

Bingley raised an enquiring eyebrow. "She told you?"

"No." Darcy swirled the brandy around his glass. "When you came to me you were afraid they were in poor circumstances. I wanted to find out where they lived and if it was a bad area I intended to see what could be done to improve their position. I would have come to you first, however I was informed that the house was average for the area and they were in no danger. That was the whole of it."

"I see." Bingley contemplated the snapping coal burning brightly in the grate. "I am glad you were concerned enough to assess the situation. There is little to worry about now, of course, as Elizabeth is leaving the house at the end of January."

"Leaving?"

Bingley looked at his friend rather sharply. "Yes. You did not know?"

"No."

"She told us at Christmas that she will come to stay with us until the weather settles, and then she is going to spend time away from London. I hope she will come with us to Scarborough before she decides where she wishes to settle."

Darcy was stunned. He finished his brandy in a swallow, welcoming the burn as it went down his throat. Elizabeth had told him nothing of her plans, although she must have been forming them before the dinner party. Why had she not confided in him? It was not like Elizabeth to keep such a plan secret unless she did not want him to know of it. Was she running away from the past, from the future—*or from him?*

"Darcy? What is it man? You look ill."

Darcy forced himself to control the churning emotions that threatened to overcome him. He'd had a lifetime of practice in concealing his feelings but this was something he had never faced before. He made a supreme effort to speak normally, carefully setting his glass down.

"I am well. It is just a surprise that Miss Bennet would leave Town for an extended stay unless it was with relatives."

Bingley said slowly, "Jane tells me that Elizabeth has been unhappy for some time. Her father's death was a great shock—she was with him when he died. I know she is happy for Jane and me but it means she will be alone, that is why we have both tried to convince her to live here. Perhaps she will when she returns."

Darcy sat staring sightlessly at the fire. He had not known that Elizabeth was with her father when he passed. Even if it was expected, the event would have been a great shock considering how close they had been. He had been with his own father when the elder Darcy passed. He remembered every moment of that time, the grief, the sorrow, the feeling of loss, even abandonment.

"She has been through so much," Darcy murmured.

"Indeed. Perhaps time away from everything will be beneficial. I am sure she will have Mr. Gardiner's assistance in finding a suitable accommodation. Jane tells me Elizabeth has always worked out problems on her own. That may be her purpose."

Darcy had little else to say and the friends parted shortly after with Bingley promising to send him a copy of the partnership agreement when it was ready. In his town coach returning to Mayfair, Darcy felt an emptiness he had never experienced before. He had been afraid to speak, to risk driving her away. He wondered if his silence had brought about the very thing he feared. They were approaching Darcy House when he abruptly rapped on the roof of the coach. When the hatch opened, his orders were short.

"Take me to Matlock House."

December 1814
Matlock House, London

Darcy found his aunt in her private sitting room looking over the menu for the supper at the Twelfth Night Ball. She smiled up at him as he bent to kiss her cheek, sobering when he turned away and paced to the windows overlooking Hyde Park. A wind blew shivering among the dry branches and winter shrubs. Lady Matlock rose and rang for a maid.

"You will be happy to know," she said as she resumed her seat, "that my Twelfth Night Ball is not a *bal masqué*. Masquerade balls have rather gone out of fashion, and I find wearing a mask, even those beautiful Italian masks one holds on a stick, to be awkward for dancing.."

Her attempt at conversation failed as Darcy did not answer her. The girl arrived shortly with a tea tray containing a fresh pot and an extra cup and saucer. She took away the old pot with a practiced curtsey. When the door closed behind her, Lady Matlock prepared two cups of tea and sat back.

"Come and have tea, Will."

Darcy looked across at her, wondering why he had come here. He had always been very fond of his aunt-by-marriage, but he was not a man to unburden his soul to anyone, even someone he respected as much as Eleanor Fitzwilliam. Even his cousin Richard who was like a brother to him did not know his most personal concerns.

"I—should not have come."

He had started for the door when his aunt spoke with a firmness he would have attributed to his cousin commanding troops.

"Fitzwilliam George Alexander Darcy, I have known you since you were born. Come here, sit down, and talk to me. That is why you are here, is it not?"

Darcy obeyed her. She handed him the tea cup and he found he was parched. When the cup was empty Lady Matlock set hers back on the tray and considered him gravely. He could not seem to form words from the jumble filling his mind. His aunt's face softened. She understood better than he knew how difficult this was for him.

"This is not something new. I have seen you struggle with some great pain or loss since your trip to Hertfordshire with Mr. Bingley. Only recently have you been more like your old self although rather less distant. There is only one change in your life that I am aware of and that is the introduction of Miss Bennet into your circle. It is she that you are disturbed over is it not?"

"Disturbed? Yes, at my wits' end." He pressed a hand to his forehead. There was a fist squeezing his heart. "I want to marry her. I have never known a woman like her and never will. She is everything to me."

"But there is an impediment."

"She avoids my overtures. She thinks because of the past…"

"Her sister's elopement, yes, I know about that." His reaction was not quite shock and Lady Matlock went on calmly. "That is an old, country scandal and best left where it began. It has no relevance to you except for Wickham, and you are not to blame for his sins, or your father's gullibility."

Darcy did not resent her assessment. He had long wondered why his father gave Wickham so many chances to change, paid his bills, saw that the young women he seduced were cared for. What was it about the wastrel his father saw that no one else did? His aunt's voice brought him back to the moment. She leaned forward looking into his face.

"Does she have feelings for you, or is it all on your side?"

"I know she does, I have seen it in her eyes. She is frightened to open herself to me, to let herself respond to what I offer her. I tried for two years to forget her. It is not possible. I will marry Elizabeth Bennet, or no one."

His aunt heard the anguish beneath the words. She gathered her thoughts before laying one of her slim hands on his chill fingers.

"Fitzwilliam, I want you to think of Georgiana."

Darcy would have bridled but Lady Matlock's voice was so gentle he waited silently for her to continue.

"Georgie was five when your mother died. She could not understand the implications, only that her mother was gone. She was eleven when George died, still a child but able to grasp the basic knowledge that her father had died. She had family and friends who love her and made her grief as easy as possible. What would she have felt if she had lost them within a year of one another? If her family and friends had turned from her, if you had married and abandoned her? I know it is not an exact parallel, but you must realize that all of that has happened to Miss Bennet. One sister is lost, her mother and father died less than a year apart, her remaining sisters married, two of them living far enough away to discourage frequent visits, and Mrs. Bingley, with whom she is obviously as close as a twin, must now consider her husband and potential children before anyone else."

"I only want to help her, to stand beside her and offer her my own strength. I love her as I can never love another woman, if she rejects me..."

His words faltered and stopped. Lady Matlock looked at him with understanding. "For ten endless years I had a son who went to war. Whenever Richard left to rejoin his regiment I felt as if a part of me sickened and would not be well until he returned alive and unharmed. Every day he was away I waited for notification that he was wounded, or lost. I worried that when the war was finally over he would not be able to live among men who are not at war. I am very familiar with the pain you feel when someone you love dearly is in jeopardy, even if it is not physical danger." She paused and Darcy saw the shadows of old pain in her eyes.

"What am I to do, then? I tried to walk away before, I cannot do it again. If I cannot help her, love her, what is left?"

"Most strong women are strong because they have to be. Life has not allowed them to lean on others for support. Miss Bennet has carried terrible burdens no young lady should ever be forced to shoulder. She has survived, however she has reached a point where she is no longer able to continue carrying their weight. She needs peace to recover herself, to know who she has become and what she wants from the rest of her life. Give her that, Will. If she decides she prefers a single life, you must honor her choice."

Darcy bowed his head, his eyes shut tightly. His mind balked at the truth in her words. How could he let Elizabeth go, even if it was what she wished? He felt as if something inside him was tearing apart.

Darcy rose abruptly. Lady Matlock still held his hand. "Think about it, Will. Think very hard, please."

He nodded once, and left her.

## January 1815
## Matlock House, London

Matlock House glowed like a flambeau in the winter night. Liveried footmen stood at the open doors, where warmth and muted jollity spilled into the snowy street. Carriages came, stopped, and departed for the mews or other locations to await their owners' pleasure. Lord Matlock always provided hot cider and edibles in the servants' hall for the servants of his guests. His own staff scurried in controlled confusion preparing for the midnight supper. Liquid refreshments were already available to the guests: wine punch, mulled cider, sherry, and for the ladies who did not imbibe alcohol, orgeat and tea; and port, Madeira and brandy for the gentlemen.

The dancing had not yet begun when Bingley, Jane and Elizabeth arrived. Lady Matlock welcomed them in the entry hall along with her husband who seemed to Elizabeth to be preoccupied. She took Elizabeth's hand, smiling with something of empathy in her expression.

"I am so happy you could come tonight, my dear. That is a particularly lovely dress, the color becomes you very well."

"Thank you, my lady."

Elizabeth wore the new gown she had kept aside, a rose pink velvet in the empire style. Instead of two of the darker satin ribbon ends there were six, falling to near the hem so when she danced they would flutter and swirl around her. She wore a simple pearl necklace borrowed from Jane and pearl earrings, her dark curls swept up with silver pins.

"Your aunt and uncle arrived a few minutes ago. I believe they are in the ballroom."

Elizabeth continued to Lord Matlock who bowed to her curtsey. He voiced a conventional welcome and she moved on, joined by Jane and Bingley a moment later. Together they entered the ballroom, large by Town standards, and already filled with color and the softened cacophony of a hundred voices all speaking at once. Mrs. Gardiner had been watching for them. She came to meet them, hugged Jane and Elizabeth, had her hand kissed by a twinkling Bingley and walked them to where her husband waited, smiling benignly.

The room was magnificent. Chandeliers cast a festive light over the company, bringing out the sheen of silk and satin, the richness of velvet, the luster of skin and hair, the liquid glow of gems, the subdued contrast of black wool and spotless white linen. Tall urns full of glasshouse flowers lined the walls, their scent mingling with the perfumes of the women and colognes of the men. Chairs and sofas had been placed between the pillars for the comfort of those not dancing. Drapes covered the windows except for the glass doors at the far side of the room that led to a terrace and the gardens. Those had been left open to allow air to enter, something Elizabeth appreciated immediately. Dancing for hours in a closed room had often brought on a headache by evening's end.

Elizabeth's gaze involuntarily moved around the room seeking a tall man with black curls and a face of masculine beauty. Surely he would attend his aunt's ball. She did not find him however, a pang of disappointment sharper than it ought to have been dimming her pleasure in the spectacle. At the far end of the ballroom the musicians were already on the dais, instruments tuned and ready. A few more guests came in before Lord Matlock approached the dais and spoke to the music master. Bingley turned to the party with a rueful smile.

"There are three lovely ladies and I can only dance with one. It is such a situation that makes me wish I had been a triplet, or a twin at least."

"I think I shall sit this dance out," Mrs. Gardiner said with a glance at her husband. "I have heard there is to be a waltz later. I shall save that set for you, Mr. Gardiner."

"I should hope so, Mrs. Gardiner." Her husband turned to Elizabeth. "May I have the pleasure, Lizzy?"

"Of course, Uncle."

Bingley offered his arm to Jane and they all joined the forming set. The musicians were excellent as was to be expected. Elizabeth made an effort to lose herself in the dance, but her eyes strayed from time to time to the entrance as one or another late arrival appeared. *He is probably delayed by something and will come later. What if he is escorting a lady and that is why he is not here yet? Well, why should he not? He is free after all, he holds no obligation to anyone but himself.* Why then did she feel this desolation?

Mr. Gardiner observed his niece make an effort to appear pleased and happy with an inner sadness. His wife had shared her suspicions about Elizabeth's melancholy as they shared everything having to do with family. He still felt a sense of guilt that he had not made it his business to look into Thomas Bennet's odd behavior rather than feeling resentment, however justified. He doubted he could have helped in any significant way with the deterioration of his brother-by-marriage's health. Perhaps he might have kept a friendly relationship with Bennet if he had tried harder to understand that grief was not the only reason for the changes in character.

They made light conversation until the set ended then found Mrs. Gardiner who was seated next to Lady Addington and enjoying that lady's lively observations on the ball. She smiled at Elizabeth's curtsey and patted the sofa where one seat remained.

"You look lovely tonight, Miss Bennet. Are you enjoying the ball?"

Elizabeth seated herself next to the noblewoman. "It is early to pass judgment on the whole evening, but everything is well at present."

"Hmm. I do not see Mr. Darcy. I supposed he would be here since it is his aunt giving the affair. Perhaps a matter of business has delayed him."

"Yes."

Elizabeth avoided meeting the older woman's shrewd gaze. Mr. Gardiner had taken his wife's hand and was leading her to the floor for the second half of the set since Elizabeth had indicated she did not wish to continue dancing. Lady Addington knew everyone present and was able to comment on their histories, relations, and dancing abilities. Jane returned to sit with them while Charles spoke to a friend nearby. When the next set began to form Sir Eustace approached. Being something of a diplomat he had thought better of asking Miss Bennet to dance, leaving him free to ask Mrs. Bingley who was soon to be his sister-by-marriage. That left Bingley able to dance with Elizabeth. Bingley had not the superb skill of Mr. Darcy, but he was a competent and amusing partner. Elizabeth refrained from asking him if Mr. Darcy intended to attend the ball, when he answered her question spontaneously.

"I expected to see Darcy here tonight. He was intending to come, I hope there has been no problem at Pemberley."

"Oh, I hope not. I do not see Miss Darcy either."

As if to belie the statement, Georgiana Darcy slipped into the ballroom with Richard and Anne Fitzwilliam. Anne looked like another woman than the reclusive lady of Rosings. She wore a butter yellow gown with lace trim and yellow diamonds in an elaborate coiffure. Georgiana, perhaps in contrast, had chosen apple green *velours ciselé* in a stylish design. Richard looked solid and self-assured. At the end of the set the three came over to exchange pleasantries with Elizabeth and Lady Addington.

"I do not see my wayward cousin," he noted, looking around at the shifting mass of people. "He does not care for balls, but he always attends mother's Twelfth Night affair."

"Mr. Bingley expected him as well." Elizabeth tried to keep her voice unconcerned. "He was afraid there is some matter of urgency delaying him."

"I have heard of nothing. Coaches do break down, although I have never known Darcy's to do so, and he could walk here from Darcy House if it did."

Elizabeth did not press the issue. She danced the supper set with Richard, she suspected at Georgiana's suggestion, and sat with them at supper. Georgiana tried to keep up a cheerful chatter and Anne, on Richard's far side, spoke more than was previously her wont. In spite of her table companions and the wonderfully prepared and served food, Elizabeth could not eat. She took a few bites and moved the selections around on her plate, all the while trying to respond to Georgiana and Richard in as normal a manner as possible. Twice she caught her aunt, at a nearby table, watching her, but the older woman only smiled and looked away.

Supper dragged on and on. By the beginning of the second part of the Twelfth Night ball Elizabeth felt a hollow pit inside her. Mr. Darcy was not coming. Either because he wanted nothing more to do with her but did not want to embarrass her publicly, or because his family had convinced him to marry a lady of the *ton* and he was reluctant to tell her.

Elizabeth made a supreme effort to put aside her feelings and draw what enjoyment she could from the remainder of the evening. When the dancing recommenced Bingley's friend requested an introduction and Elizabeth danced a set with him. He was friendly without being forward and spoke readily on the little season and his home in Dorset. She smiled and nodded and responded with a word here and there and when the set was done remembered not a single thing he had said.

After that Elizabeth remained sitting with Anne, who was not strong enough to sustain an evening of dancing, and Lady Addington who continued her comments on the dancers. When the last set approached Elizabeth sought out her aunt Gardiner. She wanted to leave as soon as their goodbyes to friends and their hostess were over. The two women sat on a sofa without speaking while couples formed on the dance floor. It had been announced as a waltz. Since Almack's had approved the somewhat scandalous dance the past year it had entered the programs of the more sophisticated members of society.

Mrs. Gardiner was scanning the room when she touched Elizabeth's arm and moved her head slightly toward the doors. "My goodness. Apollo Belvedere in impeccable evening clothes."

Elizabeth raised her head at her aunt's words. The plink and rasp of violins being tuned mingled with a surf of voices and laughter as the guests waited for the last dance to begin. She saw him immediately, striding through the crowded ballroom like a panther through house cats. A chill ran ice down her spine. He was dressed entirely in black and white, his broad shoulders filling the perfectly tailored evening coat, his shirt and elaborately tied cravat snowy, his white silk waistcoat embroidered with silver swirls, his dancing pumps mirror polished. A veneer of sophistication over raw male power, the sole product of seven hundred years of dominance as absolute in its own realm as any king's. Their eyes met. Elizabeth could not look away. He stopped before her and bowed.

"Good evening Miss Bennet, Mrs. Gardiner."

Somehow, Elizabeth curtsied along with her aunt. The sounds from the dais where the musicians adjusted their instruments ceased. Darcy held out his hand.

"Will you dance with me?"

Elizabeth put her hand in his, felt his strong fingers close around hers. The room faded into blurs of color and whispers of sound. They took their place with the others. His voice was the rumble of distant thunder.

"Do you know the waltz?"

"Yes."

He must have heard her, for he straightened. Darcy took her left hand in his right. His gloved hand on her waist, in proper position for the waltz, burned through the velvet of her gown. Elizabeth laid the back of her hand on his shoulder. As if a circuit had been connected heat rushed through her. She felt her face flush and tried to drop her gaze but his eyes locked with hers and she could not look away. They faced one another as the music began, closer than they had ever stood. She moved with him into the rhythm of the dance. Darcy's eyes held hers, compelling, hypnotic. Elizabeth lost the other couples, lost the sound of violin and cello. It was as if a wall she never knew existed fell, allowing her to read his desire, his need; to read as well his unfailing devotion.

Seven centuries of powerful men resided in those eyes. The skirt of Elizabeth's gown swirled around them, pale rose against the dead black of his trousers, the ribbons fluttering and twining. She knew in turn he saw her uncertainty, her own need. The movement of the waltz whirled with her senses, the wavering beat of her heart. On and on, endless as time. She did not want it to stop, she did not want him to leave her. It was no longer a dance, it was a ritual binding man and woman in a ceremony far older than civilization: flutes, drums, torchlight. Elizabeth felt desire swell through her body. Her mind cried out, *I am in love with you!*

"Elizabeth."

His voice held her, commanded her, enfolded her. She was not aware the dance had finished until he began to lead her from the floor. Elizabeth walked blindly, her breath came in swift little shivers. At that moment Elizabeth felt she could stand no more. The doorway to the main hall made a dark rectangle in one wall. She withdrew her hand and hurried away from him, from the polite confusion of the dancers breaking apart from the set, trying not to run as she made her way through people she saw only as colors and shadows, passing women who stared after her with varying amounts of curiosity, hauteur or animosity.

Lamps lit the corridor. Elizabeth hurried by the ladies' retiring room. She did not want to see anyone, she only wanted stillness, dark soothing stillness where she might gather her emotions under some sort of control. She passed closed doors in endless procession. The hallway came to an intersecting corridor. Elizabeth turned blindly to her left where only the low flame of a wall sconce caught pale glints of light from gilt wallpaper. Glass gleamed softly at the end of the hallway. She almost ran against the door before she saw it was not a mirror. Desperately Elizabeth shook the knob. It gave easily and she stumbled through it into a conservatory, her heart shaking in her chest.

The door closed behind her. Green smells engulfed her, filled her nostrils; tall plants in huge pots towered over her, bowed over trellises making a tunnel of verdant leaves and dim white blooms. The only light came from tall glass windows that formed two slanted end walls of the room. Somewhere nearby a heat source warmed the damp air. Elizabeth passed orange and lemon trees, orchids on their graceful stalks like flocks of exotic birds. She found a bench facing one of the glass walls and dropped onto it, clutching the seat as if she might fall off. The admission of her feelings for Darcy had shaken her to her soul.

*I cannot love him, I cannot! Lydia, relatives in trade, no dowry, no connections, his sister, it would ruin him. I have to go away. Go somewhere, find employment so he will never be able to look at me like that again. There is no choice, I must do it for his sake. Oh, God, please help me! I love him...*

In the ballroom Darcy watched her flee with mixed emotions. He wanted desperately to follow her, but duty forced him to look for his uncle instead. Lord Matlock stood with two of his cronies at the far side of the room. Darcy came up to them as one of the other men laughed at some jest. It was a moment before the earl saw his nephew, then the expression on Darcy's face caused him to excuse himself and step away from his friends.

"What has happened?" he demanded in a low voice.

"We must speak privately, Uncle, at once."

Lord Matlock turned without a word and led the way to his study. In the hall and entry guests formed small groups, bidding each other good night, waiting for their wraps or for carriages to be summoned. The two men made their way past the crowd with a few words to this or that guest. When the study door closed behind them, Lord Matlock faced his nephew, his expression grim.

"It is Chadwick, is it not? He was supposed to be here tonight."

"Adele."

"Damn the woman! What has she done now?"

"Tried to commit suicide."

The older man's face whitened. "Tell me she did not succeed."

"She did not. Her maid found her and called Chadwick, who sent for a doctor. She is quite ill, but will survive. The maid will say nothing, but Chadwick was beside himself. I stayed with him to ensure he did not let the servants know what occurred. Once we were sure she was out of danger he calmed enough to see sense in keeping the situation quiet. He gave out that she was taken with a sudden fever. The doctor, of course, will keep silent."

"Thank you, Will. The family owes you a great debt." Lord Matlock went to a sidebar and poured two small whiskies, handing one to Darcy. "I will go see him as soon as the crush diminishes. I do not want talk that I hurried from the house as soon as the ball was over. And I must let your aunt know." He swallowed half his drink at a gulp. "It is her father at the root of it, the 'Count'. He has more than enough to live an appropriate life but he is always asking for more. And in spite of what Chad says, Adele's gambling has drained his coffers to a degree that it has to stop. My threat to cut her father off was meant to curtail her behavior, not bring on this—this madness. Did she not think of her children?"

"I do not believe Adele is capable of considering anyone but herself." Darcy drank a little of the whisky and set the glass down. "If there is nothing else at the moment, I have someone I need to speak with. I will ask my aunt to join you here."

"Of course, of course." Lord Matlock finished the whisky in his glass, looked at the sidebar, and put his glass aside. "I shall let you know how we are to proceed."

"Thank you, Uncle."

Impatient now that his information had been passed to the proper person, Darcy returned to the ballroom. He did not see Elizabeth but her aunt stood with Lady Matlock. He bowed to them, glanced around for Elizabeth without success.

"Aunt Eleanor, my uncle would like to speak to you. He is in his study."

Lady Matlock knew her nephew and husband well enough to know Lord Matlock's summons had nothing to do with the ball. She excused herself and went out, leaving Darcy with Mrs. Gardiner.

"I do not see Miss Bennet. She left the dance abruptly, I trust she is well?"

"My niece probably just wanted some fresh air. She may have stepped out onto the terrace."

Darcy bowed and made his way to the glass doors leading to a terrace along the entire side of the house. Several groups and couples were still enjoying the scented chill of the night air. Elizabeth was not among them. Darcy hurried along the flagged width of the veranda to the first open door he saw. He passed through a small parlor to the main hallway, his heart thudding in his chest. A liveried and bewigged footman stood on duty near the front door. *She would not have gone that way. Where is she? What happened in there, what did I see in her eyes? Love but more—fear?*

Darcy continued along the corridor, opening several closed doors to find dark empty rooms. At the end of the hallway he stopped. To his right a short hall that had once led to an outside door showed a plastered and painted wall, a misty garden behind an arched trellis covered in yellow trumpet flowers. Before it a pillar stand held a large ceramic pot whose verdant fern exploded like a green firework. He turned left, immediately caught by the glimmer of a glass door: the conservatory.

His hand caught the doorknob before he stopped, uncertain. Emotions swirled and clashed through his mind. *She wanted solace, quiet, have I a right to disturb her? But if she is ill or in need I cannot simply leave her alone. I do not want to take advantage of her, I have no right to impose on her when she is vulnerable. I only want to see if she is well. Elizabeth...*

Darcy was inside the conservatory before he realized he had crossed the threshold. The door closed behind him. He paused to orient himself in the heavily scented darkness redolent of exotic places. Darcy passed under a trellis much like the painted one, through a jungle of verdant foliage, past tropical flowers and trees in waist-high pots. The smells of citrus and spice assaulted his senses. Darcy felt a growing panic—where was she?

He saw her suddenly; his breath stopped, Darcy did not move. The snow had ceased, moonlight fell obliquely through slanted glass walls, striping everything with opal radiance. Elizabeth sat on a bench with her back to him, arms wrapped tightly around herself, her head bowed. He knew without a sound that she was crying.

At that moment nothing on earth could have kept him from her.

Elizabeth did not raise her head as Darcy dropped to one knee at her feet and carefully took her hands in his. "Elizabeth."

She heard the soft caress of her name. He covered her hands with his, pressed them to his chest. His heart thudded against her skin.

"I only wanted to know that you are not ill."

Elizabeth tried to make the conventional reply, *I am quite well, thank you.* Her voice betrayed her, she shook her head once, unable to form the lie. Darcy took out his handkerchief and blotted the tears from her face, put it in her hands. He rose and sat beside her, wrenching pain filling his chest. *I should leave her, I have to leave her, if I do not—*

Her fingers closed around his as he started to rise. He barely heard the word, "Stay."

Darcy sank back onto the bench. He took her in his arms as if it were the most natural action in the world. For a time they sat in silence, her head on his shoulder, his face resting against her hair that smelled of lavender. At last when he had convinced himself to ask her if she wanted to return to the ball or if he might bring her aunt, she turned her face up to his and he was kissing her, reveling in the feel of her soft mouth that opened to him with the innocence of a flower. Darcy could not stop himself. He wrapped her in his arms and when they both gasped for breath he broke the kiss, still holding her against him, her head bowed on his shoulder.

Darcy gently released her taking both of her hands in his. "I want you to be happy, Elizabeth. I want to see you smile and hear you laugh again. I want to wash away all the darkness in your life. I want to share your life and have you share mine." His eyes burned with a dark fire that seared her heart. Darcy brought her hands to his lips, kissing the soft skin. "I want you to be my..."

Elizabeth pressed two fingers to his lips. They trembled like her voice. "Do not say it. We both know that it cannot happen. To go on can cause only misery. One day you will marry a lady of wealth and status to give you an heir to Pemberley. When that day comes I want you to be without regrets."

"My only regret will be to live without you. Elizabeth, do not do this to yourself, do not think that I can simply walk away and forget. I love you."

The dark thing stirred in her mind. She pulled her hands from his,, her heart seemed to stop for a beat before it began to flutter against her ribs. Elizabeth forced herself to speak past a throat that wanted to close off the words.

"You do not know what you ask. Please, do not do this!"

"I ask you to be my wife. I love you Elizabeth, why is that wrong?"

She stood up so abruptly Darcy instinctively leaned away. Elizabeth took a step backward. The dark thing surged in her, roaring, uncontrolled. Darcy rose, towering in the shadowy glimmer of moonlight on snow.

Cold fire filled her, radiated in her voice. "You do not know, you cannot know, cannot understand! Even your dearest family will turn away from you."

"My family will abide by my decision. I am my own man. There will be no break because I marry where I choose."

Elizabeth felt her body shaking with a force she could not control. Her words spilled out as floodwater spills over a weir. "Friends you have known from childhood will shun you. No one will care what becomes of you. You will be alone and Georgiana will be destroyed along with you!"

Darcy fought for control. Reason, he had no defense but reason against this violent storm, these irrational objections. "Georgiana is going to marry Mr. Worthington. She is not in danger of rejection by our family. As for the *ton* do you think me so weak that I would sacrifice a lifetime of happiness for the good opinion of people for whom I have only disdain?"

"There is no happiness." Elizabeth seemed not to hear him. The darkness had reached its crescendo and begun to sink into oblivion. Her voice dropped, she looked through him to a future without light.

"It will not stop, it will not go away, you will never draw a breath without regret for what you have done. I will not let you. I will not agree to your ruin because of—of love."

"Then send me away." Darcy's voice cut through the stillness of the encroaching dark. "Tell me to go, say you do not want to see me again. One word from you and I will leave your life forever."

"I...I do...I do not..." Elizabeth fought for breath against the crushing pain in her chest.

"Say it," he commanded.

Something in Elizabeth shattered, jagged shards ripping her with unbearable pain. "I cannot!"

Darcy dared not touch her. He spoke so gently the words were a caress. "Why not?"

"Because I love you."

Her whisper barely reached him. She was gone so suddenly Darcy was immobilized with shock. He moved forward only to see pale pink velvet as another blossom among the lush dark foliage. He ran after her; long fronds swept over him, tangling stalks obscured his path, holding him back, impeding his passage. He reached the door to the corridor to find it open. His crumpled handkerchief lay on the threshold. Darcy achieved the main hallway in three strides. Elizabeth had vanished.

# CHAPTER NINETEEN

January 1815
Meadow Lane, London

Jane had become worried when Elizabeth did not return to the ballroom to join her and Bingley, as she was to stay with them for several days. Her anxiety increased with Mrs. Gardiner's remark that her niece had seemed agitated after her dance with Mr. Darcy, although he had not followed her but left the room with his uncle. Jane checked the rapidly emptying entry without locating her sister. At last she tried the ladies retiring room. Elizabeth sat on a sofa staring at nothing. She did not look up at Jane's entrance until her sister sat beside her and took her hand.

"Lizzy, what is wrong? Are you ill?"

Elizabeth slowly turned her head at Jane's voice. "I…I have a terrible megrim."

Her voice was barely audible. Jane rose immediately. "Charles has sent for our carriage. Stay here,, I will get your wrap and tell aunt so she will not worry. Once we are home you can rest."

Elizabeth did not respond. Jane left her for the few minutes she needed to inform their aunt and uncle that Elizabeth had a sick headache and obtain her evening cloak before gathering her sister for the trip to Hephaestus House. In the carriage she sat beside Elizabeth with Bingley across from them. They had barely turned into the street when Jane felt her sister clutch her arm.

"I want to go to Meadow Lane."

Jane looked quickly at her husband. "Dearest, you will be more comfortable with us. If you do not wish to stay you can go back tomorrow."

Elizabeth bent forward still holding Jane's arm. She could not explain, could not tell her sister and Darcy's best friend what had occurred. She wanted silence. She wanted solitude. Every word from someone else, even someone as dear as Jane, was a scrape over a raw wound.

"Jane, please, take me home. *Please!*"

Bingley shook his head at his wife. He was vaguely aware that something of importance had happened with no way of knowing what it had been. To force Elizabeth to accompany them seemed wrong to him. She was not a prisoner after all. He rapped on the roof and gave the coachman instructions to the house on Meadow Lane.

"Lizzy, at least let me come in and see you settled. I will worry if you are alone and ill."

"Nettie—Nettie is there. She can help me."

"We will call first thing tomorrow," Bingley said, more to his wife than Elizabeth. "Just to see how you are faring."

Elizabeth did not disagree. She heard his words as sounds outside the shell of her isolation. Jane held her hand until the carriage pulled into the drive. Bingley got out and handed his sister-by-marriage out. Jane kissed her cheek before Elizabeth descended. He walked her to the door, heard the bolt go home, and went back to his wife. This was a neighborhood where a carriage stopping at this time of the morning might well bring someone to a window. The sooner they departed, the better.

"She is ill, Charles." Jane was worried. She had never seen her sister suffer from a migraine of such intensity. "Nettie is devoted to her, but if she is not better in the morning we will call Dr. Griswald."

"Certainly." He sat beside his wife and put an arm around her. "She has seemed exhausted of late. Perhaps the ball was simply one event too many."

Jane did not contradict him, but in her heart she knew Elizabeth's behavior was not normal. She shivered in apprehension. Bingley drew her closer. They would be home soon and his angel could rest. Tomorrow would come soon enough.

In the house Elizabeth leaned her back against the door until her knees were able to hold her. Nettie was asleep. She had no intention of waking the maid. She only wanted the sanctuary of her room, of dark and quiet space. To her leaden legs the stairs seemed to go up and up. At last she entered her bedroom, unlit, unwarmed by the clean empty fireplace. Elizabeth did not feel the cold. She got out of her gown, dropped it on a chair and removed her short stays, her hands moving without conscious direction. There was a petticoat and her stockings. She stripped off everything but her shift and wrapped her robe around her.

Elizabeth's eyes were becoming accustomed to the dark. Her body felt heavy, her limbs unwieldy. Jane's rocking chair was at hand; Elizabeth fell into it, no longer able to stand. Leaning back she closed her eyes. She was aware of nothing through the gray mist that engulfed her. An icy draft from the window drifted around her unfelt.

*Gone, he is gone. The only man I have ever loved, ever could love is gone from my life. I have sent him away. He will never return.*

The bite of cold finally stirred Elizabeth from her stupor. She still sat in the chair, stiff and shaking with cold. An indigo square of night sky told her the curtains were partially open. After several tries, Elizabeth pulled herself to her feet and shuffled to the window. Although she could not see it, the china clock on the mantel read twenty minutes after four. Over two hours had passed as if time stood still.

Freezing rain scratched at the open top of the window, a dark puddle spread on the floor where it had blown in under the eaves and dripped down. She closed the window and the curtains, tore off her robe and threw it on the wet floor. He was gone. She had sent him away and he would never return. Elizabeth stumbled to the bed and crawled in, wrapping the covers around her as tightly as she was able. Curled like a sick child she shook with tremors she could not control, too numb to cry. The dark forge within had died.

Elizabeth closed her eyes and tried to will herself warm. She had no strength to get up and start a fire. Life inevitably continued, endless years of emptiness, loneliness, pretending to be content when her soul screamed out for him and there was no answer. A little warmth began to touch her icy skin. She barely felt it. She must make decisions, plan what to do now, but all she saw was Darcy's face, white stone except for those wonderful dark eyes burning into hers, telling her her life was over.

*Gone, gone, gone…*

The gray fog filled her mind. She gave herself to it. Anything was better than that image filling her with unendurable pain. Elizabeth slid quietly into limbo.

# January 1815
# Darcy House, London

Darcy sent his coach ahead with Georgiana and walked the short distance home. By the time he reached Darcy House, wet snow had soaked through his light overcoat leaving his clothing clinging unpleasantly to his body. He entered the house using a key he had taken with him. The night footman looked at him curiously before resuming his professionally blank countenance. Darcy climbed the stairs to the second floor to find Martin waiting for him in his dressing room. The valet removed Darcy's coat and assisted him out of his clothing, as if his master coming home in such a condition at well past midnight was quite normal.

"Do you wish a hot bath, sir?"

Darcy roused from the pain that had taken over his mind since he left Matlock House. "No, it is too late. Just water for washing."

Martin said, "Yes, sir." He retrieved the jug of water from the edge of the fireplace and mixed it with cold water from the ewer on the washstand.

Stripped to his underwear, Darcy washed his face and upper body as if it would take away the memories of that night. Elizabeth burning like a torch in the wind, full of such pain he could hardly breathe. Denying him, fighting his every attempt to reassure her; at last her words *'Because I love you'* before she fled from him.

The images ripped through his brain. It took Martin two tries to get his attention and help him into his nightshirt and robe. Darcy dismissed him with a gesture of his hand. He made his way to a chair before his bedroom fire and sank into it. A groan of pure agony escaped him. What had he done? Desire, unchecked and unregulated, brought him to this nadir. He had not meant to speak, not meant to press her; he had only wanted to comfort her. Or so he told himself. When she welcomed his kiss, he thought she accepted his presence and what it meant. He had been so terribly wrong.

All his life, Fitzwilliam Darcy had lived in the iron chains of duty: to family, to his heritage, to Georgiana, to Pemberley and its dependents. He had fulfilled his obligations without demur and without resentment. Until now. Until Elizabeth Bennet opened his eyes to his own disregard for anything or anyone who did not fit into his rigid world. Until he had come to love her more than his soul. He had failed her, he had failed himself, and there was a price to pay: the loss of any happiness he might have had in his life.

Darcy woke with fingers of sunlight poking over the top of the drawn drapes. He was covered with a blanket and Martin was making discreet noises with a coffee service. Throwing off the blanket, Darcy took the cup Martin proffered and drank it in two swallows, ignoring the burn.

"Your bath will be ready in five minutes, Mr. Darcy. Will you be staying in this morning?"

"Yes."

Where else was there to go?

Darcy bathed, dressed and made his way to his study. He looked into the breakfast parlor as he passed, knowing it would be empty. After a late night, Georgiana slept until nearly noon and took tea and toast in her room rather than come down to a regular meal. His stomach revolted at the smell of food. He went on to his study and sat behind the solid block of his desk. Neat stacks of papers defined the space along with his writing materials. The miniature of Georgie watched him with a soft stare. After several minutes he rose and went to the fireplace, sinking into one of the two large leather chairs placed there.

He was still there an hour later when Mr. Burgess tapped at the door, and then, without waiting for his reply, admitted a visitor. Too lethargic to be angry, Darcy sat up at the sound of his cousin's voice.

"Thank you, Burgess. If you would organize a pot of coffee and something to eat I would appreciate it."

"Yes, sir."

The door closed discreetly. Richard strode to the hearth and surveyed his cousin with some concern. Darcy looked up at him and indicated the other chair. "If you are done giving my servants orders you might as well sit down."

Richard did so. "I am not here by chance. My mother asked me to look in on you. She tells me there was some sort of upset after the ball last night and you disappeared at the same time as Miss Bennet."

"She need not have worried." Darcy's voice was uncharacteristically bitter. He moved restlessly, slammed his fist on the arm of the chair. His head fell back and the anger went out of him. "I have lost her, Richard."

Richard did not answer immediately. Mr. Burgess brought in a footman carrying a tray with coffee and sweet rolls. When they were placed on a table within easy reach of the two men he withdrew as discreetly as he had come. Richard rose, poured two cups, added a tot of brandy to both and put one in Darcy's hands.

"Get outside of that and tell me what happened."

Darcy sipped the brew. It took him some time before he began. His cousin waited with the patience of a soldier used to waiting. At last Darcy set the cup down and ran both hands through his hair.

"Your mother gave me some very good advice that I did not follow."

"My mother has her failings, but a lack of insight is not one of them. What was it?"

"Not to press my suit with Elizabeth. To allow her time. I meant to do so, but…she was so beautiful as we danced. I saw in her eyes that she loved me. When she ran from the ballroom I wanted to follow, however I had to tell uncle about Adele."

Richard's face darkened. "Father told me when he got back from Chad's. They are employing a private nurse for the time being until some decisions can be made. Go on, Will. What happened?"

"I found her crying in the conservatory and everything just…happened. She wanted me, it was as if she accepted me, accepted what I offered. I did not mean to propose, the words just came out and suddenly it was as if she became a different woman. She was so angry, so adamant that my life would be ruined if we married. I answered her objections but she did not seem to hear me. Then I…I told her to send me away if she did not want to be with me. Her last words were— that she loved me." Darcy's voice dropped to a torn murmur. "Then she ran from me. I could not find her, so I came home. She has gone and I will never convince her to marry me now."

Richard was silent for some minutes while his cousin stared blindly at the fire. "Miss Elizabeth has admitted to her feelings for you; those are not easily put aside. She has been betrayed over and over, by her sister, by her friends and neighbors, by life. Now that Mrs. Bingley has a husband and potentially a family, the last person she can absolutely trust has left her."

"She said our marriage would destroy me. As if she was tainted by Lydia's actions."

"Not by that alone, Will. I have seen men after a battle where they fought like tigers return to camp and collapse. Sometimes it happens days later. They are like walking dead men." He refrained from telling Darcy that some had even committed suicide. "It usually passes in time. I do not understand it, however I think something of the sort has happened to her. In the heat of fighting, trying to survive, nothing else matters. When the fighting is over a reaction sets in. She may need nothing more than time to recover."

Darcy remained silent. "You are right, Cousin. I have been thinking more of myself than of her. My need, my feelings have been foremost in my mind. Not purposely, but the damage is done nonetheless." They sat in silence for a time listening to the purr of the fire and the seeking wind outside. The wall of pain inside Darcy shivered but did not break. "I have work to do at Pemberley, spring planting, field plans, tenant matters. I shall go there and do what needs to be done. Perhaps, in time…"

His voice trailed away. Richard said, "I think that may be the wisest course. It is a well-used adage, however some wounds do heal with time."

The two men rose and shook hands. After Richard left Darcy did not move. Yes, he would return to Pemberley, his center, his sanctuary. If there was any peace to be found, it would be there.

## January 1815
## Meadow Lane, London

"Oh, Mrs. Bingley, thank Heaven you've come. I was just going for Dr. Griswald." The maid's agitation was obvious. Her face was pinched, she wore her cloak but had not removed her apron.

"Nettie, what has happened. Is it my sister…?"

"Yes, madam. I didn't know she had come back, I thought she was with you. I remembered I'd left the window in her bedroom open to air the room and when I went to close it I found her in bed. I—I tried to wake her, but I couldn't. Mrs. Hobson is with her, I have to go for the doctor."

Jane felt her knees grow unsteady. Bingley's hand on her arm and his steady voice reassured her. "Go up to Lizzy. I will take Nettie in the carriage for the doctor."

She hurried up the familiar stairs to the first floor. From below she heard the front door close and increased her pace. The cook looked up then rose with a curtsey as Jane came in, putting the chair aside. Jane bent over the bed. Elizabeth had been turned onto her back under an extra blanket. The two servants had dressed her in a nightgown and taken the pins out of her hair but not tried to brush it out, so it lay in a tangle of curls on the pillow. Her face was waxen. Jane listened for her breathing, terror holding her heart in a vice. After several seconds she identified the slow rise and fall of Elizabeth's chest.

"I am here, dearest," she said softly. "The doctor will arrive soon. Oh, Lizzy, what happened, how did you come to this?"

Mrs. Hobson had withdrawn to the fireplace. She added more coal and stirred the burning lumps. Both window and curtains were closed but Elizabeth's shift lay in a sodden mass on the floor beneath a sill that gleamed with wet. The housekeeper took it with her. Jane pulled the chair back to the bedside and sat down, dropping her reticule beside it. She spoke without turning.

"My husband has taken Nettie to fetch Dr. Griswald as he does not know the way. I do not know what the doctor may need, but it would be well to have hot water ready, if you will, Mrs. Hobson."

"Yes, madam."

Mrs. Hobson left the room without comment until she was in the kitchen. "Unlucky house, or unlucky family. Take your pick."

Bingley was back with Dr. Griswald in a quarter hour. Mrs. Hobson let them in and was asked by the doctor for hot water. He went immediately to Elizabeth's room where Jane indicated the bed and its unmoving occupant. After washing his hands, Dr. Griswald set his bag on the night table and began to examine his patient.

"Has she shown any symptoms you are aware of, Mrs. Bingley?"

"We were at Lady Matlock's ball last night. At the end she complained of a severe megrim and wanted to return here. I tried to convince her to come home with my husband and me, but she was so insistent—I have never seen her like that. She assured us Nettie would take care of her. I have found that Nettie thought her with us and only found her this morning in...in this condition."

The doctor straightened. "I am not absolutely certain, but I do not believe she has had a brain seizure. She is very young for such a thing, and she does not have the symptoms. Did anything happen at this ball to frighten or upset her badly?"

Jane held her hands tightly before her. "She danced the last set with Mr.—with a gentleman. As soon as it was over, she left the ballroom. My aunt said he remained to speak to his uncle, then they left together. I found Lizzy in the ladies' retiring room a few minutes later. She seemed dazed."

Dr. Griswald studied the floor for several moments. He met Jane's eyes. "I want to make a more thorough examination, if you will permit me."

Jane tried to understand his meaning and failed. She nodded stiffly. "If it will help Lizzy."

"Please wait over there." He indicated the door to the dressing room. It took him five minutes to satisfy himself that she had not been violated. He pulled the covers over her and turned to Jane. "I have seen people in this condition once or twice before when something completely disrupted their lives, a fire, the death of a spouse or child. It is a form of shock. The mind cannot accept what has happened and so it retreats to silence and sleep."

"What happens then?"

"If they regain consciousness in a day or two, they will gradually recover. I would not advise moving her until she is fully conscious and able to get around under her own power. Make sure you do not let her go too long without at least drinking water or broth. I will call tomorrow to see how she progresses, if you like."

Jane assured him she would be grateful for his attendance. She resumed the chair when he was gone and took up her sister's hand. "Rest, dearest. Whatever caused you such distress cannot touch you while I am here."

Elizabeth did not stir at her sister's touch and words, but she sighed. Jane, ever hopeful, took it as a good sign.

## March 1815
## Pemberley Manor, Derbyshire

Darcy had thought at Pemberley, his refuge, his earth, blood and bones of his ancestors, he might find peace. But it was not possible. She was with him every day, every hour, making him always aware of the guilt he wore like an iron coat. If he lost focus on the work at hand for a moment her phantom appeared in his mind. Walking in the gardens, her face to the sun; seated at the mistress' place at dinner, her voice floating along the table, full of laughter like a carillon of silver bells; sweeping through the halls and corridors in a swirl of silk; sitting in a bay of the library with a book, her lower lip caught in her teeth as she concentrated on the text. In his bed, drowned in passion, the scent of her, the taste of her mouth, the feel of her pliant body under him consumed with rapture…

It would never be. He had learned of her illness from Georgiana two days after that terrible night at Matlock House. She knocked on the door of his study barely waiting for his response before hurtling into the room, breathless and shaking.

"Fitzwilliam, Lizzy is very ill! They would not let me see her, she cannot see anyone but family. What could have happened? She seemed fine at the Twelfth Night ball."

Darcy was out from behind his desk before she finished. Georgiana was trying not to cry, with little success. He sat her in one of the chairs before the desk and brought her a little port to sip before he took the other chair. Her color began to return after a minute. She handed him the glass and pulled out a handkerchief, blotting her eyes.

"I found out when I went to visit her at the Bingleys. I thought she was staying with them, but she is not there, she is at the house where they used to live. No one knows what happened to her, but Charles told me both a local doctor and Sir Edgar Crane believe it is some form of shock as she has no injuries."

*Shock. Yes, I shocked her. I could not exercise a little more patience and this is what I have done to my Elizabeth. Richard was right: she has carried too many burdens, one more was enough to destroy her.*

"Do they believe she—she will recover?"

"They hope so. At present she is to be kept very quiet. I have sent flowers for her, but—Fitzwilliam, what could have happened?"

Darcy bowed his head. How was he to tell his sister that he had destroyed her dear friend and the woman he loved? He temporized. "Richard said recently that sometimes soldiers after fighting for their lives will collapse when the battle is over. Miss Bennet is a strong woman," *women who are strong are strong because they have to be,* "and she has been like a soldier since the Bennet family's troubles began. If she no longer has to fight to survive perhaps the lack of that purpose has left her ill."

"I am not sure I understand the idea. Richard has seen a great deal more of life than anyone I know. If he is right, do those men recover?"

"Usually, in time." He swallowed with a dry throat. "The doctors are taking good care of her I am certain."

"Charles told me they will move Elizabeth to Hephaestus House as soon as she is able. It will be easier for her to be cared for there."

"In that event, you will probably be able to visit her in a few days."

*If she tells you what happened, will you hate me as much as I hate myself? I did not see how my offer could harm her. I did not listen to my aunt or Richard, only my own selfish desires.*

Darcy stayed locked in his study for the remainder of the day. He refrained from drinking, sitting at the hearth until the fire died and chill crept into his bones. Even after he dragged himself to bed there was no sleep for him that night. In the morning he bathed, dressed and ordered his carriage to take him to Hephaestus House. Bingley saw him in the drawing room. He looked more haggard than Darcy expected. After the two men shook hands, Bingley waved him to a chair and offered him a brandy.

"Jane has hardly slept since we found Elizabeth at the house. When she is able to be moved we will bring her maid with her. The girl is devoted to Elizabeth and will help care for her. Sir Edgar will continue to look in on her, but he agrees with Dr. Griswald, the local man there. She has experienced some sort of mental crisis. She is in a state somewhat like a coma without the more severe manifestations. He believes given her age and state of health that she has a very good chance of recovery."

"Does he know how long it may take?"

"Dr. Crane says it varies from case to case. He has little experience in matters of this kind. They are fortunately rare."

Darcy rose. "I am leaving for Pemberley tomorrow. I have abandoned it long enough. If you could allow Georgiana to see Miss Bennet as soon as she is well enough I would appreciate it. She is quite distressed."

"As are we all. Certainly, I shall send word to her when Elizabeth can have visitors."

"Georgiana is staying at Matlock House. Thank you, Charles."

As the weeks passed at Pemberley, Darcy forced himself to concentrate on the spring planting and other estate business by sheer force of will. Georgiana had elected to remain in London with the Matlocks. In her newfound maturity she had informed him that with her friend ill and Mr. Worthington deeply involved in the steam engine project she preferred to be of what use she could in London rather than worry uselessly in Derbyshire. Darcy missed her, however he was a little comforted to have a source of information about Elizabeth.

Several weeks after he left London, Georgiana had written that Elizabeth was improving and now took meals with the family and short walks in the park. Caroline's wedding date had been set for April first, which gave Darcy cause for a wry smile. He wrote a note to Rundell, Bridge and Rundell ordering a silver tea service engraved with Sir Eustace's crest to be sent to Hephaestus House for the couple. Caroline would appreciate the expense and Sir Eustace the gesture. His sister's subsequent letters detailed her days, her lessons, the books she read and the concerts and plays she attended.

Darcy had felt unable to ask Georgiana for detailed information about Elizabeth. He had to content himself with small items; she went with Georgiana and her sister for tea at Lady Addington's. Mrs. Fortesque was also there with preliminary plans for a new private library that would serve women who wished to study subjects usually only pursued by men. They drove in the park, she stayed with her aunt and uncle for several days. At least, he assured himself, Elizabeth was improving. It was his only comfort in a constant weight of regret and guilt.

Darcy briefly debated remaining at Pemberley for the rest of the summer. Georgiana could go with Lord and Lady Matlock to their estate of Foxwood to escape the summer swelter of London. And Elizabeth, always Elizabeth. If she was well enough to travel she might go north with Bingley and her sister to Scarborough to meet his family. If not, surely the Gardiners would look after her. Always the painful knowledge that one day he must face her. Darcy had begun to have the old nightmare again. Elizabeth in the freezing mist, hating him, sending him away; this time he had no defense.

On March 6th Darcy received a short letter from Richard.

*Rosings Park, Kent*
*Darcy,*
*As I feared, Napoleon has escaped Elba and landed in Marseilles. There will be a renewal of hostilities and the War Department has offered me a temporary contract to train troops. I am tempted, but I*

*served king and country for over a decade, and so I declined. I have a
wife and an estate to care for and there are enough officers on half pay
who can perform the job as well as I.*

*I am returning to Rosings to consult with my steward. When I am
satisfied, I will bring Anne from Town for the summer. Anne wants to
invite Georgiana to join us, if you have no other plans? The Bingleys
will leave for the north after Miss Bingley's wedding and do not an-
ticipate returning until later in the year. I do not know if Miss Bennet
is accompanying them. If not, Anne may ask her to visit Rosings. She
has developed a friendship with the lady and I am certain Georgiana
would enjoy her company.*

*Yrs., etc.*

*Richard*

Richard's mention of Elizabeth was a godsend. He had no
way of knowing the current state of her mind, however without
Lady Catherine in residence and with Anne's and most probably
Georgiana's company he had no reason to doubt that Elizabeth
would find Rosings a place of peace and friendship. Darcy found
himself unable to settle on a plan for the immediate future except to
apply himself to matters of Pemberley estate for long hours in hopes
of exhausting himself enough to sleep. It did not prove a success.

He spent time in the library when there was nothing to occupy
his mind. Mr. Bennet's books had been uncrated but not yet shelved.
The retired professor of literature he employed when he needed a
librarian had them neatly ordered waiting for Darcy to decide if they
were to be integrated into the general collection or set aside as a
separate group. Idly he opened a volume of Petrarch's *Sonnets*. There
was the bookplate: *Ex Libris* Thomas Carlisle Bennet. Darcy closed
the book and replaced it on the stack.

*These should be with her. Perhaps when she is settled she will accept them,
or Bingley can pay me a token sum for them and give them to her. She can
hardly refuse them from him.*

Darcy knew, as he had long known, that he would never be free of her. He also knew he must try to make his peace with her rejection, and that would not be accomplished until he had faced her. Originally he had intended to travel to London for Caroline Bingley's wedding, but Darcy knew Elizabeth would be there, and he was not yet ready to see her. He would write Charles citing pressure of estate matters that kept him from attending. His excuse would be accepted with the unspoken understanding that Darcy wanted no chance of Lady Samuelson creating an awkwardness.

Darcy continued to apply himself to Pemberley's maintenance. Rains came, there was flooding along the river when a small earthen dam failed, inundating several fields. An overset candle caused a fire that required moving the tenant family to a temporary location while their cottage was repaired. And always Elizabeth was with him.

March came to an end and April dragged slowly past. Darcy knew it was time. He summoned Mr. Niles and Mrs. Reynolds for a final conference and asked Martin to pack his trunks. He was returning to London to beg Elizabeth's understanding—he did not expect her to forgive him—and accept the final end of his dreams.

# May 1815
# Rosings Park, Kent

Elizabeth sat on an old wrought iron bench in the gardens at Rosings Park, the solidity of the rambling structure some fifty yards behind her. Hedges marked off various areas, as if the plants and shrubs could not be trusted to stay in their own set places and would ramble about if not strictly contained. The house was a relatively new building constructed for Sir Lewis de Bourgh's first wife on the site of an older mansion. Anne told her Lady Catherine was never fond of the manor house. Elizabeth doubted the noblewoman was any fonder of the idea of being a second wife.

A short way from where Elizabeth rested the hedges abruptly

stopped, giving way to a lawn that sloped down to a stream and a little folly. An old apple tree held pride of place above the swath of green, its pink blossoms promising summer bounty. Beyond the folly trees were painted in stillness on a lucent blue sky. It was a lovely scene. Elizabeth wondered if Georgiana might paint it now that her critical relative was not there to discourage her.

Anne had spoken briefly of her mother when Elizabeth and Georgiana accepted her invitation to join her at Rosings Park. Lady Catherine's residence in Bath seemed to suit her. She had friends there, elderly like herself, rigid of attitude toward their social status like herself, full of complaints about nearly every aspect of life, like herself. She did not write to her daughter, for which Anne seemed grateful in a somber way. Richard received brief reports of her activities monthly. Thus far there had been no problems.

Georgiana was too well bred and too sensitive to hover over her friend, but Elizabeth knew the younger woman was concerned for her health. She had not told Georgiana or anyone else what occurred the night of the ball. Beneath her steady emotional improvement the pain was still too raw to share. Jane had accepted her sister's explanation that all of the events of the past three years had struck her at once, causing her to fall ill. It was the truth, just not the whole truth. When Elizabeth stayed with the Gardiners her aunt had questioned her gently. Elizabeth knew Mrs. Gardiner was too shrewd to believe she was hearing the complete story, but respected her niece's right to privacy.

From the moment Elizabeth woke in her bedroom on Meadow Lane, she knew a time would come when she had to face the past and the event that brought it to crisis. Jane's drawn face was her first image. She took Elizabeth's hand, tears falling unheeded down her cheeks.

"Lizzy. Lizzy, can you speak? Oh, Lizzy, we have been so worried!"

The entire room had a green cast as if Elizabeth saw it from underwater. As the green faded and Jane's dear face came more sharply into focus Elizabeth knew a time would come when she must confront the thing that had torn her apart. It was dead, but its ghost remained. She had escaped it for a time; now she could retreat from it no longer. Elizabeth rose from the bench and straightened her skirts, thinking to walk to the little folly. Nettie's call stopped her. She turned to find the maid hurrying toward her with a letter in her hand.

"I'm sorry to disturb you, madam, but this came in the post and I thought you might want to see it."

Elizabeth took the letter with a murmured thanks. It was from her aunt Gardiner and felt as if it contained at least two pages. For a moment she wondered if something had happened to one of her sisters before common sense told her that would have come as an express not a regular communication. She dismissed Nettie and put the letter in her dress pocket. With a parasol to manage as well as her skirts she did not wish to drop it before she reached her goal.

The folly was a perfect miniature Greek temple built by previous owners of the estate. Elizabeth had visited it before and found it a quiet place to read or simply enjoy the view. The stream ran past it over an artificial waterfall which added the soothing sound of rushing water. Inside its round circumference a marble ledge provided seating. The open pillars at the front allowed light to enter without flooding the space. Elizabeth folded her parasol, removed her bonnet, and prepared to see what her aunt had to say.

She broke the seal and opened the sheet, surprised to find a second letter within. Elizabeth caught her breath at the sight of her name; just the one word, Lizzy, and recognized the handwriting on the paper. It was her father's. *"Letter...desk..."* Elizabeth began to tremble. Those were his last words. She shut her eyes tightly to dispel the images, clutching the papers until they crackled. In her distress at his passing she had completely forgotten.

Slowly Elizabeth forced herself to regain her composure. Her father was gone, surely a letter from him was not designed to upset her. Still, she took up her aunt's missive first.

*My dear Lizzy,*

*When your uncle went to the Meadow Lane house with some of his men to move out the furniture and household goods you are disposing of, they found that one of the drawers in the desk in Thomas' room was locked. Thinking it perhaps contained something of value, Mr. Gardiner opened it with a key on the ring Jane gave him. It contained the enclosed letter. We did not give it to you while you were ill in the event it might cause you unnecessary distress. Since you are better, we felt you should have it. I hope you will forgive us for waiting. I know your father loved you dearly. If it contains any instructions we can assist you with, please write your uncle and he will do whatever he is able.*

*Your loving aunt,*

*Margaret Gardiner*

Elizabeth refolded her aunt's missive and put it in her dress pocket. She held the letter from her father in both hands, strangely unwilling to open it. The writing was not as strong as it once would have been, but clearly his. With slow fingers Elizabeth broke the seal and opened the paper.

*My dearest Lizzy,*

*When you read this I will be with your mother. I cannot seem to speak these words so I will put them on paper. I am sorry, Lizzy, for bringing shame and sorrow on my family. Yes, it is my fault as much or more than Lydia's. When it came to the moral guidance and discipline I owed the children I brought into this world, I took the easy path. I never had doubts of you or Jane, or even Mary. I abdicated my responsibility to all of you, but it was worse for Kitty and especially Lydia. I let Mrs. Bennet raise them as she saw fit rather than bother with the duties of a father. It was a terrible mistake. In the end it cost all of us everything of real value in our lives. It is too late for me, but not for you and Jane. Watch over her, Lizzy. Do not let some selfish man*

*marry her for her beauty and neglect her kind and gentle heart. As for you, my favorite daughter, I ask your forgiveness and offer you this last bit of advice: find a way to be happy. Do not let anything stop you when you know what you want from life, or whom. You have the wit and intelligence to find joy in living if you make the effort.*
*God bless you.*
*Papa.*

Elizabeth sat without moving for a long time. She raised her face to the old woods spread out around the park. Dark purple shadows pooled beneath the heavy trunks. A vast swath of clouds like opal scales partially obscured the sun. The wind freshened, rustling in the leaves of oak and sycamore, promising rain by evening. She felt numb with realization of the lie she had lived for years. The letter said far more than her father intended. Yes, he had abdicated responsibility for controlling his family and he was fully aware of it. He could not have been ignorant of the potential consequences.

Memories no longer infused with the satisfaction of being her father's favorite fled through Elizabeth's mind. He taught her the farm ledgers so she would do them for him. He sent her to visit the tenants rather than insist her mother perform the task. He taught her Latin so they could discuss the histories he read and chess so he had someone to play the game with. Her father used their mutual love of knowledge and her affection as a way to put off even more responsibility. Even asking her to protect Jane, as if her sister had no will or opinions of her own, was one more attempt to make her atone for his own failings.

No longer able to sit still, Elizabeth rose and left the little folly, her bonnet and parasol forgotten. She passed through the garden without seeing it, her feet taking her automatically along the path past the Hunsford vicarage. Her destination was a small grove a few minutes' walk through the park. At some time in the past someone had cut and smoothed a fallen log to make a rustic bench. From its vantage point Elizabeth was able to look out over a meadow filled with small yellow flowers to a line of low trees where a stream ran. Light dazzled from the water in a thin line of shimmering glitter like sequins on a ball gown. Her senses absorbed the sounds of this quiet place; birds chattering and scolding, the resigned sighs of upper branches swaying together, small scufflings in the heart of the grove where squirrels worked or played.

In spite of the peaceful setting, Elizabeth could not stop the images from appearing in her mind. Her father blaming Kitty and allowing Mr. Gardiner to assume the role of father. Everything for his own convenience. Even when they moved to Meadow Lane he followed his pattern, sitting alone with a book ignoring anything he did not wish to deal with. Elizabeth wrapped both arms around herself, rocking back and forth. How could she judge him when she had benefited so greatly from his teaching?

She knew in her heart it had not been malice but weakness. Elizabeth could not even hold her father completely responsible for their destruction; her mother had played a large part in Lydia's wild nature. Perhaps if her father had tried to control his wife's behavior early in their marriage, she might have seen the danger her favorite daughter faced rather than encouraging her actions.

It was all too late. A life of indolence and self-indulgence could not be erased by pretending it never happened, or forgiving her father his failings. Elizabeth realized the dark thing inside her, the maelstrom of fury that possessed her the night of the ball, had been growing for years, hidden by her mother's rejection and her love of the father she thought she knew. As she slowly became convinced she was tainted with her sister's sin, Lydia's defection gathered her emotions into a growing pressure with no release. Elizabeth knew the dark thing was dead, but she still felt its influence telling her to hold tightly to her anger and resentment as a shield against future betrayal, against any right to happiness. Against trust, against love.

Mr. Darcy had broken through her defenses. Unable to face the realization that she had come to judge herself by the false standards of society, Elizabeth lashed out at the man whose proposal forced her to see herself through his eyes. She had vowed not to let society make her a victim, all the while doing exactly that to herself. Elizabeth slowly allowed the quiet of the grove to soothe her. There was no future for them now, the damage was done. She would meet Mr. Darcy eventually, and apologize. She would tell him she was going away so he felt no restraint in visiting Bingley and her sister. It was the least amends she could make.

Rising from the bench Elizabeth put the second letter away and began the walk back to Rosings Park. The drawing room was empty, a small fire in the hearth in spite of the fine weather. It was to accommodate Anne, who still grew cold easily. Elizabeth took her father's letter from her pocket. Without forgiveness what remained for any of them? Her father had loved her, loved all of his daughters. Tragically for all of them, that love had not been strong enough to overcome the inclinations of a lifetime.

Pressing the letter to her lips Elizabeth whispered, "I forgive you, Papa."

She felt no sadness, only a great empty void inside. Leaning, she put the letter on the coals and left the room while it burned.

# CHAPTER TWENTY

June 1815
Matlock House, London

"William! My dear it is so good to see you. When did you
return to Town?"

Darcy bent to kiss his aunt's cheek. She gestured to a chair across
from her and rang for tea. As a politician's wife Lady Matlock had
much practice containing her emotions behind a pleasant expression. Her gaze swept over Darcy and a small flare of apprehension
made her turn her face away until she mastered it.

"Last evening. I hope everyone is well?"

"Yes, quite well, with the exception of Adele."

Darcy was surprised. "I thought she would be fully recovered by
now."

Tea came so Lady Matlock did not reply until the tea was poured
and they were alone.

"Adele admitted she thought if she seemed desperate enough she
could get her own way. Her maid always comes to dress her and coif
her hair an hour and a half before they are to leave for an event. That
evening the maid was delayed for a quarter hour, or Adele would
have been found sooner."

"Was the lost time so dire?"

"In this case, yes." Lady Matlock drank a swallow of her tea. "She took laudanum as I am sure you know, only she mixed something with it. She claims she does not remember what it was. A pity, because her ploy has left her in poor health."

"Doctor Crane cannot discover what she used?"

"Not to my knowledge. It seems her father has been pressuring her to have his funds increased. Your uncle had a talk with the count. I do not think he will bother Adele again. I am afraid it will be some time before she is completely well."

Darcy said nothing. He drank his tea and replaced the cup. Lady Eleanor allowed him to come to his main purpose for the visit, although she knew what he wanted. For his part, Darcy sat in silence gathering his thoughts. Lady Eleanor refilled her cup and waited.

"I stopped by Bingley's home on my way here. The butler told me they are still in Scarborough."

"Lady Addington saw Mrs. Bingley just before they left. They intend to turn the visit into a wedding trip to the Lake District. I am surprised they did not stop at Pemberley on their way."

"Bingley is involved in a business arrangement with Lord Rathbone and other gentlemen including myself. He was probably anxious to reach his family and begin the necessary arrangements. Perhaps they will call at Pemberley on their way south."

*Did Elizabeth tell her sister what happened that night? If she did, Bingley will hold me responsible for her illness.*

Darcy rose abruptly. He paced to the windows and stood looking out at the side garden. The gardeners were expert; rose bushes showed extravagant colors against a green wall of boxwood that contained their sunny space. He returned to the chair after several minutes, his eyes full of pain.

"You gave me very good advice, which I ignored when the moment presented itself. You told me to let Elizabeth Bennet take time to deal with the past without importuning her. After the waltz she ran from the ballroom. I had to tell my uncle what had happened with

Adele before I could search for her. I only wanted to comfort her, I had no intention of anything beyond making sure she knew I would stand by her as a friend."

Darcy's voice had grown husky. Lady Eleanor reached out and took one of his hands in hers. "I do not believe she still thought of you as just a friend. Both of your feelings had gone beyond that."

Darcy's shoulders slumped. He took his aunt's hand in both of his. "She was in the conservatory crying. I held her, I told myself it was only to quiet her, but…"

The words stopped. Lady Eleanor said softly, "But you made love to her instead."

"I kissed her. She seemed to welcome it. I did not realize the state she was in, I only knew this was the woman I loved and wanted to marry. When I started to propose she became agitated. I ought to have left her then. I did not. I answered her objections one by one, I could not stop myself. In the end she ran from me. It was two days before I learned she was ill. I did not dare try to see her then. I also ran away, to Pemberley."

"And now you have come back and you think it safe to speak to her."

Darcy released his aunt's hand. "I have to tell her how sorry I am for what happened. I know she is at Rosings with Anne and Georgiana. I take full responsibility for my actions, I only wish to see Elizabeth before anyone else knows the root of her illness."

"My dear nephew, you are a fool."

"How well I know it," Darcy said bitterly.

Lady Eleanor sat back on the sofa, folding her hands in her lap. "Not in that way. You have always been too responsible. You take on problems in which you have no direct interest because you believe it is the right thing to do. Miss Bennet was ill before you began seeing her with her sister and Mr. Bingley. Your actions in the conservatory did nothing worse than force her to admit her feelings for you to herself. I do not doubt that revelation pushed her over a wall of regret and guilt she had built around herself like a house of cards. She fell, hard. If you had not confronted her that night she might have gone on as she was for a time, but eventually the cards would have collapsed."

Darcy knew his aunt was right. It did not assuage his sense of responsibility. "If I had remained her friend I could have been there when it did, instead of precipitating it."

"If you wish to blame yourself," Lady Matlock said with some asperity, "you are free to do so. But that is not thinking of Miss Bennet's needs, it is thinking of your own." She stood and Darcy followed suit. "Anne wrote to tell me her friend is doing quite well, so if you wish to speak to her, I am sure they would welcome another guest."

Darcy watched her leave the room as gracefully as always. *You gave me good advice before that I did not follow. This time I shall.*

## June 1815
## Rosings Park, Kent

"I say," Richard Fitzwilliam looked up from perusing the morning post, "a note from Darcy."

Of the three other people at the breakfast table, only one looked startled. Anne seemed mildly surprised, no more. Georgiana was eager to hear what her brother had to say. She had not received a reply to her last letter, causing her some concern. Elizabeth schooled her face to show nothing of the sudden hitch in her breathing. Richard opened the missive scanning it rapidly.

"Darcy just returned to London. He wants to know if it would inconvenience us for him to visit for a day or two."

Anne sent one swift glance around the table. "I do not know why Darcy feels he must ask permission to stay with us. Of course he can come."

"Very well." Richard put the note aside with a grin. "I will send him an invitation. Should I make it a formal one?"

"Certainly not."

Richard and his wife smiled at each other. Georgiana said, "I will wager he has been so involved with the work at Pemberley he has not rested or eaten properly. He never does if I do not nag him."

"Think of it as practice for marriage, Georgie. When you marry you will already be expert at nagging your husband."

They bantered back and forth with Anne adding an occasional word. Elizabeth did not join in. She drank tea, the remnants of her breakfast forgotten on her plate. There was no doubt in her mind he was coming here to see her. Not to renew his addresses; he was beyond any such humiliation after her violent rejection in the conservatory. Perhaps to offer her friendship once more, although that seemed even more farfetched. They were no longer able to be even friends.

*To say goodbye. This is what I told him I wanted, after all. To be free of his love so I could go on feeling myself as tainted as Lydia. So I did not have to blame my father for his failure, by taking on his burden as I had always done. I could not let myself believe I was worthy of Mr. Darcy and what we might have been to each other.*

Elizabeth spent the day busying herself with whatever she found to do. She sat with Anne sewing and mending garments from the basket for the Hunsford parish poor. Georgiana joined them after a morning ride, excited to see her brother.

"He will have gotten Richard's note this morning I am sure, and will be here today or tomorrow at the latest. I have not seen him since he left in January. I have so much to tell him."

"I am sure he will want to hear it all so I will allow you to monopolize the conversation at dinner for one night. Then the rest of us need to have a turn."

Georgiana smiled brightly at her cousin. "I am sure he will want to hear from all of us, so I will only monopolize half the conversation."

After a light nuncheon Anne retired to rest. Georgiana went to practice the pianoforte. She was working on a new piece acquired from her music master and wanted it perfected before she played it for them. Elizabeth found herself unable to settle to any occupation and went to sit in the garden. She found it increasingly hard to calm the agitation of her mind. Pewter clouds formed and reformed above the woods, blocking then releasing shafts of sharp sunlight to stab the trees. The wind rose, leaves shivered along the lines of hedges changing their color from pale to dark green.

Elizabeth rose. She had more than enough time for a walk before it was time to change for dinner. Her favorite path took her past the lane by the parsonage. She had met the new vicar, a widower in his fifties. He was from a neighboring village and knew the people and their concerns well. Pleasant and knowledgeable, Elizabeth had no doubts that he would serve Hunsford and the Fitzwilliams well. It only seemed strange that she should be at Rosings, and Charlotte at Longbourn.

Once at the grove Elizabeth sat down, took off her bonnet and let the wind play with her hair. Nettie would make it presentable later; for the moment, Elizabeth wanted the freedom of enjoying nature without restraints. Absorbed in thought, she did not hear approaching footsteps. The shadow fell on her without warning. Elizabeth startled, half rising. Mr. Darcy stood a few feet away, his dark eyes on her face.

"I am sorry if I startled you, Miss Bennet. I was not sure if you were here or not."

"It is quite alright, Mr. Darcy. I just did not hear you approach."

He moved slowly near. "Please do not be alarmed. My only reason for seeking you out is to apologize most humbly for my behavior at our last meeting. I do not ask you to forgive me, my conduct was unforgiveable. I only want you to know that I never meant you harm."

"Mr. Darcy," Elizabeth tried to speak twice before the words formed, "please do not think you harmed me. Any harm was of my own doing. I lied to myself, a very foolish and dangerous thing to do. When confronted with the lie I—I lost control of myself. If your behavior was unforgiveable, mine was surely reprehensible."

"No, never." He was standing in front of her, his face drawn with strain. "When I had time to consider everything you have been through, to think I importuned you for my own selfish reasons showed me a man I never expected to be. I have bitterly regretted my words with no way to heal the damage they did. Please say, at least, that you do not hate me."

Elizabeth could hardly breathe. He was not apologizing for his words, only for the effect they had on her. *Find a way to be happy.* If she was ever to know happiness she must step out of the past. This man, this wonderful man offered her far more than security and social acceptance. She would never have married only for those things. He offered her love.

She rose abruptly; her limbs trembled so badly she was afraid she might fall if she tried to move. Darcy was so close she felt the warmth radiating from his body. How wonderful to be held against that strong, comforting form, wrapped in the safety of his arms.

"Miss Bennet?"

The pained uncertainty in his voice gave her courage. Elizabeth raised her face to his; she saw there everything she desired in life. She had only to reach out to him, only to make that last gesture. It did not even take courage.

"How could I hate you? Shall I repeat my last words?"

Darcy felt a welling exaltation shake him to his soul. His voice husked. "Miss Bennet, if you still feel about my offer as you did that night please tell me now. I have no greater desire in life than to share all my days with you as my wife. But the choice is, and always has been, yours."

Elizabeth raised her hands to enclose his face. "It is my greatest desire as well. I love you, Mr. Darcy."

Darcy kissed her willing mouth carefully until he felt her raise her arms around his neck and respond with natural passion. When they parted he enclosed her in his arms. She rested her face on his chest, content. Darcy knew she would never again be the woman he had fallen in love with three long years ago. Suffering had taken its toll on her spirit. With love and care he hoped to restore her joy in life in spite of the shadows of old pain she would never completely lose.

*I will stand with you, Elizabeth, whatever comes. Together we have strength enough to meet anything life brings.*

Unnoticed, the darkening clouds had drawn nearer, spreading a blue cloak over the meadow. Darcy offered his arm and Elizabeth took it.

"We had best get back to the house, or you will be soaked."

Elizabeth picked up her bonnet. "Yes, let us hurry. Georgiana will scold me if you catch a cold."

They reached the shelter of Rosings manor as the first large drops of rain patterned the walkway. Richard met them in the entry. He did not joke about their somewhat disheveled appearance which told Darcy his cousin was careful of Elizabeth's sensibilities. Too full of emotion to act as if nothing had happened, she excused herself to dress for dinner. With a great sense of peace Darcy watched her cross the hall and mount the stairs. He turned to Richard, who still remained silent but raised a questioning brow.

"I need to talk to you," Darcy said with a certain grimness. "Privately."

"Enter my study, sir. We shall not be disturbed there."

Darcy was happy to see the old Richard emerging. His cousin shut the study door behind them and went to the sidebar to pour brandies. "I think congratulations are in order."

Darcy accepted the glass, touched it to Richard's. "Elizabeth has agreed to marry me." Both men sipped their drinks before he continued. "That means an announcement will be in the *Morning Post* when the date is set. I do not know how long it will be before Wickham contacts me. I am debating whether it is better to stay in London after the wedding if I have not heard from him, or return to Pemberley."

Richard considered. "London is preferable. I am close enough to reach you in several hours, and we both have resources there that are not available at Pemberley."

"I dislike dealing with the cur when Elizabeth and Georgiana are in Town, even at Darcy House. However you are right, we can both call on loyal men in London and the law is organized, rather than depending on a constable used to handling no one more dangerous than a local tosspot."

Richard took another swallow of his brandy. "Do you think he will contact you directly, or by post?"

"By post. He knows better than to confront me. I think he will set up a meeting somewhere he feels safe. It may be on very short notice."

"I think it best if I am in London when the notification is published. I can stay for a few days, it should not take more than that for Wickham to act, unless he truly is out of the county."

Darcy finished his drink. "This time I want it over and done, Richard."

His cousin's face hardened. "Let Wickham stick his head out of his rat hole and I promise you it will be for the last time."

The measure of Darcy's anger was that he did not disagree with the implication of Richard's words.

Darcy and Elizabeth strolled in the gardens after dinner. The rain had been short and the evening was soft, a light breeze stirring the scent of roses and lavender. At length they sat together on the wrought iron bench in the rose garden. Darcy took her hand, twining their fingers.

"My love, I am the biggest fool in the history of foolish men. If I had waited a little longer, been a little patient..."

"You would have found me gone. It was my intent to leave London for some quiet place where I could find peace. I told myself it was more for your sake than mine, another lie. I believed you would return to your friends and I could not bear the thought of watching you marry a grand lady, even while I denied what I felt for you."

Darcy's eyes clouded. "I knew you planned to leave, Bingley told me. Your escape would have been for nothing. I would not have married anyone but you." He raised her hand to his lips. "In any event, I cannot think of a place in the entire country where a beautiful stranger would not be an object of interest. You would have been besieged by curious ladies wanting to know your history and besotted gentlemen begging an introduction."

Elizabeth's lips turned up in the smile he loved. "Then I should have made up a history like the plot of a novel. They would soon have left me alone."

"I would have found you, you know." His voice lowered, he held her eyes. "If only to see that you were well and safe. I—did that after Bingley saw you the first time. He could not tell me where exactly it happened so I looked into it and discovered you lived on Meadow Lane. I never went near. I only made sure it was a safe neighborhood."

"The house is called Willow Cottage. Papa chose it for his own reasons. I cannot say I liked the house particularly, and now I suppose someone else will be living there."

Neither spoke then, enjoying the evening and their silent rapport. Darcy was the first to break the silence. "I do not wish to press you, my love, however we will need to speak of the date for the wedding. If you wish to wait for a time I have no objection."

Elizabeth felt her chest tighten. She took several slow breaths. "I expect you will wish to return to Pemberley before too much longer. I shall write Jane and our aunt Gardiner before I decide. I do not want to interrupt Jane and Charles' wedding trip."

"As you wish. Will you want to be married from the Bingleys' home or your uncle's?"

"As I am living with Charles and Jane, I think from Hephaestus House."

He brought her hand to his lips for a gentle kiss. "Richard knows of our betrothal. Shall we tell the others in the morning?"

"Yes, let us tell them. It will certainly enliven breakfast."

That proved to be an understatement. Georgiana could hardly contain her delight and approbation. Anne smiled serenely and gave quiet congratulations. Richard welcomed her to the family with more dignity than Darcy might have expected. The role of landowner had begun to infuse his cousin with an authority much like his former military command. He was a man used to taking responsibility for other men; soldiers or tenants and staff would be handled with the same calm assurance. Richard would be an excellent landlord, Darcy thought, and if there was a child, an excellent father.

Elizabeth wrote her letters that evening to be posted in the morning. She had no doubts how the news would be received by her loved ones. She found it possible now to accept society's disdain without pain or regret. It was her life, she intended to live it as she chose, not as strangers dictated. She was safe in William's regard. Nothing else had influence over her. It had been a long, painful lesson but Elizabeth had learned it well. She was her own woman at last.

## June 1815
## Hephaestus House, London

They remained at Rosings for another three days. While the ladies talked of wedding plans, Darcy and Richard made plans of their own. By the time Elizabeth, Georgiana and Darcy entered the traveling coach for the ride to London, it was settled that wherever Wickham chose for the meeting would have trusted men surrounding it long before the appointed time.

The coach reached Darcy House at noon on a warm June day. Elizabeth joined Darcy and Georgiana for the remainder of the afternoon before deciding she wished to go to Hephaestus House as Nettie and her luggage had already been delivered there. Darcy insisted on accompanying her. He took Georgiana's maid with them for propriety's sake, so they were not able to discuss any personal matters. If Bingley's butler was surprised to see her he was too well trained to show it. Mr. Hastings had news of his own to share.

"The master and mistress arrived half an hour ago. If you will wait in the drawing room Miss Bennet, Mr. Darcy, I will notify them that you are here."

Elizabeth felt a surge of happiness that she would see her beloved sister so soon and be able to share her betrothal with Jane in person. The drawing room showed the results of a partial redecoration in new chairs and reupholstered sofas, all in variegated shades of green and blue. Cushions bright with needlepoint flowers and botanicals embroidered in natural colors added to the air of elegant comfort. Elizabeth took a seat on a sofa, looking around.

"I think my sister has done very well here."

Darcy joined her also scanning the room. "I do not know. I used to have no trouble finding the drawing room, the colors reached out and dragged one in. Now…"

Elizabeth nodded sagely. "I know exactly what you mean. Perhaps we ought to have Charles post a map near the front door so visitors can find their way without bothering Mr. Hastings."

His chuckle warmed her. Before she could reply, Jane hurried into the room and Elizabeth rose to hug her tightly. "My dearest sister, it is so good to see you. You look very happy."

"I am most happy." Jane curtsied. "Mr. Darcy, welcome. Charles will be along in a moment, he sent for refreshments when Mr. Hastings told us you were here. He is still not used to having a wife, I am afraid."

Bingley entered the room at that moment and Elizabeth curtsied. He came to take her hand, kissing it lightly. He and Darcy shook hands before both men sat down. Darcy took Elizabeth's hand but allowed her to speak.

"We have news. Mr. Darcy and I are engaged to be married."

Jane sat very still. She reached out and caught her sister's free hand, pressing it. Elizabeth saw doubt in Jane's clear eyes that caused a stab of pain in her heart.

"Are you not happy for me, dearest?"

"You know I am. It is just—you were so ill. Are you truly ready to marry?"

"Yes, Jane, I am. I have looked into myself and found that it is time for me to meet only my own expectations, no one else's. This is what I want more than anything else in life. I am well and truly ready."

Jane drew her sister into an embrace. "Then I wish you all the joy in the world."

Bingley had been observing Darcy through this. His friend watched Elizabeth with tender concern. There was nothing possessive, nothing equivocal in his face. He put his hand out and shook Darcy's with vigor.

"I also wish you all the joy in the world. If it is half of what I find with my angel you will be truly blessed."

Tea came and the two couples talked of the newlyweds' trip to the north and the Lake District. Jane expounded on its beauty, and on the hospitality and friendliness of Bingley's relatives. His mother had especially taken to his bride. She was a down-to-earth woman and Jane was quite taken with her.

"The steam engine project is going forward," Bingley told them as the plates were emptied and the cups refilled. "Worthington is already working on some refinements and I expect as soon as the equipment is set up and we hire several metalworkers we can start practical operations. My cousin Stuart will manage the fabrication and his brother Joseph will start calling on potential clients. I will meet with Lord Rathbone this week to let him know how it goes."

"You seem to have everything in hand." Darcy returned his cup to the tray. "Has Mr. Worthington found a place to live?"

"Joseph is a bachelor. Mr. Worthington is staying with him for the present."

"Will you need to travel to Newcastle often, Charles?"

Elizabeth felt her sister's eyes on her as she asked. It might be difficult for Jane to have her new husband constantly going back and forth from London to his plant in Newcastle.

"Perhaps a trip or two at first, but with Stuart and Joseph handling things I do not think I will be needed often."

They talked of other things until Darcy rose to leave. Elizabeth walked him to the entry hall. He held her hands while they waited for his outerwear to be brought.

"I shall see you tomorrow?"

"Yes, Mr. Darcy, you shall. I want to call on my aunt and uncle, if you have no objections?"

"None at all. And we should discuss the wedding date. I will not wait to have the banns read, I would rather procure a special license. If you have no objections?

"None at all." She rose swiftly on tiptoe to kiss him softly.

Darcy touched her cheek with warm fingers as they parted. A footman appeared with his hat, stick and gloves. "Until tomorrow, Elizabeth."

"Until tomorrow, William."

## June 1815
## Gardiner Residence, London

When Darcy arrived to collect Elizabeth in the morning, he took her aside before Nettie joined them. In the semi-privacy of Bingley's study Darcy took a small velvet box from his waistcoat pocket.

"I am sorry I did not have this with me at Rosings. I hardly dared hope you would forgive me, let alone agree to fulfill my dearest wish."

He opened the box to reveal a ring, brilliant rose diamonds in a white gold band engraved with Celtic knots. Elizabeth did not take her eyes from his as he removed it from the silk lining and set the box aside. Darcy slipped it on her finger and kissed her hand reverently. He saw tears wet her lashes. She raised her face as he bent his head to kiss her with great tenderness.

"I had it made for you some time ago. I wanted you to have something of your own rather than part of the Darcy jewels. For a time I thought it would never be worn, for I would not have given it to anyone else. I cannot express the happiness I feel to see it on your hand."

"Where it shall remain for as long as I live."

From the hallway someone cleared their throat. The couple turned to the partially open door as Mr. Hastings tapped on the panel. "Your carriage is ready, sir."

Mrs. Gardiner greeted them with some surprise. In the drawing room as they waited for tea Elizabeth told her of the engagement without going into detail. She had never disclosed to anyone her confrontation with Darcy the night of the ball. It was both too painful and too personal to share, even with Jane. Since the Gardiners had thought Darcy inclined to their niece the engagement was not as unexpected as it might have been.

"Why do you not stay for luncheon? Mr. Gardiner will be home and you can share your good news with him then."

They agreed and Mrs. Gardiner's next question was the wedding date. Darcy looked to Elizabeth to answer. She hesitated before she did so.

"We have not discussed it, however I think it will not be long. Mr. Darcy must return to his estate for the summer harvest, and I see no reason to postpone our marriage for more than a month."

Mrs. Gardiner smiled. "You are quite right, Lizzy. London in summer is not an inviting place, although it has been cooler than usual. Sometime in July then."

"Yes. Mr. Darcy is going to procure a special license so we do not have to wait for the banns to be read."

Darcy's mouth turned up at the corners. "Indeed. If Elizabeth agrees, I shall put the notice in the paper for the day after tomorrow, that is the 18th."

"And we can be married in mid-July. I will discuss the date with Jane as they will want to hold the wedding breakfast at Hephaestus House."

"Then," Mrs. Gardiner looked very satisfied, "we will give Mrs.

White another commission for a wedding gown? Mr. Gardiner has some beautiful silks he just received. And I am sure Jane's and my modiste will be glad to prepare your trousseau."

"As long as she is not enamored of lace, frills or feathers!"

They all laughed at Elizabeth's sally.

Mr. Gardiner's congratulations were sincere and luncheon went by quickly in good food and pleasant conversation. When Darcy and Elizabeth departed, he lingered with his wife in the drawing room in a pensive mood.

"All our nieces married. And to good men who will take care of them. It is good to see that Lizzy looks so well and happy. I know you were as concerned for her as I was."

His wife patted his hand. "Yes, I had my doubts she would recover so quickly. I can still see pain in her eyes when she speaks of her family. I do not know what happened at Rosings, but something did, more than Mr. Darcy's proposal. Perhaps one day she will share it with us."

"If it precipitated her return to health, I am happy for it, whatever it was." He fell silent for a time before speaking quietly. "We have not heard from Catherine."

"No. Not since before Jane's wedding. I am afraid she resents your efforts to assist her. She seemed to genuinely affect Mr. Thurgood though."

"I do not think it is that, my dear. Mr. Thurgood is in trade, as I am. Catherine is gently born. I am inclined to believe that she has found it gives her status among his friends. Communicating with us might lessen that status."

"Edward, do you really think her so shallow?"

Mr. Gardiner shook his head sadly. "Her favorite sister disgraced her, her father abandoned her, she made a good marriage but not perhaps one she would have chosen had there been an alternative. If she has found acceptance and even deference in her new role I cannot begrudge her it."

"I suppose not. I wonder…"

"What, my love?"

"If Thomas' actions are not some part of Lizzy's problems?"

"I would never say this to Jane or Lizzy, but Thomas was a selfish man. He abdicated his obligations to his family in favor of a life that would have better suited a bachelor. A man must either lead and guide his family or suffer the consequences, and they rarely affect only him. Lizzy adored Thomas, however she is an intelligent woman. If she had not already become disillusioned by his behavior toward Fanny and her sisters before Lydia ran away, she surely sees it now."

Mrs. Gardiner looked troubled. "Do you think that is what happened, that she saw her father as responsible for at least part of their disgrace?"

"It would certainly explain a great deal." Mr. Gardiner rose. "I must get back to the warehouse. Tell Lizzy I will set aside some silks for her to choose from. There is one I think she will particularly like."

Mrs. Gardiner also rose to walk him to the door. "You are as good as a modiste, Edward. I expect it is experience of silks, and women."

He kissed her cheek. "Only you, my love. Only you."

# CHAPTER TWENTY-ONE

June 1815
Darcy House, London

Richard arrived at Darcy House on the afternoon of June 17th after a visit to the War Office. A cold collation was being served in the dining room and Georgiana immediately sent him upstairs to freshen himself before they ate. Darcy was glad to see his cousin had responded so promptly to his summons. He saw an elation in Richard's manner he could not attribute entirely to the hunt for Wickham.

"What has happened, Richard? You look as if you have news."

"I am not certain if it is good or bad, good I hope. This is from the latest dispatches. Napoleon is about to engage Wellington with a part of his forces. The bulk of the French army attacked Blücher at Ligny, but Napoleon was not there. Splitting his forces is not a wise move. If Blücher wins the battle Boney will have lost too many men to offer a strong attack. Wellington is too smart to engage the French unless it is on his own terms. With a little luck, this could be the end."

"I am grateful you are not there, Richard." Georgiana sipped her wine. "I know aunt Eleanor and Anne are as well."

"I am torn," Richard admitted. "I spent so many years chasing Napoleon and his generals all over Europe, its anticlimactic to sit at home while the whole show comes to an end."

"You do not think Napoleon can win?"

Richard considered Darcy's question seriously. "He has loyalists and he has proven himself an outstanding strategist, but his army is not what it was before the invasion of Russia or his defeat and exile. The French Imperial Guard will stand by him. Whether the rest of his men are as dedicated is uncertain."

"We shall see. I hope the war is finally to be over. Although I can see where the end of hostilities will cause problems at home."

"Indeed. There will be an influx of men discharged from the army with no certainty of work at home. If it is not properly handled it can cause chaos."

"When has the government ever handled a crisis properly?"

That question was left unanswered. They finished luncheon and Georgiana went to read, leaving them alone. Over glasses of port Richard outlined a tentative plan for trapping their old enemy.

"It will depend in part on where he wants to meet. If he is coming from outside the country it may be several months before he contacts you. When he does and we know where the place is, I will have trustworthy men all around it half a day before the appointed time. They are experienced at blending in so even Wickham will not tumble to the fact he is being watched. You will need to meet him before we move in. Go armed, Will. He is a snake, and a dangerous one if he has waited all this time to confront you."

Darcy accepted his cousin's assessment. Wickham hated him. It was not outside the realm of possibility that once he had the money he would feel no compunction about murdering his boyhood friend.

"I will be at Matlock House if you need me." Richard finished his port and rose to take his leave.

Darcy walked with him to the entry hall. "If—or I should say when—Napoleon is defeated there will be massive celebrations here at home. That may complicate matters if Wickham acts now."

"I had thought of that. We will have to deal with the situation as it arises."

The cousins shook hands and Richard left a pensive Darcy to return to the drawing room. Georgiana looked up, then closed her book. "What is wrong, Will? Is it something with Anne?"

"No, sweetling. Nothing is wrong, we were speaking of the war. Richard thinks the fighting will be ending soon."

Georgiana ran her fingers over the cover of the book, her expression thoughtful. "The war with France has been going on since before I was born. I will be happy to see it end, but I cannot help thinking of all the lives lost or ruined by it. I hope it is the last time our country must fight another for the rest of our lives."

"I wish the same, Georgie." *Human nature never changes in the essentials. I doubt either of us will be a great deal older before hostilities of some sort arise again.*

Georgiana put her book aside. "Shall I play for you, Brother?"

"I would like that very much."

Darcy followed her to the music room. She chose a sonata by Mozart she knew he especially liked. Georgiana felt a wistfulness as she played. There might be a few more evenings like this one before both their lives changed with his marriage. Georgiana welcomed Elizabeth as her sister. Their time at Rosings had convinced her that Lizzy needed to heal from a war of her own, and there was no better place to do so than Pemberley.

## July 1815
## Bond Street, London

Mrs. Gardiner called for Elizabeth and Jane several days after the peace was announced to determine the progress of Elizabeth's trousseau and shop for accessories and personal items. In the carriage Jane turned to her sister, who looked more thoughtful than a shopping trip normally engendered.

"If I am not prying, is the letter you received this morning the cause of your silence?"

Elizabeth saw that their aunt was watching her with interest. She sighed and turned her attention to her companions.

"The letter was from Charlotte. It was sent to Meadow Lane and forwarded on to Hephaestus House. I found it curious, that is all."

"Do not leave us there, Lizzy," Mrs. Gardiner encouraged.

"It concerned Mrs. Long. Charlotte implied she has taken to imbibing more wine than she ought, and saying odd things. She seems to think that Caroline Bingley is going to invite her to London and introduce her to her friends."

"Caroline?"

"Lady Samuelson?"

The two voices chimed together. Elizabeth smiled wryly. "Indeed. That is what is so odd. I do not believe Caroline and Mrs. Long ever said three words to one another."

"Mrs. Long became bitter after the death of her husband," Jane said sadly. "She lives alone and they had no children. She may just be trying to make herself more socially acceptable by pretending to a friendship with someone of higher status."

"But, Caroline Samuelson? It is—bizarre."

"Does Charlotte give any reason for her statements?"

"No. If she receives any more information she will write me. I have sent her an invitation to the wedding, she may wait until then to speak with me."

The carriage set its passengers down near the shops on Bond Street with instructions to call for them in two hours. Mrs. Gardiner looked amazed at the press of shoppers. "It is a good thing we ordered your trousseau before the peace was announced or you might have had to postpone your wedding until Michaelmas."

Elizabeth glanced around her at the crowds of ladies on the street, some followed by footmen or maids, and knew her aunt's words were not entirely in jest. "I do not think there is a modiste who is not receiving more orders than she can deliver."

"Or a seamstress who is unemployed." Jane took her sister's arm.

"Mrs. White is working on your wedding gown, perhaps she could make another dress or two if Madame Colette is unable to complete your order."

"The future wife of Mr. Darcy does not have to worry about having her gowns completed unless a duchess supersedes her, especially her trousseau."

Mrs. Gardiner patted her niece's arm. They paused to study several pelisses displayed in a shop window. None of the ladies noticed Lady Caroline Samuelson approaching until her all-too-familiar voice assaulted their ears.

"Good afternoon, ladies. What lovely pelisses. Are you planning on moving to a colder climate, Miss Eliza? Surely the one you seem to favor is too heavy for London."

"Good afternoon, Lady Samuelson."

All of the ladies curtsied. Caroline made a small dip, her lips curling in what she believed was a condescending smile. Jane remained at Elizabeth's side. She was no longer intimidated by her husband's sister. With wide-eyed innocence she raised a brow.

"Did you not see the announcement in the *Morning Post*?"

Caroline stiffened her back, making the large velvet hat perched on her elaborate coiffure slip a little forward. "I know we are sisters-by-marriage, Jane dear, but in public I really must insist on the formalities."

"Oh, of course, my lady." Jane pressed Elizabeth's arm before she could speak. "I only thought you had already heard the news."

"The only news I have heard in the past several days, is about the peace celebrations. Lord Samuelson took a house in Bath for the summer, but with Napoleon defeated at last he *insisted* on returning to London."

"I believe what Jane meant, my lady, is that I am to be married in three weeks."

Caroline raised both brows. "Oh? Well I suppose it had to happen. Who is the lucky gentleman? Or is he a friend of your uncle?"

"He is indeed a friend of my aunt and uncle, and a gentleman. I am marrying Mr. Darcy."

"You—you are...no, I do not believe it! He would not—he would never..."

Lady Samuelson's complexion was not designed for the shock. She went rapidly from white to red to a modified lavender.

"Why not, my lady? Because he would never lower himself to marry someone with relatives who live in *Cheapside*? I can assure you it is true."

Ignoring the fact Caroline had just called her a liar, Elizabeth took off her glove and displayed the diamond ring Darcy had made for her. "It is obviously true, my lady. I believe Derbyshire is quite a bit colder than London so that pelisse will be most suitable." She replaced the glove and added casually, "I understand you are soon to have a visitor known to both of us."

"Visitor? Of whom do you speak?"

"Mrs. Long of Meryton. She has told several people of your intent to invite her to London. For the peace celebrations, I assume."

Lady Samuelson's reaction was as unexpected as it was dramatic. She stumbled a step as if about to swoon, her face draining of color. Jane reached out instinctively to steady her while her maid hurried forward.

"My lady, are you well?"

"Y-yes. I just...I—I hardly know the woman."

"So we understood. Still, it is strange she should name you since as you say, you are barely acquainted with her."

Caroline recovered enough of her composure to move a little away from Jane. "I believe—I will call for my carriage. I am indeed not feeling well."

Her maid scurried off to find the carriage. With an effort Caroline straightened although her face remained deathly pale.

"Shall I stay with you, my lady?" Jane asked.

"No, no that will not be necessary, t-thank you."

"In that case we will wish you a good day, my lady."

Elizabeth gave a perfectly correct curtsey. The other two ladies also curtsied and the three entered the shop. When they were well away from the doors they stopped and looked at one another. Jane seemed nearly as surprised as Caroline.

"That was a very strange reaction to something Caroline ought to have laughed at. She was truly upset."

Elizabeth said slowly, "Which makes me wonder exactly what Lady Samuelson has to do with Mrs. Long."

"Well, until you receive more information, let us go on with our shopping." Mrs. Gardiner continued into the depths of the shop. "We must have a look at that lovely pelisse."

Elizabeth and Jane followed her after one significant shared look.

## July 1815
## Darcy House, London

The note came on the morning after Elizabeth's shopping trip. There was no return direction on the coarse paper and only Darcy's name and direction printed in block letters. In his study Darcy opened it with a grim face.

*MEADOW LANE TOMORROW NIGHT £5000 10PM ALONE*

A shiver ran down Darcy's spine. Wickham knew where Elizabeth and Jane had lived. He put the note in a locked drawer of the desk and penned a quick note to Richard for a footman to deliver to Matlock House. His cousin joined him in half an hour. Darcy handed him the communication and watched Richard's expression grow flinty. When he handed it back, Darcy saw the Richard of the battlefield.

"Only £5,000. That means he intends to continue the blackmail. He would ask far more if it was the only payment he expected."

"I am not surprised. Wickham could never be satisfied, he always wanted more."

Richard poured them both a brandy. "I will have my men in

position by noon tomorrow. I doubt he will search the house, so at least two can wait in the attic rooms. I will position one in the basement and two more outside, one in the hayloft in the stable and one across the street. There is a small grove of trees where he can wait unseen. I will be nearby on horseback in the event he somehow escapes."

They drank their brandies in silence. Darcy did not have to voice his appreciation, they were too close for that. He said when their glasses were empty, "My only question is, why Meadow Lane? To let me know he can find Elizabeth if he wishes to?"

"It is as good a motive as any. I agree it seems strange when his usual haunts are the stews of the city. He may feel safer with less people around, it should be easier to spot strangers. Wickham's great failing is that he considers himself more clever than he is. This time it will be the end of him."

Darcy followed Richard to the study door. "I prefer he be captured alive if it is possible. He is a deserter, let the army deal with him."

"If he leaves Meadow Lane alive, he will spread his vile story. He will feel no compunction not to ruin Georgie. I do not want that to happen."

They stepped into the hall and Darcy only said, "I do not want Elizabeth to hear of this."

Mr. Burgess waited at the door. His face showed a momentary alarm. "Sir, Miss Bennet..."

"What do you not want me to hear of, Mr. Darcy?"

Darcy turned sharply. Elizabeth stood just outside the drawing room door, a spark in her eyes that sent his heart racing. Richard bowed to Elizabeth's curtsey.

"Good morning, Miss Bennet. You are looking well."

"Thank you, sir. You are also looking well. My fiancé however is looking guilty."

Richard suppressed a grin. "Good luck, Cousin."

The door closed behind him and Darcy was left with Elizabeth as Mr. Burgess quickly effaced himself. Instead of returning to the drawing room, Darcy led her into his study and closed the door. The smell of leather, paper, brandy and wood polish soothed her as it always did. Elizabeth had become adept at sensing his moods. She allowed him to lead her to the sofa under the windows and sit beside her without further comment.

"What is it, William? Something is troubling you greatly. I do not want secrets between us; can you not share this?"

Slowly, in a low, unwavering voice, Darcy told her of the letter and Wickham's threat. Elizabeth reached out part way through the recitation to take his hand. He wrapped his fingers around hers and held them tightly. At the end, he pressed his lips to the soft skin of her knuckles.

"You see why I must do this. I will not have Georgie's life ruined by insinuations of illegitimacy. Wickham has been a curse on the Darcy family since his youth, he must be stopped."

"Colonel Fitzwilliam will not let him leave the meeting alive, will he?"

Her whisper was uncertain. Darcy did not answer for a time. "I will do what I can, but I know my cousin. He considers Wickham a traitor and the law condemns him as a deserter in time of war. If he is turned over to the army he will hang. I have never condoned murder, but if ever a man deserved to die, it is Wickham. We do not even know if your sister is alive."

"We—Jane and I—have wondered that as well. I find it hard to believe that if he had simply abandoned her she would not have contacted Mama. But even that does not justify murder, William. You cannot allow this."

"I do not see how I can stop it, short of letting Wickham continue to blackmail me, with the certainty of ruin darkening Georgiana's life for years. Is that truly what you want me to do?"

Elizabeth bowed her head. Darcy drew her against his shoulder, his arm around her, their hands still linked. "I do not have an answer. I only know his death at the hands of anyone but the law will haunt you. It will diminish you in your own eyes and that will hurt me, and our marriage." She tipped her head back to look into his dark eyes, desolate with a choice no man should have to make.

Before he could speak, Elizabeth straightened. "I am going with you. I do not believe Richard will do anything rash if I am there."

Darcy had half expected her declaration, still it horrified him. "No, Elizabeth, you cannot! Wickham will certainly be armed. Your presence would only give him one more weapon against me. You must see it is impossible."

"Wickham is the only one who knows what happened to Lydia. Even if we only surmise he—he did something terrible to her, it will be an end to the not knowing."

"Elizabeth, please! I cannot let you…"

"As long as there are hansoms available, you cannot stop me." The words were gentle, but Darcy heard the determination in them. "I have a right to confront the man who destroyed my family and threatens to destroy the family I am joining. I will be your *wife*, Mr. Darcy, and Georgiana's sister. Your troubles are mine."

Darcy leaned his head down and kissed her very tenderly. "I will take you with me, for the reasons you have stated. I trust you to do as I ask while we are there."

"I shall, I promise. Oh, William, what a terrible situation!"

"Wickham is a terrible man." He rose and took her hand, lifting her to her feet. "Did you call for me, or Georgiana?"

"Georgiana, but I do not think I could keep countenance and talk of wedding clothes this morning."

Darcy walked her out to where the Bingleys' carriage waited. "I will call for you tomorrow evening," he murmured. "This must be kept between us." Elizabeth gave a slight nod as he handed her in.

Alone, Darcy returned inside. A day and a half and Wickham's threat would be over, one way or another.

Darcy remained in his study until dinner. He had asked Mr. Burgess not to tell his sister that Miss Bennet called. The siblings ate in the breakfast parlor as they did when only the two of them were in residence. Darcy had no appetite for the food he forced down in small bites. Georgiana ate with relish. She no longer chattered as she had done in the past, her conversation as pleasant and more mature than the girl he had cared for these many years. He missed that bright child while he realized the changes in her outlook and behavior were inevitable.

"I will be happy to see you married, William. Elizabeth is perfect for you. She will love Pemberley, and we can be a family until I marry." Georgiana ate a little more of her sautéed cutlets.

Unwilling to show the amusement he felt, Darcy spoke with commendable restraint. "Are you making plans already? It must be my wedding that inspires you."

"Not at all. Well, not very much." She laid her fork down. "Since we are not formally engaged, I cannot write to Mr. Worthington and so must gain any information about him from Charles and Jane. I know he is staying with Charles' cousin and that the work is progressing and that is all. Once we are all at Pemberley it is not that far to Newcastle, so perhaps I shall see him occasionally."

"I am certain you will, as his work permits. The beginning of a new enterprise takes time and effort if it is to be successful. Mr. Worthington is the sort of man who will give his entire energy to the effort."

"I understand that, Brother. I am willing to wait until Mr. Worthington is established before we make any permanent plans. But sometimes it is difficult."

Darcy heard the longing in her voice. He considered for a few moments before replying. "When we are at Pemberley, I shall give you permission to announce your betrothal, if Mr. Worthington agrees. Then you may correspond with him without injuring propriety."

"Oh, William, really?" Georgiana's face lit with happiness. "Thank you!"

Darcy felt a sadness at his sister's eagerness to take up the role of wife and mother even while he understood her need for a life of her own making. He waved away the dessert course and sipped his wine while Georgiana finished her meal. They had coffee and tea in the drawing room. Georgiana saw that her brother was not in the mood for conversation so she shared the events of her day with Lady Matlock instead.

"Chadwick has taken a house in Brighton for the remainder of the summer so Adele can visit the spa and take the waters. She is getting better slowly, aunt Eleanor says. She claims it was a sudden fever, but I have a suspicion it was something quite different and much less innocent."

"So long as it is only a suspicion."

They looked at each other in perfect understanding. After tea, Georgiana played for him and sang several selections. They parted on the third floor landing, however Darcy did not go to bed immediately. He was too restless to sleep. He wished he knew a way to keep Elizabeth from accompanying him tomorrow night. He could easily question Wickham about Lydia Bennet, possibly with more success than her sister. Wickham could lie either way but he was less likely to lie to Darcy.

Darcy pondered the idea of having Richard's men keep Elizabeth from the meeting and rejected it. She was determined; she would not soon forgive him if he went back on his word. At last Darcy built up the fire and stretched out on the sofa in front of the hearth. He had no choice but to allow Elizabeth to accompany him and pray that no harm came to her. If anything went wrong, he vowed to shoot Wickham like the rabid dog he was.

# CHAPTER TWENTY-TWO

July 1815
Meadow Lane, London

E lizabeth had told Jane she was going to Darcy House and would stay for dinner. It was the truth, as far as it went. Georgiana was staying the night at Matlock House a fact that was not disclosed. Neither Darcy nor Elizabeth had an appetite for an elaborate meal. Darcy requested bread, cheese and cold meats and they ate what they could manage in the breakfast parlor. Afterward Elizabeth played to pass the time. Normally she reveled in the sound of Georgiana's pianoforte; tonight she hardly heard the notes so occupied was her mind with their meeting at Willow Cottage.

At nine Darcy requested his town coach be brought around and they departed shortly after. There was no conversation on the trip to Meadow Lane. Elizabeth was aware of her fiancé's tension and chose not to attempt to lessen it. There was a hard lump where her stomach should be; she felt the magnitude of what she had committed to. Elizabeth wrapped her arms tightly around herself under her pelisse and prayed that all went well.

Darcy knew Elizabeth was frightened. He felt fear for her more than himself. A small pistol rested in his inner coat pocket. His hand touched the shape, invisible from the outside. At any sign of danger to Elizabeth, Darcy was prepared to end the meeting and Wickham's life, even at the cost of his own.

The street was dark and quiet as they approached the cottage. Mr. Tombs had specific instructions to approach slowly and leave the coach a short distance from the house. Darcy felt his driver stop the horses and looked out to see a man slide out of the shadows of a grove of trees and approach the vehicle.

"Mr. Darcy, I'm the colonel's man. We got word somebody entered the house about an hour ago from the back. Long cloak, no other description. They lit a light in the front room."

"Thank you."

The man touched his cap and withdrew as silently as he had appeared. Darcy tapped on the ceiling trap. When Mr. Tombs opened it, he said softly, "Pull over ahead. We will walk the rest of the way."

The horses walked a few yards further and the coach halted. Darcy opened the door, jumped down and put up the steps for Elizabeth. Together they made their way to the house. Elizabeth held tightly to Darcy's arm, watching her step in the feeble light from a moon like a nail paring. Darcy felt his chest tighten until it became difficult to breathe. He forced his muscles to loosen. He needed all of his physical strength for whatever was to come.

Elizabeth turned the front door knob. It opened on a hallway like a dim tunnel with a thin blade of light from the parlor cutting across it. Every aspect seemed different: menacing webs of shadow draped the corners, the air was cold and lifeless. Darcy put Elizabeth partly behind him as they advanced. Boards complained underfoot. The house was old, empty, devoid of life. The parlor door stood wide open. Darcy took a deep breath and stepped into the room. A cloaked figure waited before the black maw of the fireplace. Darcy's brain registered instantly that something was wrong before the person reached slim hands to throw back the hood. Elizabeth clutched Darcy's arm. Her cry was barely a gasp of shock.

"Lydia!"

"Hello, Lizzy. Mr. Darcy. I'd ask you to sit down, but the furniture seems to be missing."

Darcy was caught between anger and care that Elizabeth not be hurt more by the past. He attempted to keep her sheltered by his body, but she stepped away from him to face her sister. Under the cloak Lydia wore a dress designed to inflame the lust in any man. She was still pretty, but harsh experience had impressed a hardness on her face. Elizabeth pressed a hand to her mouth, repressing a sob.

Lydia's mouth twisted. "Too late to cry for me, Lizzy. I only want one thing from your man—five thousand pounds."

"Where's Wickham?" Darcy's voice rasped. "Waiting somewhere nearby for you to bring him the money?"

Her laugh was short and ugly. Another voice cut through it. "Yes, where is Wickham?"

Richard strode into the room to stand shoulder to shoulder with Darcy, his face stony. The fact that he faced a woman made no difference at that point. His whole purpose was their enemy, his agent, male or female, represented only a barrier to his goal of eliminating Wickham from their lives.

Lydia threw her head back. "George is dead and in hell where he belongs.

"We'd been in Town about a month when one of the big men in the beau monde caught George in bed with his woman. The River Police found what was left of him at the foot of the Tower Bridge. Somebody took a knife to him. They slit his throat, among other things."

Elizabeth bowed her head against Darcy's shoulder for a moment. How could this callous woman be her lively, fun-loving little sister?

"I'm sorry to shock you, Lizzy." Lydia's tone softened a little. "He was a rat and he got what he deserved. He thought Mr. Darcy would come looking for me and pay well to take me home. When it didn't happen, he took it out on me. He could have just let me go but he didn't. When he was done with me, he drugged me and sold me to an abbess in Soho. By the time I had a chance to leave my—employment, it was too late. No one in the family would have taken me in then."

"How do you know it was Wickham they found?" Richard demanded.

Lydia's eyes flicked to his face. "One of Annie Young's girls told me."

"Mrs. Young."

Darcy glanced at Richard; this was confirmation that the former companion could have told them of the death and saved them time and distress. She had taken her revenge for Wickham's death, Darcy thought bitterly. Lydia's voice returned his attention to the present.

"She has a house in Whitechapel. I know one of her girls. Pearl said Annie had to identify him. She was sick for two days. She paid for the burial too, such as it was. You can ask the River Police if you don't believe me."

Darcy heard a note of desperation in her words. Richard shrugged. "It explains some things. If he's dead, then, why are you demanding money from Darcy?"

"I didn't think Mr. Darcy would appreciate me showing up at his wedding in my working clothes and sitting with the bride's family." Lydia wrapped the cloak around her as if she was cold. "I want to leave England. With that much I can go to Canada and start over. I can say I'm a young widow, my husband was killed in the war. That ought to create some sympathy." Her voice dropped. "I don't have a family anymore. If I don't get out of the business soon there won't be any reason to leave."

Richard said quietly to Darcy, "I leave you to do whatever you think best. I will have a look around and then call off my men."

With only the three of them in the room, Lydia lost her bravado. She seemed to slump, her hands closed tightly in the edges of the cloak. Darcy realized that she was frightened.

"I should have known it wouldn't work. I guess I learned too much from George."

Elizabeth left Darcy's side and went to her sister. "Lydie, I'm so sorry. All this time we thought he might have killed you, and you were here in London. I wish with all my heart you had contacted me!"

Lydia shook her head. "You were right, Lizzy. He did kill me. I'm Lily now. I can never be Lydie again."

The tears finally spilled from Elizabeth's eyes. Lydia touched her hair gently. "No use crying, Lizzy. I found that out a long time ago."

Darcy came to stand beside Elizabeth. "I will give you the £5,000 if you will answer a question with absolute honesty."

Both women looked at him, Elizabeth with gratitude and Lydia with disbelief. "If I know the answer."

"In the time you were with Wickham, did he ever mention a letter, or show you a letter, that he thought I would pay a large sum of money for?"

Lydia considered. Darcy did not take his steady gaze from her face. After a short time she shook her head. "He always bragged that he had something on you and he was waiting for the right time to make you pay for it, but I never saw or heard about a letter."

"He would have kept it on him or very near. In his pocket book or an inside pocket."

"No. Near the end he went out for the night, and I searched everything he owned for money to get away from him. He had a small trunk with a false bottom, there was nothing in it but dust. I went through every pocket in his clothes. And I watched him dress and undress enough times to see if he moved anything from one suit to another. He didn't use a pocket book, he rarely had anything to put in one. There was no letter."

Darcy took a breath. "Very well. Can you come here again tomorrow night? I will give you a bank draft for the money. You can negotiate it in Canada when you arrive there."

Lydia closed her eyes for a moment. When she opened them she gazed at Elizabeth with regret. "Don't come with him, Lizzy. Say goodbye now. If I make it to Canada I'll write you a note and that will be the end. Its better if we both forget we have a sister.

"I will never forget, Lydia. I still love you."

Elizabeth embraced her. Lydia stood rigid, then wrapped her arms around Elizabeth in return. When they parted, she stepped back.

"Tomorrow night. Alone."

"You have my word."

Darcy took Elizabeth's arm and escorted her out of the room. When they were once more in the coach rolling toward Hephaestus House, Elizabeth leaned into his chest and cried as if her heart were broken. Darcy could only hold her and murmur endearments until the storm passed. He felt a year older than he had two hours ago.

As the lights of Mayfair intruded into the coach Elizabeth straightened and blotted her eyes with the handkerchief he handed her. "Thank you, William. Not just for the money, but for understanding. She will always be my sister. I hope she can make a life for herself in a new place, even if she can never forget what happened to her."

"So do I, beloved. I would never have wished such a death on Wickham, but I cannot help appreciating that he will destroy no more lives. If I can give your sister a second chance it will in some way make up for not preventing his depredations."

"You could not control his actions, William. I do not blame you in any way."

"I could have exposed his character before I left Hertfordshire. My pride prevented me and look what it cost your family."

The bitter self-accusation in his words made Elizabeth turn to him. "You are not to blame, William. Not for any of this," she said firmly. "Lydia ruined my family's name, but the family was already ruined, it was only a matter of time before something irreparable happened."

"You are harsh on your loved ones." There was no judgment in his voice, only compassion.

"I am truthful. In spite of love for one another, we were not truly a family. We did not take care of each other as we ought to have done. Lydia is not the only one who will never forget the past. We have to live with who we are and who we have been. Otherwise we will never be free to live at all."

"My wise love." Darcy drew her against him, his face resting on her hair. "We will accept the past but not dwell on it. I intend to make a lifetime of memories with you so strong that what has gone before will have no power over us."

They continued on in mutual silence to the Bingleys'.

## July 1815
## Darcy House, London

Richard waited in Darcy's study when he arrived home. He handed his cousin a glass with two fingers of whisky that matched the one he held.

"You are giving her the money?"

"Yes. Her life was destroyed at Wickham's hands, she deserves a chance to make a new life for herself. And she is Elizabeth's sister. Do you realize she is only eighteen?"

"Georgie's age. If it was not for her dowry, the same thing might have happened to her. I am not sorry he's dead, even though I would never sanction the way he died."

Darcy finished his drink in two swallows. Richard said as he sipped his, "That is no way to treat good Strathspey."

Darcy put his glass on a table. "I will see her safely off to Canada, and then I can concentrate on the wedding."

"You are not afraid Miss Lydia will produce the letter Wickham claimed to have at some time in the future?"

"She says he never spoke of or showed her a letter of any kind. She had occasion to go through all of his belongings and found nothing of any value, and no letter. She was telling the truth, Richard. I saw it in her eyes. He either glimpsed the letter in some manner and read only a few words, or he lied about seeing it at all. Whatever happened to it, I refuse to let it hang over me like Damocles' sword. Perhaps my father changed his mind and destroyed it, and in the last minutes of his life forgot he had done so. It makes no difference. I am to marry the woman I adore and begin life with her, nothing else matters."

"So be it." Richard finished his drink and said goodnight.

In the stillness of the darkened and slumbering house, Darcy went up to bed. He began to feel the reaction to the night's events set in; he felt cold and heavy, and his temples throbbed. Martin assisted him out of his clothing and into a nightshirt before Darcy dismissed him. Darcy thought about another drink and rejected the idea. He got into bed, still restless.

To distract himself he mentally listed his activities for the next day. He would see his banker in the morning, obtain passage on a safe ship for Lydia, and provide her with a modest amount of traveling money for the voyage. Then he meant to go to Doctor's Commons and put in motion the purchase of a special license. As soon as the wedding was over and everything packed and on the traveling coach and the servants' coach, they would start the journey to Pemberley. Calmer for the planning, his headache faded and he was at last able to sleep.

## July 1815
## Hephaestus House, London

"Lizzy, are you well? You look exhausted."

Jane brought her tea and seed cake from the breakfast offerings on the sideboard and took the chair next to her sister. Elizabeth had only asked for a cup of tea and had not touched that. She had little color to her face, Jane thought, and lavender shadows under her eyes. *Pray God it is not her illness returning.*

"I did not sleep well." Elizabeth tried to escape Jane's scrutiny by sipping her tea, but her dearest sister knew her too thoroughly.

"How late were you out last night? I did not hear you come in."

"Mr. Darcy brought me home before midnight."

Jane's stomach lurched. "Lizzy, you did not—quarrel, did you? He did not...?"

"Oh, no, no, dearest. William was wonderful." Elizabeth reached for Jane's hand and held it tightly. "It was what happened last night. I have spent the hours trying to discern how to tell you." Tears glistened on Elizabeth's lashes.

Jane was hardly aware of the breakfast parlor around them. Bingley had gone out to a meeting with the steam engine investors. They were alone except for the servants, however she knew whatever Elizabeth had to disclose needed privacy.

"Come with me."

Jane stood and pulled Elizabeth to her feet. Together they went along the hall to Jane's private sitting room. With the door closed they would not be disturbed. She sat on a blue brocade settee and Elizabeth joined her. The room was cool at that time of the morning; a large crystal vase of white roses delicately scented the air.

"Now, Lizzy, what in Heaven's name happened that has you so upset? Did you and Mr. Darcy quarrel?"

"Nothing of the sort." Elizabeth tried to form the words, struggling with the memory of their youngest sister's face as she told of Wickham's death. "Last night...last night Mr. Darcy, Richard Fitzwilliam and I went to Meadow Lane."

Jane stared at her. "Meadow Lane? Why?"

"We thought to meet Wickham. Mr. Darcy received a note demanding money and setting Willow Cottage as the meeting place."

"Oh, Lizzy!" Jane was genuinely distressed. "You ought not to have risked it, even with the two of them there. Wickham is a dangerous man."

Elizabeth closed her eyes. "Not any more. He is dead. Instead we met with Lydia."

Jane did not move. She pressed one hand to her mouth as if to suppress a cry. When she spoke, her voice was a whisper. "Lydia."

"Yes, but, oh, Jane, not our Lydia. Wickham wanted money from Mr. Darcy to return her, but Mr. Darcy never knew what had happened. When there was no money, he took his revenge on her. He sold her to a—a house of ill repute. She has been trapped there ever since. Even when she might have left, she believed we would reject her and did not contact us. Oh, Jane, she looked so—so different. She has suffered so much!"

Jane put her arms around her sister and held her, tears streaking her cheeks. "How horrible! Poor Lydia. What an inhuman thing to do to her."

"She wants to go away, leave England." Elizabeth regained enough composure to speak more calmly. "That was why she wanted the money. She wants to make a new life in Canada. William agreed to give her five thousand pounds. If she had wanted to stay I am sure he would have found a way to help her, but she is too damaged. She said…she said she has no family now. I felt so helpless, Jane. I still love her, but she is not our Lydie, and can never be again."

The sisters held each other for a time. Jane sat back at last, wiped her eyes and stroked the damp tendrils of hair off Elizabeth's forehead. "I think she has made the right decision, Lizzy, do not you? Here there is always a chance her past will be exposed. In Canada that is not likely. It is a wild country I understand, but there are cities where she can live and perhaps remake her life. I wish I had seen her, I am sorry I could not tell her goodbye."

"When she reaches Canada she will let me know. We will at least know she is there and safe. But, oh, Jane, it hurt me so to see her!"

"I am sorry I could not share it with you. Some might say it would be better if she had—not survived. I do not believe it. I love her and I hope with all my heart she will be happy." Jane rose. "Now get your bonnet and gloves and we will go for a walk in the park. The fresh air will do us both good. I believe we have learned that some things cannot be mended but must simply be endured."

Elizabeth agreed to the walk. The pain she felt for Lydia was only one more element of all they had suffered. It would not define them, or mar their futures.

When they returned from a mostly silent walk in Hyde Park, Georgiana called and spent the morning at Hephaestus House. She was to be Elizabeth's maid of honor and her excitement spilled over, infecting the others with a little of her gaiety. The ladies retired to an empty bedroom to admire the latest additions to Elizabeth's trousseau, especially her wedding dress which had just arrived after a final fitting. The three ladies gathered around the bed where it was laid out, Nettie hovering nearby.

"I have never seen clear white muslin so fine." Georgiana delicately ran her fingertips over the fabric. "Did Madame Colette create it?"

The dress was in the latest style with a full underdress of white satin embroidered with flowers in light-colored silks and a train of muslin fastened between the shoulders with a row of white silk rosettes.

"Mrs. White made the dress," Jane replied. "She works as a seamstress for several of the modistes, however she takes private commissions."

Georgiana smiled. "I shall have to speak to her about my own wedding dress when the time comes. She ought to have a shop on Bond Street."

"I have been thinking of asking William if he might want to help her set up in business. Our uncle Gardiner knows her skill, he might also wish to assist her."

"That is an excellent idea." Jane moved away from the wedding gown and Elizabeth nodded to Nettie to put the dress away. "Charles is always looking for investments, although the steam engine plant has all of his attention at the moment."

Elizabeth's trousseau had already been put away except for the latest gowns: a figured velvet of chestnut brown with gold outlining flowers and leaves, and two muslin day dresses. When those received the praise they deserved, Jane conducted her guests to her private sitting room for tea and biscuits.

"Are you coming with us to Pemberley after the wedding?"

Georgiana held her cup in both hands, her response tentative. "I should like to, Lizzy. I can stay in Town for a time if that is inconvenient."

"You shall certainly make the trip with William and me. I will need your expertise so I do not get lost among all the floors and corridors. I have heard that the manor house is more confusing than the maze."

Georgia giggled. "Who in the world told you that?"

"Charles. He said the first time he visited Pemberley it took him over an hour to find his way from his rooms to the dining room."

"It never took Charles an hour to find a dining room in his life."

They all laughed at Jane's comment. When Georgiana's visit ended and the sisters were alone, Jane turned a serious face to Elizabeth.

"Lizzy, are you—concerned about…about being alone with your husband?"

Elizabeth colored, not as much as Jane however. "After we are married you mean. I suppose I am—uncertain. Mama would have been little help I imagine. I thought I would talk to aunt Gardiner."

Jane seemed relieved. "Yes, that is what I did. She was…very helpful."

The conversation ended there. Elizabeth knew she should speak to her aunt before the wedding, perhaps when the invitations began to be answered. She had gleaned bits and pieces over the years from overhearing married women talking; their comments only made the whole situation more confusing. Elizabeth doubted human beings mated in the same way as farm animals, yet there had to be physical contact for babies to be created. Some spoke as if it were a trial to be borne, others seemed to find it more pleasant. Elizabeth knew William would do nothing to harm her; still a nagging anxiety remained.

She determined definitely to consult her aunt.

Her opportunity came the next day when Mrs. Gardiner called to speak to Jane about the wedding breakfast. Cook was brought in and the three women finalized the menu, with Elizabeth adding a comment or approval here and there. Mrs. Gardiner waited until Cook left them before smiling somewhat sadly.

"I received a short letter from Catherine this morning. She and Mr. Thurgood intend to come for the wedding. She asked if I thought you and Mr. Bingley could accommodate them here rather than stay with us. She writes they do not want to put us to any trouble, and Mr. Thurgood wishes to speak to Mr. Bingley on a matter of business."

"They can stay here, of course." Jane hesitated a moment before she added, "I wonder why she did not write me directly?"

Elizabeth was silent. After she married, Catherine had not communicated with them at all except to send a note of condolence on their father's death, and her inability to attend Jane's wedding. She wondered with a slight pang of guilt if Mayfair was a preferable location to Gracechurch Street.

"They did not attend your wedding," Mrs. Gardiner reminded Jane. "She may be embarrassed to ask you."

"Yes, that is probably it. Shall I write her, or do you prefer to answer her letter?"

"I shall write her. If Mary and Mr. Clarke are coming they may want to stay with us, as we have a nanny who can watch the children. I think I will suggest it to her."

They had tea and talked of inconsequential matters until Jane rose. "I have to speak to Cook about several things, if you will excuse me for a short time?"

With a significant glance at Elizabeth she left aunt and niece alone.

# CHAPTER TWENTY-THREE

September 1815
St. James-in-the-Fields, London

The Gardiner carriage clicked and clopped over cobbles in the showering sunlight of a September morning, accompanied by street vendors' cries, a rattle of other carriages, rumbling carts and drays and a surf of indistinguishable noise from the thronging thoroughfares. Elizabeth Bennet sat next to her aunt who for some reason of comfort held her lace-gloved hand. Mr. Gardiner, seated across from his wife, was a solid presence without visible emotion. He was to walk his niece down the aisle of Sir Christopher Wren's graceful St. James-in-the-Fields church.

Whatever misgivings he might have harbored did not concern financial security for the bride. He had read the settlement documents several days ago at Darcy's request, although Elizabeth was of age and able to sign them without consent. Mr. Gardiner found them as generous as he expected. Everything his niece brought to the marriage was to remain in her name and for her benefit, in addition to the money and privileges her fiancé granted her, which were substantial to say the least.

Mr. Clarke sat beside Mr. Gardiner. He and Mary had arrived late the day before and would not see Jane until the wedding. Mary was a little heavier than the last time Elizabeth saw her; she looked content, Elizabeth thought, almost matronly. There was a perceptible fondness between husband and wife that spoke well for their marriage. Catherine and Mr. Thurgood had reached Hephaestus House two days ago. Their younger sister worked hard at not seeming impressed by Jane's situation, an effort her swift appraising glances belied. Mr. Thurgood reminded Elizabeth of a more ambitious Bingley. He spoke of his business with pride, something Catherine subtly encouraged, as well as his plans for expansion.

The carriage pulled in before the church's façade, Portland stone facing over red brick with a vertical bell tower rising into the washed blue of the sky. Mr. Clarke exited the carriage as soon as the footman put the steps up and assisted his wife to descend. They stood together to look up at the façade while Mr. Gardiner left the carriage.

"What a lovely building." Mr. Clarke sounded rather wistful. "Sir Christopher was a genius."

His wife quietly agreed. She would have felt it prideful to wish one as fine for him, at least openly.

In the carriage Mrs. Gardiner smiled at Elizabeth with motherly affection.

"Are you ready, my dear?"

Elizabeth raised her head. "Yes, Aunt."

She was indeed ready. The night before Elizabeth had gone up to bed early, not because she wanted extra sleep, rather to be alone on her last night as a single woman. She had dismissed Nettie as soon as the maid tidied the dressing table and gathered her clothing to be put away. The little maid lingered for a moment and Elizabeth knew she wanted to say something, encouraging her with a smile.

"Yes, Nettie?"

"I just want to say, madam—that is—I'm that happy to go with you. I know Mrs. Bingley would have kept me on here if you wanted a proper lady's maid, but I...I'd rather stay with you, madam."

"And I would rather you stayed with me. Goodnight, Nettie. Get some sleep, tomorrow will be very busy and the next day we leave for Pemberley."

Nettie curtsied as Jane's maid had coached her. "Yes, madam. Goodnight."

"Goodnight, Nettie."

Alone, Elizabeth considered the bed and rejected the snowy sheets turned down invitingly. The window was open at the top to allow a breeze entry. It meandered around the room, fluttering the candle flames. Elizabeth blew out all but one on the night table. In enclosing shadows she sat before the dark fireplace and let her mind wander over the long sequence of events that began with a country assembly and ended in a wedding her most fantastic dreams could not have anticipated.

To a man who adored her. To a man she loved with all her being. He was her strength and she was his. She did not see it as a marriage of equals. Elizabeth acknowledged her husband her superior in understanding and knowledge. She was intelligent enough to acquire the latter, and perhaps the former, however his keen mind and trained intellect were abilities Elizabeth did not covet.

She was his emotional mainstay, the counterbalance of his reason and logic. Unlike her parents, her and Darcy's different characters worked together to enhance each other. If they disagreed they would talk instead of ignoring the problem until it became a wedge between them. She would not suffer as her parents had from lack of understanding, lack of compromise, lack of accommodation. Nor would their children.

Elizabeth colored in the melting shadows. Her aunt had indeed been "helpful" as Jane said. There were still elements Elizabeth did not fully understand about marital relations but she believed she comprehended the basics. Chiefly her aunt had advised her to trust her husband. Elizabeth supposed it was enough, for she did trust William. Still she felt a certain apprehension.

*Every married woman has a bridal night. Jane is supremely happy, my aunt is happy, there is no reason I shall not be happy.*

Happier than Catherine with her newfound status separating her from the past? Happier than Mary, engaged in good works and caring for her home and children? Happier than Lydia on a voyage of escape and hope for a better life? Yes, definitely happier than Lydia, punished for all her days by one terrible mistake. A mistake whose tragic consequences Elizabeth no longer dwelt on. If she was to accept a life of happiness for herself she must let the past rest in peace.

Elizabeth rose and went to bed. She closed her mind to thoughts and concentrated on the sound of the trees outside her window sighing together in the rising wind. To her surprise she woke in the early light of morning with no remembered dreams.

Darcy stood in the vestry of the church awaiting the arrival of his bride and her party. Bingley and Jane had already taken their seats in the front pew as had Mr. and Mrs. Thurgood. His aunt and uncle along with Lord Brentmore and Anne Fitzwilliam occupied the front pew of the groom's side. Lady Matlock wore an expression of placid approval. Lord Matlock was keeping a neutral countenance for the sake of family harmony.

"At least she is not another Adele," was his only comment to his wife on the subject.

Lady Addington was in attendance; she looked like the proverbial cat with canary feathers still attached to its whiskers. Other friends and relatives made up the remainder of the congregation. Most, Darcy thought with some annoyance, out of curiosity to see the lady he was marrying. That was not, however, what darkened his gaze, fixed in abstraction on an urn of golden chrysanthemums.

"Alright, Will, what's eating at you? Surely not the wedding."

Darcy turned his eyes on his cousin. Richard wore conventional clothing, forest green coat and fawn trousers, no longer able to employ his dress uniform. Darcy's coat was black, his trousers gray, and his waistcoat jade green and silver. The two men formed a contrast that was still harmonious. Only Darcy's tension and Richard's quiet steadiness were in opposition.

"Never that." Darcy took a step away from his cousin turning to face him. "When I met with Lydia Bennet the second time, to give her the bank draft and her sailing information, she handed me a sealed note for Elizabeth. She said it was a wedding present that Elizabeth probably would not use."

"No explanation?"

"None. I left it at Darcy House. I still have not decided when I want to give it to Elizabeth."

"You are going to give it to her?"

"Yes. Not today, certainly. I will not chance her being upset on our wedding day."

Richard considered. He knew Darcy very well. His cousin would not read his wife's mail, nor keep a letter from her whatever its origin.

"Why do you not wait until you are at Pemberley? Mrs. Darcy will have so much to engage her attention the note may pass with scarcely a notice."

There was a sudden expectant buzz of voices from the church. Before Darcy was able to reply, the curate tapped on the door, put his head in and summoned them.

"The bride has arrived, gentlemen. Please follow me."

Darcy felt his stomach quiver. He pulled in a breath as they entered the church and made their way to the altar. His heart began to beat faster, every sense deepened; colors intensified, sounds sharpened, waiting faces merged into a blur. Then Darcy saw her. Small and straight on her uncle's arm, falls of transparent muslin over embroidered satin, a velvet half-bonnet resting on ebony curls like a delicate frame around her face. She was the most exquisite being he had ever beheld, and yet vibrant with life. She was his love, his other self, his Elizabeth.

Elizabeth was aware of the congregation turning to watch her progression down the aisle without focusing on the faces or hearing the murmur of voices. From the moment she walked through the doors her only thought, her only vision was Darcy's tall figure waiting for her before the altar; where they were to speak their vows, where they were to be bound together as man and wife for all eternity. She felt no uncertainty, no doubt. This was what her life was meant to be.

Mr. Gardiner put her hand in Darcy's, leaned and kissed her cheek before joining his wife and extended family. The minister spoke the familiar words, solemn yet somehow comforting. Darcy's strong voice spoke to her, his hand warm holding hers as he slipped an incised gold ring on her finger.

"With this ring I thee wed; with my body I thee worship; and with all my worldly goods I thee endow."

The final blessing, the presentation, and it was done.

Darcy stood still for a moment before he offered his arm and Elizabeth took it with more gratitude than she expected. For some reason her knees were suddenly unsteady. Outside the church they stood together in the brightening sunlight while Darcy's carriage was brought up. Several couples came up to offer well wishes including Charlotte and Mr. Collins. Elizabeth braced herself, however the exalted company and the fall of his former patroness had dampened his effusive style and he only wished them well. Charlotte indicated she wanted to speak to Elizabeth later, to which her friend nodded a brief acquiescence.

The Darcy carriage arrived quickly much to Elizabeth's relief. Someone had fastened large white rosettes to the bridles of the matched bays drawing the vehicle. To laughter and good wishes they entered the carriage for the short drive to Hephaestus House where the wedding breakfast awaited. Then they were alone.

They said little on that drive. Darcy took her hands in his, kissed them reverently, and held them until they reached their destination. Hephaestus House's large dining room shone with a wealth of flowers and ribbons. If the laden boards did not groan they at least muttered complaints. The couple moved among their guests until Darcy found them seats at the table with family members who were not circulating. Jane caught Elizabeth's hand and squeezed it, smiling with joy.

"You were so beautiful, Lizzy. I cried just looking at you."

"I hope you saved some tears for the rest of the ceremony?"

"I did not need to. Some ladies who came to make sure Mr. Darcy was actually married cried enough for all of us."

The sisters laughed. Darcy returned with their plates at that point, and Elizabeth found she was able to eat, something she had not expected. The food was superb; for a time they all concentrated on enjoying it. Across from them Bingley finally said, "You are leaving for Pemberley so soon?"

"Yes. I want to introduce my enchanting bride to her new home. Pemberley has waited for her a long time, I wish no more delays."

"You and Jane will have to join us for the holidays," Elizabeth added. "I intend to invite all of my family. I want a true Christmas celebration."

Jane glanced at Darcy. His lips were turned up at the corners in a smile of satisfaction. "We shall come if the weather permits travel."

Bingley added his affirmation. They finished eating and Elizabeth excused herself. She saw Charlotte rise to follow her. In the ladies' retiring room the two lifelong friends embraced.

"I am so glad you came, Charlotte. I will be able to write you regularly now."

"Do not put anything personal in your letters, Lizzy. My husband reads my mail, such as it is." She studied Elizabeth's face for a moment. "You have suffered a great deal, my friend. I am sorry I was not able to help more."

"There was nothing you could have done. It is all over and I have a new life, one that includes the past only as its remembrance gives me pleasure or instruction."

"Then you are blessed and I am so very happy for you." Again Charlotte hesitated. "Something happened I wanted to relate to you, only now I am not sure I ought."

Elizabeth smiled. "Is it so distressing?"

"In a way. It is Mrs. Long. She has acted strangely for the past year or more. Lately she began walking around Meryton at night, arguing with herself, talking nonsense. Sir William wrote to her cousin in Shropshire who came to see her. He has taken her back with him to live on his farm, but I fear if she grows any worse she may have to be put in some sort of care."

Slowly Elizabeth said, "Does she speak of anything or anyone in particular?"

"That is the strangest thing. She kept insisting that Miss Bingley— or Lady Samuelson as she is now—was going to introduce her to London society. I do not believe they ever exchanged two words together."

*Not where anyone saw them.* Aloud, Elizabeth said, "I suppose it was a fantasy. We shall never know."

"No, probably not. Especially since the cousin sold her house and most of the furniture." Charlotte smiled wryly. "I am just an old cynic. And I had better get back to my husband before he decides to give Mr. Darcy advice on how to be a superior husband and gets us both thrown out of the house."

Elizabeth remained in the retiring room for a few minutes, washed her hands and rejoined the festivities. Darcy had entered a conversation with Bingley and two other gentlemen, one of whom was Catherine's husband. She saw Georgiana sitting with Mr. Worthington; she looked composed except for a sparkle in her eyes when they rested on her future husband. Catherine had joined Jane and Mary. They all looked up at Elizabeth's arrival. She took a seat next to Mary and asked about the children. For the next half hour the sisters talked together much as they might have if catastrophe had never torn them apart.

*We are not the same people who grew up together, however easily we resume our familiarity. Kitty has truly become Catherine; she has assumed the place of a leader in her local society. Mary is all she wanted to be, a vicar's wife and helpmate, of use and inspiration to those less fortunate. Jane has found her perfect husband—I doubt if a cross word will ever pass between them. And I have found the most important treasure of all; not only William, I have found myself.*

When conversation waned, Elizabeth repeated her invitation to come to Pemberley for Christmas. Catherine was enthusiastic, but Mary replied with gentle regret.

"Christmas is one of Mr. Clarke's busiest times. With caring for the poor and the children's pageant and services on Christmas Eve and Christmas morning I do not see how we will be able to get away. Perhaps later in the spring if that is not inconvenient?"

Elizabeth impulsively put an arm around Mary and hugged her. "You are welcome at any time."

Mary colored, then returned the embrace. "Thank you, Lizzy. I am so pleased you are marrying a good man."

As if called by the praise, Darcy came up to them. He bowed, dark eyes on Elizabeth. "I am sorry to interrupt you, my love, but it is growing late and we are to start early tomorrow. Will you mind very much if we leave now?"

"No, Mr. Darcy, not so very much."

Elizabeth watched him stride away, her pulse suddenly racing. She bade her sisters goodbye, thanked Jane for all her kindness, and went to find her aunt. Mrs. Gardiner occupied a settee in a quiet corner with Lady Addington. Elizabeth thanked her aunt warmly for her help and support. When Mrs. Gardiner went to find her husband and spread word that the bride and groom were leaving, Lady Addington took Elizabeth's hands in her veined ones and squeezed them lightly.

"You will do very well, my dear. You have crossed the stormy sea and a beautiful land is in sight. The captain of the ship is not bad, either."

Her rakish chuckle made Elizabeth laugh in return. She said farewell and joined Darcy in the entry hall where guests were gathering to wish them well. The carriage came, they left Hephaestus House for their home.

*Our home. Mine and William's. And then Pemberley, after our wedding night. I pray I do not disappoint him on our wedding night.*

## September 1815
## Darcy House, London

The senior servants were waiting to formally welcome their new mistress, in spite of the fact most of them had met her on her visits to Georgiana. The formalities over, Darcy conducted Elizabeth to the mistress' chambers, pointing out rooms she had not yet seen. They stopped before the door to her bedchamber, delicately painted with a vase of flowers, and Elizabeth took her husband's hand.

"Before dinner I should like to speak to you in your library."

A note of mischief in her voice caused Darcy no apprehension, only a stirring of curiosity. "Of course, my love. I am always at your disposal."

He kissed her hand, saw the door close behind her and continued on to his rooms. When he descended the stairs he carried a single sheet of paper. He bore the look of a man thoroughly satisfied with life. Elizabeth was already in the venerable room. The drapes in the one bay were drawn, crisp panes of illumination sliding over the comfortable chairs and small table situated there. His wife waited near the center of the room where a long table stood ready to hold oversized volumes or maps, her gown concealing what lay on the polished wood surface.

"I have something to show…"

"I want to show you…"

They stared at each other, then burst into simultaneous laughter.

"Oh, dear," Elizabeth gasped. "We seem to be thinking alike already." She stepped aside indicating the two books on the table. "Your wedding present, Mr. Darcy."

Darcy approached the table and touched the covers of the tomes reverently. "The Shakespeare folio and the Chaucer. You kept them?"

"They were my father's favorites. He advised me to hold on to them in case of a special need. This is that time. You will cherish them as he did. They belong with you."

It had been a long time since Darcy felt tears prickle his eyes. He laid the paper he carried on the end of the table and took his wife in his arms, kissing her gently.

"They will always hold a special place in my heart, and in Pemberley's library. Thank you, my beloved Elizabeth."

He released her and held out the paper which was a letter with an official letterhead. "This is your wedding present." Elizabeth took the letter but did not read it. Darcy's hands rested on her shoulders in silent support. "Lady Addington contacted me after the dinner party. She and Mrs. Fortesque are forming a society to encourage young women who wish a more extensive education than they are presently allowed. The have leased a building in Bloomsbury to be used as a library and for educational lectures. I have engaged to pay for any renovations needed, and donate books for the library—which will be called the Elizabeth Darcy Reading Room."

She bowed her head against his shoulder, tears gathered in her eyes. "William, my dearest William, you could not have found a better gift." Elizabeth raised her head. "May I ask one more favor? I would like to donate my father's books as well."

"They are yours to dispose of however you choose. I can think of no better place for them."

Darcy again took his wife in his arms, this time only to hold her tightly against him. Neither one needed words.

Darcy stood outside the door separating his bedchamber from his wife's dressing room. Freshly shaved and, to Martin's unexpressed satisfaction, wearing nightshirt and robe, he contemplated the night ahead. Once he would have gone to her without a second thought, driven by what he believed to be love. Now he saw it with shame for the lust it had been, the drive to possess the woman he desperately wanted. Tonight Darcy's only goal was to lead her carefully into the act of love.

Darcy knew her to be brave beyond the courage of many men, but she was also a maiden, innocent of knowledge of marital relations. Depending on what advice she had received, and from whom, she must face tonight with confusion or trepidation, or both. If he failed her the damage would be difficult to overcome. He had to find a way to link friendship and passion, trust and desire.

*Pray I do not fail her on this of all nights.*

He crossed the dressing room, raised his hand and knocked lightly. At her welcome Darcy entered her bed chamber to find her standing next to the old Cherrywood full tester that had been his mother's and his grandmother's before her. Elizabeth had left only the wall sconce by the bed turned low. In its soft glow Darcy was overcome by her beauty; the creamy oval of her face framed in lustrous curls, her small strong body barely concealed in a sweep of primrose silk. She tried to smile but her lips trembled. Darcy came a careful step closer.

"You are looking at me that way again." Elizabeth sounded breathless.

"What way, my dearest love?"

"As if you want to devour me."

So easily, Darcy had the answer. He always loved it when she teased him, it made him think she felt a closeness between them. That was the connection he sought, that playfulness and the trust it sprang from.

"Hm. Sweet young bride. I have not had that before."

Darcy put his arms loosely around her and kissed the curve of her neck, running his tongue along her collarbone. Elizabeth made a small sound, not quite a moan, of pleasure. Darcy repeated his actions on the other side of her soft throat. This time her reaction was to place her hands on his chest and grip the lapels of his robe.

"Mmm. Delicious."

Darcy tightened his embrace just enough to press her body lightly to his. He continued to kiss and lick her skin until he reached her lips. The first kiss was merely a pressing of his mouth to hers. She imitated his actions, her arms rising around his neck to tangle delicate fingers in his hair. Darcy let his hands slide down her back, over her hips. She shivered but did not pull away. With a swift breath to steady him, Darcy took possession of Elizabeth's mouth. Her efforts to respond reassured him of the passion he had always sensed in her.

Darcy picked her up, lifting her into the middle of the bed. He took off his robe and dropped it over a nearby chair, joining Elizabeth as she lay back on the pillows. The embers in the firebox muttered in their sleep, sending orange flickers over the hearth. She stroked his cheek as he rested on one arm watching her.

"Do not hesitate, William. My aunt told me what to expect. I love you so much."

"And I love you with all my heart and soul, my dearest, loveliest Elizabeth. I will be as gentle as I can."

Darcy bent his head to kiss her. His nightshirts, which he rarely wore, were sewn especially for his tall, muscular frame and fit without bulk. When he got into bed the linen had seemed tight. He wondered if it had shrunk in the wash, a distracting notion given Martin's usual standard of perfection. As he shifted position it twisted, pulling against his neck and shoulder. He managed to tug it partly loose, only to have it tighten around his legs. Thinking curses, Darcy jerked at the intractable fabric, shifting his weight to free it without success.

"If it is uncomfortable, why do you not take it off?"

Elizabeth's whisper was a little thickened with what Darcy fervently hoped was growing passion but feared was more likely laughter. He hesitated a moment, then got out of bed, dragged the offending garment over his head and tossed it in the general direction of his robe. When he returned to her she lay watching him with wide dark eyes. Darcy realized his body was responding to her gaze. He got into bed for the second time, vowing to give his valet a bonus.

Elizabeth touched his chest, the motion tentative. She slid her arms around his naked body, stroking his back, reveling in the sensation of his heated flesh under her fingers. Darcy let her exploring hands move over his skin until he could no longer bear it. His heart beat so loudly he wondered if she could hear the sound. Heat ran along his limbs; against his side he felt Elizabeth's body turn a little toward him.

She reached up, pulling him down to her, breathless. "Love me, William."

A command Darcy obeyed with tender ardor.

Elizabeth lay silent and drowsy, her husband close beside her. She did not know the time, certainly after midnight and before dawn. She was content for the moment to be separate from him, listen to his deep slow breathing and think of their coupling. The heat from his body kept her warm; he was like a banked fire. A fire that had blazed when they joined in a consuming fervor.

There had been some pain as her aunt warned her. When it came she was caught up in a rapturous maelstrom that dulled her awareness, and it had not lasted long. Elizabeth shifted her position a little. She was sore, but that would pass. She was also completely unclothed. Somewhere between William's first slow stroking her body and his moving over her as she fell away into exquisite sensations, her nightgown had disappeared. When she rose a few minutes earlier to visit the commode in her dressing room it was nowhere in evidence and Elizabeth returned to bed without seeking it. At the moment a nightgown seemed somehow superfluous.

William had not controlled her. He had guided her, encouraged her, given her intense pleasure before taking his own release. She was grateful and a little awed. There was much she needed, wanted to learn; he would teach her, share with her, until she became truly his partner in the act of love. For now Elizabeth felt only a lightness as she moved closer to her husband and slipped back into sleep.

# CHAPTER TWENTY-FOUR

September 1815
Pemberley, Derbyshire

"Mr. Niles, if I might have a minute of your time?"

"Certainly, Mrs. Reynolds. How may I help you?"

The two most senior servants of Pemberley Manor, while not personally close, kept a friendly courtesy in their dealings. The butler waited for his counterpart to approach, wondering if her request had to do with the arrival of Mr. Darcy and his new bride later that day.

"Do you by any chance know what became of that lovely little Queen Anne chest Mr. Thatcher used to keep in the butler's pantry? I know you did not care for it, but I assume it is still somewhere in the house."

"Indeed it is. I did not want to put it in the attics so I had it moved to the old nurse's room."

"Excellent." Mrs. Reynolds smiled with satisfaction. "I think it would go well in the mistress' chambers. If Mrs. Darcy does not care for it, something appropriate can always be purchased."

"It is quite a nice piece," Mr. Niles acknowledged, "although not to my taste. I will send a footman to bring it down."

"Thank you, Mr. Niles."

"Not at all, Mrs. Reynolds."

They parted with their usual amicability. The anticipated arrival of the master and the new mistress had kept the great manor house in as much turmoil for the past fortnight as it ever experienced. Little was known about the lady except her name and that Mr. Darcy was said to be enthralled with her. Mrs. Hastings, the Pemberley head cook, had written her counterpart at Darcy House inquiring of Mrs. Darcy's preference in dishes, only to receive word that she was not demanding as to food, or, as far as Mrs. Adams was aware, anything else. Mrs. Hastings was unsure whether to be reassured by this or vexed at the lack of information. She settled on preparing a range of dishes until she gained more specific knowledge of the mistress' tastes.

Mrs. Reynolds was sanguine about Mr. Darcy's bride. She had known him since the age of four years old and with the exception of his friendship with George Wickham—and that only until the boy showed his true nature—he had never gone far wrong in his judgment of people. She had no reason to think, however besotted he might be, that he would err badly in a wife. After all, the much-disliked Miss Bingley had not succeeded in catching him for all her efforts.

Actually, Mrs. Reynolds had a note from Mrs. Burgess prior to the wedding to the effect that Miss Bennet, as she was then, while gently born was not a member of the *ton* and had no family but three sisters, all married, the eldest to Mr. Darcy's best friend Mr. Bingley. She also had an aunt and uncle in London, the uncle in trade but both quite genteel and well mannered. Mrs. Reynolds bridled a bit at the word "genteel" before she told herself that it was not her business to judge. If Master Fitzwilliam was happy with his choice that was all she cared about.

The housekeeper glanced at the long case clock in the hall and went upstairs to oversee the placement of the Cherrywood chest. Pursuant to Mr. Darcy's instructions before his prior visit to London, she had not only had the mistress's bed chamber and dressing room thoroughly cleaned and aired, but purchased new drapes, bed curtains, and linens; all in a neutral cream color, until Mrs. Darcy should choose to renovate the rooms. Mrs. Reynolds had also prepared a room for the mistress' lady's maid close to the servants' stairs leading to the wing where the master's and mistress' suites were located. The girl's name was Nettie, which gave Mrs. Reynolds confidence that she was not a fancy French maid and likely to put on airs.

She surveyed the delicate little chest on legs where it was situated in the dressing room. It would do very nicely for gloves and stockings and such. A maid was polishing it to its former roseate luster when she made a small exclamation.

"What is it, Laurel? You have not damaged it, have you?"

The maid immediately turned to the housekeeper with a denial. "No, Mrs. Reynolds. Its just this drawer, it won't close properly."

Mrs. Reynolds examined the offending drawer. It protruded a half inch from the frame of the chest. Its twin rested securely in place, as did the two drawers above. She pulled it out. It moved freely without the squeak or scrape of warped wood.

"Something is caught in the back," she told the maid. "Here, your hands are smaller than mine, reach in, careful now, and see if you can feel what it is."

The maid complied, kneeling in front of the chest to run a hand slowly into the drawer. She looked up at the housekeeper after a moment, her eyes wide. "It's a paper, ma'am. I can just feel the edge. Its fallen down behind the drawer. If I reach a bit further…"

Mrs. Reynolds watched the maid grope in the drawer, turning and twisting her arm. She sat back suddenly with a bent paper in her hand. The housekeeper took it from her as the maid rose to her feet. She pushed the drawer in. It fit as finely as the day the chest was made. It was only when she looked at Mrs. Reynolds that the maid saw the housekeeper staring at a folded and sealed letter, smoothing it with reverent hands.

"So that is what happened to it."

"That is Pemberley House."

The Darcy coach stopped at the top of a low rise overlooking the manor house and grounds some mile ahead and below this vantage point. Late afternoon sun showed the building in crisp relief against the high, wooded ridge behind it. Darcy got out of the coach and handed Elizabeth down. He extended his hand to Georgiana, who shook her head with a smile.

"Show Elizabeth her new home, William. I will wait here."

Darcy took his bride's hand. Together they walked a short distance to a spot where the trees around them parted fully to expose the view. Elizabeth's hand tightened on Darcy's as she looked down on Pemberley House in its bezel of lush gardens and lawns. When she raised her head to meet his eyes her own shone with wonder.

"I do not have words to say how beautiful it is. I think I shall spend my first week here in the gardens."

"Shall I have a tent put up for you, or will you sleep in the house?"

A little thrill of pleasure flitted through Elizabeth; her husband was teasing her. "Oh, I think I could be convinced to sleep in the house—by the right person."

"Georgiana?"

"Of course. Who else?"

He laughed, a deep rumble in his chest. They returned to the coach and continued on, reaching Pemberley House to find a reduced version of the household staff awaiting them on the front steps and along the driveway. Mrs. Reynolds had told the maid to say nothing of her discovery. She did not want word of it to reach the master until his bride was introduced and settled in. That letter had waited for seven years, it could wait another few hours.

Darcy handed Georgiana out of the coach first; she stepped aside and Elizabeth descended, taking her husband's arm. He offered Georgiana his other arm. With a lady on each side, Darcy approached their home. The servants bowed or curtsied as they passed. On the top step Mr. Niles and Mrs. Reynolds did the same before voicing a welcome to their new mistress.

"Welcome home, Mr. Darcy, Mrs. Darcy, Miss Darcy. We are most happy to see you arrive safely."

"Welcome Mr. Darcy, Miss Darcy. A special welcome Mrs. Darcy. We hope you will be happy here."

Elizabeth saw the sincerity in their faces and smiled, her throat tightening. "Thank you, Mr. Niles, Mrs. Reynolds. I am sure I shall be very happy here."

They went inside and Mrs. Reynolds made brief introductions to Mrs. Hastings and several of the more senior servants. Nettie waited a little apart. It was all she could do not to bounce from foot to foot with excitement. As soon as introductions were over the maid hurried away to await her mistress upstairs. Mrs. Reynolds conducted Elizabeth to the third floor wing where the master's and mistress' suites were located.

"Mr. Darcy wanted you to decorate the mistress' rooms as it suited you, Mrs. Darcy, so they have only been freshened."

"I am sure they are perfectly suited, Mrs. Reynolds."

Elizabeth stepped through the door to the bed chamber and looked around. The room was spotless with obviously new linens and drapes, but their complete neutrality gave it a feeling of being unfinished. She would certainly redecorate in time; for now the spacious room was soothing in its lack of personality. Nettie waited in the adjoining dressing room, which was an equally blank canvas. The only item that caught Elizabeth's eye was a small Cherrywood chest-on-legs. Elizabeth touched the polished surface with gentle hands.

"This is an exquisite piece. Queen Anne, is it not?"

"Yes, madam. I thought it might suit for gloves and stockings."

"It will indeed. Thank you for placing it here."

Mrs. Reynolds smiled. "You are most welcome, Mrs. Darcy. There will be tea in the yellow drawing room whenever you are ready."

With a curtsey she left Elizabeth to her maid's ministrations. Nettie was bursting with enthusiasm, but her training kept her to silently helping her mistress out of her traveling ensemble and pouring water into the Wedgewood basin on the wash stand so Elizabeth could wash her face and hands. When Nettie had helped her into a day dress and brushed out her hair she could no longer maintain her composure.

"Oh, madam, this is the grandest place I ever saw. And they've been that kind to me. My room is just at the top of the stairs so I can be here ever so quick when you ring."

"I am happy you like it here, Nettie. I find it extremely grand myself. I suppose we shall get used to it in time."

A knock on the dressing room door sent Nettie to open it and admit Darcy. She curtsied as he entered then returned to pinning up Elizabeth's curls in a simple coiffure.

"Do you want to go down to tea, my love, or rest until dinner?"

Elizabeth met his dark eyes in the mirror. "Tea would be welcome, but I will stay if you want me to."

She saw a moment's conflict in his face, then he smiled. "I think tea is indicated."

It was not until the next morning, after a night Elizabeth held ever after among her most treasured memories, that Mrs. Reynolds requested to speak to her employer in private. Darcy had found Elizabeth in the breakfast parlor just obtaining a cup of tea and a scone. He was served his coffee and sat next to her observing the rosy color in her face when she looked aside at him.

"Are you well, Mrs. Darcy?"

"Very well, Mr. Darcy." Elizabeth lowered her voice to a murmur so the impassive footman at the sideboard could not overhear her. "As you should know, sir."

"So you find my bed as comfortable as your own?"

"Comfortable may not be the proper description. Enchanting, surprising, wonderful…"

"As long as you are content you may describe it in any way you choose."

He signaled the footman and requested a plate of food and more coffee. "I have to keep my strength up," Darcy whispered to a raised eyebrow from his wife. "I married a most accommodating lady."

To renewed blushes he started on his breakfast. Half an hour later he sat behind his study desk when Mrs. Reynolds knocked. She closed the door behind her and approached with a letter in hand.

"This was found wedged behind a bottom drawer of the chest Mr. Thatcher kept in the butler's pantry. I had it moved to Mrs. Darcy's dressing room and Laurel found it when the drawer would not close properly."

Darcy felt a numbness crawl through his mind. She handed it to him, her voice carefully emotionless. "Mr. Thatcher must have put it away for safekeeping. When he passed so soon after Master George no one knew where to find it."

"Thank you, Mrs. Reynolds. I am sure this will go no farther than the two of us."

"Yes, sir. Laurel has been asked to keep it to herself, but I was careful not to put any special emphasis on finding it. She is new so the name would mean nothing to her."

"Very well. I shall deal with it."

"Yes, Mr. Darcy." Mrs. Reynolds curtsied and left.

For minutes Darcy held the letter in a limbo between reading it and simply destroying it. All of the persons involved were dead: his mother, father, John Wickham, George Wickham. Georgiana could no longer be hurt by any information it contained. More importantly Darcy knew certainly that his mother had been a woman of honor and integrity. He took up a paper knife and slit the seal, noting as he did that it was a small spot of candle wax partially obliterating a regular wax seal.

*"Dear John,*

*"I want you to know how much comfort your friendship has given me in this time of trouble. We cannot meet at present because Dr. Morrow*

*has confined me to my rooms. I will miss our walks in the gardens, although I know you took time from your work to see to my welfare and give me the comfort of your assurances that all would be well. Now that George is returning from London and the business matters that took him there for so long are resolved, your kindness will mean as much to him as it does to me.*

*"God bless you, my dear friend.*

*"Anne Darcy"*

Darcy felt a welling of love for his mother that washed away all of the lingering pain of Wickham's false accusations. His father had undoubtedly found the letter among John Wickham's effects after the steward died. He had not read the letter, nor had John Wickham. Did his father doubt his wife, or was it simply that he did not want any shadow of scandal on her good name if someone else saw that she had written to their steward? It was of no importance now. Darcy remembered that before Georgiana was born there was trouble with bad harvests and an investment that had failed, jeopardizing Pemberley's financial security. His father had gone to London and stayed several months before the matter was successfully concluded. It must have pained and upset him to leave his fragile, pregnant wife alone when she had only just learned of her condition. John Wickham's efforts to reassure Lady Anne would have been a godsend.

All those years of wondering, the weight not only of Georgiana's future but his mother's reputation threatened by a few words that meant nothing and Wickham's evil intent. He could only speculate that Wickham had found the letter while searching the desk for anything of value and read the beginning before Mr. Thatcher caught him. The old butler no doubt meant to give Darcy the letter after the funeral, before his own collapse and death made that impossible.

Darcy returned the letter to its original place in the locked desk drawer. He would share the information with Elizabeth and then decide if he wanted to burn the letter as his father originally requested.

George Wickham was no longer a part of his life. His sins died with him. As he started to close the drawer his gaze fell on Lydia's note. For a moment Darcy debated waiting a little longer to give it to Elizabeth, before placing it in his pocket. Decided, Darcy locked the drawer and rose.

Suddenly he very much required his wife's company. He was directed to the gardens by a footman and found her in the rose garden, walking slowly up and down the paths between plants, her bonnet hanging down her back by its ribbons. She turned at his step with a smile that caught at his heart.

"This is the loveliest spot in the gardens. It is my favorite of all Pemberley's displays."

Darcy's voice grew husky. "It was my mother's favorite as well. She brought in most of the rose bushes and oversaw the planting to her specifications. I love it as well."

Elizabeth sat on a stone bench under a small arched trellis covered by climbing roses of a delicate pink. After a moment's hesitation Darcy sat beside her. He took her hand and raised it to his lips before reaching into his pocket for the note.

"I have waited to give you this until we were at Pemberley. I did not want any shadow on our wedding."

Elizabeth's brow furrowed slightly. "What could have troubled our wedding?"

"This, perhaps." He gave her the note. "When I saw Lydia to finalize our arrangement, she gave me this for you. She said it was a wedding present you would make no use of."

Slowly Elizabeth took the note, holding it in both hands. "I see. You thought it might be some sort of accusation or remonstrance."

"I was not sure. I chose not to take the chance. If you are upset with me, I am sorry."

She leaned her head on his shoulder. "No, dearest, I am not upset. I believe I have some idea of what is in the note. It is something Jane and I puzzled over, and Charlotte provided at least part of the answer at our wedding breakfast."

As Darcy watched, Elizabeth broke the seal and opened the note. He said, "If you require privacy to read it, I shall return to the house."

"No, William, please stay." Her eyes perused the short contents before she handed him the paper. In Lydia's careless hand he read the last piece of an old puzzle.

*Lizzy,*

*I met with George secretly at Mrs. Long's. Someone paid her to let us meet. She did not say who but one day I saw Miss Bingley sneak out the side door. Kitty did not know.*

*I love you too.*

*L*

Darcy sat stiff and speechless until Elizabeth took the note from his hand. "We knew they had not been seen together in Meryton, and the time in Brighton was too short for a seduction to have taken place." She folded the note and put it in a pocket of her dress. "I knew Miss Bingley disliked me and opposed Charles and Jane marrying, but I never suspected she hated us enough to ruin our entire family."

Darcy said roughly, "Samuelson or no, she shall never be allowed in our home again."

"No, William." Elizabeth sighed and twined her fingers with his. "She is Charles' sister. We cannot ban her without explaining why, and that would cause a rift between them that might never be healed. Think how it would affect Jane as well as your best friend to learn that his sister was a part of all that happened to us, for we cannot blame her entirely. She only precipitated matters. It might all have occurred without her conniving."

"You would not forgive her?"

"No. She will never ask it of me in any event. I will find it difficult to welcome her into our home, but on occasion I will make the effort, for Jane and Charles' sake."

Elizabeth turned to him, her face at peace. "I have so much to be thankful for, I refuse to let the past intrude. The past no longer has power over me. Only you, my love."

Darcy did not speak; he took her in his arms and kissed her with all of the love he felt. She was his life, his sanctuary, his home. His beautiful, wonderful Elizabeth.

# EPILOGUE

The wedding of Georgiana Darcy and Giles Worthington occurred on June 5, 1816, shortly before the bride's nineteenth birthday. They spent a week at their newly gifted home in Twickenham before moving to a rented cottage in Newcastle. Eventually they would sell the house on the river and purchase a small estate near York. There they remained until Mr. Worthington, an early investor in railroads, retired a rich man. Both he and Georgiana wished to live closer to the Darcys and Bingleys which led to the purchase of another small estate, this one in Nottinghamshire. This was their home for the remainder of their lives. They had two children, both boys.

Anne Fitzwilliam gave birth to a son, Richard Lewis William Fitzwilliam, shortly after her thirtieth birthday. It was her and Richard's only child. She passed peacefully five years later, outliving predictions by a decade. Richard eventually remarried and fathered another son and a daughter. He and his second wife lived to old age at Rosings Park.

Lady Catherine de Bourgh never reconciled with either her daughter or son-by-marriage. She died of a brain hemorrhage shortly after Anne, and was buried by her request at Bath.

Adele Fitzwilliam died four years after her abortive suicide attempt having never regained her health. Viscount Chadwick remarried shortly after his mourning period ended, to the widow of an earl. They had one daughter and lived a conventional married life devoid of drama.

Lydia Bennet reached Canada safely and true to her word sent a single note to Elizabeth thanking her and Darcy for their assistance. She was never heard from again, but her sisters wished her well although they rarely spoke of her.

Charles Bingley's steam engine plant evolved into the design and manufacture of railroad engines and related equipment, as well as farming machinery, including eventually a steam-powered plow, forerunner of the tractor. He and his investors became wealthier men than any of them might have believed, leading him to buy a large estate in Derbyshire not thirty miles from Pemberley. His and Jane's two sons and three daughters were raised with their cousins in a closeness of spirit that kept the family together through the many changes in life as the Regency ended and the Victorian age began. Charles and his angel remained deeply in love throughout their lives and were honored by everyone who knew them.

Mary gave the Reverend Mr. Clarke four children before her final pregnancy eliminated any chance of there being another baby. Neither she nor her husband were distressed by the news. Mr. Clarke had just received a transfer to a larger and somewhat wealthier parish where his and his wife's abilities would be fully utilized. The Clarkes devotion to their parishioners gained them a well-deserved reputation for Christian charity that stayed with them for all their long lives.

Catherine Bennet Thurgood became a force in the social life of Manchester. With steam-powered machinery designed by Mr. Worthington, her husband made such a success of his business he was able to open several more plants. She seldom traveled to London, and saw her sisters only on occasions when they all gathered at Pemberley. Sadly, the Thurgoods had no children. Their considerable fortune was eventually left to fund a hospital for factory workers and their families.

Darcy and Elizabeth were blessed with four children, two sons and two daughters. The eldest son, William Charles Darcy, married the Bingleys' second daughter, Amanda Margaret. His stewardship of Pemberley upon his father's retirement and his son's, after his death, brought the great estate safely to the brink of the twentieth century. His younger brother, Richard George, took up a career as a diplomat, married the daughter of a viscount, and served queen and country with distinction for many years. The Darcys' eldest daughter, Jane Anne, took up the cause of women's rights. She married late in life to a widower with two children whom she loved as her own and who returned her love. Although she did not live to see women achieve the vote, her crusading efforts paved the road others traveled to that momentous change. The Darcys' second daughter, Victoria Eleanor, married the son of a neighbor and friend of the family and never lived more than ten miles from Pemberley. She presented her husband with four daughters and a son and lived happily until her death at fifty-five. Her husband never remarried.

As for Darcy and Elizabeth, they made the adjustments and compromises any two intelligent and loving people make in a marriage of partners that lasts a lifetime. Indeed, they truly created their happily ever after.

### *THE END*